BLOODY
NEWTON

BLOODY NEWTON

JOHNNY D. BOGGS

KENSINGTON
PUBLISHING CORP.

www.kensingtonbooks.com

KENSINGTON BOOKS are published by

Kensington Publishing Corp.
900 Third Avenue
New York, NY 10022

ISBN: 978-1-4967-3833-2 (ebook)

ISBN: 978-1-4967-3831-8

First Kensington Trade Paperback Printing: July 2024

10 9 8 7 6 5 4 3 2 1

Printed in the United States of America

In memory of Karl Cordova (1970–2022),
fellow baseball coach, Scout leader, friend;
and his father, Bill (1936–2020),
who liked my novels.

Kansas is in the Great West, is an important part of it, and
is destined to occupy
the central portion in the cattle business.
—*The Saline County Journal,*
July 13, 1871

In some circles, the town became known as "Bloody Newton"
because of the number of killings that occurred here. The total
was probably about 12.
—*The Newton Kansan,*
June 20, 1974

Chapter 1

All the railroads of Kansas are pushing for the Texas
cattle trade, which promises to be larger the coming
season than ever before.
—*The* (Topeka) *Kansas Daily Commonwealth,*
February 2, 1871

That morning, he awakened to her smell. She had bathed before coming to bed that night, washed her hair, and they had
made love. He treasured mornings like this, especially in the
spring, breathing in that fragrance of the rose powders she used.
Wind blew the curtains, a horse in the corral neighed, and he
rolled over, putting his right arm around her. She giggled, and
took his hand in hers, giving it that soft squeeze.

She liked to say how their hands were made for each other,
that they fit perfectly.

He pushed himself up, found her earlobe, kissed it, found her
cheek, kissed that, too. Waited for her to turn her head, so he
could dive into pure blue eyes.

When she did, he kissed her again.

"Careful now," she whispered, but her eyes told him they
both wanted to abandon any notion of caution.

He smiled. She puckered her lips. They kissed. She had the
most inviting lips. Her mouth opened. He explored it. Her arm
came around his back.

Then, from the barn, a voice shouted:

"Pa. Aren't you awake yet?"

Another echoed: "Those steers won't drive themselves."

She fell back onto the pillow.

He rolled away to glare at the ceiling.

Both voices outside yelled something unintelligible.

He groaned.

After trying, but failing, to stifle another giggle, she sat up and stared down at him. Stared with those hypnotic eyes. He memorized that nose, her freckles, the golden hair, gazed upon her, naked and beautiful and everything a man could dream of a wife.

"You're the one," she told him, "who wanted sons."

And rolled out of bed, found her robe, slid her feet into those satin slippers he bought for her last year, and went to make coffee.

"Pa! Aren't you awake?" That would be Taylor, the oldest, eighteen and already taller that Gary Hardee.

"You've already slept through the best part of the day." That was Evan, fifteen, and just as tall as his old man.

By then, Gary Hardee had pulled over his shirt, shoved on his hat, and was trying to jerk up the canvas britches. He stifled a curse. From the winter kitchen, he heard Jane getting a fire started in the Charter Oak. He had seen one in Kansas three years ago, and listened to the salesman make his case—till the skinflint figured out that Gary was a Texan and went to talk to a local lady. Not that Gary could have gotten that heavy piece of iron all the way back to Fort Bend County, and he felt better anyway after he had worked out a deal with a fellow in San Antonio, who brought in this Charter Oak from a hardware merchant down in Galveston.

Jane loved the stove. Sure beat cooking in a fireplace or over a pit outside.

The sons shouted at him again, while he was pulling on the boots. That caused his hand to slip and catch the rowels on the spur on his right boot. Right below the thumb, breaking the skin.

Irritated, he shouted back at those greenhorn kids, before he brought the hand to his mouth and tried to close the cut.

The boys laughed.

From the cook stove, Jane said, "You can't jump on those two boys for taking our Lord's name in vain when you do it yourself, Gary Hardee."

He pulled the silk handkerchief from his back pocket and pressed it against the cut. "I didn't take God's name in vain," he said.

"Oh, I am pretty sure you did, and I am even more certain that Preacher Colquhoun would agree."

"They caused me to cut my hand on a spur," he pleaded.

"And how many times have I asked you to remove your spurs before you walk into the house?"

"Waste of time," he whispered.

"Pa!"

He returned to the fight with his boots.

She came through the door. He remembered when the bed-chambers had been separated with a blanket during the winter, checkered sheet during the summer. She let him finish getting the left boot on, then he held up his injured hand.

"Almost cut off my thumb," he said.

She unwound the wrapping, looked over his hand and into his eyes, and let the end of the silk fall. "It's already stopped bleeding."

He smiled. She grinned.

"Pa!"

He sighed. She laughed, bent down, pulled off his hat, kissed the top of his thick hair, returned the hat, and walked back to the stove.

The blue silk neckerchief lay atop the back of the rocking chair, the one Jane had used to rock the boys to sleep, the same one her mother had used to rock her five sons and four daughters to sleep. He tied the scarf around his neck and grabbed the vest that the neckerchief had laid on. Finally, he made a beeline to the window, pushed back the curtains, and leaned outside.

Taylor sat on the top pole of the round pen, rolling a cigarette. At least Evan was doing something productive, cleaning the chestnut gelding's hooves with a pick. Taylor's sorrel was ground-reined near the barn. But he gave both of his sons credit. They had saddled his dun. Gary almost laughed.

Instead, he cleared his throat, and both boys—no, they were young men now—looked his way.

"Won't never get to Kansas if you keep burning daylight," Taylor said.

He nodded. "One thing both of you might ought to remember." Gary waited. "Wat leaves all the hiring and firing to me. I pick who takes a herd to Kansas. I pick who doesn't. And I say who rides drag all night eight hundred and fifty miles. And who gets to be the cook's louse."

The two glanced at each other. Taylor stared at the cigarette he had just licked, and slipped it above his left ear before he pushed himself off the corral post. Evan lowered the chestnut's leg, straightened, set the pick on atop a corral post, and started brushing his hands on his chaps.

Taylor motioned toward the dun. "We saddled your horse, Pa," he said.

"I can see that. Wash up. Your mother's making the last good meal you'll taste till we get back home." Once he came back inside, his smile come out of hiding.

Gary ran the back of his hand over his cheeks. He would have to look closer at Jane's neck. Sometimes that stubble could leave a rash. The thick mustache, Jane always said, just tickled. Had he been smart, he would have shaved before he came to bed, but when a husband's about to leave home for three, four, maybe as long as five months, more often than not, brains got bucked off in a hurry.

Bacon sizzled, and he thought he heard Jane cracking eggs, so he glanced at the mirror and wash basin. He wouldn't get a good shave for months, so he might as well clean up a bit. He was just about finished when he saw her reflection as Jane opened the door. Smiling, he scraped the last bit of graying brown from his throat, wiped the lather on the towel, and folded the razor into its handle, then splashed water on his face and toweled himself dry.

Turning, he found her staring with those intense eyes, her head cocked, a smile beginning to form. Her head shook, and she sighed.

"I know," he said. "Should've thought to have shaved when I got home yesterday."

"It's not that," she said.

He waited. She didn't say another word. "Well?" he tried. "What is it?"

"You don't take your hat off to shave?"

His eyes shot upward, saw the brim of the battered hat some folks might call gray, or charcoal, maybe the color of the dun gelding. After a year, he couldn't remember what color it had been when he had pulled it off the shelf in Abilene.

"Oh." He made no effort to take it off, though.

"Breakfast is ready," she said.

Those blue eyes were turning sad now. Like they always did this time of year.

"I can leave Evan—" He didn't come close to finishing.

"Oh, no, you won't, Gary Hardee. No-sir-ree-bob. You left him behind last year—and I never heard the end of it. For the umpteenth time, Evan's going with you and Taylor, and that's settled."

"Yes, ma'am."

The eyes slowly started to lose that heat. He walked toward her, enveloped her in his arms, and pulled her tight to his chest. He felt her arms wrap around his waist.

"I'll miss you," she whispered.

"You don't know how much I'll miss you," he told her. "Wat says he'll send a rider over every now and then, and if you need anything, you know where to find him."

Major Walter Pool "Wat" Anderson usually organized the gathers in the county between the Brazos and Colorado Rivers. Since Wat owned the biggest spread, the smaller ranchers left all the decisions to him. That is, until the herd started north. At that point, Gary Hardee took command.

"Hugh's still going with you?"

Hugh, a bit older than Taylor, was Anderson's youngest son.

"Last I heard."

"Rich?"

That was Wat's oldest boy.

"No."

"Good," she whispered. Word was that Rich had killed a man down southeast a ways in DeWitt and Karnes Counties in a feud that had started up a few years back between two muleheaded families.

"Last I heard," Gary told her, "Rich was down in Indianola. He never took to cowboying anyhow."

She pulled her head from his chest, and stared into his eyes.

"And Hugh has?" The sarcasm could not be missed.

"He's the Major's son," Gary said, "and Taylor's best friend." He read the worry in her face. "I don't think any Suttons will be following us to put a bullet in Hugh's head."

"You'll be careful," she whispered.

"I always am."

He bent down, kissed her. Her arms tightened around his waist.

"I thought you said breakfast was ready." That was Taylor, who must have just stepped in off the porch.

"We keep Major Wat waiting," Evan chimed in, "and he'll likely send those beeves north without us."

Pulling away from him, Jane shook her head and let out a long sigh.

Gary Hardee smiled. "You're the one who bore me sons."

Chapter 2

The A. T. & S. F. railroad will make the terminus of
their road for the coming year at a new town called
Newton, situated on section 17, township 23, range
one, east, in Sedgwick County. They will also build
cattle yards near the trail, one mile west of town.
—*The Neodesha Citizen,*
April 7, 1871

"Sis, where we goin'?"

Three miles out of town—no, she had to remind herself, that Neodesha was a city now—and those were the first
words her brother had spoken. Denise Beeber had prayed that
Arthur would have remained mute another one hundred and
twenty miles or so.

Sighing, she flicked the lines, which the two jacks ignored as
they pulled the wagon along the trail. "Newton," Denise finally
answered.

"Where's that?"

"North of Wichita. We'll be there in a week or so."

"What's in Newton?" he asked.

"I'm hoping nothing when we get there," she told him. "But
the Santa Fe Railroad is supposed to reach there this summer."

He sniffed, pulled a frayed handkerchief from his vest pocket, and blew his nose. She had not glanced at him once since leaving Neodesha.

"Sis . . ."

Denise knew Arthur stared at her, but she kept her attention on the backsides of the mules, and the road. She didn't dare look her kid brother in the eye. If she had, she might blacken the one that wasn't already raw and bruised. Knock him out of the wagon onto the road, and still not look back.

"I'm sorry."

Biting down the curse, she drew in a breath, exhaled, and still focused on the road.

"Arthur," she whispered after a long moment, "you're always sorry."

How many times had she heard that? Growing up in Little Rock . . . then that brief stay in Eureka Springs . . . over to Fort Smith . . . then up to Missouri—Carthage, Springfield, Nevada—finally into Kansas at Fort Scott, down to Baxter Springs, and then Neodesha, where everything seemed to be going just fine. Until Arthur had to start being Arthur again.

Mayor A.K. Phelon's voice rang through her head one more time.

"What you have to understand, Miss Beeber, is that Neodesha is not just a town anymore. We are a third-class city with more than one thousand people. Good people."

Then A.C. Nycum, who won the election as constable in a landslide, added: "Except for one black sheep."

Yes, Arthur Beeber was the black sheep. He had always been the black sheep. He kept a job about as long as he stayed sober, a trait that reminded Denise of both her mother and father. Her brother had tried religion—four of them, by her count—and had even visited that witch down in the Indian Nations just south of Baxter Springs—but the bottle and many of his friends enticed him back to wickedness. She would have liked to have blamed it on the recent unpleasantness, but both armies had drummed

Arthur out of their corps. He had served eight months wearing butternut, and six months donning the blue, returning to Little Rock with the only scars on his right ankle and both wrists from iron manacles.

"He was playing billiards on the Sabbath," she had told Neodesha's duly elected officials. That sharp tongue was a product of being her mother's daughter. She knew that was a mistake before she even opened her mouth.

"One day, Miss Beeber," the mayor said, "the state of Kansas might lawfully stop such a violation of public decency, and maybe the owners of our saloons shall come around to showing some regard for the feelings of their fellow citizens. But your brother picked up a billiard ball and threw it hard into the face of the Reverend Ross."

Denise would always wonder if the good preacher had stepped into Urgel Soney's place for a friendly game or to buy a cigar that he often called "the Devil's weed."

The constable had picked up the list of complaints.

Arthur threw a stonemason through the billiard saloon's window.

Spit tobacco juice onto the shirtfront of lawyer Yoder, who last month had gotten Arthur Beeber off from a lengthy jail stay with a dazzling defense before Police Judge Hays.

He threatened Mr. Harkullas with a razor and refused to pay for a shave and haircut at the kindly barber's tonsorial parlor.

Urinated into the well on the lot on Wisconsin Street, then tried to throw the real estate agent into said well.

All of that might have read like some whimsical story reprinted in the *Citizen* had it not been for the fact that Arthur wound up on Main Street, where he punched Mr. Roberts in the stomach, brought his right knee up into the poor man's face, then threw him through the front window into the new restaurant he had opened.

She could hear Judge Hays again:

"Roberts inquired if the assault on him was your idea."

Denise had labeled that statement as ridiculous.

Now she knew better than to take her eyes off the road. She tried to dam the tears that wanted to flow like the Verdigris and Fall Rivers. She wanted to lash out at her brother the way her father and mother had until their dying days. She heard again what she had heard just a few days ago.

Hays: "Miss Beeber, I asked Arthur himself, and he did not deny William's statement. In fact, your brother laughed and said, 'Ask Denise.'"

Phelon: "You both compete for business."

Denise: "There are more places for hungry men and women than Mr. Roberts's place and mine in this town . . . I mean, *city* . . . gentlemen."

Nycum: "But William has certainly cut into your patronage, ma'am, since he opened."

Denise: "I have frequented his place myself, sir. I can better him when it comes to pies, cakes, and bread, but his confectionery is extraordinary. I have complimented Mr. Roberts many times."

And it might have gone on and on like that till Judgment Day, but Hays leaned forward, his eyes sad, his voice quiet but strong.

"Denise. He called Annie Bass a whore. In public. You know Missus Bass. She's as fine a lady as you'll find in all of Kansas." Denise did know Annie. Now she knew why the dressmaker hadn't been into Denise's restaurant. Her heart started pounding against her ribs, and she slipped her hands under her thighs to keep her arms from shaking.

"He put a knife against Mr. Cowgill's throat. Now you've got the Masonic Lodge against Arthur—and you. He might have cut Cowgill's throat had it not been for Missus Bass's scream. That turned his attention back to her. And that's what gave me the opportunity to bust your no-good brother's head with my walking stick."

"Missus Bass has approached James McHenry about a lawsuit," Mayor Phelon said. "That lawsuit would name not only your brother, ma'am, but you, too."

"The *Citizen* would be forced to publish articles on such a trial, ma'am." Until that moment, John Gilmore, who had been dining at Denise's restaurant for as long as Denise had been in Neodesha, had not spoken. "And it is undetermined as of this moment if there shall be an article in Friday's paper."

Her hands came from beneath her thighs. Her elbows found the end of the mayor's desk, and she rested her head in her hands.

Constable Nycum cleared his throat. "There's a lot of trees around here, ma'am. And Baxla and Windowmaker sell a lot of rope in their store."

Hays again spoke with that calm voice. "Denise, we decided to meet with you for your own sake."

"We should have run Arthur out of town months ago," Nycum cut in. "Or called on the—"

"Shut up," Hays barked. He smiled the saddest smile Denise had ever seen. "I thought grits were biscuits before you came to town, Denise. Guess that's the Yankee in me. And Roberts might make fine candies, but you wallop him in everything from coffee to pot roast. And your pies . . ." He sighed.

She waited until she thought her voice would not crack. Then she found the real estate agent, the one Arthur had threatened to throw into the well.

"I guess I know why you're here, J.W.," she said. "How much will you give me? But savvy this: the stove's coming with me. So are all the copper and all the cookware. And no way are you getting my recipes."

She smiled. "Because I never put them on paper."

Three days they traveled. Denise cooked breakfast; Arthur hitched the team. They stopped only to rest the mules, or let them drink. And whenever they passed some wayfarer who asked about Neodesha, Denise told them how far away it was, and agreed that it was a fine city. You couldn't call it a town anymore.

"Any hard cases around?" one hard-shell Baptist woman asked.

"No, ma'am," Denise told her. "They've driven out the hard cases."

Arthur pouted the next four miles.

On the fourth morning, just after they crossed the Little Walnut, Denise heard galloping hoofbeats behind her. Arthur's head had slumped forward, sleeping again. The boy could fall asleep anywhere, yet he never once toppled over the wagon's side. She looked back, and pulled the two jacks off to the left, to give the two men an easy pass.

They passed, and she pulled up the scarf, pulled down her hat, and lowered her gaze to let the dust pass.

Arthur jerked awake, and Denise saw the two men slowing down, then stopping their horses at the creek's edge. But they turned their mounts around and walked them a few yards back down the trail.

She didn't recognize them, but Arthur's soft curse told her that he sure did. They had reined up by now, blocking the road.

"What'd you do?" Denise whispered.

"Nothing," Arthur answered. But he was already sweating. And this morning wasn't hot enough to sweat.

Both men smiled. One wore the blue shell jacket of a soldier, but she didn't think he belonged to any of the Kansas forts. He could have been a Yankee from the late war, or he might have been a deserter. The other was big and tall—so tall he looked ridiculous on that small mustang he rode—dressed more like a farmer than anything else, though he did have a pistol stuck in a holster underneath his left shoulder.

She couldn't run over them. So she pulled hard on the leather and held tight to the lines after the mules stopped.

"Mornin'," said the one in the blue jacket.

Denise answered with a nod. Arthur stared ahead, his blue eyes darting between Soldier Coat and the Shoulder Holster.

"Arthur," the tall one said. "You never told us your sister had hair like a Kansas sunset."

Flattening her lips, Denise gave her brother a brief yet intense scowl; then she looked back at the two men. She waited for her brother to say something before she gave the two riders a chance to explain. When no one spoke, she did.

"You got business with my brother?"

"Yes, ma'am." Soldier Coat tipped his battered hat. "We surely do."

"Arthur." But Denise did not take her eyes off the two riders.

The wind stilled. No prairie hens sang, and the creek gave no sound. The only noise came from the heavy breaths of tired mules and hard-ridden horses.

"Well, we got business with you, too, ma'am," Soldier Coat said, grinning and standing in his stirrups, looking Denise up and down.

"Rex." The big one pushed back his hat. He started to dismount, thought better of it, and put both hands on the horn of his saddle. "Lady. Arthur, Rex, and I, and a few others, had a dice game going inside that run-down old frame house nobody's lived in on Mill Street. Your brother was hot for a while, but then his luck ran out like his whiskey."

"He bet your eating house," the other one said. "And I won it."

Arthur started breathing in and out in short breaths, but Denise did not look at him.

"He didn't own my place of business, gentlemen," she told them. "It was never in his name. So you were misinformed."

The mules snorted.

"We don't see it that way," Soldier Coat said.

"Arthur running off like he did, and you running with him, well . . ." Shoulder Holster shrugged. "You see how it looks."

"Word around Neodesha is that you sold your eating place for a right smart of money," Soldier Coat said.

Her mouth and throat turned into a desert. And for a cool morning, now Denise started to feel the beads of sweat popping out on her forehead. Her heart pounded. She tried to work up enough moisture in her mouth, tried to get her brain to be re-born, tried to make her stupid brother say something that would straighten out this entire mess.

Another mess in which she found herself right in the middle.

"You were misinformed." It sounded like the lie it was.

Soldier Coat lowered himself into the saddle, then dis-mounted, and handed the reins to his partner.

"Rex," the big one said.

"Shut up." The man kept smiling as he walked toward De-nise's side of the wagon. "Arthur, you should've told us that your sister didn't look nothing like you. Just put her up instead of her lousy victualing house."

He stopped at the side of the wagon and offered his hands to help Denise to the ground.

She felt confused. This had to be a dream. She was twenty-five years old, on her way to Newton, Kansas, simply because of one paragraph she had read in the *Citizen*. On her way from a suc-cessful victualing house in a fine third-class city in a pretty town in Kansas where she had neighbors and friends.

Well, she had had neighbors and friends and a successful busi-ness.

Then she caught a glimpse of the revolver, a Navy Colt, at the side of her head. Not pointed at her, though. She was staring down at the man called Rex. The revolver was . . .

It roared before she made the connection. The flash of white smoke and orange flame blinded her, and the roar so close to her head left her eardrums throbbing. The last thing she remem-bered seeing was Rex's blue eyes—widening in horror, his mouth opening to scream, as his right hand shot down toward the butt of a revolver shoved inside his waistband. His left hand came up in a fruitless defensive gesture.

The mules jerked the leather lines from her hand, and she felt herself falling over the wagon's side. Maybe she fell. Perhaps Arthur pushed her. She knew she had not jumped. She didn't have enough muscles to do that.

Somehow, she managed to stretch out her arms to break her fall, flipped over, landed.

Echoes popped around her. Hooves pounded sand. Her left wrist hurt like the devil. Mules snorting, the wagon lurched forward while a horse splashed across the creek. When she could breathe again, when she thought she could move, she opened her eyes and put the nightmare behind her. Until she rolled over, pushed herself up with her right hand, and looked into the face of Soldier Coat, his eyes staring straight up, mouth open, and a small hole in his left cheek.

Somehow, Denise fought down the bile in her throat, and sat up. She found another hole in his chest, just below ribcage.

Arthur.

She realized she hadn't said anything. Now she turned where the wagon should be, but wasn't. She looked toward the creek and saw the back of the stove, still on the wagon, the mules stopped in the shallow water. The horses Shoulder Holster and Soldier Coat had ridden were gone. Which way, she didn't know, didn't care. Her eyes swept over the road, and she saw Shoulder Holster lying in the grass on the north side of the trail, on his side.

"Arthur." This time she shouted loud enough for one of the mules to answer with a bray.

She didn't realize she had managed to stand, but she stepped onto the road, started for the one in the grass, but stopped. There was no need to look at him. She had already seen one dead man.

"Help."

That was stupid. Only the mules heard her.

"*Arthur.*" This time she screamed, and then she realized where her brother was.

She ran to the wagon, climbed into the back, skirted around the big stove, over the boxes, the trunk that still held her grandmother's wedding gown and the daguerreotype of Mama and Daddy. Onto the bench, and there he sat, slumped against the side wall. She sank into the box.

He looked up at her and pulled a bloodstained hand away from a crimsoned shirt. When his mouth opened, blood dripped over his lips. She kicked his left leg accidentally, but he didn't feel it. Somehow, she twisted and sank beside him, took his bloody hand in hers, and looked at the holes in his belly.

"Stupid," she whispered.

His lips formed: *I know.*

Her head shook. That wasn't what she meant. She felt the tears streaming down her face and pushed herself closer to him. His head rested on her shoulder, and she brushed the bangs out of his eyes with her bloody fingers. His blood.

He coughed slightly, then let out a long sigh. Her brain started working again. Wichita. If she pushed the mules, she could reach Wichita today. Maybe tonight. She glanced at the sun. She had no idea how long she had been lying on the roadside, stunned. Her wrist still hurt like blazes.

The dead men? No time to move them, or load them onto the wagon. There was hardly any room with the big stove and everything anyway. Maybe she'd find some small settlement before reaching Wichita. Maybe there would be a doctor. Or an Army patrol. Or a farm.

"Arthur," she whispered. "Try not to move. Try not to move." She moved her lips closer to his nearest ear. "I'm going to get you to a doctor. You're going to be fine. Just hang on, brother. Just hang on."

She started to move away from him, looked into his eyes, and felt that heart break into a million pieces. Sinking back into the box, she pulled Arthur's head onto her shoulder and wailed. She cursed and cried, mourning for Arthur and cursing, not her brother, but herself. The fool kid was always doing something that would get him in trouble. Even Daddy had predicted that Arthur would come to a silly end.

"It wasn't silly at all, Daddy," Denise managed to choke out. "He was protecting me—protecting me."

She kissed his head and hugged him tighter, rocking as much as she could in the cramped confines of a driver's box in a farm wagon. She begged God to forgive her, begged Arthur to forgive her, because the last words he ever heard from Denise had been his big sister calling him *Stupid*.

Chapter 3

The Messrs. Perry Brothers called on us this week,
while on their way to Newton. They are preparing to
start a paper at that place. There will soon be four papers in Sedgwick County, and we may have a German
paper in Wichita, which will make five. This speaks
well for our county, for there must be something to
induce newspaper men to come or they would not
come. We bid them welcome.
—*The Wichita Tribune*,
April 20, 1871

Since the wind sucked smoke through the window, Cindy
Bagwell did not complain about the man with the stovepipe
hat who kept firing up one cigar after the other. Nor did she carp
about the drummer in the sack suit, who, every time he fell
asleep, kept dropping his head onto Cindy's shoulder. She would
just nudge him gently, and he would sit up, mumble some apology, and stare out the window, before he dozed again.

There was nothing to do about the dust, so she did not grum-
ble about that, either. Besides, the Dutch Reformed preacher in
the center bench complained enough about the dust. Close the
curtain, and the smoke would fill the entire coach—pipes from
the preacher and the quiet man in the black broadcloth suit; cig-

arettes from the cattleman who called Kansas City home, and the burly man with greasy buckskins who said he was a hide hunter and certainly smelled like some dead animal; and some sort of slim Mexican thing that seemed too small for a cigar and too big for a cigarette that the brazen woman with a powdered face kept puffing while playing cards with the gent from Chicago who used his lawyer's briefcase as a table.

Besides, the dust wasn't so bad. It smelled like sage. Not the swamps and tobacco and cotton that she had been breathing in all those years down in Alabama.

And she knew better than to criticize the jehu who drove this coach. He seemed intent on hitting every rock, every limb, every hole in the road. No matter how many times the other passengers cursed, yelled, or threatened the driver, that Concord never missed running over something. It leaped up, landed hard, and tilted to the right, sending Cindy slamming against the dozing drummer and the cigar-smoker who pinned her there, but just for a moment. Because the coach landed back on all four wheels, then listed on the left side so that Cindy slammed against the cigar smoker, and the drummer's head cocked Cindy's cheek so hard she was certain she'd sport a bruise.

Cards flew in her face. The hide hunter fell to his knees, and he must have shoved the Dutch Reformist forward—or backward, depending on how one viewed the seating arrangements— and the preacher's face planted right between Cindy's breasts.

He pushed himself back as the coach righted itself, and Cindy shoved him harder. That sent him back toward the hide hunter, who caught him. Everyone then bounced up and down a few times before the jehu, after uttering just about every foul word Cindy had encountered, yelled:

"Y'all all right down there?"

The hide hunter just about matched the driver's mastery of profanity. The sassy woman called the jehu a bigger jackass than those pulling the Concord.

The jehu laughed.

When things quietened, the Chicago man started regathering the cards, and people settled back into the nearest thing to comfort they could find.

"We'll be arriving in Wichita, folks, in about twenty minutes." That was the messenger, the fellow with the big mustache and linen duster who never let go of the double-barreled shotgun he carried. He even took it with him to the privy. Cindy had hoped he might grant her an interview, but when she finally had summoned up enough courage to approach him at the last home station, he had laughed, shook his head, said, "Ma'am, I ain't never heard of no lady newspaperman." And then he walked away.

Before that, the Chicago lawyer had volunteered to be Cindy's escort, chaperone, and protector. She had thanked him for his kindness but did not accept his invitation, because she thought he had other motives. It didn't really matter, though, because he lost interest in Cindy when the sassy woman boarded the coach at Burlingame.

Passengers resettled themselves. The man in the stovepipe hat lighted a new cigar. The drummer yawned without covering his mouth, shifted around, recrossed his legs, and nodded off to sleep. Eventually, his head rested on Cindy's shoulder.

She sighed, but figured he would wake up soon enough. There had to be fewer than ten minutes before they would arrive at Wichita and Cindy Bagwell might never have to take another stagecoach ride for the rest of her life.

This time, the drummer's left hand fell atop Cindy's thigh. She was reaching over to remove the hand ever so gently when she felt the fingers give her a tight little squeeze.

She drew a breath. The hand relaxed, then squeezed again. Cindy put her hand on his wrist and dug her nails deep into the drummer's flesh.

The head jerked off Cindy's shoulder and the hand off her leg, and he cursed while clamping his right hand over the blood oozing out of his left wrist.

"Next time," Cindy said, using her iciest voice, "I cut off your hand."

The hide hunter tilted his head back and let out a ragged laugh. "Bully for you, missy," he called out. "Bully for you."

She peered out the window and felt the relief of seeing frame buildings, curtains, and people. Blessed people—folks with whom she had not been rammed inside a compact stagecoach for what felt like months.

"Wichita, folks!" the jehu shouted. "Then south to Arkansas City."

He pronounced it ARE-kan-zas. That would take some getting used to.

"Changin' teams. Changin' crews."

"Thank God," the Dutch Reformed preacher said.

Laughter filled the Concord. Even the drummer, still nursing his gouged wrist, smiled. Probably because the stagecoach slowed, creaked, and moaned to a stop.

"Toilets be behind the station," the driver said as he opened the door and helped the drummer out. "You have time to guzzle down some of Joe's coffee, maybe have a bite of sowbelly stew."

Young men were already leading the team of mules away from the wagon and bringing another to it.

The hide hunter jumped out without the jehu's help, but Cindy let him help her.

"This is the end of the road for you, right, missy?" the jehu asked.

"Yes."

He pointed to the back of the stagecoach. "Mike's fetching your bags. Make sure he don't make no mistake."

She started, stopped, and after the Dutch Reformist climbed out, she asked, "Might you know the way to *The Wichita Times?*"

The man was helping the sassy woman off.

"The what, missy?" the jehu asked. The Chicago lawyer and the man in the stovepipe hat exited without his assistance.

"*The Wichita Times?*" Cindy repeated. "It's the newspaper run by Ralph Bodie."

"Oh." He shook his head. "Can't help you, missy. I don't read."

"Well, thank you, sir," she told him. The Alabama in her made her thank him, even though she wasn't sure her backside, back, or neck would ever recover from the ride he had given her since taking over the run at Fort Scott. Carrying her valise, she moved to the boot, where the messenger handed her a brass-studded leather suitcase and a satchel hatbox. No trunk. Nothing overly heavy. Three pieces of luggage was all she needed—all she had, carrying everything she had to her name.

No one offered to help her carry anything, but the messenger pointed toward the west.

"Just walk toward the river, ma'am," he said. "The Arkansas River." He too called it ARE-kan-zas. "You're on Douglas Avenue, ma'am. When you get to the last block before the river, turn north. That's right. That's Wichita Street. Two blocks up, head back thisaway on Second Street. The *Times* is somewhere there, if I ain't mistaken."

"That's right," she told him. "Mr. Bodie says he's on Second Street. I have the address in the telegram."

She was going to thank him, too, but he was already walking away, and the new team was beginning to be hitched to the Concord.

When she found a spot of shade, she searched through her valise until discovering the telegram Ralph Bodie had sent her, offering her the job, boasting that he was excited to meet her, and that Wichita was a booming city that could use a woman's touch and Cindy's gift for words. Besides, Ralph Bodie had worked with Cindy's father back during their brief but glorious enterprise together as correspondents for the *Southern Punch*.

Lugging the suitcase, hat case, and valise, she finally made it toward the edge of town. She could see the Arkansas River—

"ARE-kan-zas," she tested her tongue, shrugged. No bridge, and the river looked wide. Someone emerged from the river.

Her mouth fell open. Luckily, he was too far away for Cindy to get the entire picture, but, by thunder, that man was naked. He was taking a bath, in a river that looked like it carried more mud than fresh water. Quickly, she turned onto Wichita Street and walked past stores. Even quicker, she forgot that image of a naked man taking a bath in a river. Carpenters busied themselves putting up another frame building. A carriage rolled past. At First Street, two men galloped horses right down the middle of the street in the middle of the day, shouting, laughing, one of the riders hitting his horse's rump with a battered hat.

More dust.

Cindy hoped the house Mr. Bodie told her about had a place to bathe. She was already covered with dust from the journey across Kansas.

She turned on Second, and looked for the number six. There it was, across the street. She looked both ways, found not galloping horses, just a mule tethered in front of one building, and a freight wagon parked across the other.

More carpenters gathered around *The Wichita Times*. Only, one of the men on a ladder was removing the shingle that hung from a post.

Through the open door, two men of color carried out the printing press.

She set the hat satchel and suitcase on the boardwalk.

"Excuse me . . ." The men straining with the press did not even look at her. But the man taking the sign from the fellow on the ladder turned, still holding the sign, and smiled.

"Yes'm."

"Is . . . is *The Wichita Times* moving?"

That had to be the reason. Of course, Mr. Bodie needed a bigger office for his newspaper if he were hiring a staff or reporters and editors. He . . .

"You might could say that." The man coming down the ladder chuckled. The one holding *The Wichita Times* sign just stared blankly.

A burly man with a silver handlebar mustache came out of the building.

"I'm paying you boys two bits to work. Not gab."

He glared at Cindy.

"I'm looking for Ralph Bodie, editor of *The Wichita Times*, sir."

The man blinked, smoothed his mustache, and looked at the blank-faced man as if the latter might have the answer. But the fellow who had been on the ladder answered.

"Bodie got kilt, ma'am. Three days ago. Shot dead at his desk and—"

"Shut up," the man with the big mustache said, and he faced Cindy again. "What business did you have with Bodie?"

She blinked and stared, and tried to assure herself that either the man had been playing a joke, though his humor showed poor taste and bad judgment, or she had simply misheard.

"He promised me a job." She swallowed.

"As what?"

"A reporter," she whispered.

The man now laughed. "You funnin' me, missy?"

But her face must have told him the answer, and he cut the laugh short.

"You were gonna work for Ralph Bodie?"

She didn't answer. Instead, she asked, "Is he really . . . dead?"

The man holding the sign decided to put it in the wagon with the rest of the stuff being removed from the office.

"He's dead." The man smoothed the ends of his mustache, and looked at the one who had removed the shingle from the post.

"But . . . he was going to pay me fifteen dollars a week." She wished she could have stopped that sentence before it escaped, but it was the first thing that struck her. More than nine hundred miles on riverboats, wagons, and coaches. She didn't have enough money to get back to Alabama.

"Fifteen dollars," the one now removing the ladder said with a chuckle. "By thunder, I ought to become a newspaperman."

"How?" she coughed out that question. Heart attack, she guessed. That must have been it. That's how her father had died, which was how he said all newspapermen died. Clutching a quill at the desk, or marking up all the mistakes the tramp printer had made setting type. That shot-dead comment. That was . . . Western humor.

"Bill Schlichter put a bullet in his belly," the man said.

Her mouth moved to form the question, but nothing audible came out.

The man with the big mustache answered anyway. He must have read her lips. "Because that piece of Southern trash wrote once too often about Yankee raiders. It's a wonder nobody gunned the blowhard down before Bill done it."

"But I was to be—"

"Lady, it ain't none of my affair. You lost a job. I lost a tenant. I can find me a new tenant, and it sure won't be another newspaper editor. We got enough papers already. But don't bother trying the *Vidette*. It's Republican to the core, the way a Kansas paper ought to be. And I don't think Sowers or Hutchison will be charmed by that Southern drawl you got. And Albert Yale over at the *Tribune* won't risk a scandal by hiring a petticoat reporter. So if I was you, I'd hightail it back to South Carolina or wherever you secesh come from. Print your lies back to folks who actually believe the libel you say."

She tried to tell him she came from Alabama, not South Carolina, but he was already back inside what once had been a newspaper office.

"You might try the *Herald*."

She turned to the voice. It was the man, still holding the ladder. He wasn't laughing anymore, not kidding. He probably saw the tears in her eyes.

"Arby McBane's hired himself a young whippersnapper of an editor," the worker said. "Can't recollect his name. McBane, he's the publisher. Paper comes out every Thursday. Evenings. Today's Thursday. Everybody ought to be working right about now."

"Oh," she said.

Chapter 4

We hazard nothing in saying that Texas cattle did
much to prolong the struggle about Richmond. Up to
the very last, Lee's ragged battalions were actually
kept alive by Texas cattle rations. . . . But, with the
close of the war, this trade took a new shoot, and now
serves a more profitable purpose. The cattle no longer
sustain men that they may kill their fellows, but are
themselves slain for the mutual benefit of all parties
and sections of the country . . .
—*The Leavenworth Bulletin*,
March 10, 1871

Major Walter Pool "Wat" Anderson usually organized the
gather near the bend of the Brazos, twenty or so miles
southeast of Richmond. Here, one never worried about water or
rain, and the grass always grew green and tall on the coastal
prairies. There was plenty of shade in the live oaks. Cattle were
easy to find, since the elevation usually changed from flat to flat-
ter. Cattle didn't have many places to hide, and the only danger
was losing a steer in a mud bog, or a cowhand losing an arm, leg,
or life to an alligator. Every rancher must have had a good year,
Gary Hardee thought after reining up after he and his sons forded
the river.

Evan pulled along Gary's right, and Taylor stopped on Gary's left. Evan let out a whistle.

"Gosh a'mighty," he said. "How many steers, you reckon?"

Which was what Gary was wondering.

"Last year we drove two thousand," Taylor told his younger brother. "We probably started out with a couple hundred more. Pa says you're always likely to lose some on the drive north."

Pushing his hat back, Gary stood in the stirrups.

Taylor sought out confirmation. "Ain't that right, Pa?"

Two fires, one on the northwestern flats, the other off to the southeast, closer to most of the shade. Cowboys brought in roped steers to both camps. *Two* camps. That's what dumbfounded Gary. If some rancher had decided to take a herd up to Kansas himself, Gary would have heard that kind of news—because the Major wasn't the kind of man to let that happen without raising a commotion and busting a few heads.

"Pa?"

Gary settled back into the saddle, smoothed his mustache, and tried to make out which wagon looked like the one he was used to. But his eyes couldn't find any difference—wagons, even chuckwagons, pretty much all looked alike—and the wind wasn't blowing this way, so he could not detect the smell of coffee, for no one in South Texas brewed better than Moises Dunn.

"Pa?"

This time Gary heard. "What?" He did not bother trying to hide his irritation. If Wat Anderson had changed things up, without consulting Gary, the old soldier would rue such poor judgment.

"I was telling Evan that we usually take more than two thousand head. Because we might lose some. Stampedes and river crossings and such. Ain't that right, Pa?"

Now, becoming a father again—not a contrary trail boss and cattle drover—Gary made himself grin. The older brother, letting the kid brother know how ignorant he was. Being the middle brother while growing up, Gary could remember being on both sides of that equation.

"That's right." He looked over at Evan and gave the boy a wink. "'Course, there have been times when we arrive with more steers than we left with. It's amazing how many farm cows just like to join our herd, and try to court the boys."

The boy blinked. "You don't pay the farmer for his cow?"

That was Evan. Ever the idealist. A trait he inherited from his mother.

Gary shrugged. "Half the time, we don't even notice the newcomer till the tally man gives us a head count in the stockyards." He studied the action down below, adding softly, "And you don't find too many farmers with enough sand to ride into a trail crew's camp and make accusations of rustling and the like."

He kicked the dun into an easy walk and rode northwest, toward the tallgrass, then turned southeast and the live oaks. That's where the Major usually set up camp, and Wat was as superstitious as Gary Hardee and Moises Dunn when it came to trail drives and gathers. Fifty yards later, he reined in, twisted in the saddle, and looked back at the other camp. He smoothed his mustache, the way he often did when trying to figure something out that didn't make sense, and finally jerked his thumb toward the usual camping ground.

"You boys ease your way to that cook fire. I'll be back in a jiffy."

He pulled the hat down harder and spurred the dun, leaving his sons staring as he raised dust across the grasslands, not slowing down until he neared the camp. For a moment, he thought he had guessed wrong, as he watched Miguel Sanchez bring a roped steer toward the branding fire, and Bill Bailey rise from a squat, but keep the iron in the hot coals till a couple of cowhands walked up to the roped steer and tossed it to the ground.

Miguel Sanchez had been riding with Wat Anderson for as long as Gary could remember, and Bill Bailey had moved between cowboy and lawing since the end of the war. But Gary saw the chuckwagon clearly now, and that was not Moises Dunn's rig.

Bailey gave a brief nod before he turned around and walked with the hot iron to the moaning steer. He slapped the iron against the hide. Smoke rose, hair and hide burned, the steer bawled, and Bailey pulled back the iron, as the other cowboys released the animal.

After handing the iron to another cowhand, Bailey stepped toward Gary.

"Good to see you ag'in, Capt'n."

Still looking at the steer that had been branded, Gary wiped the dust off his mouth and chin and nodded at the chuckwagon. "That's not Moises Dunn's rig." He hooked his thumb toward the other campsite. "You not working for the Major this year?"

The look on Bailey's face told Gary what he needed to know.

"Times change, I reckon," Gary said.

"It ain't that bad, Capt'n." Bailey pointed southeast. "The Major'll be sippin' Moises's good brew over yonder. He'll fill you in—since I can see he ain't already tol' you his plans for this year."

"Who's cooking your coffee?" Gary asked.

"Adam Pollock. He cooked for Shanghai Pierce, till he got sick of Shanghai or Shanghai got sick of him. You know Shanghai."

Everybody in Texas knew Shanghai Pierce. Pierce was a cattleman, and he would let anyone and everyone know that when it came to cattle drovers and cattlemen, few came better, or tougher, than Shanghai Pierce.

"And who's bossing your outfit?"

"Reckon I ought to leave that to the Major, Capt'n." Suddenly, he beamed. "Hey, I spied two young rascals ridin' down that hill with you. You bringin' the kid this time?"

"Reckon I ought to leave that to the kid to tell you." He was already turning the dun around when he started the sentence, and spurred the horse into a lope to put a period at the end.

* * *

Some things, at least, remained the same. Hugh Anderson, looking cocksure, stood by the fire at the other camp, chatting with Taylor and Evan, and that was Moises Dunn's chuckwagon. When the old cook saw Gary slowing the dun to a walk, he limped over with a cup to fill. He would bring that one over to Gary, but that was the only cup he would serve for the rest of the drive.

If there were a drive.

Major Wat Anderson sat on his folding stool, but he pushed himself up when Gary stopped the horse.

And Carlos Morales walked over, smiling that sunny grin he always had. This would be his third time wrangling for the herd, which meant he had to be sixteen years old now. He stopped on Gary's left, waiting.

Gary made himself smile at the young Mexican.

"You trying to match Wat in the mustache department, Carlos?"

The boy smoothed the black fuzz above his lip and said, "I have many years before my hair turns white, Señor Hardee."

Gary chuckled before he swung down and handed the reins to Carlos.

"I wonder," the boy said, "how long it took the major to grow a mustache like that."

"He's had it as long as I've known him," Gary said, "and I knew him since I was your age, back when his hair was black as yours."

The boy led the horse to the picket line, but stopped when Gary called out his name.

"Don't unsaddle him, yet," he said as he started walking toward the crew around the chuckwagon. "We'll see how long I'm staying."

Wat Anderson turned toward the teenagers by the fire. "I pay for work, not gossiping around a cookfire. Pick your poison, boys, branding or roping."

"Pa . . ." Hugh started.

The glare from his father silenced the kid. Taylor and Hugh strode toward the picket line, while Evan smiled and hurried to the branding fire.

After taking a few steps toward Gary, the Major stopped. His hair was white as snow, but the face bronzed from years in the sun. The mustache hung all the way to the top pockets on his corduroy vest, and he pulled a cigar from the top pocket, found a lucifer in a lower pocket, and struck it against the buckle of his chaps.

By then, Dunn had reached Gary with the cup of coffee. They nodded their greetings without a spoken word, and the cook limped back to the Studebaker.

Gary took a sip—one that usually would have relaxed him, but not this time—and he strode toward the Major.

"Didn't recognize the road brand they were slapping on that herd," he said, and pointed the tin cup toward the far camp.

"Registered it two weeks ago," the Major said. "It's Hugh's brand."

Which might have made sense if it weren't a road brand. Hugh had to be closing in on his twentieth birthday, if Gary remembered right. But this was a road brand, a sale brand, not a brand registered to a rancher.

"We had a good calf crop, a good winter and a good spring," the Major said after removing his cigar. "I'm sending two thousand head with you, and Hugh's taking twelve hundred. Ride the market while it's still good."

Ride the whirlwind, Gary thought about saying, but for once, curbed his tongue.

"Major . . ." He decided a respectful tone might be in order. "Hugh rode drag last year, the year before, and the one before that, he was Moises's louse."

"He was at point," the Major said, "when you brought the herd into Abilene last year."

Which was true. But that had been for show, to give Wat something to brag about at The Drovers Cottage to the other ranchers,
drovers, trail bosses, and cattle buyers. After eight hundred and
fifty miles over seventy-two days, those two thousand beeves
weren't going to do anything but drag their worn-out hides into
the Great Western Stockyards, for forty-two dollars a head.

"You got a good man over yonder." Gary gestured with his left
arm. "Bill Bailey. He could show Hugh—"

"Bill's riding point."

Well, that was something.

"I'm sure Hugh wants Taylor riding with him," the Major said.

Gary had thought about letting Taylor and Hugh ride flank instead of drag on this drive, while keeping Evan on drag for the
entire trip.

"Gary."

He looked up at the Major, those usually fierce green eyes
now looking sad and old.

"I figured you could keep an eye on Hugh. Our deal stands,
same as always. And I'll up the percentage two points for whatever Hugh's twelve hundred bring. Your trail leads, his follows. I
know it'll be a heavy load, but you're the one man I know who
could help this old soldier out."

That was as close as the Major would come to playing the Carolina debt. *Help this old soldier out.* Gary looked at the whiskers
and the mustache, the long white hair that hung to his shoulders.
The whiskers and mustache grown to hide the grapeshot that
had knocked out teeth and tore through the face, and the mangled ear that was hidden by the white hair—all done while drag-
ging Captain Gary Hardee out of fire on that idiotic last charge at
Bentonville.

His right hip started aching, like he could feel that splintered
Minié ball rolling around.

Turning, he stared across the valley. Taylor was already bringing a roped steer toward camp. Gary turned to the branding fire

where Evan stood gripping a branding iron—the G-H Con-nected—and ready to burn the road brand onto the hide.

Gary also was figuring out the best plan. Send Hugh Anderson out first? If Hugh's herd stampeded, the cattle would likely run in the direction they were pointed. North. Providing they ran after dark. Gary's two thousand most likely would not get caught up in the run. On the other hand, if Hugh led, Gary would have to move upstream to find water not muddied up by Hugh's steers and horses, but that was a selfish thought. And Bill Bailey would know enough to move the herd to cleaner water. On the other hand, Hugh would have to find the camping grounds—and that hard-headed boy, Gary guessed, would be too proud to listen to any advice Bailey or another seasoned trail hand gave him. But at least the kid would have Bailey riding with him.

He looked back at the fire, where Evan was squatting. Deke Brown was there. He had been riding up the trail back when they took beeves to Sedalia, before Missourians started bellyaching and bushwhacking after claiming that Texas Fever kept killing their milch cows. Deke knew cattle and horses. He was also a jackass and a bully. But Jacob Cooper was at the fire, too, and he had been hiring out to the Major since '68.

Trail bossing wasn't all that complicated. By thunder, if Gary Hardee could do it . . .

"I'll up it to two and a half percent," Wat Anderson said.

Gary shook his head and sipped the coffee, now cold. "You don't have to do that, Major."

"I don't have to, Gary," the Major said, "but I just said I was going to, so it's done."

Gary sighed, and nodded. "All right."

"I hate to surprise you like this, Gary." The Major sounded much older now. "But I want Hugh to be as far away from his brother for a spell."

Most likely, Hugh's mother wanted her baby not to follow in Rich's tracks.

"How's Lou?" Gary asked.

The Major shrugged. "Fine. Except when she's meaner than a mad dog."

Gary smiled. The Major asked, "And Jane?"

"Happy to have the house to herself." He smiled, knowing it was a lie, but thinking how at least Jane didn't have to worry about having one son who had killed a man, and another who had always wanted to best his big brother at anything.

"Thanks for sticking with me," the Major whispered.

Gary somehow managed to keep his smile. "We're like an old married couple, Major. But you're not the only one with some news."

After handing his cup to the Major, he started toward the picket line, where Carlos had tied up Gary's horse.

Chapter 5

Sirs:—In compliance with your request that I should write a communication for your paper descriptive of this section of Texas, the manners and customs of the people, the nature of the country and its chief resources, I now set about the task . . .
Cattle being the principal wealth of the country, boys here learn to ride, and read cattle brands before they have learned the alphabet.
—*The Saline County Journal,*
September 21, 1871

Evan had already burned the road brand onto the hide of the steer Taylor had roped, while Gary's oldest son recoiled his lariat.

Gary stopped walking. "Taylor." When his son looked over, Gary gave him orders. "Head back to Hugh's camp." He was sure Hugh had already told his best friend since they were toddlers about his rise in cattle-driving prominence, probably rubbing it in Taylor's face. "Tell Bill Bailey to ride over here on the double."

That might trouble Bailey and Taylor, not to mention Evan, who was leaning against the branding iron and eavesdropping on the conversation. Gary needed to add an explanation, and he never had been fond of explaining things. But there were exceptions.

"I need to talk to him about our drive." *Our* drive. That still didn't sit well in Gary's stomach.

"Hugh." The Major called out to his son, who pitched a cigarette to the ground and started walking toward his father.

"Stomp that smoke out, boy," the old soldier roared. "We've seen enough wildfires." He shook his head and sighed.

Hugh did not argue. He stopped, turned, and stepped on the butt he had discarded, twisting left and right, left and right, left and right, then strode over.

"Captain Hardee has agreed to the plan, son," the Major said, softening once Hugh stood. The kid was taller than his father, and muscled, too, the freckles he had as a boy faded, and he had started a mustache—thicker than Carlos's—but no match when compared to Gary's or, especially, Major Wat Anderson's.

Criminy, when you start comparing your thick mustache to a kid's, you know you're getting old and crotchety.

"I got something Hugh and Bill ought to see, Major." Gary said. "You need to see it, too."

He continued toward the picket line, and began fumbling with the buckles to the saddlebag, but stopped to watch Taylor hook his lariat around the horn, then spur the sorrel gelding into a lope across the valley. The boy centered a horse right well, and carried himself easy in a trot, lope, or gallop.

After finding the circular in the saddle bag, he pulled it out, and walked back.

Wat Anderson had news, too, and he shared it with Gary before he could unfold the broadside.

"Did you hear about Tom Smith?" the Major asked.

Stopping, Gary shook his head.

"He's dead." The Major held out a clipping from a newspaper. Gary took it with his left hand, keeping the circular, still folded, in his right.

The paper had been torn, from the top of the November 10 *Weekly Times*. It wasn't a local newspaper, and just two columns from the top of the paper had been ripped. His eyes went to the headline in the second column.

TERRIBLE AFFAIR.

He sighed when he found the smaller headlines.

Marshal Tom Smith of Abilene, Murdered.
His Head is Cut off with an Axe.

One paragraph, nineteen lines, wrapped up the foul murder of a dedicated public servant. Smith had been sent to Chapman's Creek, roughly fifteen miles from Abilene, Kansas, and apparently, while Smith struggled with one of the men, the other found an ax and struck the lawman on the back of the neck. The wanted men, at least as of November 10, months ago, had not been apprehended.

Gary blew out a long breath and returned the clipping.

"My lawyer in San Antonio mailed it to me," the Major said. "Someone found it in a stagecoach. Paper was from Leavenworth. That's what J.D. Day told me."

"That's a shame," Gary said. "Smith was a good man."

"That's what he gets," Hugh said, "for trying to take guns away from we Texans."

Gary ignored the boy. "Good lawman. Hard to keep the peace in a cowtown, but Smith, he sure knew how to do it."

Smith enforced a policy that few Texans—Gary Hardee included, at first—thought possible. No cowboy rode into Abilene's city proper carrying a firearm. Deke Brown, ornery as a stepped-on rattlesnake, had tried, and that redheaded Kansas lawman had mopped up a saloon's floor with Deke's face, then dragged Deke and one of Shanghai Pierce's cowhands to what passed for a jail in Abilene.

After that, Gary had no problem collecting every short gun from his trail crew. They didn't ride into town with even a hide-away gun, and Carlos Morales had asked Gary to keep his pock-etknife before he went to ride in for a bath, haircut, and a shave—that being before Carlos had decided to grow out a mustache, or what he thought was the beginnings of a mustache.

"Well, Abilene will be free for us to hurrah this year," Hugh said, "now that that thick-headed fool . . ."

"Son." The Major sighed. "No man, even a Yankee, deserves to die like Marshal Smith died."

The boy pouted.

"Besides," the Major added, "those Kansans will probably hire another hard rock for a law dog."

"Likely," Gary said. "But I'm not sure Abilene is going to be welcoming us back this year. Us . . ." He started to unfold the circular. "Or any herds from Texas."

Gary handed the broadside to the Major, who settled onto his folding stool. Gary went over to the coffeepot to fill two cups. By the time he was back, Bill Bailey was reining in his black gelding, swinging down, and handing the reins to Carlos.

Wat Anderson finished reading the circular.

"Taylor said you wanted to see me," Bailey said.

After sipping coffee, Gary looked at the Major, who sighed and held up the paper for Bailey to take.

We, the undersigned, members of the Farmers' Protective Association, and officers and citizens of Dickinson County, Kansas, most respectfully request all who have contemplated driving Texas cattle to Abilene for the coming season to seek some other point for shipment, as the inhabitants of Dickinson will no longer submit to the evils of the trade.

Bailey shook his head.

"I can't believe Mr. McCoy would let them get away with

that," the Major whispered as Bailey returned the broadside to Gary.

Joseph McCoy, an Illinoisian, had lured Texas cattlemen to Abilene back in '67, with massive stockyards and a cowboy-friendly environment.

"Imagine he was outnumbered," Gary said. "The *Chronicle* never cared much for our trade, despite all the fine articles we gave them, not to mention lots of money we left in Abilene."

And not just money at saloons, brothels, and gambling dens. Just about every cowboy off the trail spent money on baths and shaves, and new duds. Cowhands might not be able to afford a room or a meal at The Drovers Cottage, but they would eat at smaller grease pits. The married ones bought presents for their wives. The fathers found something for their kids. Abilene, just like Baxter Springs in '66 and Sedalia before, wasn't just a Sodom or Gomorrah.

Bailey nodded. "I figured this'd happen, and if the citizens of Abilene wasn't sick of the gamblers, prostitutes and, yeah, our rowdy boys, the farmers would've started up on Texas Fever. Just like they did in Missouri."

"Do you think they will close off Abilene?" the Major asked.

"Maybe not this year," Gary said.

"I heard Ellsworth has sent out some riders encouraging us to try them," Bailey said. "Great Bend, too."

The Major nodded. "Should we try Baxter Springs again?"

"We need a better railroad," Gary said. "The Kansas Pacific was good to us in Abilene."

"There is the Santa Fe," Bailey said.

Gary nodded. The Major sipped his coffee. "Where's this Ellsworth?"

"West of Abilene," Gary answered.

"Closer, then." The Major began absently twisting the left mustache.

"I reckon," Gary said.

"I say we take the herds to Abilene," Hugh said, "whether they like it or not. Because we know that the Kansas Pacific and the buyers from Chicago and Kansas City want our business, even if those dandified grangers and shopkeepers don't." He cursed grangers and shopkeepers.

"Your mother would not approve of your profanity, son," the Major said softly. "You are free to curse when you are driving cattle, as I told my soldiers they were free to curse in battle, but when we are speaking civilly about important matters, profanity is unwelcomed."

Hugh let out a sigh of exasperation, but the Major ignored that and looked up at Gary. "What do you think?"

"Well, first we have to get the herds to Kansas. That's never easy. And I imagine, just like last year, by the time we're over the Red River and in the Nations, we'll be called on by many a Kansas businessman with a railroad official tagging along, praising all the virtues—"

Bailey interrupted with a "But mostly the wickedness."

They all laughed before Gary added, "And telling us what their town—I mean, *city*—has to offer."

The Major nodded. "You'll pick what you think is best, right?" His old eyes focused on Gary.

"Well, Major, I have my herd. Shouldn't Hugh . . . ?"

"No." It was a whisper.

"Pa!" His son shouted.

"No." The Major's voice became strong, and the old man pushed himself up. "No. Hugh will be bossing his herd, but you'll be in charge of the business end. Hugh will have a letter of credit with him. That is for both his herd and yours. But you know the business, Captain. You have final say in those matters once you are in Abi—well, wherever you wind up. Telegraph me at Richmond. They will bring the message, and my reply."

They finished their coffees, the Major fired up another cigar, Bailey returned to his camp, and Hugh stormed to his horse.

Gary walked with the old man to the buggy he had ridden into camp. Back in the day, Wat Anderson could ride everything with four legs, but *back in the day* had been years, a long war and a bad horse wreck ago.

The Major groaned as Gary helped him into the wagon, where Wat found the whip and laid it across his thighs as he reached for the lines to the big gray Oldenburg pulling the rig.

"Give Lou my best," Gary said.

"I shall. And I will send a rider over to your place to look in on Jane every few days."

"I appreciate that."

"I know what you're thinking." Wat Anderson looked down into Gary's keen eyes.

Gary opened his mouth, but decided there wasn't anything to say.

"Hugh's too young to head a drive," the Major said. "Probably too young to even take the point. But I won't be around much longer, and I need someone to take over. And I know I cannot depend on . . . on . . ." His lips trembled, and Gary felt blessed that he had two solid sons. The Major recovered. "We had to make boys into soldiers."

And we killed many a boy trying to do that . . . for nothing.

"Do the best you can," the Major said, and he gathered the lines tighter. "And take care of your own two boys." He nodded. "When you get back, I'll break out the good rye."

He faked a smile, flicked the leather, and traveled north toward his home. Looking back, he called out, "I'll be back to see you off in a few days."

After the Major left, Gary found his cup, walked to the pot, filled it, and strode over to the wagon, where Moises Dunn was cutting out biscuits with the floured edge of an old airtight of peaches.

"When I heard the old man had made Hugh boss of one herd—without tellin' you first—I figured you'd quit him," Dunn said, without looking up from his biscuit-cutting.

Gary did not bother to say anything.

"Man like you could name his own price. Man like you ought to be givin' Shanghai Pierce or Ike Pryor some competition in trail drivin'."

The coffee tasted like it always did. Satisfying. Not too bitter, not too sweet, not too weak but not too strong.

"Know what a Grover and Baker is?" Gary asked after a long while.

Frowning, the cook shook his head.

"Jane and I went to New Orleans once." Gary smiled at the memory. "Saw one on Canal Street. It's a sewing machine. Won some hifalutin medal in Paris. She always fancied a sewing machine."

"Fancied a cookstove, too, I recollect." The cook stopped cutting biscuits with the tin can, to roll a smoke.

Gary smiled. "Trail bossing got her that stove. She's a good cook. Doesn't mix cigarette ashes in her biscuit dough like you do, mind you, but her biscuits turn out pretty good." He touched the end of his bandanna. "Well, Jane likes sewing, too. Made this for me. She might be able to make you a shirt without so many holes in the front."

Snorting, Dunn licked his cigarette, stuck it in the corner of his mouth, and lighted it with a lucifer that he shook out and flicked toward Gary's coffee cup.

"Things a man'll do for a woman." Dunn shook his head.

"Some women—most of them, I warrant—are worth it." Gary took a drink of coffee.

"They give medals to sewing machines?" Dunn asked with contempt.

Gary smiled over his cup. "Old man," he said, "they gave me three and breveted me captain."

"Hard-pressed, weren't they?"

The smile remained, even as he sighed and shook his head. "Not as hard-pressed as we might be to find enough men to fill two trail herds."

Catching a glimpse of the wrangler out of the corner of his eye, Gary spun around and called out Carlos's name.

The boy stopped, turned, and hurried over.

"Carlos," Gary said, "I got a chore to lay on you, amigo. I'm gonna have to do a lot of riding from my herd"—he pointed vaguely at the other camp—". . . to that one, and that's after we get both herds moving north. Means I'll be wearing out more horses than I usually do. Do you reckon you could keep a string of four—no, three should do—and take them to Hugh Anderson's remuda?"

"Señor, it will be my honor."

"Who's wrangling for Hugh?"

"Whit Barlow," Carlos answered. "He is older than me. Knows horses better than me. He will please you, señor."

"Well, tell him what he'll have—three extra horses—and that he'll get a bonus in Kansas."

He smiled at the wrangler.

"You know what I like, Carlos. I'll let you pick out the horses for me, and I'll see that you also get a bonus when we sell the herd." He pushed up the brim of the boy's sombrero. "Maybe enough so that you can buy yourself a strop and a razor when we hit trail's end."

He wore out two horses a day just during the gather, and strained his eyes to near blindness keeping the books straight.

Logging what rancher's steer got road-branded, so the Major would know how much each of the cattlemen would have coming to them once Gary Hardee made it back from Kansas. Gary might have doubts about Hugh Anderson's competence as a trail boss, but he didn't trust his own bookkeeping. Just last year, the Major had done all of the bookkeeping at the end of each day in that camp, but Wat Anderson's eyes were so bad now that he could scarcely make out the color of horse approaching at a trot fifty yards away.

So Gary rode horses morning to dusk, then pored over ledgers at the chuckwagon, and Gary, like his father, was a mighty poor mathematician. Usually, he went over the Anderson ledgers with Bill Bailey reading over his shoulder. In his camp, he let Evan check his figures.

Filling the crews, however, didn't come as hard as Gary had feared. Turns out Adam Pollock had a reputation as savory as Moises Dunn's. Gary knew Hugh would want Taylor riding in his crew, and figured that might work out better anyway. Evan wouldn't have to be trying to best his brother—not that Evan would be thinking of anything except trying to keep from choking to death riding drag behind two thousand northbound beeves. Bailey would keep an eye on Hugh and Taylor, and Deke Brown, as long as Bailey didn't find any liquor, and wasn't provoked.

Carlos Morales was right about Whit Barlow, too. The youngster had served as a wrangler on Emerson Lockheart's drive to Salina in '69 and to Junction City last year, and would have hired on with him again except a horse rolled over on Lockheart back in September and they buried him in October.

They filled out Anderson's crew with mostly local boys—most of them Mexicans and freedmen—cowhands from other ranches, a couple of drifters from as far away as Pleasanton. Gary kept the Negroes, Hunter Clarke—as fine a point rider Gary had ever worked with—Jimmy Batten, Alex Warner, and Adam Dozier on his crew. Like a number of ex-Confederates, the Major had a strong dislike for men of color, and that dislike had been inherited by his son. And plenty of freedmen had remained in Fort Bend County after the surrender. Most of them knew how to ride and rope.

The night before they started north, Gary and Evan rode over to the Anderson camp. Evan found his brother near the cookfire, and Gary and the Major went over the tallies one final time, then shook hands.

"Got everything you need?" the Major asked.

"I could take some luck if you have any to spare."

Wat snorted out a laugh, but the face quickly turned serious.

"Take care of my boy, Capt'n." It sounded like an order, and the Major turned and walked to his rig. Gary finished the cup of coffee and watched the old man climb into the rig, and ride off toward his big house three miles up the river. Through all the drives Gary had made for Wat Anderson, the old man had never given anything that sounded like an order. In fact, the last order Major Walter Pool "Wat" Anderson had given Brevet Captain Gary Hardee had been the best order Gary had ever heard.

"Stack arms."

This one might be a lot harder to carry out. But he said: "You know me, Major. I make a point, sir, to take care of all my men. Part of my job."

Chapter 6

To Newton.—The A., T. & S. F. road is now being graded between Florence and Newton, which point, according to contract, must be reached by the 1st of June.—Commonwealth.
—(Lawrence) *Western Home Journal,*
April 27, 1871

Cindy Bagwell quickly determined that she would not have called Arby McBane's new editor at *The Wichita Herald* a young *whippersnapper*. What came to her mind were four words that, had she uttered them in earshot of her mother or father, would have left her tasting lye soap on her tongue for likely a month.

Inside the newspaper office that reeked of cigar smoke, ink, and sweat, Bobby Knott looked Cindy over up and down several times, stopping often at her breasts for a thorough study and then focusing a good while on her dress and ankles, eyes moving down, then up, down, then up, always stopping at the ankles beneath the hems of the dress and her breasts. She did not blush because, well, she would not let this pig intimidate or embarrass her, and, more importantly, she needed to find a job in a hurry.

Now he studied her neck.

Well, I am a handsome woman.

He studied the luggage she had left next to the door. She saw that smirk, and she wished this jackass had riled the man who had killed Mr. Bodie. A moment later, he looked at the letter she had handed him. He scanned it again, before dropping his right hand to his side. His left hand came up to his chin, and he scratched the underlip beard with his thumb.

"If you came in before we went to press," he said, "I could have used you to fill us in on that dead editor who wanted to hire you." He pointed to the stack of newspapers that were growing as the printers dropped more four-page sheets onto the piles. "Rafe Cody, rest in peace."

"Ralph Bodie," she said.

"What's that?"

"His name was Ralph, not Rafe." Cindy nodded at the letter. "And Bodie, not Cody."

Bobby Knott brought the paper up, saw the letterhead, and let out the four words that had just flashed through Cindy's mind, when he turned and yelled at one of the ink-blackened printers in the back of the noisy shop.

"McNelly, you worthless reprobate. If you can't spell no better than that, your career will be deader than *The Wichita Times*."

"I type what I'm given." The printer used a few words, too, that Cindy's parents would not have appreciated.

"Any better," Cindy whispered.

Knott had been about to bark at, or maybe fire, or—seeing the revolver stuck in the editor's waistband—murder the tall printer, but Cindy's soft comment turned his attention back on her.

"How's that?"

"Nothing," she whispered.

"How's that?"

She swallowed. "It should be 'If you can't spell any better than that . . .' No better . . . that's . . ." Well, it would be a long walk back to Alabama.

"Go on."

"That's a double negative."

Now Bobby Knott smiled.

"Rafe Cody—since that's his name now—got killed for talking too much, you know. Is that a habit all you Georgians have?"

"*Ralph Bodie* was from Virginia," she informed him. "My father, his good friend, lived in Alabama."

One day, she told herself, she would learn to shut up. Yet the mouth kept on opening, and words just sang out. "But I did not answer your question so—"

"I believe you did answer it." He glanced at the letter. "Missus Bagwell."

"Miss." *Cynthia Marie Bagwell,* she heard her mother scolding her, *when will you learn to speak only when you have to.* "I am Miss Bagwell."

His grin was lecherous, and now she understood that Bobby Knott, editor of *The Wichita Herald*, had been fishing. Well, she was tired. And upset. She wasn't thinking clearly.

She heard her mother again. *Yes, Cynthia Marie, you certainly are not using the brain the Good Lord put inside that thick skull of yours.*

He returned the letter to her, and Cindy figured she would have to try the *Vidette*. Republican paper or not, she needed a job, and she certainly could not dance the way those women were on the balcony of that house she had passed after leaving the former office of Ralph Bodie's newspaper. She tried to remember the names she had heard. Bowers, Showers . . . ? She stifled a curse. Well, Hutchison, that was definitely the other name. Or had it been Murchison?

Perhaps she could also seek out the *Tribune*. She could find that publisher's name, which she had already forgotten.

But Bobby Knott wasn't leering at her. He started adjusting the black garters that covered his white shirtsleeves and was calling back to the printer he had just cussed out.

"What do you think, McNelly? You think she can fill a column the way she fills a dress?"

Western newspapermen, she decided, lacked the civility and chivalry of those from the South.

"She hasn't blowed your head off," the printer said, "which anybody else would have done. And Arby would have already thrown your arse onto the street if he heard you speaking like this to any lady."

Unfortunately for Cindy, Arby McBane was not in the office, this being Thursday. She had been misinformed about everyone being in the office on the day the newspaper was printed. The printers were there, and some delivery boys and men had entered the office to gather their newspapers, but the publisher never showed his face on the Thursday the paper was published and on the Friday after the paper was first read.

"Restraint." Knott's head moved up and down. "She's got restraint."

"I shall seek employment at the *Tribune* or the *Vidette*," she said, turning from the crude man and bowing slightly at the filthy printer. "Thank you, Mr. McNelly, for your kindness."

"Don't get your dander up, Cindy Bagwell," Knott said. "Cindy Bagwell. That name sings. But don't think I'm giving you a byline. But I will give you a test. An assignment."

He pointed at the stacks of papers. "Those newspapers get mailed, sent to Emporia, Abilene, Topeka, or we deliver them to subscribers in Monroe, Payne, Minneha, Grant Township, by horseback. Second District towns, or wannabe towns. We don't circulate too much into the Third and First districts. We have another edition that we sell only in Wichita, Park City, and Delano Township."

He stroked the underlip beard again.

"I got four-and-a-half inches of wretchedness on page two for this edition. I'd like to fill it with something that will grab some attention. Get picked up and reprinted by papers across the continent. So, Miss Bagwell, if you think you can find me a story worthy of four and one-half inches, and can deliver that to me in less than two hours, I might have use for you after all."

Her heart must have stopped beating. Or her ears were playing tricks on her. She remembered the story her father had said about playing poker one night. He swore he had a straight flush, and he had not been drinking too much on that particular night, and kept raising against three fives, only when the bet was called and he showed his hand, he barely had a straight, and certainly not enough to beat four fives. That was her father's eyes, not Cindy's ears, but she always worried that she might see or hear what she wanted to see or hear.

"I'll pay you a dollar, too," Bobby Knott told her. "*If* you bring me back some news."

"There was a man bathing in the Arkansas—" She stopped, but not before she let that cussword come out, then corrected herself. "The ARE-kan-zas River, I mean."

Bobby Knott almost doubled over, he laughed so hard, and when Cindy turned toward McNelly, she saw both printers grinning widely. Even a teenage boy in brogans and dungarees stared at Cindy with his mouth open and eyes bulging.

"I don't know what kind of lurid, scandalous material your father printed in Alabama, Miss Bagwell," Bobby Knott was saying, "but our Christian readers do not wish to read filth, my dear lady—so maybe you should go talk to Albert Yale at the *Trib*."

She remembered something else her father had told her. "Think with your brain, rarely with your fingers, and never with your lips."

Yet that lecherous gaze and ugly smile told Cindy that Bobby Knott enjoyed Cindy's comment, and that if he did hire her, he would never let her forget what she had just said. But he quickly turned serious.

"Don't think you can make something up, either. I have a nose for news. And I'll send McNelly out to verify whatever you bring back to me. But let's not have any mention of any baths taken in rivers or water troughs, if you please."

"All right," she said. "May I leave my baggage here?"

He bowed. "By all means. I won't even go through your stuff while you're gone."

She didn't believe him for a second, but she had no seconds to spare. She grabbed her pencil and a notebook, and hurried out onto English Street. The stagecoach office, she knew, was at the Wichita House. Her father had always gone to the river landings and hotels, to find out who was visiting. He went there before he went to see the sheriff or city police chief or the courthouse. He also knew that barbers knew everything that preachers and preachers' wives didn't. She hadn't found a barbershop yet, but she knew where the stagecoach stopped. So she moved in that direction, only to find herself completely lost. Where was Douglas Avenue? Which way was Main Street? Or was she on Main Street? Or Douglas? She swallowed down bile and fear, and saw a man waving at a lumberyard. Not at her. But another man crossed the street and began talking on the corner. A wagon was parked out front. A woman sat on the tailgate, stroking a dog.

Cindy walked closer.

No, she realized as she neared the corner. That was not a dog.

More people started gathering around. The man who had been called over wore a shield on his blue coat. He glanced at the woman and the dead man. Cindy came closer.

"She wanted to buy lumber, Paul," the man told the peace officer. "To build a coffin for her brother."

Cindy's heart pounded, and she studied the dazed woman, in her twenties, fiery orange hair, young, pretty, blood staining her hands and front of her dress as she just kept stroking the hair on a ghastly young man's head. She made herself get closer. Dark brown stains covered the wagon bed. Dried blood. Cindy found her notebook, pulled the pencil from the top of her ear, and started taking notes.

Horses . . . *MULES* . . . *lathered. Worn out.*
Big stove in wagon.
Red hair. Face pale.

"There's not a law against that, J.B.," the constable told the lumberman.

"There is against murder," the lumberman whispered urgently.

"You mean she said she killed—"

"No, she said they got attacked down at some creek crossin'. Her brother killed the two bushwhackers before they done him in."

Cindy looked again at the two mules. They had definitely been driven hard. Sensitivity got the better of her, but this time, she did not let the lumberman or the lawman hear her concern.

Somebody should get this team unleashed, she wrote, *before mules drop dead in their traces.*

"Then that," the lawman said, "happened outside my jurisdiction, J.B. If there was a holdup, that's Sheriff Walker's—"

"A dead man in the wagon, Johnny, is your department."

The man sighed, cursed, spat, and turned back to the wagon.

"Lady," he said, softly, respectfully, at first. "Where did this shooting happen exactly?"

The woman just stroked her brother's hair.

"Lady?" he tried again.

No response.

Then he barked, "Lady, you come in here with a fellow shot all to pieces and deader than dirt. But I got a job to do and—"

Cindy Bagwell forgot that she was a journalist.

She broke the commandment her father always broke on deadlines, the one about taking the Lord's name in vain, and she called the lawman and the lumberman a few words that left some other gawkers chuckling, which led her to give the onlookers a piece of her mind, too.

"Is this how you Kansans treat a woman who has witnessed the foul murder of her brother?"

They shut up.

The lumberman stared at his work boots.

The lawman, the least moved of the group, put his hands on his hips and asked, "And just who the devil are you, ma'am?"

"My name is Cindy Bagwell, sir, and I am a reporter for *The Wichita Herald*."

One man snorted. The lumberman looked up with curiosity. The peace officer sighed, then whispered a curse, but stared again at the redhead on the tailgate. Quickly, he turned back to Cindy.

"Miss Bagwell," he said, his voice pleading now, "do you think you could talk to her?" He nodded at the woman. "Maybe see what happened? And exactly where, so I can tell Sheriff Walker? We'd be most appreciative, ma'am."

Chapter 7

DISTANCES—From here to Cottonwood Falls it
is one hundred miles, in an air line; to Florence,
eighty-five miles; to Newton, seventy-one miles.
The latter will soon be our shipping point, being the
nearest point on the A., T. & S. and F. R. R.
—Arkansas Traveler
We will bet you a gill of buttermilk, Mr. Traveler, that
you ship your goods to Florence.
—*Walnut Valley Times*, May 5, 1871

Looking down at her brother, Denise drew in a deep breath and held it, exhaling slowly as the woman with light brown hair walked away from the group of men. The woman held a notebook in her left hand and looked about as sick as Denise figured she herself must look right about now.

She stopped fingering Arthur's hair. He was dead. Wasn't coming back to life. And these men in Wichita weren't about to sell her lumber for a coffin. That had to be a blessing, Denise began to realize. When was the last time she had tried to drive a nail? Probably when she wanted to hang a painting in the restaurant in Neodesha. Which had cost her a thumbnail for a spell.

The woman stopped about a couple of feet from the back of the wagon. She had blue eyes. Pretty eyes. A pretty face, too. Maybe

Denise's age, perhaps a year or two younger or older. She wasn't like most of the women she had met in Neodesha. Her face and hands had not been dried out by the Kansas sun, and in these parts, that harsh wind that seldom died down.

"Miss," the blue-eyed woman said, "my name's Cindy. Cindy Bagwell. I . . ." Cindy Bagwell made the mistake of looking at Arthur. Color drained from her face, and her lips flattened, but she did not throw up. She turned her head away from Arthur, regained something that resembled composure, and focused again on Denise. "I . . ."

She spoke with the sweetness of a Southern accent. Deeper South, without Arkansas's harsh twang. Softer, almost musical. She spoke softly, respectfully. She wet her lips, tried to say something, but had trouble forming the words, so she turned away, looking back at the men who wouldn't sell Denise any lumber. Denise thought she would just walk back.

"Maybe they'll sell you some wood."

The woman named Cindy Bagwell sharply spun around and stared hard at Denise.

It took several seconds before Denise realized what she just said. She tried to stop herself from speaking again, but her lips were already moving. "They won't sell any to me."

The brunette turned back toward the men. "There has to be an undertaker in this town. Isn't there?" Cindy Bagwell called out. "Or at least a coffin maker?" Her voice rose. "Or do you just throw your dead out on the plains and let the buzzards do their work?"

Well, now. That wasn't sweet as honey or musical like Grandma Sue's melodeon. Cindy Bagwell could sound like Denise Beeber when someone got her dander up.

The man with the shiny badge on his blue coat turned and pointed at a man in a straw hat and checked trousers. "Malachi," he said, "run over to George Johnson's furniture store. Have him send one of his ready-made coffins here. Tell him to hurry." The badge-wearer looked back at Cindy Bagwell. "I don't know how much George charges for coffins."

"I can pay his price."

Denise had spoken again.

Maybe she had not completely lost her mind.

The lawman started toward the wagon, but stopped when this Cindy Bagwell turned around and asked Denise, "Can you tell me what happened?"

Cindy's words came easier. Her confidence rose. "I know it's difficult. I really don't like to pry. But we really need to know." She tilted her head back toward the lawman. "He needs to know."

Denise sighed. Yes, she had lost her mind there for a bit, but the madness was leaving now. Maybe she would get a coffin for Arthur. And the brown-headed woman with the nice eyes was right. The law had to know everything that had happened.

Well, maybe not everything.

"We were on our way to Newton," she said. "Arthur and me . . ."

Cindy Bagwell started writing in her notebook. As Denise began speaking, the blue-coated lawman walked up and stood at Cindy's left. The rest of the crowd kept a distance. One man put his hand over his ear to hear better. Halfway into the account, another man wearing a different kind of badge pushed through the audience, which had to number thirty by now, and joined Cindy and the constable in the blue coat.

As soon as Denise finished, this Cindy Bagwell asked a few questions, still scribbling in her notebook when Denise answered.

For the most part, Denise told the truth. Actually, everything she said was factual, but she didn't say why the two dead men at that creek had stopped them. She didn't tell them why she and Arthur had left Neodesha. They must have figured she was like everyone else, pulling up stakes, pulling up roots, heading west to find a better place—for a while—then heading west again.

Once Denise had finished answering all of Cindy Bagwell's questions, the blue-coated lawman said he figured that the dead men were at some creek, the name of which Denise forgot a few seconds after hearing it.

"Yeah," said the man wearing a different kind of badge pinned to his vest. "I'll send Terry and Vern out with a pack mule. If the wolves haven't gotten to them yet." At some point, this man had removed his hat.

"The name's Walker, ma'am," he said, and bowed slightly. He sounded like a Yankee. "W.N. Walker. I'm sheriff of Sedgwick County. My condolences, Miss Beeber. My sincere condolences. We will need you to make an official statement to Judge Brown."

He frowned. "Well, maybe we can have Missus . . . Missus . . ." Sheriff Walker stared at Cindy Bagwell.

"*Miss*," Cindy Bagwell told him. "Miss Cindy Bagwell. I am a . . . reporter . . . for the *Times*—I mean the *Herald*." She wet her lips. "Bobby Knott . . . hired . . . me." She swallowed and whispered, "Sort of."

A reporter? Denise blinked. For a moment, she felt her temper rising. But a calmness quickly settled over her, and she found herself smiling. Arthur always wanted to get his name in a newspaper, and now he would. As a hero. Protector of his sister. People he had never met were calling him a hero. And he was a hero. He had protected Denise, given his life for her. The people of Neodesha might never read about Arthur Beeber, but, at least for a little while, his name would be bandied around in Wichita.

"The *Herald*." The sheriff put his hat on. He looked as if he had swallowed spoiled milk. "I see. Well . . ." He glanced at the other lawman, who had not introduced himself. "Maybe we can just run through your notes before Judge Brown at the inquest. After my deputies tell us what they find at the crossing."

By now, more people had gathered around the wagon, though the men, and a few women, kept a respectful distance, maybe twenty feet from the wagon.

A red-bearded fat man in sleeve garters kept running off the boys who climbed up on stacks of lumber to look down at Arthur.

Denise began to worry now. *Inquest.* She had sat in courtrooms in three states with inquests involving something Arthur had done—and they never turned out well.

But Cindy Bagwell flipped to a clean page in her notebook. She started to ask another question, but didn't get a chance, because another man stepped closer to Denise and the wagon and removed his bowler.

"Miss Beeber," he said. "I am deeply sorry for the loss of your valiant brother. Wichita and Sedgwick County typically are not places of violence. We are not Abilene and Dickinson County. George Johnson is bringing a fine coffin. If it suits you, we would like to bury your brave brother here. In Wichita."

"I'm heading to Newton," Denise said. Maybe she could get out of Wichita before any inquest.

"Yes, and one day, Newton might grow into a fine town. But for the moment, there is next to nothing there."

"That's why I'm going. To establish myself."

The man nodded and smiled. "Yes. I am certain you will. But we have preachers of many denominations. And we have a cemetery that is not a potter's field. I don't think Newton has a cemetery yet, ma'am, and certainly no preacher. Not yet, anyway. Perhaps, never. There's not even a church there at the moment."

"And perhaps," a voice from the crowd drawled, "never."

The stranger laughed at his own joke, but not for long, for women and quite a few men glared at him, and he pulled his hat down, took a few steps back, and hung his head.

"Your mules are played out," Cindy Bagwell said softly. She had lowered her notebook and her pencil. "Newton, I'm told, is twenty-five miles or so north. You wouldn't get there today."

Sheriff Walker joined the conversation again.

"We'll give your brother a hero's funeral," he said, and glanced at Cindy Bagwell. "And then . . ." He cleared his throat and dropped his voice to a whisper. "We shall need to hold a coroner's inquest—merely a formality. Perhaps tomorrow morning." He turned to Cindy Bagwell.

"Miss Bagwell, might you be so kind as to take this poor lady into your home for the night?"

The notebook dropped to the dirt. Cindy Bagwell's mouth shot open, quickly closed, and she bent her knees and lowered herself to pick up the notebook. "I . . . I . . . I . . . just arrived in Wichita myself."

The man stared.

"Bromwell will put them both up at the Southern Hotel," someone called out.

"Maybe the redhead can show Bromwell how to run his restaurant," said another man—and not the one who had been shamed to the back of the gathering—and this man started to guffaw before two women gave him an earful about human decency.

Cindy Bagwell left Denise in the company of some matronly Wichita women, though she said she would be back as soon as she could. Probably had to go back to her newspaper. The women took her to one of their houses, filled her with coffee, and tried to make her eat soup and biscuits, but Denise said she could not eat now. And the coffee was terrible, but she made herself drink some of it.

Someone gave her a black silk band to tie around her arm, and another handed her a veil. She took both, wore both, but only so she wouldn't insult the women. They meant well. And Denise let them help her into a buggy, which a dark-skinned man drove to Wichita's graveyard.

Because the Methodist minister had ridden over to Delano, a Presbyterian led the service. That was all right with Denise, and Arthur wouldn't have minded, since she couldn't remember the last time he had set foot in a church of any kind.

The newspaperwoman arrived halfway through the funeral, and scribbled more notes, and she walked up afterward, expressed condolences like everyone else, and said she'd meet up with Denise as soon as she had finished writing the article for the *Herald*.

After the donated casket was lowered into the ground, the preacher escorted Denise to the City Bakery and Confectionery on Main Street. The reverend ordered a slice of pie, and Denise asked for bread. She wished the Presbyterian had taken her somewhere else—any place but a confectionery—but tried not to think about Mr. Roberts back in Neodesha and his candies. After eating, the preacher walked Denise to the Southern Hotel, where the clerk—not the owner—gave her a key to a room and said that she would be sharing the room with Cindy Bagwell.

Denise didn't care. She didn't frown when she unlocked the door to learn that the one bed in the room was small. The room was free, and she was dead tired.

She woke early the next morning to the sound of a bullwhacker's curses, tossed off the thin sheet, and realized she lay alone in the bed. Hearing the soft snores, she wiped sleep from her eyes and saw Cindy Bagwell, the reporter for whatever the paper was called, sleeping in the rocking chair in the corner. Denise hadn't even heard her enter the room.

After washing her face in the basin on the dresser, she pulled on the same dress she had worn yesterday, spent that eternity of getting her shoes laced up, and grabbed her valise.

Denise opened the door and stepped into the hallway. A tabby cat hissed for a moment, its cold eyes daring Denise to take another step. Then the cat let out a little purr, turned around, and trotted down the hallway.

Cindy Bagwell slept in the rocking chair. After quietly closing the door, Denise started down the hall.

You still have manners.

That inner voice stopped her, and she bit her lower lip. After a long sigh, Denise set the valise on the carpet and took the few steps back to the door, opened it, and stared at the woman snoring softly in the rocking chair. The bullwhacker's whip kept popping, and his baritone of profanity rang louder than church bells, but Cindy Bagwell slept undisturbed.

Denise covered the distance quickly, put her hand on the reporter's shoulder, and gave it a squeeze, then a little shove.

Cindy jerked awake.

"It's just me," Denise reassured her, and waited for Cindy's eyes to focus, the brain to move from half asleep to moderately alert.

"Oh," Cindy managed to say.

"Why don't you go to the bed?" Denise suggested. "I'm getting an early start for Newton."

"Oh." Cindy leaned forward. The chair squeaked. Outside, a dog began barking at the cursing bullwhacker.

"What time is it?" Cindy asked.

Denise shrugged. "Morning. It's a long way to Newton. I best be leaving."

"Oh."

She wasn't like Denise, who woke up alert and moved right into her day, but then Denise had never worked for a newspaper, and she did not know when Cindy got into the room. By this time most days, Denise would have already made batter, coffee, and would be cracking eggs or seasoning meat.

Denise sighed and held out her hand. "Come on. You need more sleep."

"I'm just . . . sleepy."

Grinning, Denise took hold of Cindy's wrist and stepped back, pulling her to her feet and nodding toward the bed.

"Think you can make it?"

Cindy yawned. "I guess so."

Denise stepped out of the way, and watched Cindy walk to the bed, sit on it, lay her head on the pillow, and fall asleep. Cindy likely wouldn't remember a thing about what had just happened. She would wake up later and wonder how she had gotten into bed. Shaking her head again, Denise walked to the bed and knelt to pull Cindy's legs and feet, still wearing the shoes, onto the bed. Once she had pulled the covers up, Denise went back to the door.

There she stopped and looked at the sleeping woman.

"Thank you, Miss Cindy Bagwell," she said before pulling the door shut behind her. Denise picked up the valise where she had left it and headed for the staircase.

Chapter 8

Newton is said to be the point where the road will
terminate, and where a great railroading and
speculative town will be built up.
—*The* (Lawrence) *Republican Daily Journal*,
April 7, 1871

Gary thought about turning in the blood bay for the pale gelding, but as soon as he dismounted and Carlos Morales rode
over to take the reins, Gary swung back into the saddle.

"I'll have Whit Barlow swap this one out," he told his wrangler. The bay had enough left in him to ride back a couple of
miles and see how Hugh Anderson had made out on his first day
as a trail boss.

Trail boss. That still stuck in Gary's craw.

He spat dust from his mouth, turned the reins, and eased the
gelding away from the remuda. He first rode to his camp, where
swing rider Collin O'Hearn was pouring a cup of Moises Dunn's
brew. Seeing Hardee, the hand brought the cup and offered it to
Gary.

"Thanks." Gary took a swallow, the strong brew cleansing his
tongue and throat of dust. "How'd it go for you?"

O'Hearn shrugged. "Glad I listened to my wife and wore my
winter underpants."

Hardee grinned. "First day's always the longest." He drank again.

"This one seemed a mite longer than long."

It had been. Gary had made sure of that. "We'll keep them moving hard another day or two," he said, and drank more coffee. "Then settle down into something that won't wear out your britches."

"Don't mind you wearin' out my britches, boss. As long as my buttocks don't bruise."

After finishing the coffee, Gary handed the cup back to the cowboy, regripped the reins in his gloved hands, but now he smiled as the drag riders walked in from the picket line.

For drag riders, they weren't that dirty. But this was coastal country. That would change in the coming weeks. They had sweated, though, and shirts and wild rags remained soaking wet.

His son pulled off his hat, slapping it against his chaps.

"Pa." Smiling, Evan hooked his thumb toward one of his fellow drag riders. "Do you know what Casey's last name is?"

"Awwww," the young man with the battered hat said. "He knows. I had to write it down in that book of his'n."

Hardee nodded at the young hand about Evan's age.

"It's Steer," Evan said. "Casey Steer. *Steer*. I told him with a name like that, he had to cowboy. I thought he just made it up, Pa, but he didn't."

Gary's top teeth dragged across his bottom lip. He wet the lips and looked at his son, silently, just staring.

"What's the matter, Pa?" Evan said. "I ain't making fun of Casey. We're pards. I just like his name." He looked at the filthy teenager beside him. "I mean, Casey Steer's a name you'll never forget. Evan Hardee is just . . . well . . . dull."

"I'd rather be Casey Bull," the boy said.

Which made Gary grin. "Some cowhands I know change their names with the seasons," he said. "But I must be getting old and lazy. I'm losing my touch."

Both stared up at him.

"Never had drag riders who could stand up straight and talk like a Fort Worth barber after the first long day on a trail drive." He turned the horse and kicked it into a walk. "I'll have to push y'all harder tomorrow."

He rode easily over the flattened, churned trail. It struck him that he had never really seen what two thousand head of Texas longhorns left behind. Well, he had followed other herds, but those had been days or weeks ahead of him.

Math came to him. Two thousand steers. Eight thousand hooves. Twelve horses. He didn't count the team of mules pulling the chuckwagon or the horses in the remuda, because those cut their own trail to the west of the herd.

The grass had been trampled, and flies swarmed over the mashed manure. In some places, the ground looked as though steel harrows had been dragged by farmers. In other spots, one might have guessed that moleboard plows had disced the land.

At least the spring had been wet, the winter—like winter ever came this far south into Texas—mild, so the grass still grew high.

He found Hugh Anderson's camp where it should have been, saw the smoke rising from Adam Pollock's cook fires and heard the lowing of cattle. His gut unclenched. Hugh and Bill Bailey had done a good job. Gary let the horse pick up the pace and trotted the last mile, and rode to the picket line, where he removed saddle and blanket, stacking the saddle underneath a stub of a tree, and laying the wet blanket to dry.

The wrangler walked toward him.

"Whit," Gary ordered, "cut me out a good night horse, but no hurry. How'd things go today?"

"Fine for me, sir," Barlow said, "but I don't have to deal with nothin' but geldings."

Gary grinned, though something in the boy's face told him the comment had not been meant as a joke, and made his way to the chuckwagon.

Adam Pollock saw him, found an extra cup on the table of the chuckwagon, and tossed it to Gary, who caught it, looked around, and asked, "Where's Hugh?"

"Checkin' the herd." Bill Bailey pulled off his hat and slapped it against his chaps.

That was a good sign, too.

"How'd things go?" Gary walked to the coffeepot and filled his cup.

"Today was fine," Bailey said. "Ask me when we get farther north and the dust kicks up."

Gary understood, and thinking about Evan and Casey Steer, he almost smiled. Then it would be easy to tell who had been riding drag. They were the filthiest, coated with dust and grime from the crowns of their hats to the soles of their boots.

"Find enough graze?"

Bailey shrugged. "Trail's wide enough here, and there ain't no shortage of grass, so we could skirt east or west. When we get to country with more people, the pickins might get slimmer." He sipped coffee. "But we'll make out all right. How far you think we covered?"

"Thirteen miles." Gary shrugged. "Fourteen. Do it again to-morrow, then both herds ought to be tired out enough to settle into something not as hard on my backside. If not, we should slow down the day after."

"Ain't nothin' hard on your backside, Boss," Bailey said.

"Hardee!"

Gary turned to the tall, stringy cowhand who dropped his bedroll by another fire, and pushed back his dirty hat. Deke Brown looked sober, at least, as he strode over, found a tin cup, and filled it with coffee, then walked until he stopped a few feet in front of Gary.

"You tell me somethin', Hardee. How does your boy rank a point position, and I get stuck on swing?"

Hardee handed his cup to Bailey.

"That's something to ask your trail boss," Gary said.

"That snot-nosed runt?" Brown spit coffee onto the grass. "I'm askin' you."

"You want to draw your time?" Gary reached inside a vest pocket and pulled out a crumpled treasury note worth a dollar. He held the bill out between his thumb and forefinger. "Take it and ride out."

"I ain't no quitter." Brown took another sip. "You know me better than that. You also know that I belong at point while that boy of yours—and I ain't sayin' he's no cowhand—but he sure don't deserve to be ridin' point."

"And you know me better, Deke, to think I'd tell another trail boss what he ought to be doing."

"Brown." Hugh Anderson loped toward the picket line, dismounting before the horse stopped completely, and dropping the reins instead of handing them to Whit Barlow.

"Have Whit catch you up a horse, Brown," Hugh ordered. "Take the first watch with Taylor. Don't worry. We'll save you some supper."

Deke Brown's eyes hardened, and he breathed in and out, never looking over at Hugh Anderson, just staring at Hardee, who did not blink.

But the cowboy did not snatch the U.S. note from Gary's hand. He finished his coffee, pitched the cup into the wreck pan, and walked toward the picket line, yelling for Barlow to find him a horse that a man could sit on forever.

Hugh strode over and glared at Pollock. "I expect you to have a cup of coffee waiting for me when I get to this cookfire," he said.

Pollock wiped his floury hands on his dingy apron.

"This is my cookfire, son." He slowly turned around. "And when you're at my cookfire, you'll say please and thank you. I ain't your manservant. That's why you pay men seventy-five dollars a month."

The pale face flushed.

"Your coffee tastes like muddy water anyway," Hugh said, and turned quickly to Gary. "And what do you want? This is my camp. Shouldn't you be with your crew?"

Gary took another sip of coffee.

"My men know what to do," he said softly.

Bailey dropped his cup in the tin basin and walked toward the picket line, and Pollock mumbled something about missing a cook's louse on this drive and having to do every blessed thing he didn't want to do, and he moved to the wagon and began opening and closing drawers and cabinets.

That left Gary and Hugh alone.

"Hugh," Gary said softly. The boy's eyes shot toward Gary. The anger was easy enough to read, but Gary kept his voice calm and level. "Deke Brown can be a pain in the ass, but you do your job, you'll earn his respect."

"I did my job."

Gary nodded. "You did a good job. Herd looks good. You're as far back as you need to be. We'll keep the same pace tomorrow— fast, hard—and you stay a bit east or west of my trail."

The kid looked at the chuckwagon.

"Barking orders, yelling, that's good for a sergeant, and it's needed when you're pushing steers up a trail for three-four months," Gary said. "And sometimes, it's needed for a cowhand. Sometimes."

"I don't need your advice."

"That's where you're wrong, Hugh. You do need my advice. And you'll get it." Now Gary moved over to the boy, stood right in front of him. Gary was lucky. Hugh Anderson wasn't as tall as even Evan Hardee, so Gary had a couple of inches on him—and the heels of Gary's boots were taller than Hugh's heels, too. That gave him another inch and a half.

He waited till Hugh finally breathed out and glared at his elder.

"People respect your pa because he earned that respect. Respect isn't something you inherit; it isn't something that gets passed down like a watch or a knife or a Bible."

This was a conversation the Major should have had with his son—and perhaps he had. Gary had to figure that Hugh Anderson had too much wax in his ears to hear anything that he didn't want to hear.

"You can boss your men, or you can lead your men. That's your call. But you will listen to me when I tell you what to do with your herd. Because I get two and a half percent of what these cattle will fetch in Kansas. And medal-winning sewing machines don't come cheap."

Hugh blinked, confused.

"My herd leaves before daybreak. Give us an hour, then move yours out. I'll ride back when you're nooning."

"You don't need to nursemaid me." The arrogance had returned. "I can make a noon camp without you checking on me and my herd."

"I reckon you can, but I'll be seeing you then just the same. For one reason. I like that blood bay gelding I'm leaving tonight in your remuda. And I'll be wanting to ride him tomorrow afternoon."

He left his cup in the wreck pan, nodded his thanks to the cook, and walked to the picket line, where Whit Barlow was saddling the claybank the wrangler had picked out for Gary.

Chapter 9

Mr. H. Bulmer, late of the 'Parks House' North
Topeka, was busy this morning packing up his effects
to move to Newton, at the end of the Atchison,
Topeka & Santa Fe Railroad, where he proposes to
furnish entertainment for man and beast as aforetime.
—(Topeka) *Kansas State Record,*
May 12, 1871

Her eyes shot wide open, and she stared at the ceiling of
wooden planks over her head. Cindy Bagwell's heart pounded,
and her lungs worked furiously. Almost instantly, she forgot the
nightmare, and tried to gather her wits.

Hotel. Wichita. Funeral. Dead man. Redhead. The hotel. *The
Herald.* Beeber. Yes. Denise Beeber. Sitting up, she looked across
the room. Room. Right. Hotel. Southern Hotel. But where was
Denise? There was the rocking chair. Cindy had gone to sleep in
that chair. The bed was too small to fit two people—even if
Cindy and Denise were far from plump—and after all Denise
Beeber had gone through, Cindy figured she should have slept in
the chair. She was used to sleeping sitting up. In stagecoaches, if
one could call that sleeping. And on trains, since she certainly
could never have afforded a Pullman sleeping berth.

Foggily, a dream came to her. Denise helping her out of the

rocking chair. Saying something like, "Why don't you go to bed?" Her groggy response: "I'm just sleepy." That reminded her of the countless times she had told her father that, or her mother, when one or the other—sometimes both—tried to get her up, for church, or to rush her off to school, or to do chores. That was all she could recall about the dream.

She swung her feet off the bed. No one had taken off her shoes. After rubbing her eyes, she tried again: "Denise?"

Her head shook. She rose. Denise Beeber wasn't here. Her luggage was gone. Cindy stumbled to the dresser and found her items, made sure the coin purse was where she had left it, then got mad at herself for suspecting that Denise Beeber might have robbed her. Which didn't stop her from opening the purse. But the bills and coins looked just about right.

Certainly no one had added any money.

Her watch was where she left it, too.

Stop being a jackass, she had to tell herself. *Stop acting like Daddy. Nobody robbed you. Especially not Denise Beeber, who had just seen three men shot dead—one of which had been her kid brother.*

Cindy drew in a deep breath and looked at the watch. Of course, it had stopped. What would you expect from a broke newspaperwoman's watch?

Maybe that wasn't a dream.

She had gone to sleep in the rocking chair. That much she remembered. Denise had been in a deep sleep when Cindy finally found the room, after dang near tripping over some wretched, ugly cat on the stairs to the second floor of the hotel.

Snippets of the previous day came to her now. The shocking news that Ralph Bodie was dead—and so was the *Times.* That dreadfully smug Bobby Knott at the *Herald,* and the challenge to find something newsworthy to fill a hole on Page 2. She had done that. Interviewed Denise Beeber, hurried back to the *Herald,* told Bobby what she had found out. He thought she was lying, till he sent that printer, McNelly, out to verify the story. When

McNelly returned with a solid confirmation—Cindy felt certain that that rapscallion Knott would take the story for himself and send Cindy to the poor house, but he surprised her. Told her to get to the funeral—it would be worth at least a paragraph or two—hurry back and get to work.

She glanced out the window. It certainly wasn't early morning.

Finding water in the basin, she washed her face and rinsed her mouth. For a moment, she thought about changing clothes, decided against it, started gathering her luggage. When she reached the door, she dropped the bags.

She wasn't that desperate. Well, yes, she truly was. But her father had taught her well.

"Every newspaperman is desperate, Daughter. Runs in our blood. Desperate for the story. Desperate to get it right. Get it first if there's more than one paper in your town. Desperate to make words sing. Desperate for that morning bracer to get us through the day. The afternoon bracer so we don't forget what good rye tastes like. And the evening bracer before we lay us down to sleep."

She didn't want a drink. Couldn't understand how anyone could take a slug of rye or any kind of whiskey till the sun was down. But she wasn't going out wearing what she had been wearing since she got on that stagecoach.

So she stripped off the dress and everything else, washed in cold water from the basin. Cold water revived her. She found she still had some paste for her teeth—no brush, but she used her pointer finger. Rinsed her mouth.

Finding nothing resembling a towel or washcloth in the room, she found a relatively clean camisole in her suitcase to dry herself off. Used another camisole when she started dressing. Fought back curses as she combed the tangles out of her hair, then put it up into a bun. Found her cleanest dress—red-checkered gingham. Dug around till she discovered her mother's brooch, and pinned it on. Pulled on the socks and those shoes. Even dug out a bonnet, her mother's favorite.

After she repacked everything, she opened the door, shoved the suitcase, valise, and hatbox—everything she owned, except her handbag, brooch, purse, and the clothes she wore—into the hallway, came out of the room, and picked up her luggage.

Again leaving her luggage by the door at *The Wichita Herald*, Cindy looked around the office. McNelly, the printer, smiled at her, and motioned to a bench.

"The boss just stepped out to find a better cup of coffee than I brew, Miss Bagwell," McNelly said pleasantly. "Take a load off. because Bobby'll probably chase his coffee with whiskey."

She scanned the office, but did not spot what she wanted to see. When she looked back at the printer, he was smiling, understanding, and nodded again at the bench. "Have a seat, Miss Bagwell. I'll fetch you a copy of today's paper." He walked to the partition that separated the business part of the office from the printing presses, bent, rose with the four-page sheet, and came through the gate.

Cindy met him before he covered three more steps, and she thanked him as she unfolded the paper and looked at the front page.

"It's on Page Two," McNelly told her.

She frowned.

"It's Arby McBane's policy, Miss Bagwell," he explained. "He figures since most folks living in Wichita hail from other states, he wants national news on the front page and at least one little item that will make a reader or two smile. Local news on the second page. European news on Page Three. Advertisements on the last page and anywhere else if we get enough of them."

She turned to the second page.

"Y'all appear to be doing quite well with advertising, Mr. Mc-Nelly." Five of the eight columns were filled with advertisements, not that many big ones, but a lot of small ads.

McNelly laughed. "Those are dead ads, Miss."

She looked up. "Dead ads?" For the daughter of a newspaperman, that was a foreign term to Cindy.

"Oh, Arby and Knott-Head will run business cards they find, and they'll have me make something up to look like an ad for a business here in town, or Delano, Park City. Anywhere but Minneha. Arby says nobody reads in Minneha. Likely right, I suspect." McNelly pointed to the bottom of the first column. She saw the headline.

RED AND DEAD

Her mouth hung open after she read the first sentence. "This is not what I wrote." She almost burst into tears.

McNelly gave her an apologetic look. "Bobby Knott's the editor, Miss Bagwell," he said.

The editor of *The Wichita Times* picked that moment to walk into the office, and Cindy came up like a wildcat, almost knocked the printer down as she stormed across the room and held Page 2 in front of the cocksure young man.

"You printed this?"

Knott shouldered past her and headed for his desk. "I paid you two dollars, didn't I?" He dragged the chair out and settled into it. When he looked up, she stood towering over his desk.

"You got six-and-a-half inches," Knott said, "for the dead-man story. Then three more for the funeral. I asked for four-and-a-half inches. Remember. You got five more inches. And I paid you two silver dollars. Pretty good pay, lady. Now why don't you run back to Mississippi."

"But these aren't my words," Cindy said.

"Because I made them better." Folding his hands behind his head, Knott leaned back in his chair and propped his brogans on the desk. "'A redheaded damsel from the eastern part of our state arrived in our fine city today bringing news of a fantastic shoot-out at the crossing at Eight Mile Creek that sent two men to the Pits for their felonious intent and the orange-haired maiden's younger brother to join among the greatest Greeks— Achilles, Theseus, Coriolanus. and Hector.' It sings."

"It stinks," Cindy said. "And Coriolanus is Roman. Not Greek."

Bobby Knott brought his feet off the desk, leaned forward in the chair, and, his face reddening, pointed at McNelly.

"The rest of the article is pretty much what I wrote," Cindy said, "but that headline, and that opening paragraph—"

"Is what readers want in newspapers, you hayseed wench," Bobby Knott said. "You got your two bucks. Now get out of—"

His eyes widened, and he sprang out of his chair when the door opened, and a man in a black suit with a bowler hat entered. He held a copy of the *Herald* in his left hand. His right hand held a cane.

Knott forgot all about the printer. He even ignored Cindy. "Mr. McBane. What on earth are you doing in the office—*it's Friday, sir!*"

Mr. McBane was an old man. Cindy couldn't make an educated guess. Sixty. Eighty. Methuselah. The door closed behind him, and he held up the newspaper.

"Robert," the old man said in a voice that creaked with age, "I want to talk to you about this story on Page Two. It seems to me to be . . ." His old eyes found Cindy. He stopped in midsentence, straightened. For the first time, Cindy saw the cane the old man used. He used it now, to straighten his posture.

"Oh, Robert," he said. "I did not know you had an advertiser. This can wait." He started to leave.

"She's nothing, Mr. McBane!" Bobby Knott roared. "Certainly no advertiser. She's a . . . she's . . . she's just passing through."

"Oh." His smile, his eyes, reminded her of her father, only his eyes were brown, not blue, but they held that warmth. "That is Wichita's loss," he said, bowing so low, Cindy feared he would topple over and break into a thousand pieces. Bracing himself with the cane, he straightened, and stood there, struck dumb, not knowing what he should do.

"Please, sir." Cindy dragged forward the chair in front of Knott's desk. "Sit, Mr. McBane. I shall be on my way."

"I should hope not." The old man shuffled to the desk, patted Cindy's hand that held the chair, and settled into it. The copy of the *Herald* he held was yesterday's, and he turned to the second page. Once the old man was comfortable, his right index finger tapped at the headline over the last story in the first column.

"This article, Robert. About the gun battle at Eight Mile Creek, the woman, the funeral. It is a touching piece. But . . . this headline. And this dreadful first paragraph. It smacks of . . . of . . . of . . ."

McNelly came through with a barnyard epithet.

McBane grinned. "Yes, Liam. That is what I smell."

"I can explain," Bobby Knott sang out. "I . . . I . . . I . . ." His face paled. "Well, Mr. McBane, she wrote the article. This is her doing!" His index finger looked like a dagger.

Mr. McBane slowly turned around and managed to lift his head and his eyes, and he smiled politely at Cindy. "This is your writing, Miss . . . Miss . . . I'm sorry, child, but I have forgotten your name already."

"You did not forget, sir," Cindy told him. "For we have not been introduced." She held out her right hand. "My name is Bagwell, Mr. McBane. Cindy Bagwell. Cynthia, actually. Cynthia Ann. But I don't think anyone but Grandma Bertha called me anything but Cindy."

"I like that name." He smiled again. "Cindy. My oldest daughter was named Cynthia, and we called her Cindy, too." His head bowed. "The diphtheria took her in fifty-seven."

"I am so sorry," Cindy told him.

In his chair, Bobby Knott stared at his boss and Cindy like a mad dog. "She wrote it, sir. Every word."

Sighing, Mr. McBane readjusted his grip on the cane and started to ask Cindy a question, but then looked back at Bobby Knott.

"Are not you the editor of my newspaper, Robert?"

Bobby Knott opened his mouth, but sucked in air instead of answering the publisher's query.

"Isn't *edit* part of your job, sir?"

Bobby Knott exhaled. His face revealed the look of a man who desperately needed some ardent spirits.

McBane returned his attention to Cindy. He smiled. "Did you write this, child?"

It is a touching piece. That's what he had said. He just didn't like the headline and the first paragraph. Which Cindy had not written. And Bobby Knott was a jackass. Cindy played a hunch. "I did, sir. I . . . well . . . Mr. Knott promised me a job if I could bring in a story worth running in your fine newspaper."

He stared at her with those eyes of Cindy's father. Well, she thought, her hunch hadn't played out. Maybe she could start a newspaper in Minneha.

"It was an assignment," she said. "Mr. Knott"—she spat out the words—"gave it to me." She paused, tried again. "Well, he told me to find a story, and if I did a good job, I'd have a job. I guess I overwrote that first paragraph."

He smiled again.

"Coriolanus is not Greek, Miss Bagwell, but Roman."

"I should have known that, sir," she said. "I will remember it the next time."

His hand slapped the top of the desk. "By thunder, my dear, you have a job."

Her mouth opened. The old man laughed, laughed too hard to hear Bobby Knott's foul mouth. "You have a job for as long as you can find stories like this."

He turned, beaming, his voice sounding twenty years younger, and nodded at Bobby Knott. "Watch those headlines, Robert, and let's keep out Romans and Greeks—except on Page Four. But this . . . this . . . this kind of reporting and writing will help us lure advertisers and readers from the *Tribune* and the *Vidette.*

"This is what I want in my newspaper. News. With feeling.

With . . . with . . . with . . . with words." He pushed himself up. For a moment, Cindy thought he would topple over, but color returned to his pale face, and he smiled, and took Cindy's right hand in his own. Fearing he would fall to the floor, she rose and let him bring her hand to his lips. When he released his grip, he looked down at the reddening face of Bobby Knott.

"Pay her fifteen dollars a week," Mr. McBane said. "And give yourself a two-dollar bonus."

He started shuffling toward the front door. McNelly the printer rushed over to open the door for the old man, and when the door closed and, several moments later, the old man was past the front window, Bobby Knott grunted.

Cindy turned and smiled at him.

"I don't know what the devil just happened," Knott said. "But I need another whiskey."

"I'll tell you what happened," Cindy said. She could not help but feel like a queen. "You'll be paying me fifteen dollars a week."

Knott recovered quickly, and his eyes turned cold like a rattlesnake's.

"No, Arby McBane will be paying you fifteen a week. But I'm still editor of the *Herald*." The smile widened; the eyes turned deadlier.

"And I know exactly what I want you to write about."

Chapter 10

Newton, in Sedgwick County, seems to be the objective point. It is 31 miles west and south of Florence, and is almost sure to be a town of considerable importance. $200 have already been paid for choice lots. This road is already doing a large business, and will eventually be as important as any in the state.
—*The* (Topeka) *Kansas Daily Commonwealth,*
April 16, 1871

When she saw dust rising behind her, Denise turned her wagon off what passed for the trail and reined in the mules. She had never been good at estimating distances—Arthur had never mastered that talent, either—but she didn't think the traveler was far behind. And since the dust behind her kept blowing south, she figured the rider, herder, driver, or whatever, was heading north from Wichita and maybe bound for Newton.

Or maybe a herd of buffalo had stampeded. Or antelope. Wild mustangs. But most likely it had to be a wagon coming north from Wichita.

She found a canteen and washed down a stale biscuit and tough jerky. Wind dried the moisture on her lips before she even corked the canteen. Slowly, but surely, that dust kept getting closer.

Maybe it's just a dust storm.

No. That wasn't likely. She had seen dust storms aplenty in Kansas, but never this genteel.

What if it's being raised by Indians?

That troubled her, but not for long. She recalled that old Indian fighter who had been partially scalped—or so he claimed—in a tussle on Rose Creek. He had regaled her customers with tales of butchery and savagery and hard gallops and gunsmoke. He had said, "Injuns never raise no dust. That's what makes 'em hard to catch and kill."

It can't be Indians.

But then, that crusty, sun-bronzed fellow had been in his cups and had entered the Neodesha restaurant to "put some grub in my belly to soak up all that whiskey I done drunk."

Glancing at Arthur's revolver, holstered right at her feet, she remembered the two riders at Eight Mile Creek. And recalled what she had read in *The Wichita Herald* this morning before she fled town.

A redheaded damsel from the eastern part of our state arrived in our fine city today bringing news of a fantastic shoot-out . . .

That Cindy Bagwell called herself a writer? Denise could have done a better job, and she had written hardly anything other than recipes and bills for her customers.

After wrapping the leather lines around the brake, she bent to pick up the holster, then tugged the walnut grip of her brother's Navy Colt. After the graveside service for Arthur, one of the deputies in Wichita had cleaned and reloaded the revolver for her, showed her how to cap the nipples, and said it was a handy weapon.

Before long, the dust grew closer, and Denise relaxed. That wasn't a party of Indians, because before the sounds of jangling traces, a popping bullwhip, the turning of wheels and clopping of hooves, she heard oaths of vile profanity. Denise didn't put the .36-caliber pistol back by her feet, though.

One of the mules turned its head and brayed.

She waited a long while before the oxen came into view. The whip kept popping, but the profanity stopped. Denise's mules started acting skittish, but she hushed them, and turned again to watch the wagon and oxen.

Just one wagon. One man.

About two hundred and fifty yards away, the driver stood, but did not stop the team. It was a six-up, and the oxen moved slowly, pulling a large freight wagon—no, two wagons. The whip cracked again.

"Haw," the man shouted. "Haw." He resumed his cursing.

The wagon came along, moving toward the left.

Denise wasn't sure how long it took the wagon to pull up alongside her, but she was glad she was going just as far north as Newton. And not Nebraska.

The bearded man stood, revealing blue-striped trousers and knee-high boots as he pulled hard on the leather lines and yelled, "Whoa. *Whoa.*" And punctuated his command with more curses as the oxen finally came to a stop, with the driver's box about twelve feet ahead of Denise's mules.

He looked back, pushed up the brim of what some Kansans might call a hat, and slowly stood, his joints popping, then wrapping the lines around his brake, and hooking out the tobacco he had been chewing, tossing it into the rank green grass. Quickly, he whipped off his hat. He might have even bowed, but one of the oxen lurched, so he might have been regaining his balance and trying not to fall into the trail.

"Havin' troubles, lady?" he asked, after recovering his balance.

"No, sir." She tried to smile and look pleasant. "I'm heading to Newton. I aim to open a business there."

"Yes'm."

His lips moved, but he found no other words. With the wind blowing toward the south, she caught the scent of the oxen and his own foul stench. He was as filthy a man as Denise had seen, but she did not fear him. Dirty and profane, he seemed to have a gentleman's nature.

But it suddenly struck Denise that the man was thinking about another kind of business. "I aim to open a restaurant," she said. "My name is Denise. Denise Beeber."

His expression did not change. Neither did his vocabulary. "Yes'm," he said.

She waited for more, and when nothing came except for one of the oxen urinating, she said: "I was wondering if I'm going the right way."

He scratched his side whiskers, caked with dust. "Yes'm." His head tilted up the road. "None of my affair, lady, but . . . well . . . *Newton?*"

She smiled. "Newton."

He cocked his head to the left.

She waited for him to introduce himself.

Instead, he just blinked. "Oh. Yes'm." He scratched the other side of his chin whiskers. "But, ma'am, there ain't that many folks in Newton. To feed no how."

"But there will be." Her smile felt triumphant. "There will be."

Now he grinned, showing off yellow- and brown-stained teeth, with one missing incisor. "Yes'm." He nodded and let his smile widen. "Yes'm."

She studied the two wagons the oxen pulled, nodded, and turned back to the bearded man, who remained standing in the driver's box. "By chance are you headed for Newton?"

"Yes'm." He nodded at his wagons. "Mr. Ewing . . . of Wicks and Ewing . . ." He gestured south. "Down in Wichita. He— Mr. Ewing, I mean—hired me to haul this lumber up there. Mr. Wicks rode up there yesterday. That's his partner. Mr. Wicks, I mean, he's Mr. Ewing's partner. Plans to sell all this lumber for top dollar."

Smiling, Denise looked east, then west. She could count the

number of trees she had seen on one hand. "I warrant," she said, "lumber is in short supply."

He shrugged. "Oh, you can find timber. Some. Mostly along creeks and rivers. Got two lumberyards in Wichita. That's where I live now. Right good bit in Newton, too. Trees, I mean. For now. Probably why the judge and the land boss—and the railroad—picked it for a townsite."

He stopped to catch his breath. He probably hadn't spoken this many words, without a single profanity, in his entire life.

"Wicks and Ewing got a lumberyard," he continued. "In Wichita." Again, he pointed south. "That's who hired me. And Smith and English. They run the other lumberyard. But I ain't never hauled nothin' for them. And some other stores and such, they sell a bit of lumber, too. Like George Johnson. He's got a furniture store. Sells lumber, too. Not much. And even sells coffins already built."

Her smile vanished. "Yes. I know." She wasn't sure he heard. He kept right on talking.

"And I read in one of the papers that some fool's comin' down to this county with a sawmill."

She made herself forget about ready-made coffins and gave the driver another pleasant smile. He could talk more than she had figured.

"Most of the lumber comes by train," he said. "Emporia. Railroad ain't reached this far yet. But it will."

She smiled. "That's why I'm bound for Newton."

"Yes'm."

"I was wondering, Mister . . ." She waited, giving him the opportunity to introduce himself. He just scratched and stared, so she gave up. "I was wondering if I could follow you to Newton."

Now he used his right hand to tug on the beard below his chin.

"Well," he finally said, "yes'm. But might be better for you if I followed you." He pointed at the oxen. "These critters raise up a lot of dust. And the wind don't help none. I'm used to it. Wind, I mean. Been in Kansas when it was nothin' but a ter'tory. But I wouldn't want to get you all dirty, lady."

She understood what he meant, and smiled again. His hand pointed farther up the trail.

"It ain't hard to find, lady. Six miles up, maybe just five, there's a fork in the road. You turn them mules of yourn right. Not left." He held out his right hand, which had been scratching his whiskers. "Right."

Denise nodded.

"I'll holler at you to stop if I see something peculiar," he said. "Like a bull buffalo or Kiowa or some such." He put his hat back on. "But I can't move these wagons too fast, lady. You'd make better time without me weighin' you down."

"It's quite all right, Mister . . . ?"

That just got a blank stare.

She smiled. "I will enjoy your company and protection."

He nodded. "Yes'm. A lady like you shouldn't travel this country alone."

Her face tightened. She remembered Arthur and the two rogues at Eight Mile Creek.

"Yes, sir," she whispered.

He frowned. "Thing is, lady, slow as I go, we'll likely have to stop a few miles before we get to Newton. For the night, I mean. I try to stop before dark, you see. But you could ride in them last miles by your lonesome and . . . well . . ."

"No," she said, smiling again, "Mister . . . ?"

And this tall, bearded, burly man stared at her like he had been struck mute. She wondered if this were a mistake. Her mother, father, grandparents, the preacher back in Arkansas, even Arthur would have likely tried to slap sense into her. But . . . she looked back at the wagons and the lumber.

"I shall cook you supper, sir," she said, and faced him again, smiling. "With hopes that you will tell everyone you meet that when in Newton, they should visit my restaurant."

"Yes'm," he said.

* * *

By the time they made camp, with the sun well above the endless plain that stretched west, Denise still didn't know his name, and for all she could tell, she remained just Yes'm to him.

Yet she insisted on cooking supper, and coffee, although he insisted on providing the coffee beans.

She found the grinder, and he marveled as she cranked the handle, then withdrew the grounds and saw him staring with those dark, childlike eyes.

"I'll be da—. . . danged," he said, shaking his head.

Denise smiled. "You have never seen a coffee grinder?"

His head shook.

"Not even in a store?" She was using a Champion No. 1, one of the newest models, but as far as Denise knew, coffee grinders went back hundreds of years.

"How do you make your coffee when you're out here?"

He shrugged. "I just grab me a handful of beans, wrap 'em in a bandanna, put that in the pot, and fill the pot with water."

Denise nodded. "I suppose that would work. Sugar?"

"No, ma'am."

"Milk?"

He snorted. "Not since I was sucking—" He blushed, dropped his head, and whispered. "No, ma'am. No milk for me."

Denise had not been asking if he wanted sugar or milk in his coffee. She would have had to search for sugar, and milk was a long way from here. She wanted to know what they did to sweeten or soften the coffee. Apparently, nothing. So when she reached Newton, she would know. Make the coffee strong and black.

She fed him sourdough biscuits, fried bacon, and a cobbler made with canned peaches. From the look on his face, he would be her champion in Newton, though she went to sleep—with him unrolling his blankets about a hundred yards past the picket line, to avoid anything impolite—wondering if she would have to name her new restaurant The Yes'm Café.

*   *   *

She let him make the coffee for breakfast—just to see how his brew turned out—while she warmed up the biscuits and fed him thicker cuts of bacon and found a jar of apple jelly she had made in Neodesha.

He smacked his lips and wiped his mustache and beard.

"You ought to do right fine, lady," he said as he rose, chugged down the rest of his coffee, and went to hitch both teams.

Ninety minutes or thereabouts after they broke camp, Denise reined in the mules, and stared at what, she had to guess, was Newton.

The driver of the wagon had been right. There didn't look to be enough people to fill a table, let alone a restaurant. But she could see men working, and when her guide cursed and stopped the six-up, she pointed to one building.

"Looks like someone has beat Misters Wicks and Ewing to selling lumber in Newton," Denise told him.

"No, ma'am." Yes'm nodded at the frame building. "That's A.F. Horner's place. Brung it with him from Florence, which is where he was livin' before he got the itch to try Newton. Just took it apart and hauled it here. And before that, he was livin' in Brookville. In that very same buildin'.."

He pointed to a tent. "That's the lumberyard, lady. Reckon I ought to unload these wagons and head back south." He tipped his hat. "You cook good, lady. Real good. Make good coffee, too. You ought to do well here."

"Thank you, Mister . . ."

He was getting a better hold on the lines.

"Sir?" she called out.

When he turned, she smiled, and tilted her head toward the lumber.

"How many buildings do you think that lumber could make?"

He chuckled. "I ain't no carpenter, lady. I just know how to harness and handle a six-up."

"Enough to build a restaurant?" Quickly, she added, "A small one . . . at first."

"I reckon."

She dismissed the idea of trying to buy the lumber from him. Yes'm was honest, from that miserable hat and all the way down to the holes in his boots.

"Could you tell Mr. Wicks that I would like to make an offer on enough lumber to build a suitable restaurant in this town?"

He nodded. "Yes'm." Now he pointed. "But you see that Sibley tent over yonder?"

She saw three tents, but he seemed to be pointing to the big canvas structure shaped like a teepee.

"Yes, I do," Denise answered.

"That's the Atchison, Topeka, and Santa Fe headquarters—for this section, at least. The railroad, ma'am, owns all the land here and around the town. You got to buy the lot from that ol' jasper."

She thanked him again.

When he got the oxen moving again, pulling the two wagons, she looked at where a town was being born. There was water. A river, or at least a creek, flowed here. She saw the timber, too. Yes'm had been right about that, but she wondered how long those trees would stand with a town being built.

This was Newton. Three tents. A wooden home that had already been moved across Kansas twice. A soddy, or some home or business made of dirt or mud or whatever. The wind picked up, and one of the mules decided to let its bowels loosen. That seemed fitting, because Denise was wondering what she had gotten herself into.

Chapter 11

Efforts are being made at some points in Southern
Kansas to divert the bulk of the cattle trade from the
line of the Kansas Pacific Railway. But the parties en-
gaged in these efforts have not succeeded in drawing
away any considerable portion of the trade.
—*The Abilene Chronicle*,
June 22, 1871

Most folks—at least those living in Texas—still called it The Texas Cattle Trail. The previous year, however, entrepreneurs and ink-slinging newspapermen in Kansas had started referring to it as the Chisholm Trail, named after some Scotch-Cherokee trader who did blaze a path from his trading post in Indian Territory into Kansas. Texans weren't ready to brand their trail after some half-breed squaw man who wasn't a cattleman. Most trail drivers, Gary Hardee included, usually used the words *Texas*, *cattle*, and *trail*, but between the nouns, generally added a few adjectives that would make a lady blush. Some folks labeled it the Great Texas Cattle Trail, but Gary hadn't found anything great about eating dust and spending sixteen to eighteen hours in a saddle every day of every week, including Sundays.

Gary didn't think Chisholm would stick as a name. Folks might confuse that Chisholm with John Chisum, a store clerk-

turned-cattleman who had driven some cattle to Vicksburg during the late war and, not caring much for the value of Confederate currency, driven herds to some Indian reservation in New
Mexico Territory.

Whatever name one wanted to give this trail, Gary often
amused himself dreaming of how some mapmaker would sort it
all out.

Trail had to be used loosely. In this part of Texas, especially, a
number of footpaths led to what might pass for a main route.
Then you went wherever the trail boss found enough grass and
enough water. Farther south and west, herds might skirt around
San Antonio, where faro dealers waited to cheat half the trail
crew, and the priests and nuns might waylay the other half and
send them back home to their mothers, sisters, or wives. If herds-
men started from the Río Frío down Uvalde way, they might
make a beeline to Fort Graham.

The area between the Colorado and Brazos had been prime
cow country, but Gary often thought the herds that came from
the western part of the state were better suited for the full drive.
Those longhorns knew how to scavenge, could get by on little
grass, and less water. The Major had always called his cattle
spoilt. Too much rain. Too much grass a foot tall.

The Major had a point.

The two herds Gary oversaw loosely followed the Colorado
River north and west. At least till Austin. Some drovers argued
that Austin was worse than San Antone. Said a drover would be
wise to stay as far away from Austin as you could, or risk being
taxed with fines from the police force or interviewed by legisla-
tors up for reelection who wanted your vote. Gary didn't believe
that.

Farther north, Waco wasn't much to look at, as far as Gary
could see, but the ferry came in handy in the early years when
the Brazos was raging. Last year, a suspension bridge had opened,
but those thieves running the bridge charged five cents a head

for cattle. Gary was already thinking about bypassing Waco, and trying to cross at Fort Graham upstream. The Army had abandoned the fort before the war, but the settlement had a general store and a blacksmith—and no toll bridge and no toll-taker. Five cents at thirty-two hundred head of cattle, not to mention two wagons, two dozen horses and riders, and plenty of extra horses—that was an expense Gary wasn't about to pay.

After that, a drover usually found a smooth ride to Fort Worth, as long as he could keep his crew—two crews this trip—out of the saloons and jails. Then people thinned out, and if you could cross the Red River with no loss of time, cattle, or lives, you'd find yourself in the Indian Nations.

Criminy, old man. We're just riding into earshot of Austin. Remember what the Major used to tell you: Don't count your heifers before they're hatched.

Seeing a grove of trees, he spurred the gray to shade, swung out of the saddle, wrapped the reins around a bush, and paid the price for living on coffee all morning and into the afternoon.

Unbuckle the gun belt and hang it over the lowest limb. Reach around the back, find the buckle, loosen the chaps, lower the chaps. Start with the hard buttons on his britches. Remember, this is why he didn't wear suspenders on a cattle drive. Jerk down the britches to where the chaps were bunched up. Find the trapdoor and drain that bladder.

He never figured out how Jane, or any woman, managed any of this with their petticoats and crinolines, stockings and drawers, corsets and chemises.

Two hard, long drives had worn the rank off both herds and trail crews. Then they had slowed down, averaging ten miles a day. He had soaked his chafed hide in the Colorado River, surprisingly low after a wet spring, then again in some little creek. Tiring out four horses each day, and another at night. Riding back to Hugh Anderson's herd, and back to his. Fording creeks he knew the names of, streams he gave new names every year, swimming some, splashing through others more than once just to tell Hugh to keep his twelve hundred where Gary wanted those cattle to be.

Now he turned and looked west. If not for the lowing cattle, the jingling of spurs, snorting of horses, crackling of fires, and cussing, griping, worn-out men, they might have been able to hear a tinny piano from an Austin saloon.

Twenty-three days, if his math was right, and they had covered roughly a hundred and sixty miles.

"I told Hugh to stay on that side of the Colorado," Gary told Dunn. "Maybe it'll keep most of his crew out of the saloons. And out of jail."

"Yeah." Dunn took Gary's empty cup. "What I figured. Too bad we couldn't have just kept ridin' past it."

Gary shrugged to loosen the muscles in his back, then pushed up the brim of his hat. He turned and found Carlos Morales bringing a fresh horse, and Gary sighed.

"Tell Conner that we'll move out same as always, just before daybreak. Let him figure out the nighthawks." He took the reins from the wrangler, nodded his thanks, and somehow managed to pull himself into the saddle without his arms falling off or his legs disintegrating. "Biscuits and bacon for breakfast, Moises. I'll try to be back before you've dished out all the grub."

A two-mile ride into Austin found no letters at the post office, but he went into a mercantile, glanced through the window to make sure no one had followed him into camp, walked to the counter, and stared at the bottles, sacks, and cans stacked neatly on shelves against the wall.

He didn't need Edward Walder's Sarsaparilla and Potash as he didn't think he was suffering from Scrofulous Sore Eyes, Pimples on the Face, or Constitutional Syphilis. Another medicine that allegedly tasted like wild cherries could cure coughs, colds, laryngitis, asthma, and even consumption. He didn't have worms—at

least, as far as he could tell—so another bottle didn't seem to be
what he needed.

Salts and sulfur, coal and castor oils, quinine, oils, seeds . . .

Now he could use an aspirin for the headache that was starting. He rubbed his eyes.

"Calomel."

Gary lowered his fingers from his eyes, and shook his head as
he turned to the man leaning against the counter.

"I don't have any bowel complaints," Gary said, "and I remember that sawbones telling Luke Crystal to drink that calomel
after Shiloh, and Luke's teeth had fallen out and his cheeks were
rotting before Chickamauga."

"That's why I was glad Luke left me to join you and those
other fools rangering with Colonel Wharton," Jesse Driskill said.
"When he came back after the Yanks paroled him, he didn't talk
too much."

Driskill held out his right hand, which Gary gladly took and
shook.

"Figured you'd be heading north by now," Gary said.

"Billy's working the gather," Driskill said. "Be done in three-
four more days."

Jesse Driskill, and William H. Day, his brother-in-law, had
been working cattle together since before the war. They had sold
beef to the Confederate Army—and went broke because they
had been paid in Confederate script. Billy Day's father had
drowned at a river crossing on a drive back in 1860.

"You still working for the Old Man?"

"Who keeps getting older. What brings you into a . . . ?" He
didn't know what to call the mercantile.

He held up a wrapped package. "Nancy sent me. Where you
bound this trip?"

"I don't know," Gary told him. "Have you seen the—"

"Every cattle driver in Texas has seen that circular, but Billy and I still think Abilene's good for one more season. That's where we're bound. Till we learn different. Though to be honest with you, after all these years, I'm fed up of dealing with Kansans. How 'bout you? Where you figure to sell?"

Gary shrugged. "The Major told me to find out which town looks like the best deal."

"Come on, Hardee." Jesse Driskill turned and headed for the door. "You might want to meet this fellow who got off the stage yesterday evening."

The Kansan, dressed in a green and gold plaid sack suit and a derby hat, called himself Preston Rucker, and said he was an associate of Judge Muse and Commissioner Lakin. He offered Gary a shot from the bottle of rye he held in the saloon, but Gary shook his head, and asked the bartender for black coffee.

"Wouldn't be right," he said politely. "Me drinking whiskey, I mean, while my men are getting just coffee."

"I see." He poured a shot for Jesse Driskill.

"Gary's been driving cattle for Major Wat Anderson and a group of ranchers so far south, Mr. Rucker, that if he went any further, he'd be in the Gulf of Mexico," Driskill said. "Been driving cattle for many a year. He has a herd east of town along the river."

"Is that so?"

If Jesse Driskill said so, you can bank on it, buster. Gary kept his mouth shut, though, until the pewter cup of coffee came into his hands.

"Two herds," Gary corrected, and turned to Driskill. "The Major sent a smaller herd behind mine. His boy's bossing it. Hugh. Not Rich."

Driskill pursed his lips, spoke not a word, but his nod, frown, and eyes said it all.

"How many head?" Mr. Rucker asked.

"Thirty-two hundred. Steers."

"And where, if I may ask, do you intend to sell your long-horns?"

The coffee wasn't bad, but it wasn't Moises Dunn's, either. Before Gary could answer, the stranger did some explaining.

"Judge Muse is land agent for the Atchison, Topeka, and Santa Fe Railroad, I should have told you. And D.L. Lakin is the land department commissioner. I am here at their bequest, trying to steer"—he laughed at his weak joke—"Texas cattle to the new town, new city, new mecca for Texas cattlemen, Newton, Kansas."

Gary sipped more coffee.

"Never heard of it," he said, and loved the reaction he saw in the Kansan's face. Driskill tried, but failed, to stifle his laugh.

But Mr. Rucker recovered. "Few have now. Up until last August, it was nothing but Kansas prairie and buffalo gnats. When I left there two weeks ago, there were scant few buildings, one moved from Darlington Township and other from some town I can't recall. And Captain Sebastian. That's Captain *John* Sebastian"—as though the name meant anything to Gary or Driskill—"was living in a tent on the banks of a creek."

He stopped to sip his rye. Gary waited.

"Surely," he said, "you have seen the circular issued by the citizens of Abilene. They no longer want your trade. Newton does."

Gary drank more coffee. "The thing is, Mr. Rucker," he said quietly, "Abilene has stockyards and a railroad."

The Kansan grinned like he had just hooked his fish. And perhaps he had.

"The Atchison, Topeka, and Santa Fe must reach Newton by the fifteenth of May. That is in our contract. We are certain that it will."

Gary finished the coffee. "Railroad's one thing. Shipping yards are another."

Now the man beamed like a kid on his birthday. "When I left

town, Joseph McCoy was beginning to oversee the construction of our shipping yards. Mr. McCoy is getting fed up with Dickinson County politics as much as you and Mr. Driskill are."

Gary set the empty mug on the bar. "How about buyers from Chicago, Kansas City?"

"Judge Muse and Commissioner Lakin are working on that. I was sent south. My associates have been dispatched elsewhere." He finished the rye, set the tumbler near Gary's coffee cup, and hooked his thumbs in the pockets of his vest. "I seek no contract, sir. I brought no papers to sign. I don't even have a fountain pen on my person. I just came with the news and the invitation to bring your herd to Newton. We are closer than Abilene, and we shall definitely be more friendly to the butter that we put on our bread. Mr. Driskill is bound for Abilene—this year—but I dare say I believe he will see the errors of his ways and bring his herd to Newton in seventy-two."

"And if the railroad tracks don't reach Newton?" Gary asked.

The man smiled. "Ellsworth is roughly eighty miles northwest. Abilene is some sixty miles due north." He held out his hand.

"We'll see, Mr. Rucker," Gary said. Rucker did have a firm grip for a businessman. "We'll see. And I thank you for the coffee and conversation."

"Hope to hear that you are successful in Newton this summer, sir. And perhaps I shall meet you there next season." He tugged on his hat and turned around to pay the bartender.

Outside, Driskill tucked the package underneath his left arm and extended his right hand. Gary shook it firmly, thanking the cattleman for introducing him to Mr. Rucker.

"If the *Abilene Chronicle* and Dickinson County's finest start bickering, I might see you in Newton."

Gary smiled and started to turn.

"Dodd's Nervine, Hardee," Driskill said. "Dodd's Nervine."

Gary looked back. "What's that?"

"Dodd's Nervine. Soothes the mind. Soothes every achin' muscle. And, there's no strychnine, no mercury, no opium, but it'll do wonders for all that's aching you." He pointed at an apothecary's shop two blocks on the corner a block down.

Gary looked at the lighted window, then back at Driskill.

"How do you know where I'm aching?"

Driskill pulled his hat down and stepped off the boardwalk. Laughing, he walked across the street, bound for a saloon, but called back:

"Son, I was driving cattle long before you got the itch."

Chapter 12

Men Wanted.
One hundred men wanted between Florence and
Newton on the Atchison, Topeka & Santa Fe
Railroad. Apply at the Santa Fe depot Topeka.
—(Topeka) *Kansas State Record,*
May 29, 1871

The agent for the railroad didn't let Denise buy the lumber, which did not surprise her. "That wood is earmarked for our first hotel," he told her. "The Newton House." He made a vague wave as to where this Newton House was going to be built. She didn't even feel annoyed. As soon as Denise saw the potbellied, pale cuss behind that desk, looking out of place in the middle of nowhere Kansas with his Eastern hat, sleeve garters, and cleaning his spectacles with a silk handkerchief, Denise understood that she would not have a roof over her head for a spell.

Denise just returned the man's smile, and asked about buying a lot.

"Where's your husband?" he asked.

"Haven't found him yet," she answered.

He frowned, began chewing the end of his fountain pen. She hoped he might chew too hard and wind up with ink over his chalky face, but that didn't happen.

Knowing what the cur was thinking, Denise reminded him: "I'm opening a restaurant. You know: Bacon and eggs for breakfast. Potatoes, boiled corn, and roasted pigeon for dinner. Steaks and hot biscuits or cornbread with beans for supper. Coffee, tea, or water to drink."

"I see." He lowered his pen. "But I do not—"

She cut him off. "Sir, I owned my own place in Neodesha. I am not married. If I were married, I couldn't own this restaurant that I *will* open. Couldn't even keep any money the place brings in. All that would go to my husband. Couldn't sign a legal contract. And I know I can't vote—at least not in Kansas. But I can own my own place, sir. And, again, I *will*."

He began tapping his incisors with the end of his pen.

She smiled. "Are not you tired of eating your own cooking, sir?"

His expression turned smug. "The Atchison, Topeka, and Santa Fe has hired a darky to cook for us."

"I suppose she cooks a fine meal, too."

"*He*," the agent corrected. "He does."

She nodded. "Well, you come over to where I set up camp. Come over for supper. I'll give you the first meal on the house. And then we'll talk about what lot you are going to sell me."

Now a redness replaced that smug look. He started to push himself out of his chair. "Now, see here—"

But Denise was already walking out of the tent.

To Denise's surprise, the railroad land agent did not follow her out of the tent.

About thirty yards later, she stopped and surveyed the town. Trees could be found along Sand Creek. Mostly, all she saw was grass waving in the wind. She could tell the land wasn't flat as it seemed, but certainly she could find nothing that she would call even a hill, and barely a rise. Another creek forked off from Sand Creek before petering out. That semicircle of water, or mud from the smaller creek, would probably be where the town would grow.

A Negro man shouldering long, two-by-four pieces of pine walked east-to-west about fifty feet in front of her.

"Excuse me," she said.

The man stopped, turned, nodded, but did not look her in the eye.

"Yes, ma'am?" He used his free hand to remove his straw hat.

"What's that creek called over there?" She pointed.

"Mud Creek, ma'am."

Fitting. She asked: "And where will the railroad tracks be?"

"Don't rightly know, ma'am. Sorry."

"That's all right. Thank you, sir."

"Yes, ma'am."

She studied the locations of the tents, then red-flagged stakes, and the pile of lumber that, by her guess, would be the Newton House. Newton, Kansas, seemed to be laid out by throwing leaves in the air and seeing where they landed. But her wagon was here, the railroad man had not emerged from his tent, and this spot looked as good as any. It was in that semicircle between the creeks. And she didn't see any red-flagged stakes nearby.

She paid four burly men in hotcakes, fried pork, and sweetened coffee to get the stove off the wagon. If the railroad man objected, he could try to put the stove back in Denise's wagon.

The aroma of her cooking brought the railroad man out of his tall tent. In fact, her cooking brought everyone in Newton—all fourteen—to her camp. Even with the four complimentary meals, she made four dollars and fifteen cents before noon. Of course, the railroad man handed her some papers to fill out, and she had to pay him a filing fee. And he told her to check with the freighter when he brought in the next load of wood.

A.F. Horner liked the way Denise "doctored up" her beans. Best he had ever tasted, he said, except for his grandma's. "Well,"

Denise had told him, "I've never been able to match my grandma's beans, either. Tried to get her recipe for years. She would just say a pinch of this, and you don't know how much of salt till it tastes just right."

Right proud of his building, Horner said he planned to turn it into a storage and supply place.

Denise allowed that he had a real nice building. She liked how that false front looked. He said one of these days he hoped to put a second story on top, as he already had half of the front of the second story already built. She said that was a fine idea. She didn't say that it would be a really small second story if he didn't add to that whitewashed false front.

He bragged that he was getting a cash prize from the Atchison, Topeka, and Santa Fe for having the first real building in town.

She winked at him and said he was welcome to spend all of his prize money on her beans and cornbread.

He grinned and explained how he and some good folks in Florence had taken down all the wood—even managed to save most of the nails that weren't bent too badly—and his pals had helped him load it up and bring it all the way down here. He pointed off to the northeast.

"Almost thirty miles," he said.

"You'd never know by looking at it, Mr. Horner," she lied, and poured him a bit more coffee.

"Before that," he said, "I was in Brookville." This time he pointed off to the northwest.

"You've already cut a triangle," she said. "Speaking of triangles, how about a slice of dried apple pie?"

He accepted. Another ten cents for her money box. When she checked on him again, he asked: "What is the secret to your pie crust, Miss Denise?"

"If I told you that, it wouldn't be a secret."

She left him with a wink and refilled a railroader's coffee mug on her way back to her stove.

* * *

Cooking had always made Denise happy. That had to be something she inherited from her grandmothers. It certainly didn't come from her mother, who hated to even scramble eggs. But cooking had been a passion for both her father's mother and her mother's mother. She could spend hours each day with one of them, and around Christmas time or birthdays, both of them.

Some of her best recipes came from her grandmothers.

She traded four jars of plum preserves for a tent, and a hide hunter heading for some trading post gave her a buffalo robe. Wasn't much of a robe, the stinking man told her, but it would be a lot more comfortable than sleeping on the ground.

"Ain't got no ticks, missy," he told her. "And I reckon my p'i's'n got rid of 'em graybacks."

She spent two more nights on the hard ground before deciding to test the buffalo hide as a rug. Ticks or lice had to be better than the gnats and ants that attacked her each evening and morning. Turned out, the strychnine, arsenic, trader's whiskey, or whatever the hide man had used on the hide had done its job quite well, although she covered the hide with a canvas tarp and one of Grandma Beatrice's quilts before lying down her bedroll.

On her fourth day in Newton, Judge Muse rode in with a party of men—speculators, Denise figured, from the attention the railroad's land agent gave them. The first place the Atchison, Topeka, and Santa Fe agent brought them to was Denise's restaurant.

Not that it was a restaurant, though she had managed to buy a rectangular tent and some tables and chairs. She had had to sell the furniture from her Neodesha place because none of it would fit in her wagon. Meals were fine to be taken around the stove or cookfires in the mornings or evenings, but the noon sun and wind made eating outside an unpleasant experience. Not that many men ate at noon.

Judge Muse's eyes widened after he forked in a mouthful of mutton stew.

He chewed, swallowed, smiled, and laid down his fork and looked up at Denise.

"Thyme?" he asked.

She returned his smile. "Just a very little." Denise admired a man who could taste what he was eating. Most of her patrons in Newton shoveled food into their mouths, chewed a few times, then washed the grub down by guzzling piping hot coffee.

"And?"

Denise cocked her head. "Now, Judge Muse, if I shared my recipes, I would be out of business."

Everyone at the table, including the judge, laughed. But she knelt and whispered into his ear:

"Some peppercorns. And essence of celery."

He looked up at her and said, covering his mouth with the cup of his hand and speaking as though he were in church, "I have never heard of essence of celery."

She whispered again: "You can take three, maybe four heads of celery. Boil those with the thyme."

Judge Muse looked like she had given him the location of a gold mine. He picked up his fork, then suddenly turned toward and pointed his fork at the land agent.

"Redfield," he demanded, "why is this goddess confined to a tent?" He gave Denise another smile and a nod. "I see two framed structures, one of which is going to be, I have been informed, a storage and supply house. Do not you think that a fine eating establishment would be a priority as we build a great mecca on our prairie?"

Redfield opened his mouth, but no words came out.

"This town is named Newton, sir. Newton. After that fine city that has produced a great many of the men who have built the Atchison, Topeka, and Santa Fe Railroad into the valuable and moneymaking enterprise that it is. And if I am not mistaken, your father lives in Newton, Massachusetts."

Mr. Redfield's lips moved up and down several times before he could think of something to say, which turned out to be: "He does, sir, with my stepmother."

"Well, why is Miss Beeber serving my dinner in a tent, sir?"

"We are waiting for another supply of wood from Wichita or Emporia, sir."

"Bosh." He shook his head and let out a sigh of exasperation. "I see timber on the banks of the creek, boy. In my day, we built homes and business by cutting down the trees that grew to make this country great. By thunder, in Kansas, I have seen homes made of nothing but dirt." He slammed his fist and fork on the table, rattling many coffee cups and bowls of stew, and opened his mouth again, but Denise smiled at him, and put her hand on his shoulder.

She leaned close to him and whispered. "Don't ruin your dinner, sir. I don't want you to suffer from any indigestion."

Denise straightened, and when he looked up at her, she gave him another smile, then looked across the table and asked, "Who wants dessert?"

She had just begun to set the batter for the next morning's breakfast, counting campfires and heads, to make an educated guess at how many would be coming over for breakfast. After then making a quick tally of her supplies, Denise knew she wouldn't be able to cook many more meals.

A.F. Horner happened to be walking by, so she called out his name, set the bowl and spoon on the back of her wagon, waved him over, and wiped her hands on the apron.

She gave him a cup of coffee—saying, "On the house," with a smile—and then asked him where she would find better supplies, Florence or Wichita. They were both about the same distance, the way she had things figured.

"Wichita," he said, and smiled. "One reason I pulled up my place in Florence and came down here."

"That's what I thought." She poured herself a cup of coffee.

They talked about weather, wind, then heard the clopping of hooves, and stared down the southern trail.

Smiling when she recognized the oxen, Denise suddenly laughed and wondered when was the last time she had recognized oxen. The six-up pulled two wagons, both filled with lumber. She might get a real roof over her head before long.

The smile died, though, when the driver, who was too rail-thin to be Yes'm of Wichita, and did not handle a bullwhip with much authority, stood in the box and yelled:

"Murder. Murder."

She spotted a saddle horse hitched behind the last wagon.

"Oh," Denise whispered, and set her cup on the tailgate of her wagon. "No."

Nine men and Denise stared down at the corpse. At first, Denise tried to stop the tears, but quickly gave up.

"Where did you find him?" Redfield asked.

The stranger, dressed in buckskin britches, a homespun shirt, and an old Army campaign hat, had introduced himself as Frank Oates, and said he was riding from Wichita to Emporia to visit his mother.

"Two miles south," Oates said, pointing.

Captain David Payne, who was digging a well on Main Street, had two of the Negroes turn the body over, and Denise saw the bloody hole in the center of the body's back.

"Shot from ambush, I'd say," the captain said. "Rifle shot. From a distance. Fairly large caliber. But why?"

"There was a bunch of these two-by-fours and planks scattered all over the road," Oates said, but Denise was looking at his horse. There was no scabbard, no rifle. Only a valise strapped behind a bedroll. Frank Oates, she decided, was not the murderer.

Besides, would a murderer bring in the body of the man he had killed?

"Like maybe who did the dirty deed was looking for, I dunno, a money box, some valuable." Oates shook his head. "I picked up what I could, tossed the wood back into the wagons. Might be some small pieces I left behind. He had shingles in some boxes. But I got most of the big two-by-fours and the heavy planks."

Redfield shook his head. "What a shame."

Captain Payne nodded at the thinnest of the railroad men. "Harry," he said, "could you ride hard to Wichita? Tell Sheriff Walker what happened. This will be his jurisdiction."

"Sure, Capt'n," the man named Harry said, and he looked at Oates. "Did you see any tracks, see which way the killer—or killers—rode off?"

Oates shook his head. "Mister, I'm a druggist."

"That's kind of like a doctor, ain't it?" a big railroader said. "Can't you do some kind of examination on him? Make sure he's dead?"

"Vernon," whispered the man beside him, "for the love of God . . ."

Redfield said. "We'll have to bury him."

The captain told Harry: "You best saddle up, ride out now." Then he turned to Redfield. "Where should we make the cemetery?"

Another man cleared his throat. "Which cemetery?"

The captain put his hands on his hips and glared.

"Well," the man explained. "A town—city—cemetery? Or a potter's field."

The men exchanged glances. The dead driver just lay on the dirt, staring at them blankly with unseeing eyes.

"We don't even know his name," one man said. "And it ain't like this old hoss had no family. Or money."

"I'll have to . . ." Redfield scratched his chin.

"We could just plant him on the other side of Mud Creek," a

man Denise knew as Benton said. He pointed. "Get them two colored boys to dig the grave. Put a stick in it in case some family wants to dig him up and—"

The curse Denise shouted got their attention.

First she went to the dead man, knelt, closed his eyes, then found enough of a tarp they had laid him on to at least cover his face. She rose, her face hardening to match her eyes.

"You're burying him in wherever this Newton man decides to put our first graveyard. So pick a place in a hurry, Redfield." She whirled and jabbed a finger at Captain Payne.

"You're mighty good at digging. You dig the grave."

She turned again, and pointed at the druggist from Wichita. "And you. No. You're too small." She looked at the two men of color, who still squatted by the dead man.

"You men," she said, "I know you helped put up Mr. Horner's house. Can you make this poor man a coffin?"

They glanced at each other, then looked at Denise and nodded.

She pointed at the last wagon. "Use the wood from the wagon." She cried for just a moment before damming those tears again and wiping her face.

"Who has a Bible?" she asked.

"I do," someone called meekly.

"Who can sing?"

A few hands rose with a great deal of hesitancy.

She looked back at the wagon.

"Saw off one of those planks," she said. "He'll need a tombstone. I'll need someone to carve in today's date. And the word *murdered*. And his name. Who can read and write?"

To her surprise, Redfield said: "I'll do it."

She sniffled, gave her eyes another quick wipe, and made herself look at the dead man. The edge of the tarp had slid off his face. He just lay there, bearded, ugly, and suddenly looking so small, so lonely, so sad.

"What was his name?"

Realizing no one had heard her whisper, she looked up and re-peated the question.

A few men looked at each other. Two merely shrugged. Most just stared at their boots.

"Surely, one of you know his name. He has been hauling wood up here for . . . for . . . I don't know how long."

She found nothing but blank faces.

"He lived and worked in Wichita," she said, her voice cracking as it rose. "You must have known him." Now she was pleading. "Someone here has to have . . ." But she remembered that she never could get a name out of him herself.

"Miss Beeber," Mr. Horner said softly. "Out here, you don't ask a man his name. You wait for him to give it. If he wants."

Denise wet her lips. She tried to stop shaking. Finally she turned and looked again at the dead man. She smiled sadly, breathed in, exhaled, and nodded.

"All right," she whispered. "For now, just carve his name as Yes'm. Y-E-S-Apostrophe-M."

Chapter 13

The A. T. & S. F. Railroad will be completed to
Newton, early this Summer, making the shortest and
most direct route East, by which to ship cattle. The
above road will use every endeavor to secure the
Texas cattle trade this Summer; and the people of
Wichita and other points along the line of this
proposed trail to Newton should co operate with the
Company to retain the trade to themselves, and
secure the shipping of them at a near point, where it
will be the most benefit to the people of Sedgwick
and Sumner counties.
—*The Wichita Tribune*,
May 11, 1871

Her feet hurt; therefore, Cindy silently cursed Ralph Bodie
for having the audacity to get himself killed over some stupid article he had printed in the *Times*. Audibly, she cursed herself. She could be back home in the South. Alabama was green. It
had blessed humidity, so her skin never felt like sandpaper. She
had wakened to the songs of mockingbirds and wrens, not cursing bullwhackers or jehus driving stagecoaches. She remembered a bluebird chasing away a pair of crows, but here in Kansas,
giant ravens flew about, feasting on whatever had been dropped

into a street, or ransacking the trash bins outside of J.M. Martin's Restaurant and Sample Room, where Martin also let out rooms. His rates, as advertised, were reasonable, but those advertisements he ran in the *Herald*—even paid for them—weren't lying about the proclamation "Refreshments At All Hours," because freighters and hide hunters and just about every unmarried man in Wichita came to sample liquor or beer or a chippie from sundown to sunup.

It was hard to sleep, but she did sleep. She also kept her window closed—easy, as it was painted shut—and her door locked, with the dresser pulled in front for added security.

She even cursed her daddy, for having the audacity to be a newspaperman and winning that argument with Cindy's mother that there was no reason their daughter should not follow in her poor old pa's footsteps. She had a gift for words. For storytelling. For news. And with her looks, she could probably bring in a lot of advertisements.

Bobby Knott, of course, would not let her sell advertising.

Upon reaching the *Herald* office, she looked through the window. Knott-Head wasn't there. Likely having one of his many bracers, the lucky dog. She might have shot him dead if he were working this afternoon. Still might if he showed up. She could have done herself a favor when she had walked to Delano today. Instead of ferrying across the Arkansas there and back, she should have just walked into the river and drowned herself.

But considering her luck, some naked man taking a bath would likely have saved her. And what a story that would have made in the *Tribune* and *Vidette*—and God knows how Bobby Knott would have written it up in the *Herald*.

She opened the door to the *Herald* offices, nodded at Liam McNelly, and found the desk and chair, dragged paper and pencils out of the top drawer, and laid her notebook on the desk. After flipping to the right page in the notebook, Cindy started writing.

Which is what she had been doing for the past eternity.

* * *

Hotel Guests registering this past week:

Wichita

Southern Hotel: Judge W.W. Emerson, Topeka; Capt.
  Emerson Malette, Ft. Wallace; Mrs. L. Harris, Arkansas;
  Wm. D. Culbertson and daughters, San Antonio, Tex.;
  Beng. Buchanan & O.P. Rumsey, Fort Smith, Ark.; Hon.
  Alex. O'Leary, Emporia; Dr. Perry Wonderly, Baltimore; D.
  Stanford & A.P. Powell, St. Louis; D.K.K. Moore, Sherman,
  Tex; Albert Sisson, Chicago; C. Magrievy, Kansas City.
Harris House: Capt. B.B. Kinney, Old Franklin, Mo.; Judge
  C.J. Robbins, Ste. Genevieve, Mo.; Mrs. Andre "Ann"
  Louisa Cannon, Coushatta Chute, Louis., & sister
  Miss Irma Jean Lee, Coushatta Chute, Louis.; Russell
  "Rusty" Abbott Sr. & son, St. Paul, Minn.; Maj.
  E.M. Rozier, Ft. Hayes; Jos. G. McCoy, Abilene, Kans.;
  J. Mitchell, Chicago.
Munger House: Mrs. B.G. McFarlane & Sons Theodore &
  Neill, Salt Lake City, Utah; E.M. Gundlefinger,
  Cottonwood Falls; Sir Murphy Henworthy, London,
  England; Rev. Lester LeRoy Young, Philadelphia, Penn.
Wichita House: S. Frazee, Chicago; Dep. Marshal H.
  Shown, Lawrence; Mrs. J.G. Kennedy, St. Louis; Dick
  Jones, Emporia.

Delano

Jennison & Walker's Hotel: W. Erp, Indian Ty.; Black Bill
  Keyes, Sherman, Tex.; I.P. Olive, Williamson Co., Tex.;
  Niles Van Horn, Emporia; Mr. & Mrs. Frank Thurmond,
  Ft. Griffin, Tex.; F.K. Vogt, Waco, Tex.; Barry Carter,
  Memphis, Tenn.; Mrs. M.J. Schmucker, Baxter Springs.

She laid her pencil down, rubbed her eyes, then her right
wrist, and picked up the paper, reading over the names, checking

them against what she had copied off the registration books in the hotels.

Sighing, Cindy rose and carried the copy to McNelly, who smiled and said, "A fine job of reporting, m'lady. I can tell even before I start finding my type."

Maybe Liam McNelly had been drinking, too.

"Thanks." She made no attempt to disguise her sarcasm, and walked back to her desk. She wanted to unbutton these miserable shoes and rub her feet, but that would not be becoming for an unmarried woman. Or even a married one.

So far this week, she had written a paragraph about the new stagecoach that was beginning to make stops in Newton, even though there was no stagecoach station there—which Bobby Knott had wadded up and tossed onto the floor.

"We don't want our readers to get on a stagecoach and move to Newton, Miss Bagwell," Knott told her. "Newton's getting the Santa Fe Railroad. We want the railroad. Wichita needs a railroad—to survive. The *Herald* needs a railroad—to pay you your fifteen bucks a week—which you haven't earned yet. We don't like Newton. We loathe Newton."

She had gone back to J.M. Martin's Restaurant and Sample Room to buy a bottle of rye whiskey for Knott-Head, but at least her boss gave her paper currency for his purchase.

She had gone to the post office every evening at seven to pick up any newspapers that had been mailed to the *Herald*. She had read some of those papers at night and circled anything that might be worth being "lifted" to fill some holes in this week's edition.

She had read a dreadful piece of poetry a Mrs. Beatrice Shannon had delivered and paid three dollars if Bobby Knott would run it, which he did, even though Cindy found the verse, rhyme, and meter pathetic.

She had found a few sentences that could help fill page four about the County School fund and a lumberyard being started in

Delano, and that Mr. S.C. Johnson had recently visited Cotton-wood Falls and returned with flour and feed for his store for the "Spring Trade."

She wished she could walk back to J.M. Martin's Restaurant and Sample Room and buy a bottle of rye whiskey for herself, and drink herself into oblivion. Her benefactor, Arby McBane, had not been in the office since he had told Knott-Head to hire her.

"Miss Cindy."

Two bottles of rye might work. Or even the forty-rod one could find at other saloons in Wichita or Delano.

She let out a heavy sigh, and did not care that the printer heard her. Slowly, she pushed herself out of the chair and walked to the partition. McNelly smiled that fatherly smile he had when it was needed, and showed her where he had marked one of the pages she had handed him.

Cindy saw what he had marked, but he explained. "There's no 'e' in Fort Hayes," he said. "That's west of here, not that it matters. H-A-Y-S. And here." He slid his finger over. "And you don't need to put K-a-n-s after Abilene. We're all in the same state. Even if Abilene is in its own peculiar world."

Not boasting. Not gloating. Not showing his superiority. McNelly spoke more like a father than some of the schoolmasters and schoolmarms she had had back in Alabama.

"Thank you."

He nodded. "You know, I never point out the errors Knott-Head makes." He smiled. "I let him make a horse's ass out of himself as much as he'll let me. And the way he writes, he lets me a lot. But I want you to have everything perfect." He picked up the papers. "Or as perfect as can be in a cheap newspaper. So our readers, the few that we have—and good old Mr. McBane—will know what a good reporter and gal you are."

She gave him a warm, but tired, smile. "Thank you, Mr. McNelly, but I don't think anyone's going to ever notice anything I write here."

He shook his head. "Mr. McBane noticed the first thing you wrote, Miss Cindy. And he's not one to come to the office the day after the paper is published. Good, bad, or average. And he has never bragged about anything Knott-Head writes."

"Thank you, again. You're too kind." She limped back toward the desk, then stopped, thought for a moment, and turned around.

"Mr. McNelly." She had already started back.

"Yes, ma'am." He turned and met her at the gate.

"May I see that page again?"

"Certainly." He shuffled the pages, and handed her the one he had edited.

Maj. E.M. Rozier, Ft. Hayes; Jos. G. McCoy, Abilene, Kans.; J. Mitchell, Chicago.

"Joseph G. McCoy," she said. "I know that name."

"Everyone in Kansas and Texas knows that name," McNelly said, and looked at the paper Cindy held. She let him take it, turn it around, and bring it closer to his face.

"Abilene." He drew in a breath and lowered the page.

"Isn't he like the mayor or something?" Cindy asked.

McNelly nodded. "Mayor, yes. And he is something. Everybody from Chicago to Texas knows that name. He pretty much started the cattle trade in Kansas by himself." He laid the paper on the table behind him and stared hard at Cindy.

"He got Abilene—which was nothing back then—to build stockyards to hold cattle. He got the Kansas Pacific to stop there. And talked a bevy of Texas cattlemen to bring their beef to Abilene to sell—after he talked beef buyers in Chicago and packing houses to buy that beef in Abilene."

Cindy suddenly grinned.

"I haven't seen hotel registrations in any issue of the *Tribune* or the *Vidette*," she said. She had been reading old copies of all the Wichita newspapers she could find, even some old *Times*. That's about all one could read in Wichita. There was no bookstore. And no library.

"They don't run them. Knott-Head wouldn't either, except Mr. McBane wants to know who's in town, and eventually hopes that'll get those hotel owners to run ads in this paper." He looked at the paper again just to make sure he wasn't seeing things. "The *Times* didn't run them, either."

The paper lowered again, and he whispered, "Joseph G. McCoy."

Cindy shook her head. "Well, it's not like it's President Grant, Queen Victoria, P.T. Barnum, or Jesse James."

"Aye." His head nodded in agreement. "Cattle herds will be coming up this way in a few weeks. Like as not, he just came to Wichita to let them know that those Texians are still welcome in Abilene—as long as they come with thousands of ugly long-horned cattle."

They stared at each other.

"What exactly is a stockyard?" she asked.

"Cattle pens," he told her.

"That's what I thought. How big?"

McNelly shrugged. "When I was in Abilene in sixty-seven, McCoy had one built that could hold a thousand steers."

"My goodness."

He smiled. "Wasn't big enough. Suspect it's even larger now. McCoy bought a lot of acres around Abilene, too. He's a smart man. Visionary, high-toned folks would call him. He even got the railroad to build a sidetrack big enough for a hundred cars to get filled with Texas cattle."

"My." She didn't know what else to say. Her father had milked their cow before he went to the newspaper every day. That's all she knew about cattle, although she liked roasted beef, but pre-ferred fried chicken.

"He had a hotel built in Abilene, too. Maybe you've heard of it. The Drovers Cottage?"

She had no recollection of such a place, but she nodded as though she had.

"But here's the biggest thing he did," McNelly continued. "Joseph McCoy got Crawford—who was the governor of Kansas back then—to let Texas cattle come through the quarantine boundaries." McNelly smiled. "Every person has a price, Miss Cindy. Governors and businessmen."

At least she knew about the quarantine. She had heard enough farmers coming through town complaining that no Texas cattle should ever be allowed anywhere in the state of Kansas—especially Delano. To which a cattle buyer on his way to Baxter Springs had shouted that Texas cattle were good for the Kansas economy.

Which led one farmer to qualify: "Only if you're a whore or a beer-jerker."

Which led to a fight.

She had tried to get that in the paper, but Knott-Head had told her that fistfights weren't news unless it involved a peace officer or a man of importance. Or two women. Two women fighting would sell plenty of *Herald*s.

Cindy wet her lips. Her eyes met McNelly's and held. He was thinking. So was Cindy.

"Might McCoy want to build stockyards here?" she asked. "In Wichita? Or Delano?"

With a polite smile, McNelly shook his head. "Our civic leaders have tried to lure a railroad here for some time now, Miss Cindy. No luck. You have to have a railroad line, a spur, some way to get the cattle to Chicago or Kansas City or wherever they can be butchered and shipped off to big cities. We might get one someday. A spur from Newton is certainly an idea being bandied about. But I warrant I'll be at another paper by then. Especially if Knott-Head doesn't drop dead of apoplexy soon."

They laughed.

She turned again for her desk, but stopped, and looked back. The printer had not moved. He was smiling, waiting for her to speak again.

"But wouldn't an interview with Joseph McCoy be something Knott-Head would want in the *Herald*?"

Liam McNelly answered with a giant grin, and Cindy grabbed her pencils and her notebook and ran out the door.

Chapter 14

Our exchanges are filled with accounts of murders,
robberies, suicides, elopements, terrible accidents,
and other things exciting and shocking, more than
has been the case before for many months. Such
things seem to spread as epidemics, at certain
times, and make numerous victims, and then lull
again, as suddenly as was the outbreak, into
commonplace quietude.
—*The Lyndon Signal*,
May 4, 1871

Her feet no longer hurt. She didn't need a drink of rye—by
thunder, she had never really cared much for whiskey. She
almost knocked over a lady coming out of a grocery store as she
rushed to the Southern Hotel. She almost got run over by a
buggy, and stopped before she reached the corner.

"Stupid." She turned around. McCoy hadn't registered at the
Southern Hotel. He was at the Harris House, across from the lot
owned by L.M. Hall, the contractor and builder—the man who
told Cindy three days ago that he would neither pay a penny nor
give a sentence or a business card to anyone associated with a
foul, mean-spirited publication like the *Herald* unless it was to
move that irresponsible and pathetic sheet to Montana Territory,
preferably in the middle of Sioux country.

At least both hotels were on Main Street. The Harris House just wasn't on the first block.

She stepped on horse droppings, but did not curse, shriek, or stop running. Crossed the street, and saw the stagecoach in front of the Harris House. A man stepped out of Corbett's Millinery, and she almost knocked him into the street. Worse, she dropped her pencils and her notebook. He dropped a hatbox.

She reached down, muttering an apology, picked up what she needed, started for the hatbox, but he had it in his hands and was straightening. She came up, caught her breath, looked past him at the hotel.

Yes, the Harris House was still there.

Looking at him again, she offered one more apology, started to move around him, and stopped, turned back, and shouted.

"Mr. Rouse. I am so sorry."

"It's all right, Miss Bagwell." Rouse was one of the owners of the Harris House. His partner was . . . well . . . she never could remember how to pronounce the name, but she could spell it. Cindy Bagwell was a good speller. S-r-o-u-f-e. Well, she couldn't spell Fort Hays right, but she'd get it correct the next time.

She tried to smile, then tried to run to the hotel, but stopped, straightened, and caught her breath.

Mr. Rouse smiled again, then asked, like a good Kansas gentleman: "Are you sure you are all right, Miss Bagwell?"

"Yes. I . . . yes. I am fine. But . . . can . . . can you tell me? . . . I desire an interview with Mayor McCoy. Of Abilene. Do you know if he—"

"He checked out as I was leaving." Turning slightly, Mr. Rouse pointed at the stagecoach. "He is bound for Newton—but what would bring him to that blight on the plains is beyond me."

The clerk at the Harris House closed the street-side door to the stagecoach. Mr. Rouse started to offer Cindy some assistance. The jehu stood in the driver's box and grabbed his whip. As far as Cindy could tell, no messenger was on this run.

Cindy dodged another pedestrian, whispered a thanks to Mr. Rouse, and stepped into the street.

"Hey." Her voice boomed. The wiry man in the driver's box of the mud wagon started to bring the whip up.

"Bus-ter!" she shouted. "If you whip those mules, I'll whip . . ." Cindy did not remember every curse word she yelled, but she did not think she would ever forget the look on the face of the plump redheaded milliner who had just stepped out of her shop. Or how Mr. Rouse just stared in disbelief. And that a cat across the street screeched.

There was no time to apologize, though, for the jehu had turned around.

"Hold up there, buster," she barked again and ran through the street till she reached the mud wagon's boot. This time, she thought to look and make sure she wouldn't be trampled by another buggy. She hurried to the front wheel, and looked up at the rawboned man with silver hair and a massive mustache.

Now she caught her breath.

"I'm going with you."

"Not till you pay."

Pay? Money. Right. She did not bother asking how much the fare was to Newton.

"You'll bill it to *The Wichita Herald.*"

"The devil I will. You go in there and buy yourself a ticket."

She opened the door.

"Hey, you little hussy. You buy yourself a ticket. And you catch the next stage. 'Cause I got me a schedule."

She tossed her pencils and notebook onto the flooring and tried to figure out how to get into the coach. The jehu was climbing down. He still held the blacksnake whip.

Hard hands stuck out of a blue coat and took Cindy's hands into his own. She felt herself being lifted into the coach, ducked her head, and sighed with relief.

She almost collapsed into the rear bench. The hands released her own. She wondered if she was about to keel over from a heart attack.

The silver-mustached jehu started inside the coach. Cindy turned and tried to tell him that this was important, that the *Herald* truly would pay for her fare, and any other lie she could think of.

Then Cindy saw the long, silver barrel of a revolver that flashed past her and pressed into the jehu's nose.

"You got a problem, buster?"

Cindy could not take her eyes off the slender hand that held the revolver, the thumb pulling the hammer back till it clicked three times. Three soft clicks—but each one sounding like a hammer striking a nail in Cindy's mind.

"No." The voice almost squeaked. "No, sir, Mr. Hickok."

"Good. I got an appointment in Abilene." The revolver did not move.

"Yes, sir, Mr. Hickok. But . . . well . . . she ain't paid her fare."

"I heard her say, 'Bill it to *The Wichita Herald*.' You deaf?"

"No, sir, but the company—"

"You are deaf."

"No, sir. Yes, sir. I'll bill it to the *Herald*, Mr. Hickok." He backed away, closed the door, and turned away. The wagon rocked a bit as he climbed back into the driver's box. The thumb on the slender hand moved slightly, and the hammer slowly, and much more quietly, lowered back into place. The revolver disappeared into a red sash around the thin man's waist.

"My apologies." The voice was higher pitched now. "I abhor rudeness to a lady."

She turned and looked at him. This could not be Joseph G. McCoy. Could it? No, no, it couldn't. The jehu had called him . . .

"J.B. Hickok, ma'am." He reached up and touched the brim of a flat-brimmed black hat. "At your service, Miss . . . ?"

"Bagwell." The whip cracked like a cannon, and she slammed against the bench, and almost fell forward, but the long left arm of J.B. Hickok stopped her from falling into the empty middle bench.

"Thank you," she said. "Again."

The mud wagon settled into something less rough, and another man, sitting across from Cindy and this J.B. Hickok, came off his bench and picked up the notebook and rolling pencils. Smiling, he held up the recovered items to Cindy.

She took them, nodded, found her voice, offered her thanks to him, and tried to piece together what she had just witnessed.

A silver-plated revolver, cocked, had been inches from her face, pointed at another human being. No. Not pointed. The barrel had been pushing into his bulbous nose.

She looked at her . . . what? Savior?

His curly, sandy hair fell to his shoulders. His mustache waxed and long. Not much of a chin. No coat, but a gray one was folded in the empty space next to him. A blue shirt, tan pants stuck into tall boots. His eyes were clear, but cold. He twisted one end of his mustache, then looked at his fingernails. Well-manicured. He seemed such the gentleman—except for those revolvers. And how he had looked when he had pressed one of those weapons against that poor jehu's nose.

Then she looked at the other man. He didn't appear older than J.B. Hickok. But he had no silver-plated revolvers stuck in a red sash around his waist. He was long-faced, straight-nosed, his hair short, parted neatly, a dark mustache and long, triangular beard underneath his chin. He was dressed like a professional, black Prince Albert, black vest with a fine watch chain. White shirt. Bow tie. Pressed striped britches. Black boots.

This man smiled at her.

"Are you really with *The Wichita Herald*, Miss . . . ?"

Her lips moved, but no words came out. She swallowed. Coughed. Swallowed again. Then tried: "Bagwell. Cindy Bagwell. Yes. I work for *The Wichita Herald*."

He nodded. "Well, I applaud your determination, Miss Bagwell. That took a lot of gumption, but I'm sure Wild Bill will tell you plenty of blood-and-thunders for your newspaper."

She nodded, bounced up and down as the wagon rolled over something, and turned toward the man with the two revolvers.

"Wild Bill?" she asked.

"It's a handle that has been branded on me." J.B. Hickok sighed, as if he were suddenly old and tired.

She blinked. "I think I've heard of you."

The man on the other side of the coach laughed, then tried to disguise it with a cough.

This handsome man named Wild Bill shook his head and looked into Cindy's blue eyes. "If you heard it from George Ward Nichols, don't believe it, Miss Bagwell." He winked. "If you heard it from me, don't believe it, either."

She stared into his eyes. His hair smelled like lilacs. She thought she might get lost in those eyes, but then her wits returned, and abruptly, she turned away from him and looked across the coach at the other man.

"Are you Joseph G. McCoy, the mayor of Abilene?"

His head cocked. Hickok chuckled. "Looks like I am not the only celebrity in this springy conveyance," Hickok said.

"I am Joseph G. McCoy." He bowed slightly. "As far as how long I shall remain mayor of Abilene, that I cannot say."

"They won't let you go, hoss." Hickok pulled a file from a vest pocket and began working on his fingernails, almost as though the coach wasn't rocking sideways and bouncing up and down.

"Well." Cindy glanced at Hickok, then looked back at McCoy. "Well, Mayor, I was hoping to talk to you, sir. About . . ." She had no idea what to ask. "Cattle." She turned back to Hickok, who kept working on his fingernails. "But I'd like to talk to you, as well, Mister—"

"Marshal," McCoy said. "Mr. Hickok is to be appointed marshal of Abilene."

"Oh." Cindy blinked. Then she opened her notebook, found

a pencil, saw the point was broken, took the next pencil, found it acceptable, and turned to a blank page. She scribbled. "Congratulations," she told him.

"Congratulate me if I'm still alive come October, Miss Bagwell." He did not even look up from his fingernails as he spoke. "After the Texans are headed back home, busted and hung over."

She looked back at McCoy.

"I am interested . . ." She looked back at Hickok. This was going to be tougher than she had expected.

McCoy smiled again. "Talk to Hickok first, Miss Bagwell. He rides on to Abilene. I get off in the new settlement of Newton." The coach bounced up and down again. This time Hickok had to stop filing his nails, and he glared up toward where the driver sat. But he did not make a move for one of his revolvers.

"If any of us get there alive," Hickok whispered.

Joseph McCoy helped Cindy out of the mud wagon, while Hickok stayed inside. The jehu only opened the door for them, while men pulled the team away from the coach and others brought fresh mules to be hitched.

Someone handed McCoy a valise, and he walked toward a tall, mountain-shaped tent. Cindy started after him, but then stopped. She looked one way, then the other.

This, she thought, *is a town?*

The bullwhip cracked, the jehu cursed, and the fresh team pulled the mud wagon, and J.B. "Wild Bill" Hickok out of nowhere, bound for nowhere. Cindy stopped to write that in her notebook.

It sounded like poetry.

But then it had been a bruising long, hard ride from Wichita.

She hurried to catch up with Mr. McCoy. He was now inside the big tent, but the flaps were open, and he was pointing at a big map on a table. Three men stood around him.

"Here's what we'll need," McCoy said. He had changed. Not

physically, but the smile had disappeared. He pointed at the map, or plat, or whatever it was. "The stockyards are going to go right here. And you're going to build them. We'll have six chutes. And these yards will hold four thousand head."

The gasp came in harmony from the other men.

"That can't be—"

McCoy cut the gray-bearded man in the bowler hat off. "It will be."

"The expense of the lumber alone . . ." That man sighed.

The youngest of the men smiled and said, "But I have a brother-in-law who runs a lumberyard and—"

"You'll get the hard wood from Lanape," McCoy said. "And the pine from Hannibal, Missouri. We're talking about longhorns, gents. Texas longhorns. These are *not* your grandma's milch cows. They are tough and ornery—like the waddies who push them north. You bring in your brother-in-law's wood, it'll be kindling in two weeks. And you'll use railroad ties for the chutes."

He looked each man in the eye. "This is a shipping yard, boys. Not a treehouse for your daughter."

The young man turned around. That's when he saw Cindy.

"Criminy," he said. "The first whore has already arrived."

McCoy grabbed the speaker by the shirtfront. Cotton ripped. The man cried out in a girlish shriek as he was hurtled out of the canvas tent. Cindy had to scurry out of the tumbling man's way. McCoy stepped out while the other men just stood there, eyes bulging, mouths hanging open.

The man rolled onto his back, started to push himself up, when McCoy leaned over and jerked him to his feet.

"This woman is a writer for *The Wichita Herald*, and you will apologize to her for your rudeness. And if you ever insult any woman in my presence again, I will kick your sorry hide all the way to Atchison."

He backed up, nodded at Cindy, then spun around and walked back to the tent. "Any questions, gentlemen?"

* * *

Straightening his tie, McCoy smiled as he walked out of the tent and walked toward Cindy.

"Miss Bagwell, please accept my apologies for talking business with these fools who work for railroads. I have not meant to ignore you, and if you want this interview, I am at your disposal."

She opened her mouth to say something—she hadn't figured out what—but he held up his index finger.

"But there are a few things we must get straight before we talk, and you start writing things down." He did not wait for her to agree. "I am mayor of Abilene, Kansas. You can't write anything about me being in Newton. It is true that I have sold my Great American Stockyards in Abilene last May to Mr. E.H. Osborne of Quincy, Illinois, but as mayor, well, it would not please the citizens to learn that their mayor might be moving the cattle business out of Abilene to a friendlier city to the west, and away from those quarantine lines. Even if the citizens have grown to despise Texas cowboys and, to a degree, me."

"I see."

"Now, before you start peppering me with questions, I have something to ask you?"

Cindy blinked.

"Are you hungry? I am famished." He pointed to a smoke fire about a hundred yards away. "Mr. Ross tells me there is a woman who cooks the finest meals this side of his grandmother's—and his grandmother was Italian."

Chapter 15

The entire country east, west, and south of Salina and down to the Arkansas River and Wichita, is now filled with Texas cattle. There is not only cattle "on a thousand hills," but a thousand on one hill, and every hill.

The bottoms are overflowing with them, and the water courses with this great article of traffic. Perhaps not less than 200,000 head are now within the precincts of the State, 60,000 of which are within a day's ride to Salina. And the cry is "still they come!"
—*The Saline County Journal,*
July 20, 1871

Denise stood behind the tent, scrubbing dishes and wondering when she'd ever get Redfield to give her a lot. Three more tents had been erected, and four new buildings were going up. Denise had made an offer on part of Yes'm's last load to Newton, but two men had outbid her. She had made a decent profit in Neodesha, and kept making some money here, but certainly not enough to keep her tent restaurant going for much longer.

She also wondered why in blazes she ever thought running a restaurant was a fine idea. There were no days off—and finding any help in a settlement of railroad workers and speculators had proved impossible.

Oh, sure, she could get someone to chop firewood, or bring water from one of the creeks for coffee and a free breakfast. That's how she had water to clean up after breakfast now.

She withdrew the last plate, wiped it clean with a towel before laying it on a table to dry, then shook her hands. The towel was too wet to do that job, but the wind would dry her pruney hands quickly.

A stagecoach had started making stops on its way to Florence, Cottonwood Falls, and Emporia, but about the only people getting off here were more railroad men, who were promptly shipped off by wagon to help finish the grading and surveying.

Captain Payne kept telling her that once the railroad drew nearer, folks would start arriving in droves.

"Just bide your time, Miss Beeber," he said, "just your time."

She almost told him that if he would just stop biding his time, he might get that well dug on Main Street.

After moving to the coffeepot, she filled a cup for herself and realized she would need to boil a pot before supper. These men drank coffee all the time. Spittoons also needed emptying. That she could hire someone to do—one of the carpenters from Wichita, most likely, who were putting up another false-front store.

She stepped away from the coffeepot and tried to guess how many people would stop for supper. And she exhaled and shook her head when she heard that little bell ring whenever someone pushed open the flap in the canvas tent.

Another miserable customer. One without the decency to join the dinner or supper rush.

After guzzling down enough coffee to fortify her to serve one more meal, she set the empty cup aside, removed the rag she had tied over her forehead to keep her hair from turning into a crow's nest, and came through the rear opening.

A man she did not recognize was helping someone into a chair. Both backs were to Denise until the man turned around and smiled.

"Good afternoon," he said cheerily. "I hope we're not too late for dinner or too early for supper."

He was no surveyor, no hired hand. Surveyors did not wear Prince Albert coats and seven-dollar hats. Nor did he have the look of a railroad man, unless he was a stockholder. He could not have been older than forty. His haircut and facial hair were well-groomed.

The woman was much younger but with hair the same color.

"Not at all," Denise said.

This gent might even give Denise a tip.

"What can I get you to drink?"

"Coffee for me, ma'am."

The woman started turning around, but the man stepped in front of Denise to ask his female companion what she would like.

"The same," came a soft Southern accent.

"I'll bring the coffees right out," Denise said.

She even gave the coffee mugs another wipe—the wind often coated everything with dust—before filling them with coffee and bringing them back into the tent.

The couple talked softly while the woman, her back to Denise, wrote in a notebook. That's when recognition began.

The man stopped talking, straightened in his chair, while the woman asked a question.

Yes, Denise recalled that voice.

She served the man first—knowing that was bad form—and then slid the other cup toward Cindy Bagwell.

"Good day, stranger," Denise said.

Turning her head, Cindy quickly smiled. "Well, good day, yourself." She started to rise, almost spilling her coffee, but Denise had turned to the well-dressed man.

"Dinner is fried chicken," she said. "With pickled vegetables and cornbread. There is a bit of mutton stew left if you'd prefer that. And wild plum cobbler for dessert."

"Chicken sounds good to me," the man said.

"I'll have the same," Cindy Bagwell said.

"Let me heat it up." Denise started away, but felt Cindy's grip on her arm.

Slowly, Denise turned and looked down.

"How are you doing?" The newspaper reporter appeared sincere. Denise had learned to read people's faces fairly well, and Cindy Bagwell would never have a career as a thespian.

"Oh," Denise said. "I'm just 'Red and Dead.'"

Cindy's hand fell to her side. Her face paled.

Denise turned and headed back to her outdoors kitchen to warm the chicken and vegetables and cut up some cornbread. She hoped she had enough for two.

Before she reached the other side of the tent, the well-dressed man said, "Red and dead. That's pretty funny. Red hair. I get it."

Cindy's reply was harder to hear.

"No, Mr. McCoy, you don't get it at all."

After kicking her right foot against the trash barrel, unleashing a few oaths, picking up the correct cast-iron skillet, and setting it on the stove, Denise knelt down and went about getting a fire going to heat up dinner for two.

That was another thing she had learned about Kansas. You cooked with dried dung. Oh, the Atchison, Topeka, and Santa Fe would let you pick up some small branches that had fallen off a tree, or deadwood wherever it could be found, but no one was going to chop down a tree just to burn it when that tree might be needed for a house or business or shade.

Denise's mother—and both of her grandmothers—would have had a conniption to find her burning dung to cook food. But the chips, which is what everyone called those dried, plate-shaped manure, burned quite well. Better than wood. Buffalo chips gave off no odor. That was something Denise missed. Not the smell of dung, but woodsmoke, hickory, walnut, pine. There was something pleasing about the smell of burning wood.

She had some big ones—three inches thick, ten or so in diameter. They burned with almost no smoke, and burned hot.

While the stove heated, she made more coffee. She was following Yes'm's recipe. With no help in the kitchen, Denise didn't have time to grind coffee, so she wrapped beans in a square scarf that she set in the bottom of the pot, which she then filled with water. She had developed a taste for that brew herself.

The grease in the skillet began sizzling, so she walked over to check on the chicken no one had eaten for dinner. Behind her, a throat was cleared, and Denise slid a thigh around and exhaled.

It was Cindy Bagwell.

She knew that before she turned around.

"Listen, I apologize for what was written in the *Herald* about you and your brother," Cindy said, "especially the . . . 'Red and . . .'—the headline. But that, and the first paragraph—that's not what I wrote. A lot of that wasn't what I wrote. I have this . . . this . . . this . . . *jackass* for an editor."

"No need to apologize." Denise turned back to the food. "I shouldn't have snapped at you in there." She turned the thigh over and slid the breast to a better spot. "I'm just . . ."

She looked for the cornbread.

"Have you been cooking like this since you got here?" Cindy asked.

"Pretty much."

"I thought you'd have a real building."

She found a knife to cut some larger than usual triangles of cornbread and let out a humorless chuckle. "So did I."

The bread made its way onto separate plates.

"I see some buildings going up," the reporter said. "Is one of them yours?"

"If one is, I have yet to hear that news."

She balled a fist, mad at herself, but not because of anything she had said. *The pickled vegetables. Don't forget the pickled vegetables.*

Denise wanted to blame Cindy Bagwell for that, too, but she wasn't to blame.

"Men." Cindy spat out the word.

Denise had the pot of vegetables and had started to replace the simmering chicken with it, but now looked over her shoulder at Cindy.

"Speaking of men, isn't yours lonely in there?"

"Oh." Cindy smiled. "Yes, I should—well, I just didn't want any hard feelings between us. And I wanted to thank you for letting me crawl into bed after you left. I had hoped we would have had a chance at saying goodbye."

"Not much good at goodbyes." She focused on the vegetables.

"Well, thank you."

Denise stirred the vegetables. Pickled. She loathed pickled vegetables, but the men here ate them with relish.

"You didn't crawl to bed," Denise said.

She smiled, even though Cindy could not see that. "It was more like a blind stagger."

"Well . . ." Cindy started back toward the tent. "Oh. That's not my man." She practically snorted. "I don't have—I'm interviewing him for the *Herald*."

I hope your boss doesn't make him mad with something like "Red and Dead" or a bunch of hogwash instead of facts.

She wondered if they would want the cobbler.

"Thanks, again," Cindy said.

Denise kept her eyes on the food, but she heard the reporter walk away.

You could be sociable, she told herself. *People who eat in restaurants like to be served by friendly faces.*

She speared the breast so hard, hot juice almost sprayed her cheek.

Those people aren't eating in a restaurant. They're eating in a ragged tent.

*   *   *

When Denise brought them the last slices of the cobbler, the man Cindy said she was interviewing wiped his mouth with the napkin he had placed on his lap—and not with his shirtsleeve. That was a sight rarely seen in Newton. Redfield didn't use his shirtsleeve, but he didn't use a napkin, either. He never wiped his face. For all Denise knew, he just let the wind do that for him on the way back to his tent.

"Miss," the well-dressed man said. "I have not had a meal that divine in some time. In fact, the last time I tasted something that rivaled your fine meal—and I do not say bested your chicken—was back home in Abilene. The Drovers Cottage could use you, Miss . . . ?"

Cindy Bagwell had not told him her name.

"Beeber," she said. "Denise Beeber."

He laid the napkin back on his lap and extended his hand.

"A pleasure to make your acquaintance. I am Joseph G. McCoy."

That was a name she had heard, even in Neodesha. Everyone in Kansas knew of Joseph G. McCoy. She had heard of The Drovers Cottage, as well.

She felt her mouth move, but heard no words come out.

"This tent." McCoy waved his hand. "This is temporary, of course, but is that because you plan to move along? Up the trail? To a more inviting city?"

Denise briefly studied Cindy, but her eyes trained on McCoy, and her expression said she had nothing to do with his queries. She seemed almost as shocked as Denise thought she looked at the moment.

"I don't know," Denise finally answered.

"Newton could use you, Miss Beeber." He laughed. "By thunder, every cowtown in Kansas could use your talents." He found his fork and eyed the cobbler. "And I think I am about to taste your *piece de resistance.*"

She looked at Cindy Bagwell. Back at Joseph McCoy. Saw

their cups. And said, "Let me refresh your coffee. I'll be right back."

She was pouring coffee into the cup of Joseph McCoy of Abilene, trying to think of something intelligent to say, when a high-pitched, skin-crawling *Yeeeeeeee-hawwwwwwwwww*, rang out somewhere off to the south. A more intelligible *Longhorns, boys . . . long . . . horns*, followed.

Joseph McCoy rose first, swallowed a bite of cobbler, tossed his napkin over his plate, whispered, "Excuse me," and strode toward what passed for a door in Denise's restaurant. Cindy Bagwell sprang from her chair, started after McCoy, stopped, turned around, grabbed her pencils and notebook, and ran after him. Denise followed them through the tent flap.

She didn't realize she still held the coffeepot until she stood beside McCoy.

One of the beefy railroad men ran twenty yards, stopped, pointed down the trail, turned back, cupped his hands over his mouth, and shouted:

"Longhorns! Texas cattle!"

He raised his right arm high, waving back and forth, then turned and pointed.

"Texas longhorns, boys! They're here. They are *here*!"

McCoy started forward. Cindy Bagwell stayed just long enough to scribble a few words; then she ran to catch up with McCoy. Denise followed. She went about sixty yards before she realized that she still carried the coffeepot. She stopped just long enough to set it on the ground, then lifted the hems of her dress, and caught up with the man from Abilene and the Wichita newspaperwoman.

Behind her rushed every man still in the settlement. Even Redfield ran, coatless but trying and failing to bring his suspenders up over his shoulders, stumbling over the prairie grass.

They reached the waving man, who turned and pointed. "Here they come, fellers. Here they come. Cattle, boys. Long-horned Texian cattle. Here they come!"

Denise stopped to stare.

She didn't see any cattle. She saw two mules pulling a small covered wagon.

One of the railroaders cut loose with every foul word he could direct at the man who had gotten them all out of their tents or buildings and under the broiling Kansas sun.

But a Negro cleared his throat and said, "Boss, that wagon yonder . . . it ain't raisin' that much dust."

He was right. The wagon churned up a fraction of the dust that trailed far behind it. Denise spotted more dust off to the east, but even that cloud was dwarfed by the massive sand and grime that lifted off toward the heavens.

Minutes later, Denise realized a man on a horse rode alongside the wagon. A long while after that, she could tell that a large herd of horses was responsible for the dust cloud to the east.

They waited. And waited. Forty-five minutes. Maybe an hour passed before the rider on a sorrel gelding and a wagon pulled to a stop only to be swarmed by the welcoming party from Newton.

"Hey, fellows," yelled one A.T. & S.F. man, "it's Capt'n Rynders, boys. It's Capt'n Rynders."

Newton's men cheered the rider on the sorrel as if he were President Grant.

But the man stood in his stirrups, removed his hat, and slapped it against his leggings. "By thunder." He pointed the battered hat. "Don't tell me that's you, McCoy. Has Abilene growed this far out?"

McCoy smiled and shook his head. "You've got eight-ten days to go yet, Captain. You're too early to ship out from Newton, my friend. But next year. Next year you might try here." He paused. "You are bound for Abilene, aren't you, Captain?"

The man sank back into his saddle and settled his hat—gray, or maybe black but covered with hundreds of miles of dust—onto his gray hair. "Well, we did get a generous offer from a committee from Ellsworth, but I reckon my boys have grown fond of

Abilene." He eased the sorrel up to McCoy, leaned over to shake hands, then straightened in the saddle and pointed to the wagon.

"My cookie could use a few supplies if any are to be found," he said. "Don't rustle any of my steers, McCoy. I hear they'll fetch top dollar in Abilene."

"Next year," McCoy said, "you'll come to Newton." He waved his hand to the settlement of mostly tents. "We'll have bigger stockyards than Abilene. More whiskey. And . . . more whiskey."

The man smiled, and kicked his horse into a lope.

By then the wagon had pulled to a stop.

"What the devil is this contraption?" Redfield asked.

The driver, a rail-thin man with a high-crowned hat, kept his gloved hands on the leather lines.

"It's a café on wheels, mister," the man said.

"You feed people out of that?" a surveyor asked.

"Not people. Cowboys." He laughed. "Got all I need. Tail gate lays out like a table. Got shelves and drawers in the back, easy to get to."

"I'll be da—" Spotting Cindy and Denise, a railroader behind the wagon stopped. "Danged," he corrected. "You come up with this idea?"

The man smiled, nodded, then shrugged. "Well, I can't take credit for ever'thing. Charlie Goodnight had one I seen a year or two back. I just done some of my own modifications. Works out right well. Most of the herds that you'll see comin' up to Kansas this year got somethin' 'long these lines."

"Well," Redfield said, "maybe you'd like to leave Captain Rynders and open up your own wagon in Newton."

Joseph McCoy strode between the chuckwagon and the railroad agent.

"And maybe you'd like me to take my stockyards to Wichita," he said. "Maybe you'd like me to tell your railroad to go to the devil. Maybe you would like to explain to your bosses why I pulled out of this deal, buster, because I'm starting to like Ellsworth a lot better, and I've made my pile in Abilene and can keep making my pile there."

Redfield paled.

Cindy Bagwell took up the cause. "Maybe you'd like Denise Beeber to take her recipes and her food and find employment at . . . at . . . at . . ."

"The Drovers Cottage," McCoy filled in.

The man in the wagon looked completely confused.

"Don't leave us, Miss Denise," someone wailed.

Men raised hats in their hands and cheered.

Redfield's face paled.

Denise saw a smile on Cindy Bagwell's face. A few moments later, Denise realized that she was smiling, too.

Chapter 16

The "Chisholm Trail" is now a great public highway,
rivaling the famous Santa Fe road of old. It is
conceded by all drovers and freighters to be the best
natural road in the west. Trading houses (ranches) and
settlements have already been built on most of the
numerous streams on the road.
—*The* (Topeka) *Kansas Daily Commonwealth*,
October 11, 1870

As drives went, Gary Hardee had to think, this one rated better than most. Except for all his daybreak-to-moonrise wor-
rying, and how much his feet, thighs, calves, buttocks, backbone,
and neck ached. Here he was, pushing forty years old, and already feeling like he was as ancient and stove up as Major Wat
Anderson.

Both herds got past Austin, and across the Brazos River northwest of Waco. Spring in Texas, especially northern Texas, could
turn as wild and unpredictable as Spanish Monte. Now they had
reached Fort Worth. So far, they had met no other drovers, expe-
rienced no tornadoes, no thunderstorms, just a morning or
evening drizzle, hardly enough rain to wet down the dust. As far
as Gary and Bill Bailey could tell, the losses of any cattle in both
herds had been few, and maybe none.

Gary didn't like it at all.

"Criminy," point rider Hunter Clarke said as he and Gary waited for Carlos to bring them new horses for the afternoon. "You're worser than my grandma, frettin' when things got bad, and frettin' more when things were finer than a ripe peach because if things got too peachy, they'd turn sour sooner."

"You ought to have listened to your grandma more." Taking the reins from the wrangler, Gary swung onto the blood bay and tried not to show just how much that hurt. "Sounds like a right smart woman."

He let the gelding trot a ways south before kicking it into a lope and rode south toward the rising dust of Hugh Anderson's herd. Grinding his teeth reminded Gary that this new habit had made his jaw sore like the rest of his body. If that boy did not stop the herd to noon, Gary might not have enough ivory in his mouth to eat oysters when they hit the railhead in whatever Kansas town they picked.

Worn down my molars for nothing, he thought an hour later when he reached Anderson's noon camp. He swung out of the saddle, and handed the reins to Whit Barlow.

"He's fresh," Gary told him. "Keep him on the picket line."

That pleased the wrangler.

Gary turned and walked to the Studebaker, where Taylor, Miguel Sanchez, C.J. Merrifield, and Nicky Witt were waiting in line for their biscuits and beans. He could see distrust in some eyes—Witt and Merrifield rode drag—which almost brought a smile to Gary's stubbled face. They thought he would pull rank, cut in line, get noon chuck before they could. But Gary focused on the coffeepot, found a cup, filled it, and moved toward Adam Pollock and the chuckwagon.

The cook didn't skimp when it came to filling the plates. Smelled good, too.

Maybe I should have cut in line.

He walked ahead of Merrifield, but moved to the other side of the serving line.

"Hungry, boss man?" Pollock asked.

His mouth watered, his stomach growled, but Gary shook his head and held up the cup. "This'll do. Where's Hugh?"

"He said something about a head count."

Gary sipped coffee. He was getting to like Pollock's brew about as much as Moises Dunn's.

"Cattle? Horses?" He took another swallow. "Or men?" He grinned, letting the cook think Gary was joking.

The cook cracked a smile as he filled Nicky Witt's plate with beans, let the ladle slide back into the pot, and said: "And folks told me that Gary Hardee didn't have nothing resembling a funny bone."

Gary lifted the cup as in toast. "Good coffee can bring out the humanity in many a hard rock."

The cook reached for his own cup.

"Cattle," he answered. "Him, Bailey, two others." He drank a couple of swallows, put the cup back on the folding table, and wiped his mouth. "Sent Deke Brown to scout ahead for water."

"Was that Hugh's idea?"

"Reckon so."

Gary should have felt the tension leave his shoulders. The Major's boy was doing all right now. Almost a month on the trail maybe had burned off that cockiness, the stubbornness of youth. But Gary did not relax. He felt no relief, just sore and old.

He gave Pollock a nod, turned, and walked toward a shade tree, where Taylor Hardee was eating his noon meal.

"Sure I can't fix you some food?" Pollock asked.

"Don't want Moises spitting in my breakfast tomorrow," he answered, heard the cook chuckle, and covered the last twenty-five feet till he stood before his son.

"Don't get up," he told Taylor when the boy—*the young man*—started to rise.

Taylor settled back into the dirt, his back against the tree trunk, and made a gesture with his fork. "You want to sit down, Pa?"

Gary smiled. "If I sit down, who'd help me stand back up?"

Returning his father's grin, the boy worked furiously on the food.

"How are things going?" Gary asked.

"Pretty good." He started mopping up bean grease and juice with a big, square biscuit. He lifted the bread and grinned. "Point sure beats riding drag."

"Don't tell your brother that. He'll be hammering me for that spot on my herd, and we got a long ways to go yet for me to be hearing that the rest of the drive."

Taylor chewed on his biscuit, swallowed, found the coffee cup to wash it down. He grinned. "I miss seeing Evan," he said. "Miss it a lot."

Gary cocked his head.

Taylor's smile stretched. "Miss seeing him covered with dust from hat to boot. You sure you don't want to move him to this herd. We could swap you with Astudillo. He doesn't eat as much as Evan, either."

Hearing hooves, Gary turned, saw four riders loping in, then slowing down, and trotting toward the picket line. "I'll keep that in mind," he said, and started walking away. "We're just outside of Fort Worth," he called back. "Wouldn't hurt you to drop a letter in the post back to your mother."

"Already written," Taylor sang back. "Even sealed the envelope."

"Well, give it to me or your cook." He liked the sour look that suddenly masked Taylor's face. "You know how I don't like my hands going into town till we hit trail's end."

Hugh Anderson beat the dust off his chaps with his hat, which he pulled back onto his head, and nodded at Gary when they met at the chuck line.

"Adam said you were doing a head count." Gary moved to the coffeepot and refilled his cup.

"Yeah. Lopez says we're right where we was when we started. Bailey's tally agreed."

Gary let the wind cool the coffee. "We're about the same."

As Pollock began piling food on Bailey's plate, the point rider turned back toward Gary.

"You got that look on your face."

"What look is that?" Gary lifted the cup, but it felt too hot to drink.

"The look of a worried man," Bailey said.

"You've never seen me look any other way." Gary made himself drink.

"Don't think I ever will, either. Till you get out of the trail-driving business."

Gary stepped toward Hugh. "God willing, we'll be in Fort Worth tomorrow by noon."

Many eyes brightened. "Can we ride into town?" Nicky Witt, the young drag rider, asked. "Have a whiskey?"

"Gary Hardee ain't one to stay in towns." Deke Brown had ridden back into camp. Everyone turned as Brown eased the buckskin toward Whit Barlow.

"Towns and drovers don't mix," Gary said.

They didn't even mix at the trail's end. Cowboys and towns had never mixed, not on trail drives, anyway. Not in New Orleans . . . not in Shreveport . . . not in St. Louis . . . not in Sedalia . . . not in Baxter Springs . . . not in Abilene.

"Well, Fort Worth ain't what I'd call a town," Deke said as he slid out of the saddle.

"Sure looked like one to me last time I was there." Gary decided that Moises Dunn made much better coffee than Adam Pollock. "Getting bigger all the time." He tossed out the coffee, dropped the cup in the wreck pan, and stopped Hugh Anderson before any argument began. "Stop your herd about an hour early.

Then head to my camp. You and I will ride into town. If Pollock needs supplies, bring a mule and you can fetch back what he needs." He stared hard at Deke Brown. "Just you. And a mule if needed."

Hugh Anderson didn't show up with a mule.

Gary exchanged glances with Moises Dunn, then managed to push himself to his feet. Hugh Anderson swung down and called, "Hey, wrangler, take my hoss." He dropped the reins and headed for the coffee.

"Finish your dinner," Gary told Carlos Morales. He stared hard at the Major's son. *How could that jackass be the son of Wat Anderson?* "Carlos is eating," Gary told Hugh.

"Well, then have one of your darkies take care of my hoss."

Gary took a step toward the snot-nosed punk, who started filling a cup with Moises Dunn's coffee that had been boiled for working men. But Evan was up, setting his plate near Alex Warner's, his spurs singing as he trotted toward Anderson's lathered gelding. "I'll take care of him, Pa."

Warm air filled Gary's lungs. He held it for the longest time, till the blood stopped rushing, till he figured he wasn't quite ready to drop dead from a stroke, and he breathed in and out, in and out, and tried to lure a calmness over him.

Why didn't the Major leave me lying where I fell in North Carolina?

"You good on grub?" Gary made himself ask.

"We've got enough to last till Burlington." Hugh filled his own plate. He had to. Moises Dunn had walked away to find a place to answer nature's call.

"Prices will be cheaper in Fort Worth."

Hugh stopped ladling beans onto his plate. "Well," he said, smiling that grin Gary had wanted to wipe off the punk's face since . . . criminy, he had forgotten how far back. "That'll come out of your earnings, I reckon."

Now Gary laughed. And it felt good. Real good. He drank

some of Dunn's good brew, and, with a smile on his lips and a gleam in his eye, told the Major's son, "No, Hugh, it won't. I get paid on how many head we sell at market. Nothing else. So when you and your daddy are figuring out how much money he just put in the bank in Richmond, you'll have to explain to him how all these little expenses tallied up."

He remembered when Fort Worth wasn't much more than some sleepy hamlet. The Army had closed the post back in '53, and the settlement on the Trinity River might have been wooly before that, but all Gary could recall were a few scattered buildings—more businesses than homes, and not very many businesses—that seemed to have been arranged with the randomness of apples falling off trees.

A vendor was selling apples. Gary paid five dollars for a bushel, and Moises Dunn slid the basket into the back of the chuckwagon.

Hugh Anderson stopped his horse and looked at the crowded hitch rail in front of a picket building with a cheaply painted sign over the door that read SALOON.

"There's no bacon to be bought there," Gary said.

Twisting in the saddle, Hugh glared. Gary kept his horse walking down the street, when the batwing doors banged open and a man Gary recognized stepped out, holding a half-filled tumbler.

"Mr. Hardee. I thought that was you." Preston Rucker held his glass out as in toast. He must have been standing in front of the doors to have seen Gary. "It appears that traveling by stagecoach is faster than pushing thirty-two hundred head of Texas beef north."

He laughed at the dumb joke, but Gary knew that the Atchison, Topeka, and Santa Fe employee was no idiot. How long ago had they spoken in Austin? Three weeks? And yet the businessman still remembered how many longhorns Hardee was pushing north.

"How about let me stand you to a drink, sir?" Rucker sipped his whiskey. "I have news to report from Newton, Kansas."

Gary frowned. His mouth opened, but Hugh Anderson's proved quicker.

"You can stand me to a drink, Mister." Hugh swung out of the saddle, and, seeing there was no room at the rail, and too lazy—as most cowboys would be—to find another place to leave his horse, wrapped the reins around the corner post that held the awning. "Since twelve hundred of those beeves belong to me."

His horse blocked the alley, but city lawmen usually didn't police this part of town until gunshots sounded. And then, they would come with great reluctance.

Preston Rucker seemed confused as he turned toward Hugh, who went under the rail and stepped onto the boardwalk, spurs chiming as he approached the railroad man and extended his hand.

"The name's Anderson, sir, Hugh Anderson. I run a ranch down in Fort Bend County."

Rucker shifted his whiskey to his left hand, gave his name, and the two men shook.

Frowning, Gary glanced at Dunn, who said, "Give me some money. I'll get what we need."

The doors to the saloon banged again, and Gary looked to find that Hugh had gone inside, but Preston Rucker stood, his glass empty, his eyes focusing on Gary and the chuckwagon.

He swore softly, found a gold coin in his vest pocket, and held it out for Moises Dunn to take.

"Meet you back here?" the cook asked.

"Or jail." Gary swung out of the saddle and pulled his gelding toward the other hitch rail. "If I wind up throwing Hugh Anderson through the window."

"Ain't no window that I see," Dunn said.

"There will be after Hugh goes through the wall."

He shook hands with Rucker and followed him into the dark

saloon. Cowboys crowded the bar, and two mustached men in sleeve garters and black ribbon ties worked behind the bar. Gary found a few tables where no one sat, then tried to find Hugh Anderson. It took a while to make him out, but he pulled away between two dust-caked waddies in striped britches and tall boots. Holding a bottle of whiskey, Hugh smiled and called out, "I put this on your tab, Rucker."

Rucker turned to Hardee, who shrugged.

"His pa pays me" was about the only explanation Hardee could give.

"Not enough." Somehow, Rucker summoned his salesman smile. "But for thirty-two hundred head of prime Texas beef . . ." He stepped aside and let his right arm wave Hugh, then Gary, toward a table near the batwing doors.

That suited Gary. There would be light enough coming through the doorway, which would be easier to throw Hugh Anderson through than the shabby picket walls.

"Have a seat with Hugh," Gary told the railroad man. "I'll get a cup of coffee."

"Oh." Rucker straightened. "I'm sorry, Hardee. I forgot."

Gary gave him a friendly smile, but he seriously doubted if Rucker forgot that Gary did not drink till a sales contract had been signed. Preston Rucker, he had determined, forgot nothing.

When he returned to the table, holding a steaming cup of coffee that was stronger than a circus brawler and thicker than pine sap, Hugh was refilling both tumblers. Gary dragged an empty chair between the two, took off his hat, laid it crown down on the table, and sipped coffee.

"As I was telling young Mr. Anderson, Hardee," Rucker said, "much has been happening in Newton since last we spoke."

The coffee was terrible. Gary managed to swallow it and looked at Rucker.

"Iron rails are being laid from Florence, sir, and Mayor McCoy has finalized the plans for the shipping yards. We shall be able to load six cars at a time."

Gary smiled. "By the fifteenth of May?"

Rucker sipped whiskey. "Well, we might have been a bit overeager, but Newton and the railroad will be ready by the time you have reached Kansas, sir."

He turned to smile at Hugh. "We already have a fantastic eating house, earning splendid praise from Mr. McCoy himself, and a Wichita newspaper."

"What about whiskey?" Hugh asked.

Rucker had been lifting his glass but now looked at it and set it back on the table. "I am sure you shall be able to—"

"Better yet, how about women?"

Gary made himself drink more coffee. Preston Rucker likely was not used to dealing with a cattleman of Hugh Anderson's . . . *priorities?*

"I . . ." Rucker turned back to Gary.

"A lot of my associates believe that Abilene, despite the circulars making rounds here in Texas, will be open to Texas beef this year," Gary said.

Rucker felt more at ease now, talking about cattle, not whiskey and women. "That well may be the case, if the quarantine line is not moved, or is at least enforced, but you know that the range there is undesirable as cattle country. Why the flies are so bad in Dickinson County that they can drive the price down per pound the longer cattle graze before they are sold. Sedgwick County is much more suitable."

"How many cattle wintered up there? In Dickinson County, I mean."

Rucker sipped whiskey. "Not many, but some. A great many that did, though, are dying. But we will have a splendid yard in Newton, my Texas friends. There is no doubt in my mind that Newton will become a permanent cattle point, as the country is perfectly adapted for cattle—now that the buffalo are gone. Rich soil. Good grass in Sedgwick County, sir, enough for thousands of cattle. Unlike Dickinson County. And our rates will do as well, much better than any competing road."

He tried the coffee again. Still horrible. For a moment, he even considered sweetening it with some of Rucker's whiskey. But he wasn't certain he could get the bottle out of Hugh's hands without coming to blows.

"What day is it?" Gary suddenly asked.

"Oh." Rucker had to think. "The twelfth of May. Friday."

Gary set his cup near his hat. "I figure we're a few days over a month from the crossing at the Arkansas River." He could tell Rucker was doing a bit of cyphering in his head. "Can you assure me, Mr. Rucker, that you will have stockyards that could hold my—our—thirty-two hundred head of beeves? And a train to ship them east over your iron rails by the fifteenth of June?"

His face brightened. He sucked in a breath and started to smile. But his lungs released a sigh, and he sank down into his chair, frowning and shaking his head.

"I cannot lie to you, Hardee. I mean, it took the Union and Central Pacific years and years before they united our nation."

Hugh reached for the bottle to refill his glass.

"We have no mountains to tunnel through," Rucker continued. "But . . . well, sir . . . we got a late start, at least for this cattle season. Maybe the end of June. Maybe July."

"Maybe next year." Gary smiled. "I like an honest man, Mr. Rucker." He held out his hand. "I'd like to do business with you. But . . . I have an obligation to a lot of ranchers in Fort Bend County, sir."

"I'll do business with you, Tucker," Hugh said, slurring his words. "Top dollar. Top dollar for twelve thousand cattle I'm driving. Top dollar. And a redhead with big lips and bigger . . ." He belched.

Rucker looked at Gary and shook his head.

"Come on, Hugh," Gary said as he donned his hat. "Let's see if we can find Moises and get some coffee and chow into your gut."

He put his right hand on Hugh's shoulder, but the kid shoved the arm and started to stand. "Don't you touch me," he said.

His hand started for his revolver. "I'll kill the man who—"

"My God!" Rucker yelled.

The din of conversation in the small saloon turned silent. One bartender reached for a bung starter, while the other dropped behind the bar. Cowboys turned, or scattered, or ducked.

Hugh dropped his revolver on the floor. Luckily, he hadn't managed to cock it, and it did not go off. He cursed again, fell to his knees to pick it up, and almost keeled over face-first onto the floor.

Calmly, Gary drew his own revolver.

"Murder!" a cowboy yelled.

Ignoring him, Gary twirled the Army Colt, reversing the barrel, drew his index finger from the trigger guard, and flipped the .44 around so he held it like a club. He knelt just enough to get closer to Hugh, who had both hands on the floor as he tried to find where he had dropped his pistol.

The grip of Gary's Colt came down on the back of Hugh's head, and he fell to the floor.

Now Gary used both hands to turn his revolver around. After sliding the .44 into the holster, he looked up at the men still staring at him, and not hiding behind bars, tables, or their comrades, and smiled.

"Boy just can't hold his liquor. Passed out." Gary bent and found the Navy Hugh had dropped, and shoved that near the buckle of his gunbelt. "That hangover he'll have tomorrow will sure smart."

He grabbed Hugh, jerked him up, and soon stood with the unconscious idiot jackknifed over Gary's left shoulder. Men in the saloon began standing. Many let out nervous laughter that soon turned more spirituous. Some downright howled. Two gave Gary hurrahs. Gary turned around, held out his hand, and nodded at Rucker.

"Good luck, sir," he said as they shook.

Hugh's hat fell off, but Rucker bent to pick it up, and Gary took it in his right hand, his left arm wrapping around Hugh's back.

"And luck to you, Hardee." Rucker nodded at the unconscious teen hanging over Gary's shoulder.

"I'll need it," Gary said, and headed for the door.

Chapter 17

The Atchison, Topeka & Santa Fe Railroad is graded
to Newton and two miles beyond where cattle yards
will be built. Newton is represented as being rather a
fast town. Loose characters of all kinds infest this
place.
—*The Atchison Weekly Champion,*
July 22, 1871

The skies were just turning gray when Redfield, the A.T. &
S.F. man, showed up at Denise's tent and wagon that morning. Scared the devil out of her, something Arthur had always
said could never be done.

She was scattering coals onto the Dutch oven with a small
shovel to cook the biscuits when Redfield cleared his throat and
said something. Probably just "Good morning," but she let out a
gasp, and brought the shovel up, ready to duel.

"It's me," he said. "Redfield." He stepped closer to the fire
Denise had going so she could see his face.

She didn't lower the shovel, though. Not until he said, "Let's
find you a vacant lot in town, Miss Beeber." He lifted a leather
satchel and nodded at it. When she just stared at him, he sighed,
and lowered the satchel.

"No," he said, as if answering a question, "generally I do not start my day this early. But, trust me, Miss Beeber, I won't have time during regular business hours. I'm doing you a favor."

She still didn't trust him.

So he added: "All right, I'm doing this for Joseph G. McCoy."

Of course, she didn't trust anyone. Never would, not after Neodesha. But she decided he wasn't trying to pull some shell-game con on her when he dropped McCoy's name.

"Let me tell you what is going to happen," Redfield said. He stopped, cocked his head, and asked, "Have you ever been to Abilene?"

Her head shook.

"But you've heard of it?"

She made her mouth and voice box work. "Who hasn't?"

Redfield nodded. "Cattle towns spring up overnight. The rail-road's coming here. We all know that. Everyone in Kansas knows it. And McCoy's stockyards are going up. Newton will turn into a Sodom or Gomorrah, but before that happens—and it will happen, practically overnight—first it will become Bedlam. You've heard that expression, haven't you? Bedlam. Madness. This place soon will be a madhouse."

She leaned the shovel against the wagon.

"Step inside the tent," she said. "I'll pour us some coffee." She even asked, "Would you like some breakfast?"

They didn't wait for the biscuits to cook. She fed him scrambled eggs, fried ham, and potatoes. Instructed her hired cook and servers what she wanted before she followed the A.T. & S.F. man to his big tent, where Redfield had the plat laid out on the big table. He sipped his own coffee, filled a cup for Denise—she knew, after one sip, that he would never have a career in the restaurant business—and followed him to the big table, where Denise studied the large yellow parchment.

Streets running north-south were given numbers. First Street and on up. East-west streets had no names.

"When the town is established, they'll give those streets names." Redfield snorted. "If it's anything like most cattle towns, they'll honor a bunch of Texas hard cases. Alamo Street. Texas Street. Crockett. Travis. Houston." His face soured. He walked back to his desk to drink more of his lousy coffee. Denise drank from her own cup, and found a folding table a few feet behind her that had some room on it. After setting her cup down, she leaned against the table and studied the map.

A few places had already been inked in with the new owners. She gazed upon the broad swath that dissected the numbered streets at an angle.

A. T. & S. F.

When Redfield returned and stood on her left, she pointed between Fifth and Sixth streets, north of the railroad tracks.

Redfield's head shook.

"You can't afford that and—" His right hand rose to fend off any objections.

"You have a restaurant, Miss Beeber." He tapped a spot on the east side of the main street that ran through the center of town. "The Gold Room Saloon is going up there. That's going to be Newton's grandest. That's where the cattle drovers and the beef buyers will go to celebrate—and drink. You'd be competing against that and the Newton House." He pointed out the first hotel's location. Then dragged his finger south of the railroad tracks.

Denise gave her hardest stare. "South of the tracks?"

"Hear me out," he said, his voice even. "That's where the biggest business will be had. For a while, at least. One cattle drover and one packing-house representative north of the tracks. That can be your clientele. *Or* twenty cowboys, fifty gamblers, and a hundred dance-hall girls, spending money till they have none left, hungry for food after drinking and dancing and . . ." He shrugged.

Her head shook. "Cowboys and soiled doves don't care what they eat."

"And as good as your cooking is," he said, "the buyers and sellers will still pay good money for good whiskey at The Gold Room, and they'll eat at the restaurant attached to the hotel. Ask anyone who is moving here from Abilene, and they'll tell you The Drovers Cottage had ranchers and trail bosses and the Chicago and Kansas City money men ordering oysters and fine wines. But the cowboys spent money like they were railroad barons. You'll do better south of the tracks."

"How much?" she asked.

He glanced at the plat, and pointed at a place facing north on Second Street.

"Perry Tuttle has a saloon or dance hall going up right next door," he said. "You're just down from what I assume will be Main Street. The lots between Third and Second have already been purchased. That's as close as I can get you to the north side of the tracks."

Redfield almost sounded like a human being.

"Where are the stockyards?" she asked suddenly.

He pointed far down the plat. "About a mile and a half, two miles. Judge Muse and Mr. Lakin learned from past cattle towns' mistakes. You really don't want a thousand Texas longhorns coming down Main Street, Texas Street, Railroad Street, whatever they want to call it, right through the center of town. City deputies have enough trouble picking up all the cat and dog dung as it is."

Redfield hadn't been able to keep up that façade of a gentleman for too long.

"All right," she said. "How much do I owe you?"

He gave her the price, suggested some loan officers the railroad had brought in.

"I'll pay in cash," she said.

He blinked, opened his mouth, quickly closed it, and nodded. "Very well. You'll need to have the deed registered . . ." He moved toward his desk, waved at her to follow him, but Denise's smile faded quickly. She hoped her hired help had not let those biscuits burn.

For three days, she did not have time to think about her new location, but on the fourth morning, Redfield told her she needed to move her wagon, tent, mules, and massive stove, because someone had bought that lot she had been renting, as he called it, and wanted to open a hardware store as soon as he could find carpenters to put up four walls, a floor, and a roof.

Moving a restaurant wasn't new to her. How many times had she had to do that because of her brother? But she had always closed the place, packed it up, moved to another town. Now she understood the problems businesses had when they moved from one location to another in the same town.

You had to close shop for a while. And other restaurants could take advantage of that, pull your diners and coffee drinkers to their place. They might never return. But Denise figured she had nothing to worry about, and she wasn't even bragging about her cooking. And once the trail crews arrived, they would eat, drink, gamble, and carouse till their money was gone, then ride back to Texas and make way for the next group of cowboys. The Newton House was open, but that was on the north side. There was no place to eat south of town. Redfield had been right. And most of the *construction*—if one would really use that word in all good conscience—was going up on the south side.

She remembered Grandma Beatrice telling Arthur and her about the locusts that hit western Pennsylvania back in '32 before she, Grandpa Jesse, and the young'uns had lit out for Arkansas.

"Come every seventeen years," Grandma Beatrice said. "Couldn't count 'em. Musta been millions. The trees was covered with 'em. And a hum like which you'd never want to hear. The woods just resounded with that noise. Made me come to love birds, I tell you, because the birds was the only things that would eat 'em millions of humming bugs."

The swarm of locusts into Newton had begun. Not insects, though. Human bugs.

North of the tracks, a barbershop was opening, the candy-striped pole already painted and leaning against a workbench. Caravans of wagons filled with dry lumber moved down the trail from Emporia and Florence, now outnumbering the wood haulers from Wichita.

Two covered wagons were parked on the main street in front of a lot. A man in a straw hat and sleeve garters barked at passersby to come in and see what furniture he had for sale. He said he worked for R.C. Haywood & Company, which had stores in Florence and Emporia. And, as soon as this frame building was finished, they would have a third location here in Newton. But until he got a roof over his head, he was selling everything a business, or home, needed out of these two wagons. What's more, if he didn't have what you needed, he could have it ordered from Emporia and delivered to your home, shop, or tent in two weeks, six at the most.

She fought off the temptation to see what kind of dining-room tables and chairs he had, and walked to the grocery store, but that owner had nothing to sell from his wagon. He wanted to get the building up first. With that lack of judgment, he'd be out of business before August.

She bought her lumber from Charles Pierce & Company, which, from what she could gather, was also headquartered in Emporia.

But the real swarm, she discovered, came south of the staked, marked, but not yet graded railroad tracks.

Hammers banged, saws bit into timber, men sweated and cursed and worked with their shirts pulled off and hung on nails. Spectators cheered when they would push up false fronts against posts, poles, or four-by-four pinewood. She had known carpenters. These hired men did not fill any such bill. They swore when hammers missed nails and struck thumbs or fingers. She spotted cracks, some more than a couple of inches deep, in the front of buildings.

If the roofs were constructed in the same fashion as the walls, the owners might drown come the first thunderstorm.

She stood in front of the dance hall or saloon that this Perry Tuttle was building. It didn't seem any better than what else was going up on this side of the tracks, but she understood she had better claim her lot with more than just stakes with cotton flags waving in the wind.

Six men agreed to move her wagon and tent onto the lot for three meals and two bottles of whiskey. Rye, bourbon, or Taos Lightning, it didn't matter, as long as it was whiskey. When they saw the stove, they asked for a third bottle of whiskey. Denise agreed, and even threw in an extra breakfast.

Leaving the youngest, thinnest, and smartest of her hired men in charge, she walked back to what everyone was now calling Main Street—no matter if Redfield had not yet inked that name permanently on his plat—and found the man with the two wagons in front of the lot.

He was sipping from a flask when she cleared her throat, and he turned, smiled, and let the silver-plated container drop smoothly into the mule-ear pockets on his striped britches.

"Yes, ma'am," he said, "you look like a woman with the finest taste in furniture, and let me tell you—"

"I'll tell you," she said.

He coughed as though his bracer had gone down the wrong way.

"I want four twelve-foot extension tables. Hand-polished. Quarter-sawed oak. Hand-carved. Four eight-foot tables. Matching as close as you can to the twelve-footers. Chairs that come close to matching."

The man blinked.

"And four breakfast tables, preferably with drop leaves. Forty-two by fifty-two inches. Of high quality. Two chairs to go with each table."

This time, the man's head bobbed up and down. At least he was listening to her.

"And one more thing. Can your Mr. Haywood make a twenty-foot bar? Not for drinking. I'm not opening a saloon. I'll want stools to go with this bar so that hungry men, or women, can sit on a stool and eat a good meal with some fine coffee or tea or water. Maybe when that fellow gets his produce north of the tracks, I can make lemonade."

He cleared his throat.

"Can your Mr. Hayward get that done?"

"Yes." His voice was barely audible.

"Good."

Color returned to the hawker's face, and he started to smile until Denise spoke again.

"Now, before you get one step ahead of yourself, you need to hear this and hear it good. Most importantly, you're going to name your price, and you're going to get one shot at that price, and if it's too high—and, don't worry, I know you'll have to haul this all the way down from Emporia, and I know how much a good woodworker charges, and bars are not easy to build from scratch.

"Keeping that in mind, though, if you try to cheat me, and if you say you will deliver when I tell you to deliver and then don't deliver, I will sue you for breach of contract. Because, mister, we shall sign a contract, and believe it or not, I saw a shingle for a lawyer already hanging just north of the tracks that aren't here yet. So, you give me your best offer, and we'll see if you can do business with me."

She stopped and stared.

"Is that clear?"

He barely nodded.

"Now there's one more thing. I need everything put in my building." She pointed toward the stockyards being built. "At least two days before the first train pulls into Newton."

He inhaled deeply and let it out.

"You think we can do business?" Denise asked.

The man nodded. One hand slipped inside a pants pocket and pulled out the flask.

Chapter 18

Texas cattle have begun to arrive in Wichita. Over
3000 head came last week.
—*The* (Burlingame) *Weekly Osage Chronicle,*
May 11, 1871

Cindy tried to come up with a great description for what she
was witnessing—something that Knott-Head would claim
that he had written. But words failed her, a plight no journalist
should ever suffer.

Longhorn cattle swam the Arkansas River, cowboys on both
sides, yipping nonsensical words or cursing while swatting hats or
coiled ropes against the leather-covered legs. She had a good
view of the lead cows—no, she corrected herself—*steers*. Steers.
What a butcher had told her was the same as a capon.

Like that had helped a lot.

"What's a capon?" she had asked.

Removing his cigar, the butcher had grinned. "A capon is an
unfortunate rooster. A steer is an unfortunate bull." And waited
for her to blush.

Cindy had not allowed him any such pleasure.

She saw no end of the line of beef.

One steer was black; the one next to the black one was brown.
She asked the man next to her how wide he thought their horns

stretched. Since he had told Cindy that he was a surveyor, she figured he had a good sense for things like that.

"Six feet," he told her. "At the least."

She scribbled that in her notebook.

Water dripped off horns. The cattle had been bawling before they had been pushed into the water, but now they focused with grim determination, quiet, their eyes trained on the dry sand of Wichita. *Focused with grim determination.* That sounded good. Knott-Head wouldn't dare change it.

Those eyes differed vastly from that cowboy riding behind the lead riders. His face shone whiter than the sun at this time of day, and his lips tightened like his hands clutching the saddle horn. He looked neither at the horns and hide to his right nor the river to his left, just at the banks on the Wichita side of the river.

She blinked suddenly when she noticed something else about him. He wore no boots, no pants, no shirt—just a bandanna and a hat, and, thankfully, his undergarments.

Turning her head and recovering from the shock, she focused on the gray-headed man on the left side of the herd. Fully dressed, his boots, chaps, and spurs still dripping water, he held his reins tightly in a gloved left hand, while the right one only moved up to his lips every now and then to remove a cigarette. He would blow smoke, look down the long line of his cattle, and return the cigarette to his mouth.

He must be in charge. And if she did not talk to him now, she likely would never get a chance.

"Excuse me," she told a barber, still holding his shears and wearing his apron. The man blinked and slipped aside, then shouted out her as though she were crazy when she raced in front of the wet, stinking steers.

She made it across the street easily, but gave the herd a wide berth, and cattle that had just swam across the Arkansas River did not move fast. After catching her breath, she scribbled that the legs of the animals quickly became coated with the streets of Wichita.

Good visual detail. This story might get picked up by papers in Chicago, San Francisco, Kansas City, and New York.

Breathing in deeply, she coughed, and realized something else about cattle: wet cattle stink to high heaven.

Moving to the far edge of the street, she walked past the storefronts and toward the river, descending to the Arkansas's banks, and cleared her throat as she came up to the smoking cowman's right. The horse snorted. The man removed his cigarette, blew smoke, and focused on the cattle.

"Excuse me," Cindy said.

The man looked at her, nodded, and said, "You're a bold lass."

Thanking him, she studied her pencil to make sure the point remained sharp, and flipped to a new page. "I was wondering . . ."

The man stood in his stirrups, flipped the cigarette to the ground, and yelled, "Watch 'em yonder, Jess. To your left. Your *left*." He screamed raw vulgarities, a few that Cindy had never heard. Another cowboy, she saw, nudged his horse to stop a steer from turning back toward the far bank, while the one she figured to be Jess kept moving his lips and eyeing solid ground.

"I was hoping to ask you some questions," Cindy said.

"Boy ain't got the sense God give a turnip," the old man said as he sank back into the saddle. Seeing Cindy out of the corner of his eye, he sighed and said, "Missy, you're right handsome woman but I got me a Baptist wife back in Bosque County and—"

"I beg your pardon." Her pencil came down to her right side and her notebook to her left. "I work for *The Wichita Herald*, sir, and I am interviewing you about your cattle."

The man stared. When he finally blinked, Cindy knew he had not died of a heart attack. He swallowed and pushed his hat back, shook his head, muttered something about Kansans and Yankees, and turned back to the herd.

"Beggin' your pardon, little lady," he said at last, but stopped to boss a cowboy riding alongside wet, bawling cattle. "Keep 'em goin' for three miles, Rex. Then bed them down where you see fit."

"Boys was hopin' for a whiskey, boss," Rex said as he rode by.

"Tell the truth, so was I."

"I could use one myself. But looks like Wichita has turned civilized."

He turned back and yelled at some other cowboy, who must not have been doing his job.

"Bosque County," Cindy said as she wrote that down. "How is that spelled?"

The man sighed, cursed, and pulled out the makings for a cigarette.

"B-o-s-q-u-e."

She stared at what she had written.

"It's a Mex word, ma'am."

"How many cattle do you have?"

He crumpled the paper and started again.

"We left with around eighteen hundred." He looked back at her. "I ain't never heard of no woman newspaperman."

"Well, sir." She gave him her best genteel Alabama smile. "You're neither a Kansan nor a Yankee."

To her surprise, he grinned back. "No, ma'am, reckon I ain't." He held out the cigarette toward her.

She was tempted to take it, but then thought how she would look to him when her face turned green and she vomited over her shoes. Instead of declining his offer, she asked, "And where do you plan on selling your herd?"

This not being the day the *Herald* was published or the day after, Arby McBane stood in the office when she rushed in, panting, her hair disheveled, her shoes covered with dust-covered mud. The old man smiled as Cindy excused herself, looked at McBride, who busied setting type, and muttered an apology.

"Do not apologize, child," Mr. McBane said, "I am always delighted to see a newspaper reporter running, out of breath, with pencil and paper in hand."

Which was the exact opposite of what Liam McBride had told her last week: "Never run," he had said, "unless they're shooting at you."

Bobby Knott looked as though he had bitten into a rotting skunk.

"I talked to a cattle drover," she said. "He's from Bosque County. That's Mexican. Bosque. The county's in Texas. He is pushing eighteen hundred cattle to market."

"Fine job, Miss Bagwell." McBane found his hat.

"Is he stopping here for any time?" Knott spoke in his aching monotone.

"Three miles out of town," Cindy said. "Or was it four?" She opened her notebook, but stopped when McBane paused to take her hand. Quickly, she stuck the pencil above her ear and went to shake, but he took her hand in his, patted it gently with his left hand, then raised it and pressed it to his lips.

"You are a fine reporter, child. A fine reporter. I have told Bobby to give you an assignment worthy of your talent. Good-bye, Miss Bagwell." When he reached the door and pulled it open, he turned back. "Good day, Robert." He smiled at the printer. "Stay out of low-rent dram shops, Liam."

The bell chimed as the door closed, and Cindy turned and opened her mouth to fill Knott in on her reporting. He stopped her before she got one word out.

"Dozens of drovers will be crossing the Arkansas River before the season is finished. And a drover who is camping three or four miles outside of town most likely won't spend any money in town." He walked to his desk, sat down, opened a drawer, and pulled out a bottle. "But since you went and told McBane, give McNelly sixty words and let it go. But first, you heard the old man. And I have just the job for you."

She busied herself taking down notes as Bobby Knott drank his rye and told her what was going on.

The Secretary of State had filed a charter for the Wichita & Southwestern Railroad Company. Directors had been named, most of them from Wichita, two from Topeka, one from Sedgwick City, and R.P. Muse of Newton. Judge Muse, of course, had gotten the railroad to Newton.

"The names don't matter. Don't write down those names or ask me how to spell Schlichter." Knott lifted his glass and drank. "What matters is this: the road will begin on the Atchison, Topeka, and Santa Fe line, between Peabody and Newton. It'll be Newton. The railroad is smart, and Newton's closer."

"Oh, my gosh," Cindy said. "Wichita is getting a railroad."

"Well, not yet. Don't bet on anything. The charter's just a baby step. It will have to pass a bond election this summer. I don't think that will be a hurdle. But we want Wichita to control the cattle trade. Not Newton."

Cindy stifled her laugh. "From what I've seen of Newton—"

"Bagwell." Knott emptied his glass and refilled it with two more fingers. "You saw Newton before Texians started coming through Kansas. You saw Newton when the cattle pens were just being planned. What we don't want is Newton to become is the major cattle town—another Abilene, let's call it. We're far enough west not to worry about Texas Fever—for now—and we don't have that many farmers in Sedgwick County yet." He held up his glass as in toast, smiled, and shot down the liquor.

"I want you to go to Newton."

"Newton." She repeated the word just to make sure she heard him correctly. Her smile vanished. She smelled something, and thought that she might have stepped into a deposit left by one of those unfortunate bulls.

"Stay there till the end of the season. Or till you quit and run back home to South Carolina."

She did not bother correcting him.

"Send us letters by the stagecoach. Once a telegraph wire links us, I want you to still send letters here by stage. Telegraphs are expensive. And we are a weekly newspaper. If you are mortally wounded in a gun battle, write a letter. Don't waste money on a telegram. *If* a telegraph line ever links us. Is that clear?"

He drained the last of the bottle into his glass.

"Yes," Cindy whispered.

"I don't want stories about shipping pens the size of Corpus Christi Bay, and I don't want stories about cowboys crossing the river. I want stories of death and violence and violent death. I want scandals and eyes gouged out. I want gamblers and vice. I want you to make Newton out to be a cesspool with no sign of human decency for thirty miles."

She had stopped writing.

He leaned to her. "You won't be making up fictions. Trust me. Newton will be a cesspool, Bagwell. The likes of which you have never seen."

She wanted to reach for the bottle and suck out what little liquor might remain. Somehow, she cleared her throat.

"Wouldn't publishing stories like that make people here— voters . . . in Wichita . . . wouldn't that make them less likely to want to get this railroad spur?"

His laugh came out as a snort. "Hardly. It might make people working in Newton want to get rid of the cattle trade. That will happen eventually. It happens at every cowtown. Look at what's going on in Abilene right now. But it will make every barber, jackleg lawyer, baker, cook, hotel owner, saddlemaker, dry-goods merchant—every one want to get Newton's business. For a while, anyway. Till they realize that Texans belong in Texas and nowhere else. And pork tastes better than beef."

He pushed himself to his feet.

She sat still.

Frowning, he reached inside his coat pocket, withdrew his wallet, and tossed out some currency. "Here. Find a cheap place to rent in Newton. Don't worry. Those greenbacks won't be taken out of your salary. That's to cover your expenses. Charles Meech, the grocer, is bringing a wagonload of supplies to Newton tomorrow. Everyone's shipping something to Newton. He's agreed to let you ride along with his driver. In exchange for an advertisement. Be at his store by six-thirty in the morning."

He laughed, found a silver dollar in his trousers pocket, and added that to Cindy's advance.

"Hey." He turned and weaved his way toward Liam McNelly.

"I've got a line for you, Mac. Let's lead with this on Page Two. 'Your *Herald* has joined the move to send supplies to the rawhide outpost—make that Sedgwick County's newest rawhide outpost—known as Newton. Period. Yesterday our beloved plum in petticoats was sent to that raucous new settlement to report back on any exciting news from our neighbor to the north. We hope she is good at ducking fists and dodging bullets.'"

Chapter 19

This cattle driving business is no joke, as it requires
all hands and the boss driver and the cow ponies to do
their level best, and frequently a stampede occurs in
the night, and there is hard work and some furious
riding and hard swearing done before the drove is
again brought together.
—*The Emporia News*,
March 31, 1871

It didn't seem appropriate to blaspheme about the hard rain
when his livelihood depended on good grass for cattle to eat.
But Gary Hardee cursed anyway.

The way the skies looked, this soaking would last a long time.

Twisting in the saddle, Gary unlashed the rawhide thongs to
remove his slicker, took off his hat, and managed to pull the
heavy black India rubber over his head. He ran his fingers
through his wet hair, started to pull the hat back on, but a gust of
wind whipped it from his hands.

It didn't go far, getting hung up in a limestone marl sur-
rounded by bluestem.

He bit off another curse, swung down to the earth that, for
now, sucked the rain down as deep as it could, and led the pale
gelding toward his hat. Reaching down with his right hand while

holding the reins loosely in his left, he grabbed the battered brim and straightened just as the thunder rolled.

It wasn't loud, certainly not threatening, and no lightning streaked across the sky—just a gentle, faraway sound, almost pleasing. But the noise spooked the gelding. The reins zipped out of Gary's gloved hands before he could close his fist tighter, and the horse bounded away.

"Onion," Gary cried out.

The horse did not respond.

Cursing again, Gary pulled the hat on his head and began walking, into the wind and rain.

The gelding stopped on a rise, grazed, and had the decency to work his way about a quarter of the way down the small hill. Onion looked up when Gary came about thirty yards from him, snorted, but returned to eating more bluestem.

"You're a pain in my arse," Gary said as he grabbed the reins, tighter this time, lifted his left boot into the stirrup, grabbed the slippery horn, and pulled himself back into the saddle.

The pale horse carried him two miles, when Gary spotted the drag riders of another line of Texas beef crawling north. He spurred Onion into a lope, but slowed down long before he rode to the drag riders, two Mexicans in brown hats, a freckle-faced redhead boy in brogans instead of boots, and a lean Negro he remembered from a few years back.

"Teal," he said, nodding. "Gary Hardee. Remember me?"

The man's smile turned into a chuckle. "Reckon so. Reckon Shanghai does, too."

"You still riding for his brand?"

Teal nodded. "He pays a fair wage. Knows his business."

Gary looked at the other riders. "Name's Gary Hardee, boys. I've got two herds behind you. Riding for Major Wat Anderson." He looked back at Teal. "Shanghai up ahead?"

"Pretty far ahead, most likely," Teal said. "Said something at breakfast about getting a good number at the Red."

That sounded just like Pierce.

Gary wiped rain off his face and watched the dark skies and that wall of falling rain as far as he could see.

"Got us two thousand sea otters for sure, this year." Teal nodded at the slow steers at the end of a long line.

"Looks like they'll have some swimming to do," Gary said. His voice trailed into a whisper. "Reckon we'll all have some swimming to do."

He had hoped to cross the Red before the rains hit. But lots of things he hoped for never panned out, mostly while driving cattle. He pulled his wet hat tighter on his slick head, nodded at the drag riders, and turned Onion west till he was far enough away not to spook Pierce's herd. The last thing anyone wanted to do was cause Shanghai Pierce's herd to run.

The rain had slackened into not much more than a mist when he rode to the picket line while Moises Dunn ladled stew onto plates underneath a leaky tarp that bowed from the weight of rainwater.

Carlos Morales hurried from his place next to a post oak to take the reins from Gary.

"We thought you might never return," the boy said.

"Yeah," Hardee said as he moved to uncinch his saddle. "You're gonna wish I hadn't. 'Cause I need you to fetch me a fresh mount."

Hunter Clarke, eating food from his plate as he walked forward, said, "You ridin' out again, Boss Man?"

"Onion is played out," Morales said as he slipped a rope around the gelding's neck.

"Yeah." Hardee removed his hat and slapped as much rainwater as he could off the crown and brim. "He won't be much good for a few days." He turned to the point rider. "I need to tell Hugh and Bill what's going on."

He pointed north.

"The Red's on a rampage." He sniffled. "Reckon the rain that's hitting us was doing much the same upriver. Caught up with Shanghai Pierce, and there are five herds waiting to cross. We'll be Number Six."

Bailey snorted. "Where's Shanghai on the list?"

"Ahead of us." He smiled as Evan hurried over with a steaming cup of coffee, which he handed to his father.

The tin cup warmed his gloved hand, and he did not wait for it to cool much before he took several swallows.

"Best fill your stomach," he told his son, but raised the cup in a toast. "I sure appreciate this."

Carlos brought out the blood bay, and when Hardee started for his saddle, Clarke raised his hand. "You put some of Moises's coffee in your belly, Boss Man. I'll saddle your horse for you. You look plumb tuckered out."

"I feel like a catfish," Gary said, and drank more coffee.

Drag rider Casey Steer gave Gary a biscuit, and even Moises Dunn, once he had finished making sure everyone else had something hot to eat, brought a fresh cup of coffee that Gary downed before he rode south.

Three hours later, he let Carlos take care of his horse, found his sugans where someone—Evan? Dunn? Some guardian angel?—had unrolled underneath the chuckwagon, a prime spot Gary would share with the already snoring cook, Conner Milone, and Carlos once the kid finished his night wrangling duties.

Gary managed to pull those wet boots off, but that was all. He dropped onto the bedroll without covering himself.

At least tomorrow would be a short day in the saddle.

The sun emerged from behind the clouds before noon the next day. By the time they made camp three hours later, the grayness had moved southeast, though Gary frowned at more dark skies far off to the northwest.

Evan walked toward Gary as he rolled out his bedroll to let the sun dry it out, too. Then Gary sat on the ground and struggled to pull off his boots. When Evan stood over him, Gary rolled onto his back and raised his right leg.

"Pull these off me, Son," he said. "Before the leather shrinks so tight I'll have to cut them off."

Grinning, Evan hooked one hand under the heel and the other grabbed the toe. Dozier and Warner, the two flank riders, came over, coffee cups in hand, and laughed.

The boot slipped on Gary's soggy sock; Evan lost his grip and went tumbling heels over head, landing with a thud, and pushing himself up while the flank riders—and anyone else close enough to have witnessed the acrobatics—laughed.

"That's better'n that circus we took in in Baxter Springs that time," Adam Dozier said.

His partner kept cackling.

Gary shouted at Evan, "Get up. This chore ain't but half done." He raised his other leg.

That half proved to be a struggle, too, lasting about two minutes longer but without the acrobatics. The boot slipped off, and Evan turned and laid it next to the right boot.

"Now my sock," Gary said.

"I ain't pulling that stinky, soggy thing off your foot." Evan put both hands on his hips in defiance.

The nearest cowboys roared.

Gary joined the laughter, tugged the sock off, and laid it flat on a rock near his bedroll.

Casey Steer brought him a cup of coffee.

Thanking him, Gary found a comfortable spot on the ground, and drank.

"What do we do now?" Steer asked.

"What every cowboy dreams of," Alex Warner said.

"Nothin'," Dozier said.

Steer's face brightened.

"Not quite nothing," Gary corrected. "But till the Red goes

down a mite, we camp here. Let the cattle fatten on what grass there is, dry out, put those lost pounds back on. And there are five herds waiting ahead of us." He nodded north. "They cross first."

"Who wants chuck?" Moises Dunn yelled from his Studebaker.

"Fix me a plate, Evan," Gary said, and laughed at his son's expression. "You can fix yours first. But I can't go around barefoot. Might step on a prickly pear."

He had laid his chaps, trousers, shirt, even his gunbelt alongside the socks, gloves, and boots, letting everything dry out. Wearing his hat to protect him from sunburn, along with the bandanna around his neck and his unmentionables, Gary sat on a rock, sipping coffee and mopping up the rest of Dunn's stew with what remained of his biscuit.

Milone rode up, swung down, and squatted beside Gary.

The cowhand had pulled off his shirt and undershirt to dry over his saddlebags. Most of the older riders had stripped down to their unmentionables, though they kept boots and wet socks— or what was left of their socks after all these days and miles—on their feet. Everyone wore a water-logged hat.

"How's the herd?" Gary asked.

"Good," Milone replied. "Settled down. Baca and Fernandez are circling."

Gary handed him his coffee cup, about half full.

"Thanks." The point rider pushed back his hat and drank. "How long you reckon we'll be here?"

Before Gary could answer, he heard a faint rumbling.

Jimmy Batten, sitting next to Evan, asked, "Is that thunder?"

The skies overhead remained blue.

Milone's claybank jerked him to the ground. The cowboy cursed, landing on his knees but clenching the reins with both hands.

For one brief moment, a silence fell over the camp.

Then came the cries of horses—and Carlos Morales's Spanish shouts—from the remuda.

The ground trembled.

Moises Dunn, putting away his cookware, shouted first: "*Stam-pede!*"

Barefooted, Gary ran, feeling the sharp blades of grass, stones, cockleburs biting into his feet. When he reached the picket line, three horses had already pulled away and galloped north. He saw Evan gripping hard on his reins, fighting to keep his chestnut from rearing. Saw Casey Steer being dragged across the ground but refusing to let go of the reins. Heard Hunter Clarke yell that it must be Hugh Anderson's herd that was running.

Maybe it was. But now Gary heard the pounding of hooves and muffled shouts to the west. Whoever's herd was stampeding, Gary's bunch had joined the nightmare.

"Half you turn our cattle. The rest..." Gary couldn't hear what orders someone was shouting. Momentarily, he thought maybe he had yelled the orders. Good orders, but not clear. Everyone could take off after their herd, or the cattle coming straight for them.

It didn't matter. What mattered now was survival.

He found his horse. Grabbed the tether, the reins, latched a firm hold on the horn, and pulled himself up. The gelding reared. Gary's raw feet felt strange in the stirrups.

"We gotta turn 'em," Collin O'Hearn yelled. "We gotta turn 'em."

Gary was already riding south. Trying to see who was with him. Instinctively, he reached for his Colt, but felt only flannel drawers worn to a frazzle.

The gelding fought bit and rein every step of the way.

No dust. All that rain had soaked the ground. But Gary knew at least twelve hundred frightened longhorns were thundering straight toward him.

Then he saw that wave of beef. He made out no riders. Turning east, he gave his horse its head, let the gelding carry him out
of the path, before pulling the horse to a stop. It bucked three
times before Gary regained control and pushed the blood bay
into a skittish gallop.

*Turn the herd into itself. Turn the herd into itself. Till the longhorns
could no longer run. Just mill.*

A gunshot rang out. Maybe. With tens of thousands of hooves
digging into Texas stone, sand, and grass, he couldn't be sure of
what he really heard.

Angels calling him home?

Lucifer opening the Gate of Hades for him to ride through?

Or maybe Gary Hardee was already dead. And this was what
Hell looked like.

Mud coated his undergarments, his face, his hair. His hat had
flown off at some point. Gary couldn't recall when or where. The
bottoms of both feet, still in the stirrups, felt raw, blistered,
bleeding. He gripped the stirrups with his toes.

He craved water. His mouth felt like the sandhills he had seen
when he had driven a herd to Fort Davis to feed the bluecoats
there. But he had no canteen. Had no idea where he had lost it.

A rider eased a dark horse toward him, and Gary heard his
name being called. Somehow he managed to swallow, and he
pulled on the reins, stopping the horse, and nodded.

Grit stung his eyes. Coated his tongue. Everything blurred,
and his mouth burned with thirst.

"You all right?" he whispered.

"Yes, sir. If my heart does not explode in my chest."

"Just circle the herd now, Salvador," Gary said. "I'll survey the
damage."

After leaving the herd, or what remained of the herd, or a com-
bination of many herds, Gary reined up when he recognized a
rider loping toward him, and cringed at the searing pain in his
feet. His back started to ache. He looked at the leather burns on

fingers and hands. He tried to remember his wife's name. Once again, he thought he was dead, buried, and burning in the deepest pits.

Bill Bailey reined up.

"You all right?" the Texian asked.

Gary nodded.

Bailey turned and spit. "You ain't all right at all. Criminy, you're a mess. Here." He reached down and unwrapped the canvas strap from the horn, then practically thrust the canteen in front of Gary.

By thunder, he could have kissed that hard rock right then and there.

He took two swallows, no more, splashed some into his left hand, and bathed his eyes. Blinking rapidly, he asked: "What happened?"

Twisting in the saddle, Gary looked around, giving Bailey time to think of an answer. He saw more cattle than he had seen at the roundup back in Fort Bend County. More cattle than he had seen in some years in Sedalia or Baxter Springs.

The craving for water had not been slaked, but he returned the canteen to Bill Bailey.

Another rider, flanked by two men in big Texas hats, made a beeline for him. Gary mouthed a curse and looked back at Bailey, who had not started his answer.

Gary gave him another question. "Everybody in your camp safe?"

Bailey's face tightened.

So did Gary's chest.

And Shanghai Pierce, with two scowling men with big, drooping mustaches and bigger, dirt-caked hats on either side of him, reined in his big black, and fired more curses at Gary Hardee than a Henry rifle could hold.

Chapter 20

Mr. Pierce, familiarly known among extensive cattle
dealers as "Shanghai Pierce," who has been one
of the largest and heaviest dealers at this point, says
that . . . we have the greatest stock country in the
world, not excepting Texas.
—*The Wichita City Eagle,*
November 21, 1872

He was younger than Gary by a few years, and quite a bit
taller, even without those high-heeled boots. His thinning
hair remained dark, but his beard had started to show flecks of
gray. Folks said he could find more cattle in the cane breaks than
a Tonkawa and knew more curses than all those polite words
Mr. Webster put in his dictionaries.

But even Shanghai Pierce had to stop once in a while to
breathe.

"Mr. Pierce," Bill Bailey said when Pierce paused his verbal
cannonade. "Gary didn't start this ruction."

Whirling, Pierce cursed Bailey, told him to keep his tongue
from wagging, and looked back while pointing a long, gloved figure at Gary's face. "All I know is that the steer I saw purging its
bowels on my bedroll was wearing your road brand."

"I take full responsibility," Gary told him.

Pierce spat, cursed, spat again, shook his head, and waved that gloved finger again. He hailed from somewhere back east—Rhode Island, Gary had heard—but years back stowed away on a ship bound for Texas. "You have no other choice but to take full responsibility." His curses took a hiatus, but that would be temporary. "We have five or six herds scattered and mixed—and a plenty dead. It'll take us to the Fifth Coming of the Lord to sort everything out. And you, Hardee." The finger wagged harder, stopping only as Pierce invented new curses. "You and your crew will be doing most of the sorting. And not until every herd has crossed and all those others that will be backed up till Christmas. Only then will you swim the Red." He spit, and finally looked like he was spent.

"It'll be done, Shanghai," Gary said softly.

Bailey cleared his throat and eased his horse closer. "Mr. Pierce," he said. "It was Wat Anderson's son who caused this mess." Sighing, he turned toward Gary and explained. "There was another herd pushing behind us. Hugh said he wasn't losing his place in line; he started pushing the cattle faster. And faster. I kept yelling at him to slow down, but he just got wilder and wilder. I don't know what happened. Next thing I know, the leaders just shot out like a fireball from a Roman candle on Davy Crockett's birthday."

He wiped sweat off his forehead with a shirtsleeve and looked back at Pierce. "It was—"

"You said you were in charge of both herds when we met at my camp." Pierce's hard eyes locked on Gary.

"And I just told you," Gary said, "I take full responsibility."

Pierce must have detected that Gary had reached his limit, so he gave a curt nod, and spoke as quietly as Shanghai Pierce could manage. "Good. We all have a big task before us, and we must work together." The politeness ended. "Just get that steer that

shat all over my bedroll out of my camp first. Else we shall bar-
becue the brindle bastard."

When Pierce started to turn his horse north, Bailey coughed
and said, "Wait up, Shanghai." He had dropped the *Mr. Pierce.*

The cattleman turned, glaring hard, but Bailey had turned to
Gary.

Bailey breathed in deeply and exhaled. His mouth opened,
closed, before he found the resolve.

"We haven't seen Taylor," Bailey whispered. "Since the stampede started."

Ravens and turkey buzzards arrived. In due time, four-legged
carrion would show up, too.

Gary had not found a dead man yet, but he had lost count of
mangled longhorns wearing road brands he did and did not recognize.

He had told Bill Bailey to find Evan, but not to tell him anything about Taylor. Just send him northwest to start rounding up
cattle. All cattle, no matter the brand. They'd sort later, just as
they sorted cattle during the gathers back home. The rest of the
men split up, riding alone.

His heart skipped when he found the first dead horse, till he
realized it carried no saddle. Blanket and saddle could have
fallen off, but what once was a dun had no bridle. It was a horse
from a remuda of another outfit. Again, Gary did not recognize
the brand.

When he saw Moises Dunn and the Studebaker, he wondered
just how far the cattle had run. He could not remember seeing
the banks of the Red River, and now he couldn't even remember
where the cattle had stopped. Had the cattle turned south or
west during that massive runaway? He found the sun, realized he
was riding southeast.

He considered turning the horse toward the camp, but Dunn
looked busy, feeding hands from assorted outfits. Gary could sure

use some real clothes. And a fresh horse. Get the canteen Shanghai Pierce had loaned him refilled.

He kept riding.

A centipede sat on a rock, bathing in the sun, caring nary a whit for rider or horse. Gary squeezed his burning eyes shut.

Having filled the washtub, he returns to the cabin to tell Jane that everything is ready to give Taylor his bath.

"Then do it," she calls from behind the curtain.

He swallows. "Me?"

"You haven't been invalided," she fires back. "And I'm nursing your other son."

Glancing down at Taylor, Hardee tries to smile. The toddling little boy grins and says, "I pooped in my pants."

Jane lets Gary know: "You can take care of that, too."

Retreat. That is what Major Wat Anderson would have ordered. He scoops up the two-year-old and steps outside, carrying the giggling boy to the tub.

The diaper isn't too bad. No need to wipe the boy, Gary figures, since little Taylor is going to get a bath. He flings the diaper's contents into the corral, figuring there wasn't much difference between horse apples and . . .

He rinses the diaper in the horse trough and hangs it over the top rail of the round pen to let it dry.

After getting the rest of the clothes off Taylor, he sits the fat-legged boy in the tub of warm soapy water. Taylor takes to water like a duck. He splashes around, and Gary uses his bandanna to scrub gently behind the ears, over the nose, and under the arms before retying the silk rag back around his neck.

The boy splashes, giggles, and plays in the water.

Squatting, Gary lets the boy make waves in the tub. A gust of wind blows the diaper off the fence post, and Gary walks away to pick it up.

He has just laid it back over the rail, when Taylor lets out a panicked scream.

"Pa! Please help me!"

Gary covers the short distance in seconds. Taylor has backed away to the far side of the tub, and points. Waves of water splash over the rim and back toward the bawling kid.

Gary drops to his knees, looking around. Hears Jane's voice from the doorway, screaming.

"He's all right." Heart racing, Gary scoops the boy out of the tub.

"I thought it was a toy!" Taylor points. "I picked it up."

Gary looks till he spots the floating object. By then Jane stands next to him, jerking the sobbing boy into her right arm. Her left holds the bawling Evan.

"What," Jane cries out, spacing her words between deep breaths, "happened?"

Gary takes a few steps, bends over, and picks the dead centipede up with his fingers.

"It wasn't . . . a toy . . . Mama." Taylor sniffles.

Seeing the stump he used for chopping firewood, Gary walks over and sits down.

"Oh my God." Jane has finally seen the centipede. "Did it bite you, Taylor? Did it bite, you?"

She's more hysterical than Taylor and Evan.

"No, Mama," Taylor says, and now he's crying again. "I thought . . . it was . . . a toy."

Gary just sits there, wondering if his heart will ever settle down. He realizes he still holds the centipede, which likely was dead before Gary dumped water into the tub. He flicks it into the grass.

He found another horse on this side of an arroyo. No saddle, no bridle, but Wat Anderson's brand he recognized. The gelding tried to lift its head, whimpered, and laid back down, snorting short, ragged breaths.

Gary forced his gelding, snorting, tossing its head, closer. He knew he should dismount, but prickly pear and rocks, smashed into shards by panicking horses and cattle, covered the ground, and Gary's feet were already a mess. If he dismounted, he'd never be able to climb back into the saddle.

The Winchester slid stiffly from the scabbard. He should have cleaned it when they made camp before the stampede started. Knowing he couldn't waste any time, he jacked a cartridge into the chamber. Holding the carbine in his right hand, and his left hand gripping both reins with all his might, he leaned forward until the barrel rested just inches from the dying horse's head.

His horse jumped at the gunshot, and Gary let it run several yards before pulling on the reins.

"It's all right," he whispered, and fed a .44 into the chamber, leaned forward, and rubbed the gelding's neck. "It's all right."

The distance between the carbine's barrel and the dying horse's head muffled the blast. Only someone nearby would have heard, and the signal for finding a body, alive or dead, was three shots spaced no more than two-three seconds apart.

"Let's go . . ."

But the wind carried something toward him. A faint voice. Imagination? A mockingbird? Gary kicked the blood bay into a trot, up to the edge of the arroyo. He saw a tree a hundred yards to the east and loping horses carrying riders toward him. Those must have heard Gary's rifle shot. But the voice had come from the opposite direction. He looked into the arroyo and drew in a deep breath.

He might have prayed, but wasn't sure. Kicking the horse, ignoring the pain that now stretched from his raw feet to his neck, he rode into the arroyo to another dead horse.

Only this one had a saddle and bridle, or what was left of both. Gary recognized saddle, bridle, and the gelding.

It was the blood bay Taylor had ridden from Gary's place to start the gather. Gary had paid Milford Meek fifteen dollars and a jug of Johnny Moore's homemade whiskey for five years back.

*　*　*

He was leaning over the battered carcass when the riders stopped atop the arroyo. Looking up, Gary spat and made himself stand. Hugh Anderson and Garrett McMahon, who rode flank for Anderson's herd, eased their horses down the steep slope and stopped a few yards from Gary and the dead horse.

"That's . . ." The Major's son did not finish the sentence.

Gary had to take hold of the saddle horn, and not just because of his mangled bare feet.

"It's just his horse," McMahon said. "He might could've got throwed. Could have bailed off."

Could haves . . .? The world is littered with could haves, might haves, might could haves . . .

"Live or dead," Hugh said, "Taylor's around here somewhere. Fire three shots, Garrett. This is close as we've come."

The cowhand pulled an old Spiller & Burr from his waistband, and was trying to thumb back that stiff hammer when Gary snapped:

"Wait."

That faraway voice again. Was it Gary's imagination?

No, for this time, Anderson and McMahon heard it.

"That's . . ." McMahon stood in the stirrups.

"It might be nothing more than the wind." But Hugh Anderson's eyes scanned the countryside, too.

Gary wished he could wash the grit, grime, and tears from his eyes. He wished his feet did not hurt so much. Mostly he wished . . .

"That tree!" Hugh pointed.

He could blame the tears on those burning eyes. And butchered feet.

Taylor stood, his spurred boots spread out to two branches, his back against the trunk, maybe three feet high up in the oak.

"What the Sam Hill are you doing up there?" Hugh snapped before he broke out laughing.

"I'm stuck," Taylor told him, punctuating with many curses in a dry, haggard voice. He moved his hand slightly, gesturing toward his back and the trunk. "Belt of my chaps got hooked over a limb, knob, somethin'. Get me down. I've been stuck up here for a coon's age."

His voice sounded ancient. Probably had been screaming for help since the middle of the night.

"Pa, please help me."

Not as loud, not as frightening as that *Pa! Please help me!* But Gary remembered a centipede and a two-year-old.

He started to laugh, but could not stop the tears.

Chapter 21

Men Wanted.
One hundred men wanted between Florence and
Newton on the Atchison, Topeka & Santa Fe
Railroad. Apply at the Santa Fe depot Topeka.
—(Topeka) *Kansas State Record,*
May 29, 1871

She set up a tent on a vacant lot, knowing that Redfield, Judge Muse, or someone else eventually would tell her to move it. But by then, she figured, her restaurant would be finished. Denise told the lead carpenter that she wanted two floors. The ground floor would be the restaurant, and the upstairs would cover half of that lengthwise. Two rooms with a hallway separating the rooms. One for storage. One for Denise to escape.

The carpenter frowned. "I don't like that," he said.

"You afraid of heights?" she asked, and put her hands on her hips.

"More wood."

"More money for you."

He sighed. "All right."

"One thing," she told him. "If I fall through the floor, I'll be coming after you."

"You won't fall through the floor," he said. "And I'll double up the wood facing the street. For insulation. From bullets, drunken cowboys and railroaders might be shooting after a bender."

That Tuesday, Denise decided to move her tent into the alley behind the site of her restaurant after stopping at a crowd gathered around a box-and-strip building—a common method of construction where trees were scarce—going up on Fifth Street. Railroaders, carpenters, the stonemason who had laid Denise's restaurant floor, and burly men who might have been muleskinners crowded the shabby storefront. When an opening appeared in the human wall to let a doctor slip inside, Denise followed him and Perry Tuttle, her business neighbor, for a better look at what had happened.

The doctor wasn't Gaston Boyd. Denise knew that doctor, for he took his coffee with honey and liked his hash browns crispy and often dined with his beautiful wife, Elizabeth. Not everyone in Newton, after all, was trash.

She did know the victim, not by name, but had exchanged a good morning or good afternoon with him. He had moved his dry-goods business from Florence. Now he sat on an overturned crate holding a bloody rag against his forehead. Blood caked his yellow mustache, and his nose was split open and broken. When his busted lips parted, she saw his gold front tooth was missing, too. He spit out blood and said, "I yelled for help. Nobody come. Nobody come to help me. I yelled for help. Why didn't nobody come?"

A stranger in town, the doctor, on both knees, withdrew the rag, dropped it in the dirt, and reached inside his valise. "I need someone to hold his ear in place as I can sew it back so he won't lose it."

When he came up with needle and sutures, no one had accepted his call. He turned toward the nearest spectators.

"You." He nodded.

"I ain't good at nursin'," said the saloonkeeper, who always asked for his steak to be burned blacker than his soul.

"But that bottle in your hand will deaden the pain on my patient. Bring it over."

The man brought the mouth of the rye to his lips.

"Unh-uh," the doctor warned. "You've had enough. He needs it." When the man hesitated again, the doc bellowed, "Now or you'll be in need of stitches."

A nervous laugh rippled through the crowd as the saloon-keeper stepped forward and handed the bottle to the patient.

"Why didn't nobody come to help me?" The victim took the bottle, and gestured again to his store. "They taken ever'thin', ever'thin' I owned."

He drank.

"All my canned peaches. All my buckwheat. Ten boxes of cream cheese."

The doctor brought his hand to the mangled ear.

"I need someone here to hold this ear in place," he said tightly.

"Canned peaches," someone said. "We ought to lynch the scoundrel."

"Isn't there a *man* in this town?" the doctor yelled.

Denise stepped forward, unbuttoning the sleeves of her dress and rolling them up.

"Hussy," one of the women hissed.

Denise almost laughed. A prostitute calling her a hussy.

She knelt, swallowed, felt the sweat already on her forehead, though it was far from hot.

The doctor glanced at her, but his eyes showed neither shock nor disdain, but also not gratitude or wonderment.

"Put your fingers where mine are," he said tightly, "and don't let go."

When she did, the doctor told the patient to drink.

He guzzled the last of the whiskey, coughed, and said, "Salt, teas, coffee. Smoked pig tongues. Pickled salmon. All stole. Stole. Nobody come to help me."

"I need two more men. Men. Big men. One to hold this man's arms. The other his feet."

He glanced at Denise. "You can back out now, miss, because once I start, this is going to be hell."

Somehow, she managed to swallow. "I'm here."

"Thank you," he whispered, and let out a sigh with relief when Denise's big cook and a behemoth man in buckskins stepped forward.

"Miss Denise." Grover tipped his slouch hat and knelt behind the battered shopkeeper, then wrapped his massive arms around the man's upper arms.

"Beggin' your pardon." The stinking man in buckskins nodded at Denise, knelt, and latched gloved hands on the victim's ankles.

"Shouldn't you be doing this in your office, Doc?" someone called out.

"What office?" the man said. "The back of my surrey? Every carpenter said they will be booked for three more weeks just putting up dance halls, saloons, and whorehouses."

He turned back to Denise. "Apologies for my blunt language, miss."

She gave him a smile, took in a deep breath, and squeezed her eyes shut.

"Besides," she heard him say. "I'm a dentist."

"You can open your eyes now."

She almost smiled at the voice, and slowly let her eyelids rise. The sun caused her to blink rapidly, and Denise did not look at the injured merchant, but focused on the dentist, who had turned away and was accepting a tin cup from a cowboy who told him to keep it as he walked, spurs singing, toward one of the girls in the flimsy chamise and little else.

"That show you put on was finer than frog's hair cut eight ways."

Now the dentist was shaking hands. No one seemed to mind

the bloodstained fingers and hands. He laughed at their jokes, thanked them for their cheers and support and said, yes, he did think the ear might be saved, barring infection or more brawls.

A tall man in a fine broadcloth jacket stepped in front of the surgeon next, his hair combed back revealing a prominent forehead and clear, calculating eyes. His hair was mostly silver, sideburns stretching into finely groomed chin whiskers that touched the bow tie of satin around a starched white shirt.

You didn't see many men dressed like him in Newton.

"A bully fine show, sir," the man said, pumping the right hand of the hero. "Bully fine. Surely you were jesting when you told this fine young lady that you are a dentist by trade."

"Surely I was not," the young man said. "Philadelphia Dental College. Class of sixty-six."

"By jove," the man said. "By jove, sir. Well, you'd never know that by the way you sewed that ear back into place."

"I thought I would be suturing gums after pulling teeth from brawls, sir." He sipped from the cup, swallowed, and coughed. "Oh, my." He held the cup away and shook his head. "That will wake a man up."

"From the dead," the bearded man said. "Allow me to welcome you to Newton, Kansas, Doctor. I am Robert Muse. Judge Robert Muse."

"Doctor Page Everhart, Judge. Specializing in facial neuralgia, diseases of teeth and mouth. I have laughing gas for relief of pain. But . . ." He raised the tin cup. "Nothing that can match this."

"Yes." The judge frowned. "But too much of that leads to this." He waved his arm at the ransacked store. A barber took over Doctor Everhart's job, cleaning the victim's face with a soaked handkerchief, sticking a wad of cotton where the front tooth had been knocked out or—Denise cringed at the thought—pulled out by thieves. When he was done, two other men eased the man to his feet and guided him back into what remained of his store.

"Welcome, Doctor Everhart, to Newton. We need men of your skill and example, sir. Indeed."

"What we need, Judge," came a voice behind Denise, "is some law in Newton."

The judge stiffened but turned, those eyes fastening on the man. She knew him by name, James Peterson. , who ran a saloon and was the owner of The Gold Room that was going up north of the tracks, that hoity-toity place Redfield had pointed out on the plat of Newton.

"We are not a city yet," the judge said calmly, "as well you know, Jim. We must incorporate before we can appoint or hire peace officers and, or elect, governing officers."

"When will that be?" someone shouted.

The judge sighed. "Not before the next year."

"How about a deputy sheriff?" someone suggested.

"I have written four letters to Sheriff Walker in Wichita."

"Problem is," the barber said, "Sedgwick County covers a lot of territory."

The judge nodded. "Which is why we will petition for a new county—a county that Newton shall govern as the seat of this new county. But we must follow the laws of our state."

That caused one of the scantily clad ladies to laugh. "Laws?" she said as she brought a cigar to her mouth. "You and your laws. There ain't no law in Newton. And once them Texas waddies start coming in regular like, y'all will see just how much law it'll take to keep things peaceable here."

A man in sleeve garters and a brocade vest said, "Amen."

The judge locked eyes with Gregory.

The dentist let the barber finish his cup of whiskey.

"Perhaps we should meet this evening, Judge," Gregory said. "Figure out some temporary law. At least through the cattle season."

"That might be a fine idea." The judge tugged on his beard. "Where would you like to meet?"

"My restaurant," Denise heard herself saying. "It clears out by seven—right now, anyway. I'll foot for the coffee and cake. But any meals will be on y'all."

Gregory nodded. "She cooks a fine spread, Judge."

"I have heard. And she has guts and gumption."

Denise regretted her decision long before Judge Muse called the meeting to order. The saloonkeepers and company brought their own liquor. That wasn't a problem, since she didn't sell ardent spirits, but they did not order food, either. She had not realized just how many saloonkeepers had set up shop in Wichita. Two women wearing fine dresses came, glared, and sat down as far away as they could from each other. Men found seats—the chairs, and most of her furniture, had yet to arrive, but the place wasn't finished yet—while sawdust leaked from the ceiling onto the tables and makeshift benches at the front half of the dining room.

She wondered if anyone would come back to eat when they had to pay for full meals. Who wanted sawdust in their tea or sprinkled across bacon and eggs?

Most people stood.

Judge Muse was about to call the meeting to order, when a man of color, dressed in a sharp blue suit with crimson cravat and a fine black hat, knocked on the door as he opened it, stepped inside, and removed his hat.

"Beggin' pardon, folks," he said in a Southern drawl. "But I hear y'all's meeting and was wonderin' if this was open to colored folks."

The only sound came from Mattie, her newest waitress, pouring coffee.

"Of course, sir," the judge said. "You own . . . ?"

"I call it The Dark Moon, Judge." He grinned. "A saloon . . . Moon Saloon . . ." The grin widened. "For folks of my complexion."

"We don't need no nig—"

The judge silenced the Texas gambler by drawing a Remington revolver from his holster.

"If you don't like Newton, sir," the judge said, "I am sure Abilene will welcome you."

The newcomer grinned again. "Might not have noticed, folks, but lots of those Texas cowboys be of my coloration. Lots of 'em. Now, I don't suspect most of 'em will be welcomed in your fine places, but they'll spend money same as those of your complexication." Denise knew from his smile that he was partially putting on a show with his dialect. She figured he was better educated than most of the men and women here. Including Denise. "And I know I'll be payin' taxes same as y'all. Might as well pay for . . . protection . . ." He pulled back the coattail to reveal a silver-plated revolver in a shining black holster. "Same as y'all, too."

Silence followed, but not as long as Denise thought it would last, for Judge Muse cleared his throat and said, "We welcome you, young man, and your business."

"And his greenbacks," someone called out from the back of the building.

The laughs, none boisterous, were scattered about the dining room.

The man kept smiling, and he made his way to the wall that separated the restaurant from Perry Tuttle's Dance House.

After that, Denise busied herself helping feed the few who were hungry, or bring them coffee that they sweetened with their flasks, bottles, and jugs they had brought with them.

In the end, an agreement was reached. Gamblers, owners of gambling halls, saloons, dance halls, and any "den of iniquity" would pay a monthly fee from which salaries would be distributed to night police officers who would keep the peace, especially south of the railroad tracks.

Before a month had passed, the fees became weekly instead of monthly.

"Supply and demand," Perry Tuttle called it.

Chapter 22

The rivalry among Southern Kansas towns to secure
the entrepot of the Texas cattle trade would be amus-
ing if it were not so serious—a life and death matter,
in fact, with the contestants. In the "game" that is
now in progress between Abilene and Baxter Springs,
the thriving border city of Wichita does not "take a
hand," but the results of this year's driving has proven
that Wichita has her share and a large proportion of
the traffic in "long-horns."
—*Leavenworth Daily Commerce,*
June 2, 1871

"Lord have mercy."
"You ain't gonna find the Lord or mercy here," the
driver said as the wagon approached Newton.

It had been a long, dull, hot, windy journey from Wichita.
Cindy rode in the front next to the driver. Behind them, a stout
man with a shaggy red beard, sitting atop the tarp-covered items
from Meech's grocery, reached inside his mouth to withdraw the
wad of tobacco that might have been just a tad smaller than a
baseball and tossed it into the dusty street.

"Criminy," he whispered.

On the plains of upland sand, where few trees grew only along creeks, they entered a canyon of tents and three sod structures, but predominantly wooden walls, most of which a sneeze could have knocked over. More buildings were going up, and people lined the streets.

Cindy hadn't made out anything resembling a sidewalk.

"Handsome!"

The driver, the man in the back, and Cindy looked across the street. "Mine's bigger than what you got ridin' with you," yelled a woman with dirty blond hair and wearing just a cotton robe. She opened the robe to reveal her breasts, laughed, and closed the cotton. "The peek's on me, boys, but when you come see me, bring hard cash."

The driver turned back to look over the mules.

The man in the back said, "Ain't never seen nothin' like this before."

Hers might be bigger, Cindy thought, *but mine are firmer. And I have all of my teeth.*

The wagon emerged from the shadows to cross a wide path that separated Newton. North lay more roughshod buildings, but with a modicum of decency.

"Is this where the railroad tracks will go?" she asked.

Nodding, the driver urged the mules onward.

She looked westward down the railroad's path, then turned quickly. Bringing her hands over her eyes, she stared. She thought she could make out distant figures. Certainly, black smoke rose far off across the plains. That had to be the railroad crew, laying tracks. Tracks to this . . . *city?*

She kept staring down the graded road until the first frame building blocked her view. A few blocks later, the driver pulled hard on the reins and stopped the wagon.

"Miss." The driver pointed across the street. "That's the land office for the railroad, miss. That's where you'll find that Redford fellow."

Redford. Oh, he means Redfield.

Cindy grabbed her hatbox and valise and jumped into the street. The man in the back found her suitcase and dropped it over the side into the dust.

"Sake's alive, Barnabus," the driver said. "Show some manners and help the lady."

The man tugged on his beard and just stared across the graded road, and back at the bedlam of Newton's south side.

Cindy managed her luggage all by herself.

Redfield returned the letter of introduction Knott had given her before she left Wichita, leaned back in his chair, and said, "Your editor sent *you* here?"

Cindy gave it right back to him. "The Atchison, Topeka, and Santa Fe sent *you* here?"

The regret was immediate. She would be out of a job, and stuck in this hell on wheels. But the railroad man surprised her by laughing.

"What's Wichita's interest in Newton?" he asked, refolding the letter and sticking it in the envelope addressed *To Whom It May Concern*, which he pushed across his desk toward her.

"We cover all of Sedgwick County," she said.

"I said Wichita. Not your two-dollar-a-year sheet."

"The railroad interests Kansas, Wichita, and the *Herald*."

Gunshots roared somewhere in town. Cindy spun quickly, staring out the window. This could be a murder, a robbery, something made to order for Bobby Knott.

"Just drunks, Miss Bagwell," Redfield said, and Cindy turned back toward him.

"The railroad interests Texans, too," he said and smiled. "Two herds are camped some miles out of town. Small herds. But the trail bosses are letting their beef fatten, hoping to sell when the first trains arrive." He stood, walked to the window, and looked up and down the main street. "Other herds graze and let some of their hired hands come in."

She walked to the other side of the door and looked through that window.

"Over there is The Gold Room." Redfield pointed. "That shall be the Drovers Cottage of Newton." He nodded. "And down there stands the Newton House. It will be this town's best hotel." He cleared his throat and looked at her. "Have you made arrangements for accommodations?"

"No." Her voice cracked a bit. Probably from all the dust she had been eating on the bumpy ride north. She had checked out of her place, not wanting to waste money on renting a room that she wouldn't see for . . . however long she stayed here. Until the bond election, probably. Whenever that was.

"I see. How long will you be with us?"

"I do not know," she told him.

"Well, I think I can find you accommodations, though they might not be what the Newton House is." He chuckled. "But having met a few newspapermen in my day, and seeing that you are not working for Pulitzer or Greeley, I sincerely doubt you can afford the Newton House."

She declined to comment.

"I think I know a place where you can stay." He crossed the room and grabbed her suitcase and hatbox. Cindy picked up her valise and followed him outside.

Her stomach soured when he started walking toward the graded road. Not that the north side of the tracks was much more civilized than the south, but . . .

Saws rasped, hammers banged, and men cheered as a false front was lifted against tall poles. Another addition to ever-growing Newton.

Once they crossed the railroad's path, Redfield stopped and pointed up the tracks. "The tracks will be here in a week. And then you'll likely have plenty of stories to give your editor." He stared at her. "You sure you want to stay here?"

"I have my job to do," she told him.

"Don't fret." Redfield seemed to read Cindy's mind. "I think you'll be in good hands."

He picked up the luggage and moved on. "Just a few more blocks."

They turned at a narrow, crooked, ugly street, moved down another block, and stopped at a two-story building. No, Cindy said, studying the upstairs. One and a half stories. But the construction, unlike most of the buildings she had seen, especially on this side of the tracks, appeared solid.

"That's Tuttle's place next door," he said, moved down the narrow street, and turned into the alley. Cindy saw a tent.

"I am *not* staying in a tent," she whispered, but sure enough, Redfield lowered the hatbox and suitcase, pushed open the canvas, and dragged both pieces of luggage inside. When he turned, he took the valise from her before she could protest, laid it inside, pulled back the flap, and said, "This is your home. Temporarily." He pointed at the upper story. "When that's finished, you'll be fine, and it should be done in a week. Your landlady is quite particular on what she wants in a building. Most store owners, as you have seen, don't care one whit."

She was already sweating.

"Let me show you around Newton." Redfield took her by the elbow.

Pulling away from his grip, she pointed at the tent. "That's all I have," she said. "Everything. Is . . ."

Redfield laughed. "It is safe during the daylight. All the ladies of the tenderloin, vermin, thieves, and rapscallions do not come out until the sun is down."

She wasn't sure she believed him, but he steered her toward the busier streets.

"Newton has changed much since your last visit. I'll treat you to supper at the Newton House. Then I'll introduce you to your landlady."

"How stupid of me," he said when they had reached the graded line for the A.T. & S.F. "You've already met Miss Beeber."

Beeber.

Two loud explosions startled her. This time, screams joined the echo. Redfield cursed and took off running. Cindy recovered and followed. They ran across the railroad line. Toward the Newton House.

Sounds of carpentry ceased. Redfield slowed about thirty yards from where a man in a big brown hat stood, revolver in his right hand, pointing at a man less than ten feet away. The other man lay on the ground, his hat in the dust, his right hand trying to raise the pistol he held. Cindy's mouth fell open as the cowboy still standing stepped away from a building Cindy noted as Gregory's Saloon toward the man on the ground, still struggling to raise his pistol.

The man stood over the prostrate man. Even from the distance, Cindy heard the loud *click* as he cocked the hammer and squeezed the trigger. Cindy jumped, but all she heard was a profanity.

The cowboy cursed his gun, drew back the hammer again. This time, there was no *click*, but a clap of thunder and eruption of flame and white smoke. The man on the ground ceased moving.

Turning toward the people lining in front of Gregory's Saloon, the cowboy, still holding his smoking revolver, yelled: "You heard what he called me, didn't you?"

The man nodded.

"Say it. What did he call me?"

"A foul name." Cindy could just make that out.

"A vulgar insult," the gun-toter said. "What else did this fellow tell me?"

She couldn't hear the answer.

"Louder. I want them night deputies to hear you."

"He said he'd kill you," the man under the awning said.

That seemed to placate the gun-toter, and he holstered his revolver and turned back to the dead man.

"Well." He wasn't shouting now, but Newton had turned so quiet she heard him clearly. "He got proved wrong." And the man turned around and walked back inside the saloon.

Cindy cursed herself. She had no pencil. No notes. Everything was back in that canvas tent. She'd have to borrow pencil and paper from Redfield, who, to her surprise, was walking back into his office. Everyone seemed to be returning to wherever they had been.

And Cindy remembered where she was. On the north side of the tracks. In the *safe* part of Newton.

All the ladies of the tenderloin, vermin, thieves, and rapscallions do not come out until the sun is down?

"Not hardly," she whispered.

Chapter 23

Newton . . . is situated near the northern boundary
of Sedgwick county, upon the high prairie, near the
head of Sand creek . . . with no natural advantages
except the railroad and the cattle trail. . . . These
advantages, however, will insure for Newton a
rapid growth and lively times.
—*The Kansas Daily Commonwealth,*
June 30, 1871

Newton grew, and a great portion of that growth came south
of the railroad tracks. Redfield had been right. South of the
tracks got most of the business, and while Denise's profits grew
steady, she could not match her neighbors on Block Fifty-two.

Perry Tuttle had sent two of his chippies and his big, black-
bearded bouncer to patch the bullet holes that perforated the
restaurant's wall that butted up against Tuttle's dance hall. "One
of 'em rowdy Texians had a LeMat," the bouncer explained,
"and a couple drunks carried forty-fives. Those did the worser.
Them thirty-sixes and the pepperboxes just stuck in our walls."

That didn't make Denise feel better, but she had been
blessed. She also knew that this would happen again. She'd have
to spend money to buy wall hangings—heavy wall hangings—
that might stop more bullets, because the next time, a lantern

could be hit, or someone eating supper. In this town, *in this part of town anyway,* maybe even during breakfast.

"I should have ordered bricks," she whispered.

After pouring a cup of coffee for herself, she stepped outside and walked to Main Street.

Cowboys rode past, faces pale, heads hanging down and looking as though every step their horses took hurt like blazes. They headed west, away from what people were beginning to call Hide Park—because the women here, with the exception of Denise Beeber and her two waitresses, showed off a lot of hide.

Tuttle had a couple of smaller buildings behind and next to his dance house. Thirty yards away, Ed Krum had a similar business, called The Alamo, with two shanties and one picket building surrounding it. Not to be outdone, Tuttle was putting up a new shack, and Denise recognized two of the carpenters as ones who were supposed to be finishing her private, upstairs chambers. She didn't curse them, didn't scold them, for they would have that brothel finished in less than two hours.

On this side of the A.T. & S. F. line, footpaths could already be made out on Main Street, as cowboys crossed from one business to another, searching for more fun, stronger whiskey, cheaper women.

Well, she could have kept going to Florence. Emporia. Or all the way to Nebraska. But she was making money.

She walked back down Second Street, turning onto Poplar and then into the alley to her tent, where she had neighbors, too. Two more tents, neither as big nor as nice as Denise's. Who lived in those, she didn't know or care to meet. Could be more of Tuttle's "dancers," or Krum's, or some independent hooker.

When she pushed open the flat to her tent, she found the luggage, and bit off a curse. Three pieces—suitcase, hatbox, and a medium-sized grip. Some prostitute was trying to take over her tent, although Denise did not think her pad would make a decent bed. But the cowboys she had seen in this part of town would likely pay for a roll in the dirt.

Before she could throw out the uninvited invader's belongings, the back door opened, and Grover cleared his throat.

"We busy, Miss Denise," he said.

He must have read her expression as: *That's impossible. I just turned two corners.*

"Reckon a whole trail crew stopped to eat," he said. "Before they go 'bout their regular business."

She left the luggage inside the tent, tied the flap shut this time, and followed Mr. Thomas into her restaurant. The hussy claim jumper could wait. Business came first.

She helped cook. Brought out plates of beef fried with potatoes and hot biscuits. Refilled cups of coffee and glasses of lemonade. Gave up trying to keep the cowboys from sweetening their coffee with bottles of rye whiskey, or drinking straight from the bottle. But at seventy-five cents a plate, forty cents for a glass of lemonade, and a nickel for coffee—free refills on the latter—she did not complain.

They ran out of pie and cake—ten cents a slice. The one minute she had to breathe, she spent checking her supplies. She would have to buy coffee beans and flour before opening tomorrow.

When the railroad crew came in, she held her breath.

The big-shouldered men found a table that had not yet been cleaned, but they sat down anyway.

One pockmarked cowboy wiped his mouth with his shirtsleeve, set his cup on the table, and turned in his chair, his spurs ringing and carving up Denise's floor.

"Why ain't y'all a-layin' 'em steel rails, buster?" he said in a tangy drawl.

The meatiest of the railroaders helped hand Mattie the plates. Once she had hurried back toward the curtain, the man eyed the cowhand with cold blue eyes and said, "Iron. Not steel. Iron."

Laughing, the cowboy pulled a revolver from his holster and waved it nonchalantly at the table across the room.

"Irish," he said, nodding at the men. "This is the only iron we know in Texas."

The door opened and closed as a couple of clerks from the Pioneer Store north of the tracks hurried out. Denise hoped they had left their dollar-ninety-five on the table.

She was about to tell the drunk to holster his iron and get out of her place, but one of the cowboy's partners took over.

"Harry, put that away and finish your coffee. You start a ruction and Ike'll fire all of us."

Frowning, Harry muttered a soft curse, but turned around, digging up more of Denise's floor, and the revolver vanished.

Another railroad man rose from his chair, removed his cap, cleared his throat, and said: "You all might like to hear that we just started laying iron—not steel—past Broadway Street."

*Hip-hip-hurrah*s thundered from the dining room and into the kitchen.

But when the noise quieted, another railroad man set down his coffee cup and laughed. Without rising, he said in a thick Irish brogue: "As Declan said, you might want to hear that, but, alas, 'tisn't true. We be miles still from your nice little village."

Denise held her breath, waiting for the brawl, but to her surprise, one cowboy started laughing, and another joined in. James Peterson, the saloonkeeper who was dining with his sharpers, tilted his head back and howled, and Bruce Naylor, who owned a dry goods store whose windows had been shot out the night before, paid his bill, shook his head, and said, "And folks tell me that cowhands and railroad men can't get along," before walking out the front door.

Having barely found time to sit down, Denise spent the rest of the day helping cook, serve, and make change. She fed more cowboys, railroaders, gamblers, prostitutes, Newton's special deputies, A.T. & S.F. officials including Redfield and Lakin,

bullwhackers, muleskinners, the hunter who provided the Newton House with fresh meat—which she took as a wonderful com-
pliment—barbers, the seamstress, store clerks, attorneys, the
hatmaker, Doctor Boyd and his wife, and even that dentist, Page
Everhart.

By the time she locked the front door, the west wall was rattling from the raucous dancing and louder trombone, fiddle,
piano, tuba, and drum at Tuttle's place. So far, no gunfire, but the
clock on the wall said it was only 9:33.

After blowing out the last lantern, she stepped outside, closed
the back door, and locked it. Only when she turned around and
saw her tent did she remember her intruder. She stormed to the
canvas, untied the knot, pushed the canvas open, stepped inside,
and struck a match to light a candle on her folding table.

Valise, suitcase, and hatbox remained undisturbed. She picked
up the valise. She'd toss it into the alley first, but then came the
sounds of the grunts and chortles from one of her neighbor's
tents. The night was just getting started. That reminded her to
find her carpenters and demand they finish her upstairs rooms
before this alley drove her insane.

The grunting stopped, followed by the woman's haggard
voice: "There, there, sugar. That was fine. Jus' fine. Why don't
you pull up your britches and go dance some more 'cause Mama's
gots more entertainin' to do."

Moments later, spurs chimed down the alley; the woman
coughed, cursed, and unstoppered a jug or bottle.

Denise fell into her chair. She felt like asking the prostitute for
a slug of whatever she was drinking. Bourbon. Taos Lightning.
Laudanum. Strychnine. Anything sounded good.

The hooker left, probably heading back to Tuttle's or Krum's
to find another cowboy with a dollar to spend or a wad of paper
money she could steal. Denise untied the ribbon in her hair, saw
the luggage again, and rose, grabbed the suitcase this time, and
dragged it out of the tent.

She hadn't let go of the handle when the hand grasped her shoulder. Before she could scream, she felt herself hurtled against the wall of her restaurant. Her head cracked against the pine.

"I like redheads," a voice slurred.

Her eyes opened, tried to focus. She smelled the whiskey on a man's rancid breath, then felt his rough whiskers on her cheeks.

"Me, too," he said.

Two men.

"Listen," the rotten-breathed one said, "Me and Milt gots two dollars. So let's get to it."

"Wait," she started, only to be flung from the wall into Milt's arms.

Having vomited over his woolen shirt and vest, he smelled worse than the first man. He pushed her back for a better view in the moonlight, and glow from back windows. Milt held her at arm's length.

"I like redheads," he said with a gap-toothed smile.

Milt's pard walked toward her, wiping his big mustache with his shirtsleeve.

"Let go of her," a voice cracked. It sounded like a woman. Maybe the prostitute was coming back.

Milt relaxed his hold, and that was all Denise needed. She kicked him hard in the groin, doubling him over, before he dropped to his knees and threw up again, this time on the trash in the alley.

Something flashed past Denise. Glass crashed behind her. Denise caught her breath, measured the distance, and when Milt raised his head, she kicked him underneath the jaw. He fell backward, rolled over, and began crawling back toward Main Street.

"Lemme— *Owwwwwwwwww.*"

Turning to the voice, Denise made out a brunette woman in a calico dress striking the second drunk over the head with both hands. The cowboy fell toward Tuttle's building, came up, and crawled on hands and knees, a pencil sticking through his cheek and into his mouth. The woman kicked him in his butt, and he fell down, rolled over, came up. The next kick missed, and the woman lost her balance, fell onto her backside. The cowboy pulled himself to his feet. Without looking back, he raced after his pard.

Denise found an empty tin can and hurled it after him.

Catching her breath, trying to steady her heartbeat, she looked at the woman, staggered over, and lowered both hands.

"Here," she rasped. The brunette grabbed hold, and Denise managed to pull her to her feet.

Recognition dawned in the dim light.

"You," they said simultaneously.

"Beeber," the newspaper woman said. "Of course."

"What are you . . . ?" Denise stepped back and looked at the suitcase in the alley. So did Cindy Bagwell.

"That railroad agent, Redfield, he said I was to room with you," Cindy said. "He—"

"Jackass" cut off Cindy's sentence.

They looked at each other again.

"I'm sorry," Cindy said. "He told me . . ."

Denise held up her hand. "It's all right. Come on in. We'll talk about it . . ." She sighed. The prostitute was coming back down the alley, her right arm pulling a stumbling cowboy alongside her.

"Get your stuff," Denise ordered, grabbed the suitcase, and dragged it toward the rear door to her café. "We're moving inside. Upstairs isn't finished yet, but it's safer."

Grunting and snorting, echoed by coughing, came from the neighboring tent.

Cindy found her valise and hatbox and hurried to the rear door. "I hope it's quieter, too," she said.

Chapter 24

The famous "herders" form a marked feature of
Newton society. Their long hair, their huge revolvers,
their big spurs, their slouch hats and their bow legs
are everywhere visible.
—(Topeka) *Kansas State Record*,
July 27, 1871

June 19, 1871
Bagwell:
You won't hear this from me often, bully for you. That is
the kind of news I want you reporting constantly from
Newton. Send me more blood and thunder. Give me a story
about the dead man's funeral. Need it quickly. Will run it
below your bloody shootout prose. Keep it under 200 words.
R.M. Knott
Editor, The Wichita Herald

June 20, 1871
Dear Mr. Knott:
Address all future correspondence to me c/o Denise's
Café, Second St., Newton. I have a room upstairs. Here is
my account of the Texan's funeral.

THE FUNERAL OF A COWBOY NAMED WELCH
The graveyard at Newton in Northern Sedgwick County
is growing. On Saturday last, a cowboy named Welch, killed
by two bullets fired by another Texas cowboy named
Snyder in front of a saloon on Main Street, was buried next
to the grave of a man whose name on the wooden marker
reads simply Yes'm and this year.

Welch's marker was just a rock. No hymns were sung. No
verses read. Gravediggers dropped Welch in the hole,
passed a bottle around, then covered his corpse. His assassin has been arrested by Newton's police force and is being
transported to Wichita. He might have gone unpunished
except for the final shot he put into the gravely wounded
man's chest while he lay on the dusty streets.

The cemetery rests east of town on a slope leading to
Slate Creek, now includes one prostitute who took poison
in May, two railroad men who were hit by a train five miles
from the end-of-track and a carpenter whose head was
bashed in by his own hammer.

No flowers rest on any grave.

Sincerely,
Cindy Bagwell

June 21, 1871
Dear Mr. Knott:
Here are some news briefs for your consideration:
NEW STAGE LINE
A Mr. Risor says the Southwestern Stage Company plans
to run coaches from Florence to Wichita by way of Newton.
RAILROAD LAND SALES
D.L. Lakin, Atchison, Topeka & Santa Fe Railroad's
land agent, passed through Newton today and says that land
owned by the railroad between Florence and Newton are
still selling fast. More than $85,000 worth since the land was
opened to purchase June 1.

BOXING OUT TRAFFIC

Traffic was blocked between 1ˢᵗ and 2ⁿᵈ streets in Newton Sunday when two railroad graders got into a brawl in the middle of the street. The fight lasted, says the A.T.&S.F.'s Mr. Redfield, 42 rounds, ending in a "draw" when the tiny grader named Brackeen broke his right hand. "Just like how Sayers, the 'Little Wonder,' hurt his arm in that fight with our good American Heenan back in '60."
Sincerely,
Cindy Bagwell

June 21, 1871
Dear Mr. Knott:

This news came to me after I had mailed my other letter dated today. I'll need your help with this.

Snyder, the Texas cowboy who shot down Welch on Main Street last week, was arrested by what passes as a police force here in town. Two deputies took him to Wichita yesterday, but returned today without the murderer. When Judge Muse asked what had become of their prisoner, one of the men—I do not yet have his or his fellow deputy's name—said Snyder tried to escape and they shot him dead. The deputies returned with his horse, saddle, etcetera, as well as his pistol belt, the foul weapon he had used to murder Mr. Welch, and a horsehair lariat. Can you ask the Sheriff if he plans to investigate or get a warrant for these two men's arrest? It reeks of foulness to me.
Sincerely,
Cindy Bagwell

June 25, 1871
Bagwell:

Regarding:

1. *New Stage Line:* The *Vidette* reported that earlier this month. Don't you read the newspapers?

2. *Railroad land:* Who gives a fig?

3. *Boxing:* Criminy. If I want a story about a fistfight, I can go to any dram shop in Delano any night of the week. Don't waste postage on fistfights. I want death, murder, blood, mayhem.

4. *Snyder:* I sent McNelly to ask the sheriff about that. McNelly said Walker told him that whoever is running Newton's vigilance committee ought to buy those two "deputies" each a cigar.

June 24, 1871

Dear Mr. Knott:

More violence here. For your consideration:

DEATH IN NEWTON

A man named Thomas Irvin rode in off the trail to Newton and entered Jack Johnstone's Parlor Saloon where, after a whiskey, he moved into the gambling area of the Saloon. Moments later a gunshot was fired from the bar. The bullet penetrated the partition that separates the gambling parlor from the drinking establishment and struck Mr. Irvin, who died within moments.

Saloonkeeper Johnstone admitted to firing the fatal shot, but claims it was accidental. Poor Irvin was merely sitting on a bench and watching the gamblers at the faro layout when Death struck him without warning or, apparently, ill motive.

A gambler named Modory said that Irvin was a man of mysteriousness. "I cannot say he was of bad character or intended bad business." A dancing girl from Tuttle's place said Irvin told her he hailed from Baltimore. Johnstone said Irvin was most likely a saddle tramp.

Saloonkeeper Johnstone came here from Emporia, where he also ran a saloon.

Sincerely,

Cindy Bagwell

* * *

June 26, 1871
Dear Mr. Knott:

The Wichita Herald of June 22 arrived by stagecoach today, and I saw my article about the fatal gunfight.

Do you mind telling me where you heard that Snyder received a grievous wound during the gun battle on Main Street that occurred here? Snyder was not harmed in the least.

I did think my Welch funeral story read well.

Sincerely,

Cindy Bagwell

P.S. I have learned the name of one of the "deputies" that killed Snyder. He is known here as Mike McCluskie, but some say his real name is Delaney, though that may be an alias, too.

June 28, 1871
Bagwell:

Just mail me the news. And remember that I am the editor and editors edit. And if you don't like your job, maybe Newton will have a newspaper one day.

Now, your DEATH IN NEWTON story—that's what I want. And I promise not to add too much blood and exaggerations to your account.

Remember: Blood, death, carnage, heartbreak, tragedy. That's what we need. But mostly, blood and death.

Knott

June 28, 1871
Knott:

How is this?

TEXAS DESPERADO SHOOTS UP "MAISON DE JOIE"

Perry Tuttle has moved his various enterprises, including

a "dance hall" from Topeka, but last night Tuttle danced his way out of his Newton dancing house after a rowdy bunch of Texans decided to pepper the evening with gunfire.

Tuttle fled through the back door and returned this morning to find his walls, floors, bar, back bar and windows well ventilated.

The leader of the festivities, Tuttle claims, was none other than John Wesley Hardin, the notorious Texas gun man and murderer. Hardin, it is believed, also murdered a Mexican in some dispute on a trail drive between the Newton prairie and Abilene.

Tuttle had his girls plaster the bullet holes this afternoon and hopes to be back in business tonight.

Cindy

P.S. Imagine what this town will be like when the railroad finally gets here.

June 30, 1871

Bagwell:

That's what I want. Give me more of this. But forget the French. You live in America. McBride and I had to go to a dance hall in Delano to find out what "maison de joie" means.

Knott

Chapter 25

A letter to the *Emporia News* from Park City, on the
Arkansas, dated May 5th, chronicles the arrival there
on the 4th of 4,500 Texas cattle en route to
Brookville, on the Kansas Pacific Railway. It adds that
Major H. Shanklin, of Lawrence, was there en route
from Texas, and that the Major estimated the number
of Texas cattle that would pass over the trail to the
Kansas Pacific, this year, at two hundred thousand.
—(Lawrence) *Western Home Journal,*
May 18, 1871

"You're breaking your own rules," Moises Dunn told Gary,
who handed the reins to Carlos and limped toward the
chuckwagon.

"So are you." Gary took the cup of coffee the cook had poured
him. "You always tell me to get my own coffee if I'm thirsty."

Waving off the comparison, Dunn said, "Cross a river when
you reach it, the Major always says, if it can be crossed—'cause
come mornin', it might—"

Gary gave Dunn what the Major always called *Hardee's unsmiling grin.* "The Major ain't here," Gary told him.

Their eyes met, but Gary looked down first, staring at the
tin cup.

"Want some grub?" Dunn asked.

His head shook. "What I want," Gary said, "is a beer stein filled with Old Overholt."

"Can't help you with that." Dunn hooked his thumb vaguely behind him. "There's a jug of what some folks might call whiskey hidden under some flour sacks. That's what I save for what we call medicinal purposes, and, as you already know, that ain't nothin' you wants to drink it unless you're sicker than a dyin' dog. But . . ."

"I don't want any whiskey." Gary sipped the coffee and sighed. Years back, even before he started prohibiting, as much as he could, whiskey on a trail drive, he made that rule for himself: Never taste that first sip of whiskey, preferably rye, until the drive is finished. "I just want this drive to be done."

"Boss . . ." Dunn turned back for the Studebaker. "We ain't even out of Texas."

Groaning, Gary found an uprooted scrub oak, sat on the trunk, stretched out his legs, and stared at his boots. Waiting for the river's depth to drop to something manageable had helped his feet heal, helped horses, cattle, and men, even though his cowhands had spent hours separating cattle, tallying losses, and collapsing onto bedrolls at the end of each lingering day.

His feet had been doctored with whatever salve Dunn had concocted, and Gary now wore two pairs of socks—his last pair and thick woolens he bought off Shanghai Pierce's ramrod. Getting his boots on and off proved challenging, but Gary could walk better now, and ride. He rode a lot.

The last of the herds ahead of Gary's had crossed that afternoon, and although enough daylight remained to push what was left of his two thousand head—nineteen hundred and eighteen, according to Hunter Clarke's last tally—across, and maybe even Hugh Anderson's thousand and thirty, but Gary gave the order that both herds would swim the Red come first light.

Two other herds camped a few miles behind Hugh Anderson's camp. There would likely be a third before dusk.

Now Dunn brought over beans and beef, squatted, and handed the plate to Gary.

"How many times must I tell you that I can get—"

"Shut up and eat. How's 'em feet holdin' out?"

"More I'm in the saddle, the quicker they heal." Gary shoveled in three spoonfuls of beans.

Leaning back on his haunches and sipping his own coffee, Dunn shook his head. *"You ain't hungry."*

He grinned. Gary scowled, but finished eating everything on the plate, mopping up gravy with one of Dunn's fine biscuits.

"You sure you don't need supplies?" Gary asked after setting the plate on the ground.

"Bought enough to get us by, even with this here respite, back in Fort Worth."

Hugh Anderson, who had refused to stock up in Fort Worth, was supposed to have taken Adam Pollock to the last supply stop on this side of the Red. Gary eased off the tree trunk to stretch out, resting his back against the uprooted tree. He tried flexing his feet, but cringed at the pain.

"Comp'ny comin'." Dunn, squatting to pick up Gary's dirty plate, nodded south toward the river. Straightening, the cook frowned. "Comin' at a gallop."

Growling, Gary peered over the downed oak. "That's Taylor," he said, and started swearing. "Fool kid lacks the brains God gave a turnip. Galloping into camp when . . ." He grabbed the trunk and pushed himself to his feet, growling at Dunn for trying to help him up.

By then, Taylor had stopped. He must have spotted the chuckwagon, for he turned his palomino and trotted that way until Gary found his hat and called out his son's name.

When Taylor stopped his horse, Gary drew in a deep breath, and waited for the news. It wasn't going to be good. Taylor's face was pale.

"Pa." His voice cracked on that one syllable.

"What's the matter?" Gary asked.

"You best come to Burlington. There's been a killing."

Gary anchored himself to the tree.

"It's Hugh . . ."

Gary sucked in a deep breath. How would he break this news to the Major? But Taylor continued.

"He shot Deke Brown, Pa. Killed him in one of the saloons. What passes for a lawman there locked him up. With the rest of those who rode in with us. And . . .

"And some riders for Mr. Steen are threatening to hang Hugh."

Listening, Gary tried to control his heartbeat, his breathing, but often the blood just thundered to his head. He didn't curse anymore, didn't even sigh, just glared as Taylor told the story. More of Gary's crew came in to eat, saw no one managing the chuckwagon, and filled cups with coffee and grabbed a biscuit or two before ambling to the confab around the uprooted tree.

That didn't help Gary's blood pressure, either.

When Taylor paused at the end of his summary, Gary asked, "How many riders did Hugh bring with him?"

Taylor stared at his dusty boots. "Well, me, Deke, Pollock, Bill, C.J., Nicky, Garrett—"

"Make it simpler," Gary barked. "Who did he leave behind to watch over *his* herd?"

"That's all. Hugh told Barlow to keep an eye on the remuda, put Jacob in charge of the steers."

Gary shook his head. "I told Hugh to take Pollock in for supplies. Just Pollock." His eyes showed untampered fury. "That's why we don't go riding into town to drink whiskey till after the drive is done." He paused for just a moment, put his hands on both hips, and added: "And you were eating chow with some pals when I gave that order."

Taylor nodded. "I know."

"But you went with him anyway."

The head bobbed again. "I did."

For a moment, all he heard was his exhales. Someone's spurs tolled, and Gary studied his own crew before eyeing Taylor again. "Take your horse over to the remuda," he said. "Have Carlos cut you out a fresh one. And tell him to saddle up my claybank. Then bring it here."

O'Hearn stepped forward. "Boss, you want me or any of the boys to ride—"

"No. I'll take care of it."

"Steen's hired hands usually are as ill-tempered as that old man," Alex Warner reminded him.

"Yeah. But not as ill-tempered as I can get."

"Bill Bailey's in Burlington," Dunn said. "He laws now and then. He could . . ."

"Bill is good when he's sober," Gary interrupted, "and if he's in Burlington, he sure ain't sober. Drunk, he's just downright contrary and mean."

He watched Evan slip between Warner and O'Hearn and take a few steps forward.

"I want to go with you and Taylor," he said.

Shaking his head, Gary tried to smile. "I appreciate the offer, Evan." It struck him that he no longer had two boys riding with him on this drive. They were men. Strong men. Taylor hadn't backed down, hadn't offered any excuses, and here was his kid brother, volunteering to ride into a mean little town spitting distance from the Red River.

"But I need you to get this herd across." He turned to Dunn. "Both herds. So start breaking camp." Gary drew his Colt, pulled the hammer to half-cock, and rotated the cylinder to check the percussion caps.

"That means you get this herd over first, leave a few boys to watch over it, then swim the river and cross it again with the boys and the cattle Hugh left behind."

After lowering the hammer, he found Conner Milone and

Hunter Clarke. "Try to get them at least a mile from the river. Depending on how much daylight you have left. And camp Hugh's outfit not too far behind. If the herds mix, let them. We can sort them out when we reach trail's end."

Now he really wanted that beer stein filled with rye.

Burlington had been an old Indian settlement way back when, the story went, and Spanish soldiers lost a battle there in the 1700s. Probably true. Gary had explored the ruins of an old fort, Wat Anderson had found an old Spanish bit in the mud there once, and Theo Justin, killed in a horse wreck in '69, once found a rusty old cannonball that he gave to a chippy in Abilene after losing his wages at the Alamo Saloon.

Old-timers still called the place San Teodoro, and many folks gave it the handle Spanish Fort, but the sign nailed to a lightning-struck oak read BURLINGTON.

It wasn't much of a town, but had grown a mite since last year. The adobe trading post, where Adam Pollock's chuckwagon was parked, had added a privy and a wooden storage shed. Two new log cabins had been erected—one of which read JAIL—and a new saloon had gone up to compete with Schrock's Cowboy Saloon and Boots's Place, not to mention a canvas tent with blue paint on the sides proclaiming FARO... KENO... ROULETTE... POKER. Gary counted only six cribs. And Luther & Carl's barber-shop and bathhouse still got plenty of business.

Gary rode to the jail; Taylor followed.

They did not dismount.

Cowhands drifted out of the saloons. Gary had expected most of them to be gathered in front of the jail, but no one stood underneath that awning. The heavy door opened, and a man in a plaid vest stepped outside. Gary tried not to sigh in relief.

"Capt'n." The slim man nodded.

"Monty," Gary said. "When did you start lawing?"

The man tugged on his reddish mustache and shook his head.

"When I figured saddle sores weren't worth thirty a month and found."

Gary tilted his head toward the open door. "You got Hugh locked up?"

"And Bailey and all the rest of your boys." He nodded at Taylor. "Except that one. He was too fast for me. Thanks for bringing him back."

"This is my son," Gary said. "Taylor, this is Monty Durant. One of Terry's Texas Rangers finest."

"Not as fine as your pa, son, or Hugh's pa."

Gary kicked his feet out of the stirrups and started moving them left and right, trying to deaden the pain from the ride. "Taylor gave me his version of what happened. You feel like telling me?"

"Whiskey."

Gary nodded. "What I figured."

"Yep. Usually leads to fisticuffs. This time, they brought out their guns."

"That happens, too."

"Yep." Durant looked past Gary. The songs of spurs and drumbeat of hooves told Gary that someone was riding from Schrock's place toward the jail. That was only fifty feet or so, but a cowman wasn't about to walk when he had a horse handy.

The rider stopped on Gary's left. Gary turned and nodded at the cattleman. "Steen," Gary said.

"Hardee. How's the wife?"

"Good. Yours?"

"Mean as a badger." He twisted in the saddle. "We been waiting for you."

Gary said, "I heard from Taylor what happened here. I'll hear your version."

After a quick glance at Taylor, Steen looked back at Gary. "I was in A.J.'s place, not that bucket of blood." He pointed at the newest saloon. "Swapping lies like normal. But everybody I talked to after we pulled some boys off the jackass the Major sired . . ." He swallowed. "Well, they all tell the same tale. This tramp named Brown was shoving the kid, cussing him vilely. They'd all been drinkin', and the peddler who runs that groggery don't cut down his whiskey enough. Guns got pulled. Shots got fired. Young Anderson wasn't hurt. Your other rider, he got killed."

"Sounds like self-defense," Gary said.

Steen nodded. "Sounds like. But some of my crew knew the deceased. Zeke Brown."

"Deke," Gary corrected.

The cattleman shrugged. "Don't matter. Won't be no name carved on the cross we put up, lessen his widow comes by to give him something the wind won't knock down."

"That won't be happening," Gary said.

"It'd be easier on Zeke's—Deke's—pards if Anderson didn't put two bullets in your waddie's back while he was on the floor."

Gary swallowed down bile, wiped his mouth, and said: "That's what the Major taught us. Wounded men can still kill you. Make sure they're dead."

He wondered how he managed to say that and not throw up. Part of it was true. But this wasn't a war. This was a senseless barroom brawl between drunks.

"We was fighting bluecoats," Steen said. "Not our own." He looked down the trail. "You come alone?"

Gary tilted his head toward Taylor. "Just the two of us."

"We got you outnumbered."

"I didn't come to fight. Came here to bring Hugh back." He leaned forward and dropped his voice to a whisper, looking at the lawman and the drover as he spoke.

"Deke Brown's been hounding Hugh since before we started this drive. He didn't fight in the war. Too young. And he wouldn't have lasted two weeks under the Major. Would've been shot by firing squad, most likely. What you've been telling me, what Taylor told me, what I reckon every one of my men you've locked up will tell me, is a case of self-defense in Texas. Let Hugh out, Steen." Sure, a Texas jury might have ruled self-defense, or justifiable homicide, especially in a place like Burlington. Gary turned to Durant. "Let him out, Monty. Let all my men out. We'll ride back, be in the Nations by morning. You want to draw this out, I can't stop you. I'll just send a telegram to Richmond. I've got three thousand steers to get to market. So you'll be dealing with the Major." He straightened in the saddle. "It's your call."

No words were spoken, until Durant turned back to Gary, swallowed, and said, "There's got to be a fine. And pay for the burying."

Gary nodded. "That's fair."

Steen cleared his throat. "But you'll have to whip the kid."

Shaking his head, Gary hooked a thumb back at the saloons. "Not in front of them. You wouldn't do it, either. Don't get me wrong. I don't rightly care much for Hugh myself, but I wouldn't shame any man that way, no matter how wrong he is. But I'll handle it. My way." Lawman and cattleman eyed each other again. This time, Steen turned first and nodded. "Sixty dollars," he said. "For court costs and burying. That's for all your men. Disturbing the peace." He nodded at Taylor. "Including your boy."

Sixty dollars. Gary reached behind him to unfasten a saddlebag. *A cheap fine—for manslaughter, if not murder.*

Chapter 26

The distance from Red river, the north line of Texas, to Newton, is three hundred and fifty miles, and the drive is made in thirty days. The estimated cost of driving is from $1 to $3 per head. Each drove requires two men to the hundred and two horses to each man. The average wages to the drivers is about $50 to the man. The losses sustained during the drives are from five to ten per cent, and they are occasioned from death, lameness and stampeding.
—*The Manhattan Homestead,*
October 1871

Once out of Burlington, they swam their horses across the river, and no one spoke as Gary led Hugh Anderson's crew east. The only human sounds were groaning and retching.

One mile into the Indian Territory, Gary, Taylor, and Pollock loaded Nicky Witt and C.J. Merrifield into the back of the cook's chuckwagon and tied their horses behind.

Because of the stampede, and Shanghai Pierce's orders, Gary's herds had crossed farther west than usual, and the sun was already starting to sink. At least the skies remained clear. But it would be dark by the time they found the camps. Providing nothing had stopped the cowboys from fording the Red.

Gary had hardly spoken since leaving Burlington, and silenced Hugh Anderson with a stare. Bill Bailey opened his mouth once, but quickly closed it. Taylor, riding alongside Gary, focused on the trail ahead.

Finally, Gary broke the silence.

"You learn anything?" He did not look at his son.

They covered twenty yards before Taylor found an answer.

"Reckon I know why you don't let anyone go to town till the railhead."

After thirty more yards, Gary nodded. "That's something."

Behind them, someone vomited again.

"How much did you drink?" Gary asked.

"Two beers."

"How'd you get out of town when no one else could?"

"Everybody else had a lot more than two beers."

A quick grin creased Gary's face.

"Pa?"

"Yeah?"

"I thought they were really going to hang Hugh."

The smile vanished. Gary stared ahead at the pink, orange, lavender, purple, and blue sky. He didn't see sunsets like that much back home. Or maybe he just never paid too much attention to those kinds of things.

After a sigh, Gary made up an excuse. "It's easy to talk about lynching a man. Lot harder to go through with it. Hanging's a nasty affair. So's putting two balls into a man's back when he's lying on a saloon's floor."

Taylor focused on the sunset. They did not speak until Taylor spotted the flickering light of a campfire.

Evan's spurs sang after he left his supper and ran toward his brother and grinned widely.

"They didn't hang you, I see."

Taylor said, "That's right."

"Too bad." Evan laughed.

Gary slid out of his saddle, and Carlos walked over to take the reins. "Where's the other camp?" Gary asked Evan.

Evan pointed south. "Maybe a mile. Conner, Dozier, Rosario, and Casey are with them. Along with Hugh's bunch that got left behind." He looked back at his brother, still in the saddle. "Did you bust them out, Pa?"

Adam Pollock called to Moises Dunn: "My crew? You feed 'em?"

"Yep." Dunn walked to the coffeepot.

"Appreciate it." Hugh Anderson's cook looked from Dunn to Gary. "If it's all right with you, Boss, I'll take this wagon and—" Shaking his head, he thumbed toward the back of the wagon, "those sleepin' whiskey vats to my camp."

Gary nodded. "Rest of you riding with that herd . . ." He stared at Bailey. ". . . get back to your camp." Turning around, he looked up at Hugh. "We move north at daybreak. You wait an hour or two. Then follow our dust. I'll check in on you before you leave."

"I don't need a babysitter, Hardee." The Major's son rode south.

Taylor nudged his horse forward, but stopped briefly at Gary's side. His mouth opened, but quickly closed. He turned to nod at Evan before disappearing into the dark. Other riders followed in single file. No one spoke, and Dunn asked no questions when he dished out supper.

Days never changed. Horses carried men. Wind carried dust. Two herds pushed north. Gary sent Casey Steer to Hugh's crew. He thought about picking Evan, but Evan was too good a cowhand. Steer was green, but he could ride drag, and Hugh had lost, killed by his own hand, Deke Brown. Granted, Gary had a larger herd, and could have used an extra drag rider, but Hugh Anderson needed every bit of help he could get.

Maybe Gary would pick up a trail hand to cover the last legs of the drive. Already he had met cowboys riding south, broke after blowing their wages at Abilene, Great Bend, Solomon, Brookville. None from Newton, though. Maybe the Atchison, Topeka, & Santa Fe changed its mind.

A tribal elder asked for ten steers to pass through Chickasaw country, which Gary negotiated down to five. He had Jimmy Batten cut out the steers, and Batten did a fine job. Since the cattle had not been separated since the stampede south of the Red, Batten gave the Indians two steers wearing Hardee's road brand and three burned with Hugh Anderson's iron.

Gary's feet hurt. His legs and back felt all four hundred and fifty miles he had ridden. No, as much as he had traveled from his camp to Hugh's and back again, he probably had covered a hundred and fifty more miles. He was thirty-nine years old. Felt like sixty. Cowboying was a young man's game. And trail bossing was a job only fools took on.

Before dawn the next morning, both herds stampeded again.

Bill Bailey couldn't blame that one on Hugh Anderson. The skies had been clear when Gary turned in, but the thunderhead swept in fast. One close strike of lightning headed straight down to earth—Gary's ma always called that *sharp lightnin'*—followed by a cannonade of thunder, and Hugh's herd bolted north, and when those cattle came within earshot, Gary's two thousand joined the ruction.

The storm moved fast. With dawn breaking, Gary could see the lightning, still sharp, and the clouds finally started dumping rain onto the Indian Nations. Downstream.

They stopped cattle and horses four miles from camp. Well, the Washita River had stopped them.

Gary found Miguel Sanchez, one of Hugh's top hands, humming some Spanish song while riding in nothing more than his long-handle underwear and porkpie hat.

For a moment, Gary considered telling Miguel that's why you slept with your duds on, and your boots handy. But he and many others had stripped down the night of that first stampede, though soaking wet clothes was a pretty good excuse. Pointing at the rider's filthy socks, Gary said, "You need to find your boots. Trust me."

The young man smiled. *"Es cierto, patrón."*

Garrett McMahon and Conner Milone rode up and reined in. McMahon took off his hat and wiped his forehead. "I think we're jinxed," he said.

Milone's boots were on the wrong feet. McMahon wore neither gun belt nor that patched vest that wasn't fit to be used as a dish rag.

"Patrón . . ." Sanchez had not lost his smile. "If we had this . . . *gafancia . . . los novillos* would have torn up our camp."

"I saw Evan, Boss." Milone pointed southwest. "Horse was lathered, but he was in one piece. Doin' his job." He grinned. "You taught him right."

Gary gave a quick nod and looked at the river, but he felt like kissing his point man for letting him know one of his sons had survived another stampede. He studied the river.

Here at Rock Crossing, the Washita was deep, but generally easy to cross, and the rain kept falling downstream. Chances of the river rising, Gary figured, were small. The graze looked good, the north part of the river had a rocky bottom—hence Rock Crossing—and while the chuckwagons had to be ferried, drovers knew to leave in plain view the logs they strapped to the wagons to float across the Washita. A herdsman couldn't ask for a better place for a stampede to end.

"We'll sort the herds on this side," he said as he turned back toward the cowhands. "Same as before. Just get close to a thousand for Hugh, and the rest belong to us. Don't worry about brands." He nodded at Sanchez. "Go find your boots. Then tell me how many horses and cattle we've lost." He found Milone. "Make sure nobody got bad hurt."

He turned to McMahon. "Get Dunn to put his chuckwagon downstream. Tell Pollock to set up camp upstream. At least we got spared more rain here."

Another rider came into view, riding hard enough after a stampede, and he didn't stop until he reached the parley. It was Astudillo, one of Hugh's drag riders.

"Señor Hardee." His face paled.

"You were night herding," Gary said. That much was obvious. Astudillo was fully dressed.

"Sí. With Casey and your son."

Gary gripped the saddle horn with both hands.

"Lightning. It came quick. Close. A bright light. Near the herd. Big boom. The cattle ran. I rode with them." He swallowed again, drew in a deep breath, and let it out slowly. "Señor, I have not seen Casey or Taylor since."

Southward he rode, alone, trying to keep a mental count on the dead horses from the remuda and cattle he saw. Trying. Not succeeding. At some point, he gave up. He stopped at his camp, where Moises Dunn was packing up the chuckwagon, and told the cook where to make camp. He did not mention Taylor or Casey Steer.

A mile later, Evan rode in at a lope, pulling a dun horse behind him.

The boy reined up hard, his dirty cheeks quartered by the flow of tears.

"I found Taylor's horse, Pa," Evan blurted out. He tried to catch his breath. "Hugh . . . Hugh . . . Hugh said . . . said Taylor . . . nighthawking."

"Yeah." Hardee held out his left hand. "Give me the reins. You get back—"

"No, sir." The fist clenched tighter on the reins to the dun. "No, sir. I'm coming with you. Fire me if you want, but I'm coming with you."

Gary stared hard, breathed out, and nodded. "All right. Let's go."

They rode together, the lathered, dirty dun clopping behind them, saddle leaning toward the left.

Evan sniffled. "Fool brother. I told him . . . I told him . . . same as you. Don't ride a light-colored horse at night. It attracts lightning."

How many times had Gary heard that wives' tale? Hurricane Grady had been fried by lightning two days from New Iberia in '58, and he'd mounted on a gelding blacker than six feet down during a new moon. But Gary said nothing.

They spotted Adam Pollock's chuckwagon at the same time, kicked their horses into a lope, and reined in. The wagon pulled no horses behind him, and the cook stopped and waited.

Evan asked first: "You seen my brother? Or Casey Steer?"

The cook's head shook. His eyes focused on Taylor's horse.

Evan started to ask another question, but Gary spoke first. "Herd stopped at the Washita. Set up camp upstream. We'll split the herd, cross the river."

Pollock nodded somberly. He pointed southwest. "Cattle was bedded mile or two thataway." He did not have to say that if Taylor's horse had thrown him at the start of the stampede, and he had survived, he would have walked back to camp. Same with young Casey Steer.

The cook urged his team on, and Gary rode south with his son.

Evan saw Taylor first. Just squatting.

"Thank God." He breathed out, and spurred his horse across the earth plowed by cattle hooves. Slowly, Gary followed, whispering his own thanks to the Creator.

"You hurt?" he heard Evan cry out, his voice creaking. "Why're you just sittin' here? Where's Casey? Where's . . . ?" He stiffened in the saddle and slid off his gelding, took a few steps to the east, and stopped. His head bowed.

Gary rode in slowly, and Taylor raised his head. Dried blood covered the beard stubble over his upper lips, but Gary didn't think the nose was broken. Taylor's forehead was skinned.

"Pa." He spoke in a whisper.

Gary looked over Evan's shoulder and sighed.

"Lightning, Pa," Taylor whispered. He tried to swallow, but couldn't. Gary found his canteen and tossed it to his son. Taylor took a long pull. "Came out of nowhere."

"Yeah."

Evan dropped the reins to both horses and walked to the body. Gary started to call out for the boy to stop, but no, that wouldn't do any good. He waited for Taylor to drink more water.

"Not too much," Gary warned him. Taylor listened.

Now Evan sank to his knees, and bowed his head over the corpse of his saddle pal, his friend, the kid with the funny name. Casey Steer.

"Horse throw you?" Gary asked Taylor.

His son nodded. He took one more swallow from the canteen and looked back up at Gary. "I . . . I just couldn't leave . . . him, Pa."

"You did right." Coyotes, ravens, and wolves did not deserve Casey Steer. Gary pushed his horse to the two geldings, swung down, and walked to his younger son, putting his hands on Evan's shoulders.

"I told him . . ." Evan sniffled. "I told him . . ."

The horse was brown. Or had been.

"No one saw this storm coming," Gary whispered. "He was a good man, your pard. One to ride the river with."

A good man. A good horse. And one quick bolt of lightning. Must have caught one of Casey's spurs. Maybe the horse's bit. Neither rider nor animal probably knew what hit them.

"Why don't you take your brother to Pollock's—"

"I'll stay, Pa." Evan pushed himself to his feet and, drawing his revolver, looked at the waiting coyotes. "He was my pard."

"All right, Evan. I'll picket your horse. And take Taylor with me."

He led his horse to Evan's, found a rock heavy enough to tie his son's reins around, and led his horse and the dun back to Taylor.

He had two good men for sons. And right then he hoped both of them would be smart enough not to pick cowboying for their life's profession.

On a knoll just across the Washita, Moises Dunn and Adam Pollock dug the grave. It was farther from Texas, but Gary found it proper—crossing the river, proverbial yet real, to bury a fine lad like Casey Steer.

Taylor and Evan held Steer's uncoiled lariat, and Gary and Bill Bailey used Gary's as they lowered the body, wrapped in the dead cowboy's bedroll, into the grave. Once Taylor and Bailey dropped their lariats, Evan and Gary started pulling the ropes out of the grave, recoiling them hands over elbows.

Hugh Anderson had not gathered around the grave, but stood behind Pollock's chuckwagon. Now, as Gary gathered his lariat, Major Wat Anderson's son strode up the small hill, stopping at the head of the grave.

"I heard what you did, Hardee," he said.

Silently, Gary looped another coil.

"You give digger injuns three of my cattle."

"We'll speak of this later." Gary kept gathering the lariat, methodically, eyes focused on a bedroll that had become a shroud.

"I'm speaking now. You ain't cheating me."

Hugh stood three feet away, but Gary smelled whiskey on the boy's breath.

"We haven't even quoted a psalm or sung a hymn." Gary spoke in barely a whisper.

In all his years, all those previous drives, Gary had buried, or watched buried, three men. On this drive, he had already lost two. Well, he hadn't shot Deke Brown dead, but . . .

"You won't roughshod me no more. You won't cheat—"

Crying out in pain, turning a sidestep, then toppling to the ground, Hugh hit the ground and rolled away from the grave. When Hugh came up to his knees, one cheek had been laid open. Blood poured. Hugh reached for his holstered revolver. Then he slammed facedown on pale dirt. Rope whipped his back. He yelped like a kicked puppy, rose on his knees, tried to bring his gun up. Braided rawhide slammed against the hand and the Colt. The pistol spiraled into sand. Hugh cried again, rolled over, clawed for that .44. But Gary raked a spur's rowel over Hugh's right arm.

Another shriek. Once Hugh's head lifted, a rope pummeled him to the ground.

The lariat dropped over the abandoned revolver. Hugh suddenly rose up, mere inches from Gary's face, and only then did Gary understand.

He had beaten the Major's son with the lariat. Had intentionally cut the boy's arm with a spur. And now Gary's thumbs pressed deep into Hugh Anderson's throat.

"I've had enough of your mouth." Gary breathed in the scent of blood. Like a wolf. He saw how deep his lariat had cut Hugh's cheek. "You're Major Wat Anderson's son. Time you acted like that." He jerked Hugh closer. "Maybe you're not up to it. But he put you in charge of twelve hundred head of cattle. And a trail boss protects his men. Always."

"I didn't kill Casey." Saliva and blood splattered from Hugh's lips into Gary's face.

"No. That was God's doing. But you shot Deke Brown dead."

"Deke was gonna kill—"

"Facedown on the floor in some bucket of blood? You shot him twice in the back."

He flung Hugh to the ground. Spotted his lariat in the dirt. And realized he now gripped his revolver, the hammer already thumbed back.

When Hugh rolled over, Gary squatted and jammed the barrel against the boy's bloody nose.

Words echoed in ears:

I don't rightly care much for Hugh myself, but I wouldn't shame any man that way, no matter how wrong he is. But I'll handle it. My way.

Gary blinked as reason returned. He stared at that awful cut across Hugh's cheek. He had done that. To the Major's son. This wasn't Gary's way. This wasn't a beating anyone deserved.

"Bill." The name sounded like it had been spoken in a tunnel. "Take over the Major's herd. Moises, Hugh'll need stitches. Bill, you're down two men. Need some of mine?"

"We'll manage."

Gary might have nodded.

"My pa'll fire . . ." Hugh whined.

"Grow up," Gary whispered.

He might be wrong in how savagely he had whipped Hugh Anderson, but Gary could not back down. He wouldn't apologize. Not yet.

"Your pa might fire me. That's his right. But till he does, I'm boss. Of both herds. A trail boss protects his men. Even when they're dead. But you *won't* act like a cur while we're burying Casey Steer. So shut up. Or I'll dig a third grave."

When he released his hold, Hugh dropped to the ground. Gary's right hand still held the Army .44. He couldn't recall even drawing it, but it slid into his holster. Once he turned away and stepped back toward the grave, a voice bellowed:

Rock of ages, cleft for me,
Let me hide myself in thee.

Only later did Gary realize he led the hymn.

Afterward, he took Dunn's shovel, but Evan reached over and grabbed it.

Their eyes met.

"I'll cover him," Evan whispered. "And put up that marker." Evan tugged the shovel's handle. "You got two herds to get across this river, Pa. Soon as I'm done here, I'll come help."

After Gary blinked, his younger son held the shovel.

Turning without another word, Gary walked down the knoll. With the exception of Evan, the rest of the hands, even Hugh Anderson, helped by the two cooks, followed.

Chapter 27

The first train with cattle left Newton this morning
on the Atchison, Topeka & Santa Fe Railroad. It is
said that there are 50,000 head there waiting
shipment. The road runs a special cattle train
every morning making close connections with
trains for the East.
—*Kansas State Record,*
July 13, 1871

"I do not think this is how they celebrated the joining of the
Union and Central Pacific railroads at Promontory, Utah,
back in '69."

Denise laughed and turned to see A.F. Horner shaking his
head.

They stood in front of Horner's store on Main Street, the closest building, except for A.T. & S.F. structures to the railroad
tracks.

No. Denise corrected herself. The closest building was the saloon on the other side of the street. Of course. After all, this was
Newton.

Since it had rained that night, some of Newton's finest had
laid a wooden path diagonally from the tracks to the awning over
the saloon. Something resembling a boardwalk also ran at a

straight line from the tracks to Horner's store, but railroaders must have traipsed over that path so often, it was coated with mud and muck.

Or, more likely, the owner of the saloon had paid some of his customers in free drinks to shovel slop over those rough boards.

The locomotive belched thick black smoke, steam hissed, and the band from Perry Tuttle's Dance House blasted as loud as possible. No one could tell what song the band played, and the tuba player was missing after getting his lips busted and three teeth knocked out by one of Tuttle's dancers early this morning—and he had been the band's best musician.

Three men walked toward the heaving locomotive and took the path to the saloon, but Judge Muse led a party of four men and two women, each twirling parasols, toward the welcoming committee at the side of Horner's wooden building.

Muse raised his right hand to stop the first passengers to arrive at Newton via train, and turned around. He started speaking, but the band started up again, a few cowboys began firing pistol shots in the air, and one of the prostitutes lifted her blouse all the way to her neck and shoulders and laughed.

"Yeah," Horner said. "That didn't happen when they hammered in that golden spike in Utah."

"Mr. Horner," the judge was saying, "allow me to introduce you to Paul Cohen."

A pockmarked, bald man in a sack suit nodded.

"Mr. Cohen is here to open a sister store to Topeka's F. Johnson and Son Company."

Horner's smile and handshake, Denise noted, did not seem genuine. That was the third such store to open, following Pioneer Store, owned and operated by Peter Luhn, and Horner's sprawling enterprise.

"Cheapskate," Horner whispered. "Caters to the paupers."

Denise forgot the other introductions almost immediately, but she did smile and nod her thanks when the judge mentioned her place along with the Newton House.

That was pretty much all there was to the celebration of the arrival of the first passenger train. Mr. Redfield shook hands and chatted briefly with the new arrivals, the railroad crew uncoupled the passenger cars and caboose, and the engine and tender chugged down to the stockyards.

"Where's Miss Bagwell?" Redfield asked.

After quickly answering, "She's around," Denise looked at the locomotive and told herself to remember that it was a Taunton 4-4-0. Seven men, two women. Plus the railroad dignitaries. American flags. The band. And Judge Muse's proclamation that Newton, Kansas, celebrated Independence Day twice this month in the Year of Our Lord 18 and 71, on the Fourth of July and today, July 17, with arrival of the first passenger train. And that there would be a third celebration soon, when the first cattle cars are sent eastward thanks to the Atchison, Topeka, and Santa Fe Railroad, the citizens of Newton, Kansas, and the brave Texas trail drivers.

No need for fireworks after that speech. Texas cowhands, Newton's policemen, and some saloon owners and other citizens provided that by shooting their weapons in the air.

Denise certainly could remember that.

She would also remember two cowboys riding toward Hide Park, one of them saying to his pard, "Remember that saloon in Abilene that had the dancer with that big, live rattlesnake hanging round her neck like a shawl. Reckon Newton's got anything like her?"

She turned and walked down Main Street, crossed iron rails, bound for Hide Park. It had been a slow day at the restaurant, since all the festivities were happening north of the tracks. But tonight, she figured, would get woolly.

* * *

She sat at a table with Grover, Mattie, and Darlene and Page Everhart. The clock read 7:25, and Denise's neighboring businesses were booming tonight. Tuttle's band missed the tuba player, but no one gave a fig.

Denise, her cook, two waitresses, and the dentist sat closer to the bar, away from the street, and away from where the cowboys usually shot up the walls to Tuttle's place.

Finally, she heard the back door open, and could tell Cindy Bagwell had returned by the way her shoes tapped on the floor. And her curse when the back door didn't close all the way. Grover recognized Cindy's voice, too, and filled the empty cup with coffee.

A moment later, Cindy, hair disheveled, face flushed and caked with dirt, pushed through the curtain and into the front space, came around the counter, and stopped to take in all the empty tables.

"It's Independence Day," the dentist explained.

"That was two weeks ago," Cindy said.

"Second Independence Day," Denise explained.

She understood, pulled the pencil off its nesting place atop her left ear, and walked to the table. Dr. Everhart rose and slid the chair out for Cindy, who thanked him, and flipped to a new page and stared at Denise.

"Did you get everything I need?" Her blue eyes were pleading.

Denise took a sip of coffee and set the cup down. "The train arrived at one-oh-five in the afternoon, five minutes early. Seven men, two lady passengers."

"Ladies?" The dentist rolled his eyes.

Denise ignored him. "The train was pulled by a Taunton four-four-oh. The engineer said he could gotten here sooner, but his fireman was drunk. Again. Railroad brass on the train included Judge Muse, who declared that our fine city celebrated Independence Day twice this month in the Year of Our Lord 18 and 71, on the Fourth of July and today, July seventeen, with arrival of the first passenger train. He said the third July Fourth would be celebrated when the first cattle cars roll out eastward thanks to the Atchison, Topeka, and Santa Fe Railroad, the citizens of Newton, Kansas, and the brave Texas trail drivers. That departure is set for five-twenty, day after tomorrow."

"Where are your notes?" Cindy sounded incredulous.

"I don't need notes," Denise said.

"But how do you—"

"I don't need recipes, either," Denise said. "Except those I didn't create."

Blinking, Cindy wrote in her notebook. "Anything else?"

"A strumpet showed off her breasts."

"I can't put that in the *Herald*."

"The band was awful."

"Knott-Head would tell me that's not news."

"Then that's about it. Except only one man not associated with the railroad came to hear the judge's speech. The other three men went to the saloon."

"That . . ." Cindy started writing again. ". . . Knott-Head will love."

She closed her notebook, smiled, and sipped her coffee.

"How was your day?" the dentist asked.

Her face brightened as she recalled her interview with Mrs. C.B. Hildreth, who has a farm overlooking Sand Creek where the Texas herds cross. She was so sick of the cattle and horses eating everything in the garden that when a herd went through last week, she ran onto her porch and started yelling—yelling just the way the cowboys do when they're pushing cattle, but without the profane words—ran back inside, and dragged the tablecloth outside and started waving it over her head, letting the wind blow it—the tablecloth was red—and the herd stampeded.

"She laughed and laughed and laughed. And I laughed, too. Knott-Head will run that story. I'm sure of it."

She turned in her chair and stared at the shuddering walls that butted up to Tuttle's place, shook her head, and looked back at Denise.

"Do you know what time the train pulls out Wednesday? The cattle train?"

"Five-twenty," Denise replied.

Writing in her notebook, she said, "Well, don't worry. I'll be there to get that story myself."

"Five-twenty," Denise said, "in the morning."

Cindy answered with an expletive.

Chapter 28

F.M. Lee, living two and a half miles east of town,
returned last Friday from a buffalo hunt. He says their
party went 150 miles west of Wichita and did not
even see a live buffalo. Hunters have visited that
section in large numbers and have slaughtered
hundreds of buffalo, taking the hind quarters and
leaving the remainder to decay on the plains. This has
caused unfriendly feelings on the part of the Indians
and trouble has been the result.
—*The* (Lawrence) *Daily Kansas Tribune,*
November 25, 1871

North of the Washita, Hugh Anderson's herd took the point.
Both stampedes on this drive had started with Hugh's cattle, and Gary didn't want to press his luck with a third. Well, he also thought that pushing now just more than a thousand steers, Hugh's shorthanded bunch didn't need to be swallowing the dust kicked up by Gary's herd.

"You gonna let Hugh scout for water, graze, and crossings?" Bill Bailey did not attempt to hide his sarcasm.

Gary's head shook. "I'll do that." With that swollen, stitched cheek, one eye blackened, welts on his back, and cuts and bruises over much of his body, Hugh wouldn't be doing much of anything for a week or so.

Bailey snorted. "You might want to buy extra horses for your string when we get to Sewell's Ranch—*if* we get that far. You gonna wear your horses and yourself out."

I'm already worn-out, Gary thought, but said nothing.

Hugh Anderson surprised them all.

He climbed into his saddle the next day. Didn't talk much—not with that jaw and face—and wouldn't for a few days. But he whispered the orders, studied his father's maps, and quietly told Bailey, Pollock, and his wrangler what he wanted them to do.

When Gary gave him orders, Hugh nodded quietly.

The wind blew hot. Few clouds appeared, and most of them decided against blocking the sun. Though short in miles, the trip to the South Canadian River could age many a trail hand. Gary figured they would reach the river today, so he rode that morning after having coffee for breakfast and loped for Hugh's camp. He found the cattle and remuda already moving. So much for a cup of Adam Pollock's coffee, and maybe a biscuit. Gary caught up with Bailey and Taylor on the point.

"Where's Hugh?" Gary asked.

Taylor nodded north. "Scouting ahead."

"He won't get lost," Bailey shouted from the left side. "Late as we are, the trail's easier to follow than a path to an Abilene brothel."

"He said something about fresh meat," Taylor said.

Gary frowned. You might find game—deer, antelope, or maybe just a bird or two—once you hit the Red Fork of the Arkansas, but flat as most of this country was, a body would be hard-pressed to shoot anything but a prairie dog.

"He rode thataway." Taylor pointed to a hill sprouting from the prairie.

No, Gary remembered, this country wasn't all shaped like a hotcake.

"Said something about killing a big shaggy."

Bailey chuckled. Gary rolled his eyes.

"Look at it this way," Bailey yelled. "If he runs into a Co-manch' or Kiowa, our troubles are over."

Gary found his canteen, drank some, returned it, and wiped his mouth. "River ought to be an easy crossing," he said, looking at Taylor but speaking loud enough for Bailey to hear, "so get your herd across. We'll camp ours on the south side."

"Ain't that against your rules?" Taylor grinned.

"Not today." He pointed ahead. "You'll be chopping wood, putting as much as you can in both wagons. Up ahead, wood'll be hard to come by. Unless you want to spend hours picking up cow and buffalo chips."

He pulled his hat down tight and kicked his horse into a fast walk. When he figured he had covered enough distance from the lead steers, he pulled the Winchester from the scabbard, and turned his gelding toward Red Hill.

Most of the boys would call Red Hill a mountain. Gary had viewed only illustrations of the Rocky Mountains in magazines, plus one painting—an *oil-on-canvas*, the clerk called—in a Kansas City bank, and he never really trusted a man who drew or painted pictures, but he had seen Tennessee's mountains during the War. Chickamauga. Chattanooga. No, Red Hill didn't compare to that country, but it sure stood out here, rising more than a thousand feet, Gary guessed, off the prairie.

Having lost Hugh's trail, Gary loped toward that tower of red clay and green grass. Up top, a man could see a lot of country, and he sniggered, thinking about that time years back when he went off chasing a buffalo.

Years changed. Cowboys didn't.

No one would call Red Hill steep, and it lacked the granite and thick woods of Eastern Tennessee, but climbing to the top, even on horseback, often proved challenging.

This was no mountain. The name fit. Red Hill rose, then fell. Not too steep. Gary came from the south, but most travelers crossed Red Hill while heading west, to California. Black Beaver, an old Delaware Indian and compatriot of Jesse Chisholm, had told the Major and Gary that wagons went over the hill on the California Road, or, as other folks called it, the Beale Wagon Road.

"Seems like I'd be inclined to go around it than o'er it," the Major had said.

The Delaware shook his head. Arroyos filled the low country, Black Beaver explained. Ditches, too. Wagons did not cotton to ditches. Best way to travel was by sticking to the high country. At least here, in Indian Territory.

But even wagons could have trouble.

He remembered the spring on the top of the rise. How it fed the land below, with water leaking in spots, turning clay into a bog that could sink a wagon to the axels. But Black Beaver knew those bogs, too, and the east-west road kept clear of those things.

Gary, however, was riding north today.

Stopping a ways before he crested, he turned to look south. The sky remained blue. He could see for miles, but found no dust from either of the herds. Off to the east and slightly north, he stared at another rise. That's where, Black Beaver said, wagons would camp, because they could see maybe not forever, but far enough.

Once reaching the top, Gary would be able to make out the banks of the South Canadian. Thirteen miles past that would be the North Canadian, and he'd see enough green to pick out that river, too.

"Buffalo." He snorted, and shook his head. Hugh Anderson didn't have a lick of sense. But as he sank back into the seat of his saddle, Gary had to laugh. Pond Creek, wasn't it? Shaking his head, he pictured himself.

What an idiot he had been, riding with the Major—old Wat

gave up riding with the herds after breaking two ribs and almost his neck in '68. But in 1867, someone had given him a map that would take them to Abilene, Kansas, where a railhead waited.

When the Major sent Gary to scout ahead, he found the buffalo herd. Not a big one. More importantly, he didn't spot any Indians around. A few bulls, a dozen or more cows, and some calves. That's when Gary came up with a grand idea. He'd cut out one of the bulls, a small, young one, herd him to the Major's herd. The boys would get a kick out of that. They'd be the first Texas outfit to bring a mixed herd—two thousand longhorns and one humpbacked buffalo—to the railhead.

A buffalo bull, though, especially a young one, proved a lot more agile that he figured. When the entire herd ran, he changed plans, and turned for an old bull. That got to be ticklish, too. The old shaggy lunged, Gary's buckskin took to bucking, but Gary rode that off, and kept chasing the old bull. Finally, the bull turned south. And Gary kept him going, all the way to Wat Anderson, eleven other Texas waddies, Moises Dunn, and a wrangler.

When the cattle saw the buffalo bull riding toward them, they stampeded. And, oh my, my, my, how Wat Anderson dressed Gary down till they crossed the Arkansas. But once the herd was sold, everyone regaled other drovers, cattle buyers, even Joseph McCoy himself. And everyone toasted Gary Hardee, Texas's champion buffalo herder.

Now Gary shook his head. Here he was, silently berating Hugh Anderson for trying to pull a stupid stunt when Hugh was twenty years old or thereabouts. And the Major's son had set out to hunt a buffalo, for fresh meat. Gary had tried to drive a live one back to his herd. And that had been back in '67, when Gary Hardee was thirty-five years old.

Glancing up the rise, he tapped the gelding with the Winchester he held, but let the horse pick its own path through the oozing red clay. Just before he reached the top, the gelding fought, shaking its head, snorting, but not bucking.

This high up, the wind blew, still hot, but hard, moaning like ghosts.

"Come on, boy." Gary used the spurs now, tightening his grip on the Winchester and reins. "We're almost there."

Then they were on the highest point, where the wind felt like a gale, and he couldn't hear himself think. The gelding reared. Gary bit his lower lip, tried to shove the Winchester into the scabbard, cursed the horse to stop. He just wanted to see the country. Find Hugh.

The gelding's hind legs kicked. Gary gave up on the carbine and let it fall, needing both hands. The right missed the reins, but found the horn. He gripped it with all his might. Cursed. The horse screamed, and then Gary got a glimpse of . . .

He had to be dreaming. This could not be happening. It was a buffalo. Just one. A bull with anger in its eyes as it reached Red Hill's summit from the western side.

Dream or not, Gary tried to kick free of both stirrups. The horse started to turn back. He thought he could see the bull flinging snot from its giant nostrils, lowering its head. Gary wanted to pray. Instead he cursed.

As the bull slammed into the rearing gelding.

At some point, he remembered Conner Milone talking about one of his three best horse wrecks. The one that had busted four ribs, his left collarbone, and right ankle, and gave him the scar across his right eyebrow. Milone could recall every buck, every second, striking the tree, flipping over, and crashing into the rock. It all happened, Milone said, like time stood still, where a second took a minute, maybe even longer.

Nothing moved slow for Gary. The bull's lowered head connected, just missing Gary's leg as one horn speared the gelding's side. The horse screamed. So did Gary, trying to fling himself away from the falling horse.

He hit the ground. Hard. A million pins jabbed Gary's right leg. An avalanche covered him, crushed him. Dust blinded him.

The horse, he thought. *The horse just rolled over me.* For a moment, he saw only blackness, then light.

Breathing almost killed him. A mass of brown hide raced past him. His horse screamed again. Or maybe Gary screamed.

Red dust blocked the blue sky.

Gary closed his eyes. How long would it take him to roll all the way down to the flats?

"I didn't know I was screaming till Clint Grady told me four days later," Conner Milone had said. Gary, however, knew he was screaming.

He sucked in air. Which almost killed him. Tasted blood on his lips, his tongue, felt wetness rolling down his chin, down his throat.

A face appeared.

"Jesus," Gary said. Not the way he often said it, the way that prompted Jane to scold him for taking the Lord's name in vain. He stared into the face of his Lord's son.

Jesus spoke to him.

But the voice did not belong to Jesus.

Gary's eyes closed. He did not think they would open again, at least, not on this earth.

Chapter 29

To see roughness, chaotic society and original sin, one
wants to visit a town on the plains at the temporary
terminus of a railroad, such as Newton, the present
western end of the Atchison, Topeka & Santa Fe
Railroad.
—*The* (Topeka) *Kansas Daily Commonwealth*,
August 23, 1871

"*Never run, unless they're shooting at you.*"
Remembering Liam McBride's words, Cindy slowed
to a walk, caught her breath, and found the right dance hall. It
was the one with a crowd gathered around out front. Cowboys
and merchants peered through the two windows in the front.
She'd have to fight her way through the front door. But the cowboys removed their hats and let her pass. The merchants did, too,
with some reluctance, while four prostitutes didn't have enough
muscle to block her way.

She guessed the time to be around midnight, for Hide Park
was in full glory.

The body lay on the floor, his hands pressed against a crimson
belly, head turned toward the door, bloodstains from mouth to
chin to floor, and those dark eyes looking, but not seeing.

She found a new page on her notebook. Studied the corpse
again.

"God," she whispered. "He's only a boy."

"Twenty years old," a cowboy near her said.

"A friend of yours?" Cindy asked.

He shrugged. "We rode together. For Mr. Crane. Out of Richland Springs."

"What was his name?"

"John Henry. John Henry Lee. Went by J.H. Said there was too many John Henrys in the world already."

"What happened?"

The speaker did not look older than twenty himself. He nodded at a group of cowboys still drinking at the bar. One of them patted the back of a smiling man with a waxed mustache. Another handed him a mug of beer.

"That one," the cowboy near Cindy said, "kilt J.H."

"All right," a stern voice called from behind Cindy. "Get out of my way. Let the law through."

The man looked like he had been awakened from a sound sleep. She recognized his face, but did not know his name, for Newton policemen came and quit at a ridiculous rate.

"What happened?" He pointed at the Texans surrounding the man who had apparently shot and killed J.H. Lee.

"Fool kid," said the man who had given the killer a beer, "called my pard here a nasty name, and spilt whiskey all over his shirt."

The blue-tick shirt looked dirty, wet with only blood.

The lawman turned to the cowhands near Cindy. "That right?"

None of those spoke. Maybe because there were three of them, and a dozen with the man who silently sipped his beer. Those men, Cindy observed, wore revolvers; many packed two. Only one of the three Pleasant Springs boys carried a firearm—at least that Cindy could see—and that was a pocket pistol stuck in his left boot.

Well, J.H. Lee had a revolver. Like it did him any good.

The silence stretched. The lawman swallowed, sighed, and picked out one of the bartenders.

"That the way it happened, Deger?"

"I was tapping a keg," the bartender said. "And ducked behind the bar at the first shot."

The policeman asked another bartender.

"I guess so," was the reply. "But it happened so sudden."

The lawman turned to J.H. Lee's pals. "You disagree with anything said, boys?"

None spoke.

"All right." Color started returning to the peace officer's face. "Get him out of here. Cemetery's off thataway." He pointed vaguely. "Filling up right quick these days."

He started for the door.

"That's all there is to this?" Cindy called after him. "No inquest. No—"

"Miss," the deputy said, "the first law in Heaven is order. This ain't Heaven. This is hell on earth."

"Hey, Chippy."

Her face began flushing before she stopped at the corner, and turned around to find that big brute of a railroad man waving his hat, beckoning her to cross the street. McCluskie, the louse, spent a great deal of time eating at Denise's place, and said he ate and drank free of charge because that was his right as a special policeman. Being the only woman on the street, Cindy knew Mike McCluskie was talking to her. Dance-hall girls and prostitutes rarely emerged in Hide Park before dusk.

Stopping, she turned, found the big man leaning against an awning post in front of the American House. "Did I call you Chippy?" McCluskie laughed. "I meant Cindy."

"I'm Miss Bagwell to you."

He held a cigar in his left hand, flicked ash into the dusty street, and grinned. "Remember me? I'm Mike McCluskie, but you can call me anything you want."

Her first thought was to insult his parentage, but she feared he might shoot her.

He beckoned her. "You want a story for your paper, don't you?"

She eyed him with calculation.

"It's a good one." He returned the cigar to his mouth and stepped toward the doors of the saloon, pushing one open, and waving at her again.

"Didn't you hear that gunshot?" he asked.

Which was why Cindy had took off down the street.

"I can always write me a letter to the *Trib*."

Thought Cindy: *If you could write.*

But she waited for a cowboy to gallop down the street, then crossed over. Smiling, McCluskie held the door open until she entered the saloon.

The smoke was gone, but the body lay atop the bar. Three cowboys stood off a ways, one smoking, one holding a glass of whiskey in a shaking hand, the other rotating his hat by the brim in his hands. The scent of sulfur and cordite remained strong. The bartender, a big man with massive arms, had climbed atop the bar and held the body by the shoulders. A young cowboy had flung his body over the man's legs.

Another bartender held a lantern high overhead.

A doctor—well, John Dickey, anyway, whose apothecary was on Main Street—worked feverishly behind the bar.

The body was alive. For he let out a scream that caused Cindy to take two steps back—and felt strong arms take hold of her.

"There, there, Chippy—I mean Cindy."

She jerked away from McCluskie, who laughed again.

"That be Dan Beckwith," McCluskie said. "Tends bar here."

"Who shot him?" Cindy heard herself ask.

McCluskie laughed. "Fool shot hisself."

Cindy found the notebook in her purse, took the pencil from above her ear, and started writing.

"You look peaked, gal." He pointed. "Shot of rye'll be good for you. And you'll have a good view of the show."

Pulling farther away from him, Cindy found another witness and walked to him. He looked like a cattle buyer, and he gripped the back of a chair at one of the tables a few feet from the bar. He almost knocked the chair over when she said, "Excuse me, sir."

He recovered, though, and confirmed what McCluskie said.

"He was showing those cowboys how to work that gun." He pointed at the revolver lying in front of a spittoon. "Then the gun went off."

"If that's the way Texians shoot," McCluskie called out, "my job will be easy. Shooting yourself like that. Especially in your right arm."

Cindy looked closer. Yes, it was the right arm.

One of the Texans turned, "He ain't from Texas."

The deputy laughed. "Even better. You take your shooting lessons from a feller who shoots hisself in his own shooting arm."

"Hold that lantern closer," the apothecary said. The bartender did as he was told.

Dickey turned, spit at the cuspidor, but missed, and leaned back. "One of you boys," he said, without looking at the cowhands, "fetch me a saw or a sharp knife." He sighed wearily, and turned toward the bartender. "And I'll need a bottle to disinfect."

Cindy left before the druggist began the amputation.

Denise poured Cindy a brandy when she got back upstairs. Sitting on the edge of her cot, Cindy stared at the snifter, shook her head, and whispered, "Now I know why Knott-Head and Liam McBride drink so much. Why Daddy took a nip or ten every night he got home."

She killed the brandy, set the snifter on her side table, and fell onto her pillow. But she did not close her eyes, because she didn't want to see the two prostitutes who had poisoned themselves two days ago, or J.H. Lee lying in his own blood on a sawdust-covered floor, or a bartender about to have his right arm sawed off by an apothecary at the American House. Or anything else Newton offered.

Chapter 30

The facilities afforded for the pasturing and
transportation of cattle by rail are too great in this
vicinity to be ignored by shrewd, cautious business
men, and it is just as much for the interest of Texans
to come and remain here with their herds as it is for
the people of Newton to keep them here.
—*The* (Topeka) *Kansas Daily Commonwealth,*
August 27, 1871

*Jane sits on a rocking chair. Not the Jane he left behind all those weeks
ago in Fort Bend County, but the girl he married. She wears white,
the wedding dress she always wanted but never got. The justice of the
peace married them, Gary still in trail duds he had worn on a drive to
Shreveport, Jane in a dress of pink gingham.*

*This isn't right. He didn't start herding cattle out of Texas until after
they were married. He brought cattle to the tanneries in those early days.
Did anything he could for half a dollar. Chopped cotton. Tried carpentry. Broke horses. Hauled timber. Till one morning a man came up to
him in Velasco, where Gary had just delivered a couple of stallions to
some rich cotton king's summer home, and the fellow introduced himself
as Walter Pool "Wat" Anderson, said he was driving a herd of one hundred longhorns over the Opelousas Trail to New Orleans.*

*But Gary doesn't care about history. He just wants to reach Jane. The
more he walks, the farther away she seems.*

When he runs, the porch, the swing, and Jane are almost out of sight. Out of breath, he has to stop. If he only had a horse, he would spur it hard and gallop all the way to the hitch post in front of those doorsteps. He looks for his horse, sees only bones.

Jane sighs, rises from the chair, and heads to the door. Pulls it open. Gary opens his mouth to tell her to stop, that he's coming, but she shakes her head.

"I guess I won't be getting that Grover and Baker sewing machine," she says before stepping inside and closing the door behind her.

"No."

Gary tried to sit up. He might have moved an inch before he groaned, and dropped back onto something that wasn't hard, but no one would have called it soft.

"Easy." A hand pressed against his left shoulder. "Easy."

Raising his eyelids hurt. The light blinded him, and he cringed, turned his head, tried to move his arm to cover his eyes, but the arm refused to cooperate. Even that movement made him groan.

"Easy," the voice repeated.

A wet rag found his forehead and covered his eyes. He did not know who put it there, but he would have gladly kissed his savior.

"I'm going to lift your head a bit, Gary," the voice said. "Let some water trickle from a handkerchief into your mouth. Think you can swallow some."

He croaked, and a short while later, blessedly cool water found his tongue, flowed down his throat.

His head dropped back. When the wet rag left him, he breathed in deeply, cringed, maybe even cried, and decided never to do that again.

"You busted some ribs," the voice said. "Cracked your left collar-bone, dislocated the other arm, but I think I got that back in the socket. And your right leg's busted to hell and gone."

"You ain't cutting it off." That didn't hurt at all, and he practically shouted it. Two hands forced him down.

"You keep movin' 'round like that, we won't have to saw nothin' off. 'Cause we'll be tossing you into a shallow grave."

He coughed. Regretted that.

"Where's Jane?" he asked. "I want Jane."

But Jane did not answer. "I'm gonna give you some more water. Then I want you to close your eyes and go back to sleep."

He wanted to protest, but desired water more. The cool wetness blessed him. He slept again, but this time, without dreams.

They were talking when he woke up.

"He doesn't look good."

"On account he ain't doin' good."

Someone sighed.

"He needs a doctor."

"Maybe a preacher. Good luck findin' either."

"What do you think?"

That sigh again.

"If he's lucky, we can bury him at Sewell's Ranch when we cross the Salt Fork of the Arkansas."

He climbs up Monument Hill near Stinking Creek. Laughs at Evan as he uses one of his spurs to carve his initials into a rock. His son looks up, smiles, asks, "Where's Taylor's rock?"

Pointing to a slab of red sandstone, he says, "Over there somewhere." Evan looks at his rock, holds it up, and Gary nods with approval. "That'll last longer than some cowboys'," Gary says, and stares at the two stacks of rocks. He remembers carrying some stones back in '67, marking the trail. Carving their names or initials, maybe the year, cowboys kept adding to the piles. These days, a drover could see the markers maybe ten miles away.

Now he's looking at names, letters, numbers.

"You carved your name years ago," Hurricane Grady tells him. "Gonna make a new one?"

"No." He studies Hurricane Grady, who never came up this trail. Grady got killed more than a dozen years ago. This doesn't make sense. But Gary needs to get to work. "I must find my old one. I need to add."

"Add what?" That's Jane's voice.

"This year," Gary answers. He kneels. Finds his old piece of sandstone. "The year I died."

Nothing damp covered his eyes and forehead, but he hurt all over. He knew, from a previous mistake, not to breathe in too deeply. His right leg felt like it was being sawed off, and that thought caused him to lift his head.

Not far. It fell back onto a sack of flour. He waited for the dizziness and nausea to pass.

Furloughed soldiers, Reb and Yankee, flashed through his mind. On crutches or peg legs. Or coat sleeves pinned up. Saying how a toe, finger, calf, or thigh, hand, or arm would itch, and when they reached to scratch, they found . . .

He knew he was in a wagon. The canvas cover. Chuckwagon. He could see the cabinet in the back; sacks, pails of onions, and potatoes on the right; and soogans and slickers stowed to his left. The wagon wasn't moving. He raised his right arm. Saw it. Flexed the fingers. Lowered the arm to his side and tapped just below his hip. He felt duck trousers, solid beneath, and the flash of pain from that touch caused him to suck in a deep breath. Which almost killed him.

At least, he thought, he had part of his leg. He wasn't sure about below the knee.

The wagon listed, creaked, the canvas tarp behind him opened briefly, letting in more sunlight, and a moment later, he looked into a haggard, ugly face.

"You know me?" the man asked.

"Pollock." Gary swallowed. "Adam Pollock."

The cook nodded and squatted beside him.

"You're the stubbornest son of a . . ." Sighing, Pollock shook his head. "I was ready to bury you ten times."

"You still might," Gary whispered.

"Why am I riding with you?" Gary asked Pollock.

"I might take that personal," the cook said, laughed, and finally answered.

"It was Hugh's orders."

"Hugh."

"His daddy pays all of us, don't he?"

Gary whispered a curse.

"You might hold off on that kinda talk there, Boss." Pollock stuck his finger in the bowl of Gary's soup to test the temperature. "Not for him, you'd be feeding ants and turkey buzzards atop Red Hill."

"What?"

"You need to eat," Pollock said. "So shut up. Hugh said to put you in this wagon. We're pointing the way north, and he didn't think you needed to be eating the dust ol' Dunn would be gettin'. Even though dust would probably improve his cookin'."

Gary shook his head, and regretted it.

"Hugh," he repeated. "Hugh Anderson."

"I wouldn't have bet on it myself. And had you whipped me like you done him, I'd have spit in your face, laughed, and let you rot. Now eat. You ride in *my* wagon, you do what *I* say."

He ate without much appetite. Closed his eyes. Before dozing again, heard himself saying: . . . *I wouldn't shame any man that way, no matter how wrong he is. But I'll handle it. My way.*

My way . . .

My way . . .

"Can you lift your head?"

Gary grinned. "Not to kiss you."

"You oughta. But you oughta kiss someone else first." He brought his hand down to Gary's forehead, felt it, nodded, brought it up. "No fever. That's a good sign. Can you take some soup?"

"Think so." He studied the proposition a bit more. "Not too much, though."

"Ain't Dunn's soup. You'll like mine."

Adam Pollock climbed back through the opening. The wagon rocked again like a ship in strong winds, and he heard voices, but paid little attention. He tried to recall dreams, felt the wagon lurching, and heard spurs.

Pollock wore no spurs.

His head turned sluggishly, and he saw a hideous face, stitches starting from just below the sideburns and running at an angle to below the lips and almost to the triangular underlip beard. One eye was a ghastly yellow, scars pockmarking the face, and the nose slightly swollen.

Hugh Anderson knelt beside him.

"You remember what happened?" the Major's son asked.

I don't rightly care much for Hugh myself, but I wouldn't shame any man that way, no matter how wrong he is.

"The buffalo?" Hugh said.

But I'll handle it. My way.

"Buffalo?" Gary's answer sounded far away.

The wagon sawed again back and forth, back and forth, and a moment later, Adam Pollock was on Gary's left, holding a blue-speck enamel bowl in his hands and a spoon in his mouth. Once he set the bowl on the floor and squatted, he took the spoon with his right hand.

"Hugh's gonna lift your head," Pollock said. "And I'm gonna put some buff stew in your belly."

"Buffalo," Gary said again.

"My fault." Hugh sounded different.

Of course he sounds different, Gary thought with revulsion—at himself: *I did that to the Major's son. To Taylor's best friend.*

"I was chasing that shaggy up that big hill." Hugh frowned. "Never knew how fast a buffalo could run. I swear, I didn't even see you till . . . I didn't know you were up there."

The spoon came to his face; he opened his mouth, swallowed.

"Buffalo." Gary tried to grin. "Ever tell you . . . your pa tell you . . . 'bout the time . . . I tried to bring a . . . buffalo bull . . . into his herd?"

"Shut up and eat," Pollock said.

"Once we're past Turkey Creek," Gary told Hugh, "you won't find wood. It's flat. And you have to keep clear of the prairie dog towns. You can break the legs of every horse in the remudas if . . ."

Hugh shook his head and smiled.

"No," Gary spoke urgently, grimaced from the pain. "Water's fine at Hackberry Creek, but there's nothing to burn there but grass. And the prairie dog town at—"

"Pa."

He turned his eyes, not his head, at Taylor, who was feeding Gary soup this day.

"Shut up and listen," Gary said. He couldn't remember what all he had told these two kids. "Quicksand," he sang out. "Watch for quicksand at the Salt Fork . . ."

"Mr. Hardee," Hugh said.

Gary turned his head slightly.

"We're past the Salt Fork of the Arkansas," Hugh said.

"Thank the Lord," Taylor said. "Hugh pulled me out of that stuff. I thought I was a goner."

Hugh's head shook. "Sanchez was right there. You weren't even down to your waist."

"What?" Gary's head spun.

Hugh laughed, and Taylor lowered the spoon into the bowl. "Your son's got a new handle. The boys figured after nearly getting cooked by lightning, surviving two stampedes, and then losing his saddle in the river and finding quicksand. And *not* getting locked up in Burlington. They say he must be Irish."

"Hardee's Scottish," Gary told them. "Daniel Hardee came over from Lanarkshire in 1742."

That's what Grandpa Richard said, anyway.

"Taylor's Irish now," Hugh said. "And we're all calling him Jim Riley."

Gary didn't like that. Some cowboys changed their names every season, but by thunder if his son would. That argument would wait. He had to let these fool kids know what they were in for.

"Listen to me," he said. "Pond Creek. Pond Creek. Buffalo. There are more buffalo around there. And where there is buffalo, you might find . . ."

"We're past Pond Creek," Taylor told him. "You've been out of your head for a long, long time."

Gary blinked. "You're past . . . Pond Creek?"

"We're camping near this new settlement," Taylor said. "Evan rode in to see if they had a doctor, but no luck there. They do have a saloon. That's about it."

"The First and Last Chance," Hugh said, "depending on which way you're traveling."

"First," Gary whispered, "and Last Chance?"

"That's the saloon," Taylor said. "The town calls itself Caldwell." He held up his spoon. "You gonna eat?"

"Saloons?" Gary whispered.

"Saloon," Taylor said. "The First and Last Chance Saloon. Just one. For now."

"Don't worry, sir," Hugh said. "Conner Milone and I laid down the law. You're still trail boss."

Taylor finished: "No one drinks ardent spirits till we reach trail's end."

"A town." Gary shook his head.

Taylor shrugged. "Wouldn't call it a town just yet. Nothing but copper miners, that saloon, and buffalo grass. Caldwell, *Kansas*."

"That's right," Hugh said. "We're in Kansas."

The man in black sleeve garters and a billowy white shirt frowned.

"You say he got ran over by a buffalo?"

"That's right," Hugh Anderson said.

"When?" He opened his black valise and pulled out a stethoscope.

Evan, replacing Adam Pollock as Gary's soup-feeder, answered: "Two and a half weeks ago."

The black scope pressed against Gary's chest for a good minute or more. When the doctor removed it, he looked at Hugh.

"That buffalo? It run over you, too?"

"No, sir," Hugh answered.

"Who sutured your face?"

"Sutured?" Hugh asked.

"Stitched." He reached over and put his fingers above the wound. "Criminy, what did he use? Fishing line? Horsehair?" He peered closer. "No sign of infection, though. You crazy Texans."

He moved from Hugh and focused on Gary's right leg.

"I'll have to get him in my office." He looked again at Evan. "Two and a half weeks ago?"

"Yes, sir," Evan answered. "It's hard to keep track of days on a trail drive."

"Bet it is." He turned to Hugh. "Where do you plan on selling the herd? Herds, I mean." And put his right hand on Gary's thigh.

Gary ground his teeth and stifled a curse.

"I guess that hurts." The doctor removed his hand. "Get those wrappings off his ribs."

"They's busted," Pollock called from the driver's bench.

"Yeah, and you don't want to give him pneumonia." He glared at Hugh and raised his voice. "Where are you selling your cattle?"

"We don't rightly know. Abilene . . . ? Ummm . . ."

"Well, leave him here. Pick him up on your way south. I don't know what all I can do, but . . ."

"Ain't leaving me . . . with this . . . butcher," Hardee said.

"Pa," Evan whispered.

"I go with the herd," Hardee said. Then shrieked when the sawbones started loosening the old bedsheets that wrapped his busted ribs.

"You wanna ride in the back of this chuckwagon all the way to Abilene?" Pollock asked.

"I go where . . ." he said again.

"I don't know where you were graduated from a college of medicine," the doctor said, "but the Lord looks after you and your patient. Take him to my office upstairs. I'll—"

"I go with these cattle. And my men."

Frowning, the doctor started packing his stethoscope in the black valise at his side.

"Suit yourself." He withdrew a bottle and handed it to Evan. "Laudanum. Teaspoon a day. Teaspoon at night. No more. Unless you want to put him in a grave or the State Insane Asylum in Topeka. I'll take five dollars and be on my way now. Good luck." He held out his hand.

Hugh Anderson paid him, and the doctor took his valise, his coins, and his bowler hat through the opening in the canvas after Pollock slid out of his way. He looked back inside though, frowned, opened his mouth, closed it, and sighed a long epithet.

"Listen. It'll take you nine, ten days, maybe eleven, to get to Abilene." He pointed north. "The Atchison, Topeka, and Santa Fe is shipping cows out of Newton. You can be there in two days. Just my advice. And there's no charge for that. But if I were you, and if he wants to keep that leg, and not risk puncturing one or both lungs with those ribs, I'd opt for Newton."

He moved away from the opening, the wagon lurched a bit, and he was on the street.

"There's a good chance he'll die in Newton anyway, though. From what I read, they kill a man for breakfast, dinner, and supper every day."

Chapter 31

Some of the towns in the Southern portion of the
state must be delightful localities to reside in, if the
numerous accounts of murders committed in that
region, are true. Those Texans must be an interesting
element of community.
—*Blue Rapids Times*,
August 24, 1871

"When's that bond election?" Denise asked as she pulled
the dress over her head.

Cindy finished rubbing paste over her teeth. "Week from Friday," she said.

"What are the chances—"

"Oh, it'll pass." Cindy began scrubbing her teeth.

"I was going to ask," Denise said, "of Newton not being showered with fire and brimstone before then?"

Cindy frowned, spit into the basin, and rinsed her mouth out with water. She started to wipe her mouth and say something, but a gunshot rang out. Turning right, she held her breath.

"That's close," Denise said.

A mule brayed as though it were being ripped apart.

Cindy exhaled. "Main Street?"

Now came curses. Another shot. A scream. A third blast.

Cindy made for the door. Denise yelled, "Are you crazy?" But she already knew that answer. Cindy was plumb loco. Yet Denise ran after her, down the stairs, into the kitchen, out the alley door, up to Second, over toward Main.

Three more shots rang out, and a mule brayed horribly.

"Stop it. Stop it. For the love of God . . ."

Another shot. Then a terrible cry from an animal.

"You Yankee sons of—"

Cindy turned the corner. Denise, barefooted, came right behind, and almost ran over Cindy, who, likewise barefoot, stood in the filthy street and watched the madness unfold.

"I forgot my pencil. My notebooks." Cindy swore, and quickly turned to Denise. "Can you remember all this?"

Denise didn't answer. But it wasn't likely she would ever forget what was happening before her very eyes.

Two mules were dead in their traces. The wagon was a chuck-wagon. She had seen enough of those since arriving in Newton. The wagon's driver, she guessed, knelt in the dirt and manure, left hand buried in the filth to keep him from falling facedown, right hand stanching the blood that poured down his forehead.

"My mules." He sobbed. "My mules."

A railroader had climbed up the spokes of the rear wheel closest to the east side, and rammed the top sides of cabinet box with the sledgehammer he held high up with his right hand.

Another pulled down a hinged cover that served as a table, leaped atop it, pulling the chains free, collapsing the pine wood and sending the drunk crashing into the ground. Two friends rushed over, but not to help the man, who rolled over laughing despite a bloody nose and cut lip, while his pards reached into the holes, tossing out salt, pepper, bags, or pulling drawers all the way out and dumping the contents into the street.

Another man climbed atop the other rear wheel, reached over the top of the cabinet, and began pulling from the back. The sledgehammer pounded. The other man tugged. Something snapped.

And the cabinet would have fallen atop the man who had busted the table, but his colleagues realized what was happening and dragged the laughing drunk, and themselves, away.

"For Southern rights, hurrah," said the man with the sledge-hammer as he jumped down. He went around to the back, laughing, and stopped. The sledgehammer fell at his side. His hands raised in the air. He spoke in a whisper that Denise could not make out.

She lost track of time, but no more than a few seconds passed before the man lifted his hands even higher.

"Boys," he said in a strained whisper. "Don't do nothing. There's a six-shooter aimed at my belly."

"What the—" The man who had been atop the other wheel walked around the back, stopped, and let his hands move away from his sides, then inch toward the cloudy sky.

"You blackhearts . . . killed my mules," the driver sobbed.

Cindy started toward the chuckwagon, ignored one of the rail-roaders' warning, but stopped when a rough voice barked behind Denise: "Best stop, Chippy, I mean . . . Cindy-reller."

She didn't listen. Denise opened her mouth to tell that fool from Alabama, but by then Cindy was between the two men with raised hands. She appeared to be about to ask him a question, when she turned, looked, found Denise, and said, "This man needs a doctor."

The man on her left whispered: "He's got a Colt aimed at my guts."

"Cindy-reller . . ." Mike McCluskie walked by, pulled his re-volver, chuckled again, and began crossing the street. "Two mules littering Main Street. And a jasper from Texas bleeding on my dirt. Guess I'll have to fine these boys fifty bucks."

"Mike," said the man who had wielded the sledgehammer. "There's a Texian with a gun on Ryan and me."

"Good." McCluskie winked at Cindy, dropped to a squat, and inched his way toward the wagon. Reaching the side, he raised the barrel toward the canvas, smiling as he thumbed back the hammer.

A thunder of hooves stopped him. He rose quickly, started to aim his pistol, thought better of it, and found a friend on the east side of the street. "Run, fetch Carson."

The gangling railroader in plaid trousers took off toward the railroad tracks, but a rider in a big hat turned his pony sharply and cut off McCluskie's messenger, coming so close the man yelped and fell onto his rump, the horse snorting, pawing, and the rider glaring down at the runner.

McCluskie swore, swallowed, and watched six other Texas cowboys rein in their horses.

Dust blew up the street.

Holding a cocked revolver, one cowhand kicked his horse forward and stopped in front of McCluskie. He did not point the six-shooter at the lawman, just stared, and McCluskie smiled and slowly inched his revolver back into the holster before hooking his thumbs in his pants pockets. The rider spit between his teeth and looked at the older man wailing over his murdered mules. But he did not holster the pistol.

"How bad you hurt, Adam?"

"They killed my mules, Bill. Killed 'em for spite."

His eyes moved to the crowd, stopped at Denise. "I was tryin' to find a doc."

Denise turned north. Figures stared across the railroad tracks, but none had nerve to investigate. After all, what was another shooting in Hide Park?

Two more riders rode in from the south, including a young man with a brutal wound over his cheek. The other leaped from his horse and ran to the wagon.

"Pa," he yelled.

"Stay back, Taylor," the man in the back of the chuckwagon called. "I'm all right. And these boys are acting peaceable—now."

The young man whirled.

"Easy, Jim Riley," said the one with the scarred face. He had to be the leader. But he was speaking to the young man who had just been called Taylor. Jim Riley? Taylor Jim Riley? Well, Cindy rarely got names right in her stories, anyway.

The man with the ruined cheek looked at the railroaders who still kept their hands up. His eyes swept past Cindy or Denise before settling on McCluskie.

"What are you?" he asked.

"Special policeman." McCluskie winked. "Big election comin' up."

"Special policeman my arse," the Texan with the cocked revolver said. "His name's Delaney. And he'd cut his mother's throat for a counterfeit nickel."

McCluskie's grin was pure malice.

"Now, Bill, my name's McCluskie. Mike McCluskie. And in this town, I'm the law."

The scarred man searched the crowd, frowning, but this time stopped when his eyes met Denise's. "Ma'am," he said, and touched the brim of his hat. "Is that true? Is he a peace officer?"

"He's a cutthroat killer, a cheat . . ." Bill started, but Denise silenced him.

"He's a special policeman for the election," Denise said, and when McCluskie grinned, she added, "but I do not know why."

That didn't affect McCluskie, who laughed and turned to Cindy. "Cindy-reller," he said, "you're gonna have a crackerjack article for your Wichita paper, that's for sure." The man named Bill raised his revolver but stopped when a voice boomed, "Barbarians."

Someone from the north side of the tracks had come to Hide Park after all. Judge Muse walked straight up to Bill, who still had his revolver drawn and cocked, and said, "How dare you shoot down two noble beasts of burden, you bushwhacking Rebel trash."

"Judge," Denise said, "he hasn't fired his pistol . . . at least not here."

Whispered Cindy: "Not yet."

Jim Riley/Taylor said, "You Yankee railroaders killed those mules, buster, and wrecked that chuckwagon. And my pa's inside, and stove up pretty bad."

"Calm yourself, boy," the judge said. "We will sort all of this out—without more violence."

Cindy edged closer and peered cautiously around the edge, behind the one who had used the sledgehammer.

"Gosh a'mighty." Her Alabama drawl thickened. "He looks a mess. And he's passed out."

Denise followed Judge Muse to the back of the wagon.

"What happened to him?" Cindy asked the son of the badly injured man.

"He was scouting ahead up the trail. In the Nations. A buffalo bull caught him and his horse. Killed the horse. Came close to killing Pa."

Denise blinked. "A buffalo?"

"He needs a doctor," the son said.

"By thunder, man," Judge Muse said, "why did you not leave him at Wichita?"

"Because," the one with the scarred cheek answered, "there's no cattle getting sold in Wichita."

"Denise." Cindy spoke in a rushed whisper. "Will you remember all of this?"

"Not a chance." Denise's head already hurt.

"Lord have mercy," Muse said. "We have no hospital. This is not Kansas City." He sighed heavily, and said, "Where's Doctor Boyd?"

"Redfield and some Hun took Gaston on a handcart toward Florence," one of the railroaders said. "O'Dwyer took a bad fall off a caboose."

Doctor Page Everhart walked between two horses. "I'll take a look at whoever's wounded." He glanced at the dead mules. "Those two, however, are done for."

"You're a dentist," Judge Muse said. "And there's nothing in your office but a chair used for torture."

"We've got a bed," Cindy called out.

"I got a better one," said a sniggering prostitute who had emerged to take in the show.

Cindy frowned at the hooker, but Denise glared at Cindy.

Everhart shrugged. "I have worked on more than teeth, boys," he told the scarred one. "But it is your call."

"My pa needs a doctor," the son shouted, and Denise let out a sigh. Cindy might have been offering up their room for a newspaper story, but Denise remembered her dead brother, and how Cindy had helped her that terrible day.

"The bed's upstairs," Denise said. "And the stairs are steep and narrow. But . . ."

Taylor, or Jim Riley, looked at the leader with the scar, who shrugged. Both riders dismounted, and another cowboy eased his mount up and took the reins to both animals.

"Mr. Pollock," Taylor/Riley called out to the chuckwagon driver. "You got a blanket me and Hugh can use for a stretcher?"

The scarred one removed his hat and bowed slightly at Denise. "Ma'am, my name is Hugh Anderson, and if this is an inconvenience, we'll find a way to get Gary back to our cow camp."

She was helpless. She couldn't win.

"It's no inconvenience." Denise walked past Cindy. "I'll move our stuff into the storeroom across the hall and have Grover and Mattie get things ready."

That would take a while. But so would getting that man out of the chuckwagon, down the street, to the restaurant, and up those stairs.

Chapter 32

The most important election this county ever held, took place last Friday. . . . Notwithstanding the determined opposition the bonds were carried by between 500 and 600 majority. . . . There is no doubt but that Wichita will be the metropolis of the Southwest.
—*The Wichita Tribune,*
August 17, 1871

Opening his eyes, Gary shook his head at Bill Bailey, who, hat in hand, stood in front of the door he had just opened.

"You never learn a thing." Gary's voice croaked like a Texas bullfrog. "Do you?"

Grinning, Bailey grabbed a chair, scraped the legs across the rough second-story floor, sat, and straddled his long legs past the chair seat.

"You heard," Bailey said.

Nodding hurt, but Gary managed. "Taylor told me."

"Taylor?" Bailey grinned. "You mean Jim Riley."

"Taylor."

Bailey laughed.

"What made you take a job with a Kansas police force?"

"Money." Bailey slapped his thigh and laughed like a coyote. "The judge thought I'd be a good addition. Bein' a Texan. Might

cut down on some of the killin'. And I got your wages for gam-
blin' and girlin' once you sell the herd, and the money I make
from workin' this election'll get me back to Galveston."

"Where you'll lose it all, too."

He shrugged. "That's the only reason any fool would want
money for, ain't it?"

"You make me feel like some invalid," Gary said, as Cindy and
a Chicago packing-house man named Murphy slid him up
against the pillows. He punctuated the sentence with a few of his
favorite profanities. That burning fire ran all the way up from his
knees to his brain, then spread out like a spider's web, and just
about laid him out.

"Watch your foul language," Cindy told him. She looked exhausted. Gary wondered when she had last slept.

For a moment, he felt like that jackass she was always calling
him. But the pain started subsiding, and after Cindy adjusted the
pillows, Gary managed to breathe in and out without hurting too
much.

"I do not know how you cowboys do what you do," Murphy
said, and opened his case.

Seeing the papers, the kind of contracts he had seen before,
improved his spirits. Gary tried for levity, a word Cindy Bagwell
had taught him. "Like we say, Mr. Murphy, 'Never been hurt,
never been horseback.'"

"Well, sir." The packing-house man pulled out the contract.
"Your cattle look much better than you do, sir. No offense."

Gary reached for the papers. "We'll see how much this offends
me, Mr. Murphy." A moment later, he began reading.

"You need anything?"

Well, that was like Miss Denise Beeber. Ask if he needs anything when she has just brought up a tray of tea, biscuits, and
wild berries.

He surprised her with his answer. "Yes. In fact, there is something I'd like."

She set the tray down on the table by his—or what had been *her*—bed before he had moved the two women to a supply room, not much more than a closet, he had heard—across the little hall.

Denise waited.

"I'd like a glass tumbler filled this much." He measured with his thumb and forefinger. "With rye whiskey."

Her eyebrows arched. "Rye whiskey?"

He nodded. "Old Overholt, if you can find it."

She stared. He smiled.

"Thirty-seven, seventy-five a head. You might not realize, but this late in the season, that's a mighty good price for a mite under three thousand beeves that gave me a lot of trouble."

"Old Overholt."

Gary nodded. "I hear they serve at this place called The Gold Room." His smile widened. "End of trail. The herd's been sold. I treat myself . . . only . . . after my job is done."

"Old Overholt."

He bobbed his head once more.

Bootsteps thumped up the stairs, with spurs playing a melody, and Denise turned and stepped aside as Taylor and Hugh walked through the open door.

Gary chuckled. Hugh held a bottle in his hand. "You boys must've read my mind." He wet his lips.

More steps followed, and Cindy and a stranger came inside. The dark-haired man carried a black bag, removed his hat, bowed at Denise, and looked at Gary.

"Sir, my name is Gaston Boyd. Doctor Everhart asked me to see about that leg with which you tried to kick a buffalo to Hades."

"He fixed it, Doc." Gary felt color draining from his face.

"Yes. He tried to fix it. That's what Page said. I'm here *to* fix it."

He set the bowler on a table, dragged a chair, and stared at Denise and Cindy. "Ladies, if you wouldn't mind."

Cindy scowled; Denise studied Hugh, who nodded; and then both women left the room. Taylor closed the door.

"Look . . ." Gary swallowed. "Listen . . ."

The sheet and blanket were pulled down to the foot of the bed, and Gary tensed. When the doctor sat in the chair and started feeling up and down the leg, Gary managed not to scream, but he ground his teeth so hard his jaw ached, and he felt sweat rolling down his forehead.

"Mr. Hardee," the doctor said, "here's what I'm going to do. I'm going to rebreak your leg. Set it properly. Put it in a firm cast."

"No, you ain't—"

"Yes," Hugh Anderson said, "he is."

Taylor sat on the bed opposite of Doctor Boyd. "Even that dentist told us this would have to happen. Else that leg's gonna bother you so that you won't have any use for it . . . or they'll saw it off."

"Why didn't that tooth-puller fix it right when—"

"Because," the doctor said, "he's a dentist."

The door opened, and Evan entered, hat in hand.

"Pa." The teenager tried to smile.

"Evan," Gary said, "you got to get me out of here."

The boy's head shook. "I'm here to hold you down if need be."

"You ain't breaking my leg again."

"Yes," Taylor said. "He is."

Gary turned his head toward the cast covering his shoulder. "What about this one? You gonna—"

"The collarbone is fine, sir."

"How do you know?"

"Because Page said it was a simple break. The leg was not."

Sweat dripped into Gary's eyes. He blinked rapidly.

Evan took the bottle of Old Overholt from Hugh and brought it to his father's bedside.

"You always say, Pa," he whispered, "that you don't drink till the end of the drive. Well, look at it this way. You'll get to drink more than one or two glasses."

Taylor hooked his thumb. "We got another bottle just in case."

"You ain't . . ." His voice cracked.

Hugh Anderson stepped forward. "I'm bossing the herd," he said. "I make the rules now. And I'm following your rule, sir. A trail boss protects his men. Always."

Though his eyes burned from sweat, and fear, Gary saw those stitches. He blinked. Breathed in, exhaled.

I don't rightly care much for Hugh myself, but I wouldn't shame any man that way, no matter how wrong he is. But I'll handle it. My way.

"Give me that bottle," he whispered.

"Eat those biscuits and berries," Denise told him. "Don't get drunk on an empty stomach."

The right leg didn't hurt anymore. But he was sick and tired of being invalided. In a week or two, he probably could start moving around on crutches, Doc Boyd said, just be careful.

Gary let out a hollow laugh. "Never thought I'd have such a hankering to see a privy."

"Well, that'll be a while yet." The doctor began packing up his satchel. "Those stairs are steep, and I don't want the only Texas patient I've ever had in Newton who wasn't hurt by fist, knives, bad whiskey, bullets, clubs, drunkenness, or plumb stupidity to break his neck toppling down stairs." He closed the black bag. "In fact, a wheelchair would be more useful for you." He jutted his chin toward Gary's busted left shoulder.

Gary glared.

"Don't blame me. I was not the one who tried to ride a buffalo."

He opened the door.

"It was the buffalo, Doc," Hardee corrected, "who tried to ride me."

FINALLY—A GOOD TEXAN ARRIVES

Kansans have a habit of labeling all Texas cattlemen and cowboys as ruffians of the lowest class, but citizens of Newton have earned respect for a drover currently recovering from serious injuries in a room in Hide Park over the dining place run by Miss Denise Beeber.

Gary Hardy, of Ft Bend County in Texas, brought almost three thousand longhorns to Newton despite a near-fatal accident in which he and his horse were surprised by a buffalo bull in the Indian Ty. Despite breaking bones in his right leg, several ribs, and his left collarbone, he still managed to bring the herd in, where it sold for top dollar.

While many cattle drovers give their men a "free rein" in Newton, Gary's crew maintain good order. They stopped drunken railroaders who cruelly killed a wagon driver's two mules and thwarted a near riot before Newton's always tough and reliable Judge Muse arrived on the scene to prevent more bloodshed. Gary's men, those who have not already departed for home, are quiet and act as gentlemen. One, a drover named Bailey, has even been hired as a special deputy for the upcoming bond election.

When Gary will leave Newton with his two teenage sons and his top hand, all three as splendid and stalwart as Mr. Hardy, is not known, but already Judge Muse, and esteemed doctors Everhart and Boyd, say he will be missed, and welcomed back for the season of 1872.

—Allegro

"You wrote that?" Gary lowered the paper and stared across his busted leg at Cindy Bagwell.

"I did. Do you like it?"

"Why does it say 'Allegro' at the end?"

"That's my editor's doing. He doesn't want anyone to know that he has a woman reporting for him." Gary did not even blink, so Cindy shrugged. "It's a pen name. An alias."

"I see." Nodded so she would know he really did understand. "Lots of cowboys change their names all the time."

"Do you like the story?"

"Just not used to reading about me in a newspaper." Seeing disappointment in her face, he smiled fast and wide. "It's real good. I mean, yeah, I like it a lot. Honest. I'll take it home, show it to my wife."

He was relieved that she misspelled his surname. Maybe no one would figure out that he was the one Texan Kansans liked. Most of his crew had taken what was left of their wages, if any, and ridden home. They wouldn't read this.

"You don't know how much I had to beg to get my louse of an editor to print it," she told him. "Only way it got in the paper was because I mailed it to Mr. McBane, our publisher, and not Knott-Head."

"Well, I thank you both."

"I can bring you more copies. Lots are lying around."

He patted the paper. "One'll do."

"I guess I need to go find some bad Texans to write about," she told him. "To make Knott-Head happy."

He grinned. "They shouldn't be hard to find."

The door squeaked, and Cindy Bagwell's head popped through the opening.

"How you doing?" she asked.

"Finer than frog's hair cut eight ways," he told her, pointed at the notebook she carried, and asked, "Where you off to?"

"It's election day," she answered. "I have to let my editor know all about the results and any other news here in Newton."

"I didn't know we were electing a president," he said.

She grinned. "It's a bond election. For a railroad spur from here to Wichita." Her smile stretched. "You're funning me, aren't you."

"Yes, ma'am." He nodded at the stack of newspapers. "All I do is lay here and read."

He did not remember the dream. Just woke up from a deep sleep, opened his eyes, covered them with his good arm, turned his head, hurting his ribs and leg, even that busted collarbone, and cursing.

"Gary . . . ?"

"Good God," he said, and probably added an expletive or two. "What time is it?"

"Gary . . . ?"

"What time is it?"

"It's after three."

"Denise?"

"Yes. It's me. Gary . . . I've got . . ."

"Three . . . in the morning?"

"Gary?"

"What?"

"Look at me." The pleasant voice was no more.

Turning his head, he let his forearm move past his eyes. Her face remained blurry. She carried a candle. Someone stood behind her.

He frowned. It was Evan.

Drawing in a deep breath, Gary steeled himself.

"Pa," Evan said. "It's Bill, Pa. Bill Bailey."

Gary knew what he would hear before Evan said the words.

"He's been killed, Pa."

Gary just stared.

"That rough cob of a special deputy. The loudmouth from that day we first got here. McCluskie. Or Delaney. Whatever his name is. He shot Bill dead."

Chapter 33

The society of Newton is mixed and incongruous.
Gentlemen associate with roughs, and gamblers seem
to be held in high esteem. Cattle drivers can be seen
everywhere on the streets, in the gambling shops,
drinking saloons, and in the establishments at "Hide
Park." Every device invented for gambling can be
found in these gambling shops. Each gambling house
has a bar attached, and recently some of the establishments have added fine lunches and concert music.
—*The* (Topeka) *Kansas Daily Commonwealth,*
August 23, 1871

MORE DEATH IN BLOODY NEWTON

In the early hours of Saturday last, a railroad man, Mike
McCluskie but who has also gone by the name of Art Delaney
killed a Texan named Bill Bailey in a drunken row in Newton
hours after both men worked as special deputies during the
railroad bond election.

McCluskie was arguably one of the roughest individuals to
walk the streets of Newton. He previously worked for the AT-
SF railroad, sometimes as a night policeman. McCluskie,
whom many believe came from Ohio, is said to have killed
other men.

The deceased, a Texan and officious gambler, had driven a herd of cattle from Texas, which sold, and, as a former peace office, was hired temporarily for the railroad bond election that took place Friday.

After the election, the two men, both of whom have a predilection for bawdiness and rowdiness, drank heavily and argued. Despite such longstanding and deep enmity for each other, both men entered the Red Front Saloon on Main Street together, where they drank more, and argued, bickering until punches were thrown, the two men were separated, and Bailey hurled insults and profanity at McCluskie before walking out the door.

McCluskie, it is said, followed the Texan. Shots were then fired and men rushed outside to find Bailey in the dirt. Bailey was shot in the right side, near his heart. He was lifted off the dirt and carried into the Santa Fe Hotel, where Doctor Boyd was summoned.

Two friends of the Texan, named Riley and Anderson, rushed to the side of their comrade, while other Texans began yelling for the arrest of McCluskie. A deputy said he would arrest McCluskie, if for nothing other than the mankiller's safety.

But as of this morning, McCluskie cannot be found. An informant told this correspondent that railroad men secreted the assassin onto a cattle train this morning and sent him to, most likely, Florence, where he could disembark and hide or flee to Ohio or wherever he may escape the vengeance of the deceased's friends, many who have sworn to kill McCluskie on sight.

—Allegro

Gary refolded the handwritten papers and returned them to Cindy.

"Is that how it really happened?" he asked after a long silence.

"Depends," Cindy told him, "on who you ask. Kansans say one thing. Texans another."

Denise, sitting in a chair at the head of the bed, looked at Hugh Anderson and Gary's two sons.

Evan spoke: "We weren't there."

"I should have been." Hugh Anderson looked pale, but his eyes burned with a fury. "It's my job to protect—"

"Bill quit us." Gary stared at Hugh. "Remember? He took that job as a deputy. And Bill wasn't some greenhorn when it comes to lawing. He knew what he was doing. Knew the risks."

"He was a good man," Hugh yelled.

"When sober." Gary heard his words to Moises Dunn: *Drunk, he's just downright contrary and mean.*

Hugh waited a moment. When he spoke again, his voice was high, but his eyes still burned. "You also told me that a trail boss protects his men—even when they're dead."

"Which is what we're going to do." He turned to Taylor. "They buried him yet?"

Taylor's head shook.

"This afternoon," Cindy said.

Gary nodded and looked at Denise. "I'd like to be there. Can I get down those stairs?"

"We'll get you down them," Evan said.

"And," Cindy added, "Doctor Boyd says there's a wheel-chair . . ."

He had forgotten how bright the sun was in Kansas. It felt good, though, on his face. Having survived being carried down the restaurant stairs, and somehow getting into the back of a buckboard without dying, he made it to the cemetery. For a brand-new town, the graveyard was filling up quickly.

His right leg, stretched out on a piece of planking, hurt, but Gary would not let anyone know that. Over buffalo grass and through sand, Evan pushed the wheelchair that pill-roller had left. Gary realized he had lost a lot of weight since that wreck in the Indian Nations, but he still worried that the chair's wheels would get stuck until Evan finally parked him at the grave two men of color were digging.

Finished, they climbed out of the grave, and wandered down the slope to wait till the services were over. Afterward, they would cover the body with sand and sod.

Bill Bailey had a casket, the sorriest-looking thing ever built. Sand would shift through the cracks and cover Bill's body. Those gravediggers might be shoveling till Christmas.

"Is there a preacher?" Gary asked.

"No preacher," Cindy said. "No church."

The wind blew.

"There was a parson from Emporia. Overstreet," Cindy continued. "The Reverend R.M. Overstreet. He was supposed to give a sermon in The Gold Room. But it rained, and it got called off."

Because The Gold Room's roof leaks? Gary wondered.

"If ever a town needed religion," Cindy said, "it's Newton."

"Well." He started to say something—what, he didn't know, so he stopped. The last funeral he had attended was for Casey Steer. When he had whipped Hugh Anderson without mercy. Feeling queasy, he suddenly wished he had stayed upstairs over Denise's restaurant.

Hugh stepped up to the grave, picked up a handful of dirt, and let it sift through his fingers onto the casket.

"God," he said, "we commend to you the spirit of Bill Bailey. At least, that's what we called him, and he called himself. We rode a lot of miles together. I learned by just watching him on the point. He was a good cowhand. Loyal as a hound. He didn't know when to stop drinking, Lord, and he had a temper he couldn't handle. But we ask you to forgive him, show him your mercy, put him in a good saddle on a good horse. And let him ride."

"Amen," Taylor said.

"Amen," the others answered.

Gary nodded.

Denise began to sing.

> *How firm a foundation, ye saints of the Lord,*
> *Is laid for your faith in His excellent word.*

Once she started the third verse, Gary found himself join-ing her.

> *When through deep waters I call thee to go,*
> *The rivers of sorrow shall not overflow.*
> *For I will be with thee, thy trouble to bless,*
> *And sanctify to thee thy deepest distress.*

The others sang the last two verses, but Gary hummed, having forgotten the words.

"Anybody want to say something else?" Gary asked.

When no one spoke, Gary said, "Amen, then."

Denise walked away, looking at stones, crooked crosses, fi-nally stopping at one stone over a mound. Evan started to pull Gary away, and head back to the wagon, but Gary grunted, nod-ded at Denise, and his son pushed him ahead, going around one mound—the cemetery was laid out as haphazardly as much of the town.

Denise stood over a grave, and Evan stopped. The marker, al-ready faded, read:

YES'M
D: MAY '71

She knelt, plucked some weeds, tossed them aside, brought the fingers on her right hand to her lips, then touched the weath-ered pine. Smiling, she rose, and the smile did not wane as she walked back to Gary and Evan.

"Didn't mean to intrude," Gary whispered.

"You're not." She looked back at the grave, shook her head, and stared off at the growing town.

"It's funny," she said. "This place. This town. When I first got here . . ." She sighed. "There was one building. Horner's store, and a strong wind would have blown it back to Florence. I think that's where he came from. Tents. Three tents. The blacksmith's shop was dirt, and it wasn't finished then. That was Newton. Just a bunch of dreams. Including mine."

She glanced at Gary, at Evan, at Yes'm's grave.

"He was the first buried here," said Denise.

"A lot have joined old Yes'm." Shaking her head, Denise looked toward the town of Newton. "What's Newton's population? A thousand, maybe fifteen hundred? A railroad to bring in more, till the cattle season's over." She laughed aloud. "The depot's the only building with a real foundation. What else? Six restaurants—including mine. Three hotels. Two blacksmith shops. Two doctors. A couple of apothecaries. Three dry-goods stores. Two paint shops—how many cans of whitewash can you sell? Three lumberyards, but try to find one tree. There were some when Yes'm and I rode in that first day, him hauling lumber, me bringing a big stove and plans for a restaurant to make my pile. Yes, trees grew along the creekbeds. I must have blinked, and they were gone."

He thought she was done, but when she started walking toward the wagon, she continued.

"Our friend, Doctor Page Everhart, the lone dentist. A real-estate office. We don't even have a jail, though Cindy says they are talking about turning an old caboose or some boxcar into one as soon as they can get around to it.

"Thirty saloons thereabouts, including the dance halls. I couldn't fathom how many houses of ill repute. All because of a railroad and cattle pens."

He spent most of the day in front of Denise's restaurant, sitting in his wheelchair, watching people ride by. One cowboy, loping a dun gelding, tossed him a silver dollar as he rode deeper into Hide Park. A staggering drunk found it five minutes later, picked it up, and walked across the street and into a saloon.

That night, he ate in the packed dining room, and let Evan and Taylor carry him back upstairs.

He had propped himself up on the bed after finding a book, *A Tale of Two Cities*, published by some Yankee outfit in Philadelphia a couple of years after the war. Written by a man named Dickens, the book was illustrated by "Boz," and Gary thought he'd just look at the pictures, but he started reading, kept reading, and wasn't too happy when someone tapped on the door and opened it while saying, "Are you decent?"

Denise's grin widened.

He forgave the intrusion, for she held a cup of steaming coffee.

He laid the book, still open, facedown by his busted leg. She handed him the coffee and sat down in the chair.

"I've been asked to a dance," she said.

"Need me to chaperone?" He sipped the coffee, always excellent, and said, "Because I don't see myself cutting a rug anytime soon."

Her eyes danced.

"Taylor?" he asked.

"No. Hugh."

He felt relief. For a moment, he thought she might say Evan.

"Where's this dance?"

She pointed at the wall.

"Tuttle's?"

She laughed. "He has a new tuba player."

"That's really not a place fit for . . ."

"He says it'll be different. Perry does. It's to celebrate the passage of the railroad bond. And, well, trail herds are getting fewer and fewer, and he wants to—"

"Earn as much money as he can get."

"Perry promises it'll be different," she repeated. "Decent. No paid dancers. Good girls. Or whoever wants to come. No hippity-hoppity gals looking to pick pockets, nothing indecent, degrading, or disgusting."

Gary frowned. Denise said: "Cindy'll be here. Writing stories for her newspaper."

"What do you want to know?" he said.

"Hugh. Is he . . . ?"

"He comes from good family." Gary stared at the coffee. "He grew up a lot on this drive. I wouldn't have said this a few months back. But he's a man to ride the river with."

He lifted his eyes to meet hers, and smiled.

"Have fun. Don't step on his feet. Hurt feet are no fun when you're in stirrups for eight hundred miles. Trust me on that point."

"Cindy'll be here," she repeated. "Writing stories for her newspaper."

"I don't need a nursemaid," he mumbled.

"She does."

They laughed.

He set the cup on the bedside table and picked up his book. "I won't be getting any sleep tonight. Tuba players." He grunted. Denise leaned over, kissed his cheek, and walked outside.

The worst part about this room, Gary thought, was Denise Beeber didn't put any windows in there. Oh, there was ventilation enough—not just from bullet holes—but a body never knew what time of day it was. The lamp burned, but he had finished *A Tale of Two Cities*, and Gary never thought he would finish any book.

Someone knocked on the door, and opened it before Gary could even say he was decent. Cindy Bagwell walked in, and she wasn't bringing him coffee.

"Gary?"

"Yes?"

She pulled the door behind her, hurried to the chair by the bed, and sat down.

"Shortly after Taylor, Hugh, and Denise rode off," she said, "Page Everhart came by. I was sipping coffee in the café, helping Grover and the two girls, but it wasn't busy."

"That tooth-puller and lying, leg-cracking scoundrel jealous?" Gary grinned. "Evan told me Hugh rented a buggy, and they were going to see the town before dancing till dawn." He read Cindy's face. "That dentist jealous?" She drew in a deep breath. "You aren't jealous . . . are you?"

"It's probably nothing," Cindy said after another deep breath and slow exhale. "But a bartender at the O.K. Saloon told Page that he thought he saw Mike McCluskie an hour or two ago."

Chapter 34

It must be borne in mind that the state of society in
that town is now at its worst. The town is largely
inhabited by prostitutes, gamblers and whiskey-
sellers. Pistol shooting is the common amusement.
All the frequenters of the saloons, gambling dens
and houses of ill-fame are armed at all times,
mostly with two pistols.
—*The Emporia News,*
August 25, 1871

Hugh Anderson surprised her. Denise Beeber surprised herself. She remembered the right steps and rhythm for the
galop, and Hugh could move from the Viennese waltz to the
polka. He even taught her The Boston. And that band. That
band played so well. Perry Tuttle had brought in real musicians
from Topeka. Some of his regular players did not seem to mind
as they danced, or tried to dance, too.

She couldn't remember the last time she had danced. They
had just finished a quadrille—Hugh and Denise, while Patrick
Lee, a brakeman for the A.T. & S.F., Taylor—still answering to
Jim Riley—and Evan Hardee danced with three women sup-
plied by Perry Tuttle. Hugh looked so happy. Denise's face flushed.

"What time is it?" she asked.

Evan laughed. "It's early."

Yes, it has to be well past midnight.

They had been here since eight-thirty after dining in the Newton House, which, Denise knew, wasn't any better than her place for food, and trying roulette for just a couple of spins at The Gold Room.

The door opened. A man walked inside. Taylor stiffened. "It's him," he whispered.

Everyone turned to look.

She felt sick, recognizing the big man, bearded, with a revolver tucked inside his waistband. He looked at the dancers, then the band, snorted, and yelled at the bartender, "Bring me the worst you got, and don't spit in the glass to water it down." He moved to the faro table.

Mike McCluskie had returned to Newton.

The railroader whispered, "Easy, boys. Let's keep the dance going." He laughed, but that sounded so hollow, and he turned his brunette partner around. "Something fast, boys," he yelled at the band.

Instead, the band started "Virginia Belle."

The railroader pulled his partner closer. Evan laughed, and tried not to step on the rail-thin girl's toes as he sang, out of tune, key, and everything else, but having a grand time.

> *Fairer than the golden morning,*
> *Gentle as the tongue can tell,*
> *Was our little laughing darling,*
> *Sweet Virginia Belle.*

Hugh turned toward the door, which opened and closed again. Denise saw three men stop. They stared at Mike McCluskie, who got his whiskey from one of Tuttle's dancing girls, and sat at the faro layout. The three cowboys, none she recognized, walked to the bar.

"Let's sit this one out," Hugh said. He didn't even look at Denise. He walked toward the three men who were being poured whiskeys.

> *Bright Virginia Belle.*
> *Our dear Virginia Belle.*
> *Bright Virginia Belle.*
> *Our dear Virginia Belle.*

Denise got out of the way of the few dancers.

The girl with Taylor tugged on his arm, but Gary's older son shook his head.

> *She bereft us when she left us,*
> *Sweet Virginia Belle.*
> *She bereft us when she left us,*
> *Sweet Virginia Belle.*

Evan and his partner stopped when the band finished, bowing, giggling. Taylor stood at the door.

"Come on," he called, and waved at Evan.

"You go to sleep if you wanna, *Jim Riley*," Evan said. "I'm dancing till dawn." He had not seen, or maybe just didn't recognize, McCluskie.

But Perry Tuttle knew McCluskie on sight. He slammed a bung starter against his bar. "That's it, boys. I'm closing up." He hit the bar again. "We're closed as of now."

One of the cowboys near Hugh finished his whiskey and said, "When have you ever closed?"

"I'm closing now." He was at the band stage, and the men began putting brass into cases, and the big-mustached man swung his banjo over his shoulder. "Now!" Tuttle bellowed, and scurried back behind the bar.

"*'Lorena'!*" demanded another cowhand near Hugh. "Before you go."

Smiling, the fiddler brought his instrument up and made the strings hum.

"You ain't playing that Johnny Reb song, buster," McCluskie said.

She felt the air leave the room.

The fiddle and bow came down, the musician swallowed, and he said in a meek voice, "It's not a Reb song. It's not a Yankee song. It's a beautiful—"

"Out," Tuttle screamed. He reached under the bar, came up with a handful of paper money, and hurried back to the stage, paying off the men. He found one of the dancing girls and gave her what cash remained in his hand. "Get them out of here, Lois," he said. "All of them. I'll see you tomorrow night."

Tuttle's face was whiter than his shirt.

"For the love of God, men, we are closed."

Hugh leaned against the bar. "Whiskey," he told a bartender.

A cowboy by Hugh's side laid his revolver on the bar. "You heard the man," he whispered.

Denise swallowed. She didn't think she'd have enough saliva to do so again. Taylor held the door open as the band, and the dancing girls, except for the one with Evan Hardee, filed out like obedient schoolkids.

"Evan," Taylor called out.

"I'll sing," Evan told his partner. "We'll dance together to my singing." He took her in his arms and tried to sing, but now his voice creaked with nerves, and neither one danced as well as they had before.

The years creep slowly by, Lorena.
The snow is on the grass again.

"If you keep singing that song, boy, I'm gonna blow your head off," McCluskie said. "Just how I done your pard Bailey's."

Evan's Adam's apple bobbed. The girl stopped singing.

"For God's sake," Tuttle roared, unleashing a torrent of profanity. "Get out of here or I'll get the law."

Evan sang:

The sun's low down the sky, Lorena.
The frost gleams where the flowers have been.

But his voice rattled, and his face tightened. Maybe now he was figuring out who the loudmouthed brute was. Or saw the revolvers out, and his brother's right hand resting on the butt of his pistol.

Denise never understood why Texas cowboys brought their guns everywhere. Even to a friendly dance. Or what had been a friendly dance. But she also realized that since the election, almost everyone in Newton walked around with a gun in plain sight. Even Judge Muse.

McCluskie finished his whiskey. The faro dealer slid back in his chair.

Now McCluskie stood. His right hand reached for the butt of the revolver pressing into his big belly.

But the heart throbs on as warmly now,
As when the summer days were night.

Another cowboy, but not part of the trio that had walked in, set his beer stein on the bar and hurried toward Evan and the dancer.

"Don't get in the middle of this, Happy," one of the cowboy's pards said.

The girl pulled away from Evan. She was sobbing now, her eyes wide. She hurried toward the faro dealer. Evan stopped singing. He stood, as if lost.

"Damn all of you," Tuttle said. "We are closed."

Hugh walked away from Denise and made a beeline toward the faro table.

McCluskie had his revolver almost out, his eyes trained on Evan Hardee, but he stopped when he spotted Hugh out of the corner of his eye.

After that, Denise wasn't sure what she saw.

"You are a cowardly S.O.B.," Hugh yelled, "and I will blow the top of your head off."

The cowboy named Happy ran, yelling, "Don't do it, boys. Don't do it."

McCluskie jerked the pistol from his pants. Denise did not remember seeing Hugh move, but the gun was in his hand. She heard the muffled explosion. Orange flame and white smoke belched, and blood sprayed like a geyser from McCluskie's neck.

Someone screamed. Probably Evan's dancing partner.

"No." Denise knew she had said that when she saw McCluskie on his knees, the barrel of his pistol mere inches from Hugh's chest. The hammer fell. But she heard no report, saw neither muzzle flash nor cloud of smoke. What she saw was McCluskie drop his pistol and fall to the floor, overturning his chair, and he began rolling left and right, left and right, clutching his neck, in a spreading pool of darkness.

Hugh stood calmly over the writhing man. Hugh eared back the revolver's hammer, aimed at McCluskie's broad back. The gunshot didn't sound as loud as the first one, but the flame and smoke that the pistol produced caused Denise to close her eyes.

Curses followed. More gunshots roared from the bar.

Denise knew she should drop to the floor. She opened her eyes. The saloon girl was running now, away from the faro dealer, screaming. Evan Hardee came toward her. Taylor started, stopped.

Hugh must have heard Evan's boots. He turned. Brought the gun up.

"No!"

Denise thought she had screamed the warning. She knew her mouth had opened. But the shout came from behind her. So did the pistol shot that punched Hugh over the faro layout.

"No!" That came from her throat. "For the love of God, no!" Hugh rolled over, pushed himself up, groaned, and fell beside McCluskie.

"What the—!"

The cowboys turned.

Denise saw Taylor running, a pistol in his hand. He pushed Evan forward, and the boy staggered, fell to his knees, tumbling over. Calmly, Taylor turned around, aiming his revolver.

The cowhand called Happy ran past her, both hands against his throat, but the blood still sprayed. Denise felt its warmness, its stickiness, against her neck and the top of her dress.

Hugh came up, clutching his leg. He found his pistol. Another bullet must have hit him, because the weapon flew out of his hand and he grabbed his shoulder and fell again beside Mc-Cluskie.

Evan started to push himself up, but Taylor walked to him and kicked him down. No. That wasn't Taylor Hardee. That wasn't Gary's son. That was someone else. A stranger. She remembered the first day she had seen him on Main Street. Remembered what most of the Texans called him them.

This was Jim Riley.

The cowboys at the bar were firing at him now. White smoke filled the saloon, but she could make out Riley reaching down, taking a pistol from Evan's holster, and turning back.

"You murdering Texas Reb." That came from Patrick Lee, the railroad brakeman, the man who had partnered with Hugh, Riley, and Evan when they had danced the quadrille.

He reached for a gun Denise didn't even know he had. Then he twisted around, fell to his knees. His little brass pistol had disappeared, and he was clutching his stomach, the color leaving his face, which was masked in pain. Blood seeped over his lips, and she lost sight of him.

Denise blinked. Riley held Evan's pistol in his left hand, but the one in his right cracked again.

He is a Texan, Denise thought. *Jim Riley is a Texan. And now he was shooting Texans.*

She turned. This is a nightmare. *I will wake up. I will—*

Her breath rushed from her lungs as she hit the floor. She felt a horse rolling over her and knew what Gary Hardee must have felt at that spot south of here.

She made her eyes open. The weight crushed her, but she heard faint popping. She breathed and cried. Both hands came to her face.

"I'm shot." She felt the warm blood pouring from her nose. This wasn't blood that had splattered across her dress. This came from her own body.

"I'm shot."

"You're not shot." The body still covered hers. It was not a horse, but a man. She wanted to push him off, but the body would not move.

"Lie still." She no longer heard gunshots, only the voice. Her head turned. She recognized Perry Tuttle. Sweat poured down his face.

"Lie still," he whispered.

There was silence. Except for footsteps. Coming toward her.

She started to pray. How long had it been since she had prayed? At Arthur's funeral in Wichita? But she hadn't really prayed then. Just mouthed the words. She had said only an amen at Bill Bailey's funeral.

Denise prayed now, though. Because Jim Riley walked toward them. He would use one of those pistols he carried to kill her and Perry Tuttle.

The boots did not stop. She heard them as they stepped around her. Her head turned, and she saw the back of Jim Riley. He reached the door, opened it, and walked into the night.

Now Tuttle pulled himself off Denise.

"Are you all right?" he whispered.

"My nose." She felt silly, but her nose hurt. And it still bled.

"God a'mighty." That was a voice she remembered.

"Boy." Tuttle climbed to his feet. "Boy. What's your name?"

The other saloon girl screamed like a cougar in heat.

"What?"

Denise let out a sigh. Evan Hardee was still alive.

The dancing girl's screams echoed through the clouds of stinking white smoke.

"Get Denise out of here," Tuttle said. "Get her next door. To her place. You hear me, boy?"

"What?" Evan asked.

"What's your name, boy?"

"What . . . where's Taylor?"

"Boy." Tuttle pulled the kid close. "Buck up, son. The law's gonna be storming in here in a few minutes. Once they get up enough nerve. Now get Denise out of here."

"What about . . . ?" Evan gestured toward the faro layout.

"Godich will take care of Susie," Tuttle said. Godich would be the faro dealer. Susie had to be the screaming dancer. Tuttle looked at Denise, pulled a handkerchief from a pocket in his brocade vest, and pressed it against Denise's nose. "Hold that," he told her.

She did.

"Now, get." He and Evan helped Denise to her feet. She started to turn, but Evan's hand stopped her.

"Don't," he whispered.

"I must see Hugh." Denise started to sob.

"He's breathing," Godich said. "I ought to put a bullet in the son of—"

"Get Susie out of here," Tuttle said. "Now." He looked back at Denise. "I'll take care of Anderson. Till the doctors and law get here."

She didn't even know she was walking till she saw the open door. Evan Hardee had a hand around her waist. Before they stepped into the dark Sunday morning, Tuttle whispered, "God have mercy."

Outside, Denise looked across the street. She repeated Tuttle's words.

"Don't look," Evan whispered, but that was too late. Too late for both of them.

Happy, the cowboy, lay across the street on the boardwalk in front of Krum's dance hall.

A moment later, Evan's free hand was tugging on the doorknob to Denise's restaurant.

"Oh." She remembered. "My key. It's in my purse. I left it—"

She tried to turn back to Tuttle's dance hall, but Evan's grip around her waist tightened. "Forget it."

Glass shattered. Denise jerked her head around. Evan pushed his hand inside.

"You broke . . ." She started, but Evan was working on the inside knob. The door opened, he pushed her inside, stepped in behind her, and slammed the door shut.

His chest heaved. He brought his right hand up to wipe the sweat from his face, stopped, stared down at his bloody hand and fingers.

"You're bleeding," Denise told him.

And a pathetic voice in the darkness of the dining room cried out, "So am I."

Chapter 35

It may be that a man who deals out to two legged
brutes whiskey which would eat holes in the hide of
any Texas steer in the prairie around Newton, it may
be that man is all the while endeavoring to "preserve
order," but the common sense of mankind in general
fails to recognize the fact. The high qualities of such
men, are as doubtful to us as the virtue of a prostitute
and the conscience of a pickpocket, and it is our
candid opinion that if there is anything or orthodoxy,
hell is full of just such generous, sober, orderly,
popular gentlemen . . .
—*The Leavenworth Weekly Times*,
August 31, 1871

Leaning against the wall, clutching her left arm, Cindy Bagwell watched Denise Beeber and Evan Hardee ease toward
her. One lantern on the wall still flickered, and Cindy cringed when
she saw Denise.

"Dear God," Cindy said, "you've been shot in the nose."

Denise and the cowboy leaned beside her. The cowboy
reached and gently removed Cindy's hand. Cloth ripped. She felt
a sting in her arm.

"Hey," she said.

He held a splinter of wood in front of her eyes, then flicked it away.

"A splinter," she said, "hurts that much?"

Denise began ripping the bottom of her petticoat. "No," she said sternly, "you've been shot."

Cindy's head shook. "No, no. I heard a gunshot. I grabbed my pencil and notebook and came downstairs and—ouch!"

The cowboy clamped his hand over her arm, which hurt worse now. She cursed the cowboy, then recognized him.

She didn't know what Evan Hardee was doing, but he had better stop it, or there would be trouble.

"Came through Tuttle's wall," he said. "It's a pretty mean gash." He took the strip of petticoat Denise handed him.

"I need to get outside, find out what happened," Cindy said.

"Ouch." This time she turned and cursed the Hardee boy. He was tying that cloth hard. He backed up and said, "Where's Pa?"

Cindy blinked. "Pa? My pa, he, he died . . . oh. Your father." She pointed up the stairs. Evan vanished, and boots pounded on the stairs. Her eyes found Denise.

"Are you sure you're all right?"

"Better than you are," Denise said. Both turned to look at the door. Cindy spotted torches, a lantern. Heard curses and footfalls.

"Dear God, boys, that's Happy," a voice yelled.

"Bled out like a butchered hog," someone echoed.

A door banged open. "We got dead, dying, and badly wounded men in here. Get every doctor and nurse we got in town. The druggists. Midwives. Butchers. I don't care. But my dance house has been turned into a butcher's shop."

Cindy tried to stand, but Denise pushed her against the wall.

"You don't understand." She was crying now. "If I don't get this story to Knott-Head, I'll lose my job."

"Lie still," Denise said. "You're bleeding like a stuck pig."

Boots thundered down the stairs. Evan Hardee stopped, breathing hard, his eyes hardening.

"Pa's all right." He tried to catch his breath.

"Are you sure?" Cindy asked. "He might—"

"He's breathing. Talking in his sleep. He's all right. But I gotta get out of here. Gotta find Taylor." His head shook wildly. "I can't believe . . . I just gotta find my brother."

He rose, started for the door, but Denise grabbed hold of his leg. He turned. "Let me—"

"You can't go out that door," Denise urged him. "They'll think you killed everyone in there."

Evan blinked rapidly. The doors next door banged open and closed. Profanity came through the walls. "It's Hugh Anderson!" a voice cried.

Denise's head dropped.

Cindy wanted to scream: *Where are my pencils?*

"Those Texians have murdered McCluskie." More oaths. Someone yelled that every Texas waddie ought to be shot down like a dog.

Evan's face paled even more.

Then another voice. "McCluskie ain't dead. Lord have mercy, he ain't dead."

And, barely audible: "Ain't dead . . . yet."

"Hugh Anderson!" Cindy whispered. She needed her notebook. She wanted her pencils. She had to get this story to *The Wichita Herald*. "McCluskie. Oh, lordy, Denise, let me . . ."

"Shut up," Evan snapped. His right hand dropped, came back up. "Where's my pistol? Where the Sam Hill is—"

"Jim Riley took it," Denise said.

Evan sank down, slowly cursed. He looked through the window. Shadows moved about the curtains over the windows and the door.

"Somebody's going to notice that pane I busted," Evan whispered.

"What pane?" Cindy looked all around her. "Where is my notebook? I need pencils."

Denise came up. She wiped her nose.

Cindy gasped at all the blood on the front of Denise's dress. "You're lying," she yelled. "You've been shot. You're bleeding to death."

Denise kicked Cindy's ankle.

"Shut up." She looked back at Evan, pointing. "Through the curtain to the kitchen. The back door. But be careful, Evan. Be careful."

Gary Hardee's son vanished.

"That hurt," Cindy told Denise. "You kicked me." She started again to stand, but now her ankle hurt, and a fiery pain in her upper left arm almost had her crying.

The front door slammed open, and a man backed by many carrying torches stepped inside. Cindy saw the flash of a badge on the first man's coat.

Her left arm hurt from her fingers to her shoulder, but she made herself step outside at dawn. It looked as though Newton had hired more special policemen than had been paid for that bond election, the one in which voters had overwhelmingly approved the subscription of $200,000 in county bonds to link Newton and Wichita with a Wichita & Southwestern Railroad. The peace officers made a line across Second Street that no one dared to cross.

Well, Bobby Knott would have his wish. With a railroad spur, Wichita would become a booming cowtown. They could have it all.

"Hey, lady." She looked across the street, saw saddle blankets covering a body that lay in front of Krum's dance hall. He motioned her over.

With a sigh, Cindy walked toward him and his cigar-chewing grin. She stopped before she got to the false-fronted building.

The deputy removed the soggy cigar with his left hand and let his right fingers clutch one of the saddle blankets. "Want to see what a man looks like when he's been shot through his jugular?" He whipped off the blanket and rose.

Cindy looked at the body, locking her eyes on his unseeing one, and then stared at the deputy, who seemed disappointed when Cindy did not pale or faint.

"This is what all them dirty Texas cowboys deserve," the man said, and dropped the blanket back over the man's head, shoulders, and chest.

"Too bad it wasn't you," Cindy told him, and walked back toward Tuttle's dance hall. She had to stop and close her eyes to let the vertigo pass. Her arm really hurt now, but she made it to the open doors of Perry Tuttle's Dance House just as another body was brought out.

She fought down whatever wanted to climb up her throat.

"Go ahead," said a man holding a shotgun, "take a look-see. It's mostly cleaned up now."

She stepped inside. The place smelled of blood and rotten eggs. Chairs were scattered; cards remained on the floor near the overturned faro layout. She looked to her right, wondering if she could find the hole the bullet made before it came through in Denise's dining room and plowed a furrow across her upper left arm.

Ruined a pretty dress, too.

Judge Muse walked to her, cleared his throat, and breathed in and out.

"Hugh Anderson, a Texas cowboy, is grievously wounded, but perhaps not mortally. A warrant has been issued for his arrest for the murder of Mike McCluskie." He frowned and waited for Cindy to stop writing. When she looked up again, he added: "McCluskie died an hour ago."

Another man came up to the judge, whispered something, then walked away.

After clearing his throat, the judge continued: "Billy Garrett, a cowboy, just died. He had suffered bullet wounds in his shoulder and chest." Muse cleared his throat. "Garrett was shot by a Texas cowboy known as Jim Riley." He paused to exhale. "Riley is responsible for the rest of the carnage."

Cindy frowned as she wrote.

"Two men are wounded and will likely live, a cowboy and a shovel man," Muse continued. "The railroader suffered a gunshot wound through his calf. The cowboy took a bullet through his nose and leg."

Now the judge reached inside a coat pocket and pulled out a piece of paper. He held that as he also withdrew a pair of spectacles and settled them on his nose and ears. Leaning closer to the paper, he read:

"Henry Kearnes—I don't know how his name is spelled." Shaking his head, he looked up from the paper. "These Texas waddies are mostly an illiterate bunch, and many of them change their names with the season, or even the day." His eyes fell back on his notes. "Kearnes has bullet wounds in his chest. Patrick Lee has a bullet in his gut. He worked for the railroad as a brakeman. His wound is mortal." Muse cleared his throat.

She wrote down the last name and looked up at the judge.

"What started the fight?" she asked.

Judge Muse let out a contemptuous snort. "What always starts bullets and bloodletting? Whiskey. Cards. Dancing. The fact that McCluskie killed a Texan a week or so ago. Ill-temperance. The wages of sin."

He started to walk away, but Cindy sang out one more question: "What are you doing to apprehend this Jim Riley?"

The judge stopped, but did not look back. "A warrant has been issued for his arrest for murder and assault. How many murders will depend on how many men die. But we will bring Jim Riley to justice. As we will Hugh Anderson. Murder most foul can never be tolerated, Miss Bagwell. Never."

He made it another step.

"Like the murder last week of Bill Bailey?"

Now he turned. His eyeglasses had been returned to his coat pocket.

"The man who killed Deputy Bailey is now dead, Miss Bagwell," he said. "Isn't he?" Judge Muse walked outside into the streets of the town he had created, and likely, for the moment, regretting he had anything to do with . . .

Bloody Newton.

She sent a short telegraph to Bobby Knott, and knowing he would complain about the cost, wrote her report about the gun battle at Perry Tuttle's dancing establishment to be sent by post. Cindy could not think of how to title this gory bit of prose. Finally she just scratched, at the top of the page, three words in all caps.

NEWTON'S GENERAL MASSACRE

Patrick Lee died Tuesday morning. Cindy wrote a quick letter to the *Herald* and got it in the saddlebag for delivery that afternoon. With luck, Bobby Knott would get it in time to update the tally in the Thursday newspaper.

When she got back, she went into the kitchen, poured two cups of coffee, and walked upstairs to find Gary Hardee, covers thrown off, staring at his plastered leg. He almost blushed, and pulled the covers over his legs.

"You don't look too good," he said.

"This will help both of us." She came to him, handed him the cup, and sat on the bed by his side.

"Is it Hugh?" he asked.

"No," she said, started to sip coffee, but thought she might throw it up if she did. Why had she even poured herself a cup? "The brakeman died today."

"How many does that make?"

"Four." She tried, and failed, to fend off a shiver. "They don't know how Kearnes, or whatever his name is, has lasted as long as he has."

"So it'll be five." Gary shook his head. "And Hugh just killed one of them."

Isn't one enough?

Gary must have seen the hurt in Cindy's face, because he tried to change the subject. "Is Denise cooking?"

She let out a mirthless sound. "Nobody in Newton is eating these days. The streets are like a ghost town."

He said nothing, so she looked at him. "Cowboys are saying that if anybody tries to move Hugh to the jail, if they even get a hint that someone's going to arrest him, bodies will be ornamenting telegraph poles."

His chin fell to his chest.

"Where's Hugh?" he asked after a moment.

"Back of Hoff's store." She tried the coffee now. She had made it, not Denise, and it tasted that way. "They don't want to risk moving him." The thought of how that must have sounded to Gary made her shake her head. "They don't want to risk opening up any of his wounds."

Gary held out his cup. She took it.

"Give me that book of pages you're always writing in," he said. "And a pencil." She found her notebook and pencils, flipped to a blank page, and gave both to Gary.

He frowned, then started writing. Stopping for a minute, he said, "I need you to send a telegraph to Walter P. Anderson. Richmond, Texas. The clerk there will get it to the Major." He kept writing, ripped out the page, and handed it to Cindy. He read her face and smiled. "I didn't ask him to bring what's left of Terry's Texas Rangers up here, darling. Just himself."

She had no idea who Terry's Texas Rangers were.

"There's money in that rawhide pouch on the dresser." He pointed. "Pay the telegraph guy. Pay him extra to keep his mouth shut." He found the coffee cup on the nightstand and took another sip. Cindy went to the dresser, pulled out a note, and looked back at him.

But he was staring at his covered leg, frowning, feeling helpless. When she reached the door and opened it, he cleared his throat.

She looked back at him.

"Any word from . . . my sons?"

Her head shook. "They haven't been caught, Gary. That's all I can tell you."

His eyes shot back to his leg, and his fists clenched.

Cindy closed the door behind her.

Chapter 36

Newton, with all its faults and wickedness, will
some day outgrow them and become one of the
most important towns in southwestern Kansas.
There are good solid men among those who follow
legitimate callings there, and it needs only the
influence of the church to eradicate the vice and
gross immorality of the town.
—*The* (Topeka) *Kansas Daily Commonwealth*,
August 23, 1871

He had been moving around on those torture devices that
Kansas sawbones called crutches. He even wore britches.
Denim, though. Pants worn by sodbusters, not cowboys. And
way too big for him, but he could pull them up over that con-
founded cast. On the other hand, if he could ever meet the man
who had invented suspenders, he would buy him a shot, maybe
even a bottle, of Old Overholt.

Gary Hardee hobbled to one wall, then back to the bed. The
doc said he had to get used to these, had to start moving around
before all his muscles atrophied. Whatever *atrophied* meant.

Someone tapped on the closed door. He growled something,
stopped, and turned around. Denise and Cindy took Gary's growl
for permission to open the door. After all this time, they could

speak the language of his tribe. They stood outside what had become Hardee's Room.

Neither smiled at him, and Gary waited for grim news.

"He's here," Cindy whispered.

He exhaled audibly. That was better than what he had feared they might tell him.

Denise said: "I can bring him up."

"No." Gary started moving on crutches toward them.

"Gary." Cindy stepped inside. "Those stairs. You'll—"

He laughed. "I've lost track of how many horses have bucked me off. So if that staircase bucks me off, well, I'll get down to the café a whole lot quicker."

Neither woman smiled at his humor. But they let him hobble out of the room. It was starting to stink with his odor, anyway. Maybe he could go outside, find a barber, even a bathhouse.

But first, he had to see the Major.

Going downstairs proved harder, and took a lot more time, than Gary had figured. He wanted to blame it on the two women, hovering around him like he was a three-year-old getting in the saddle of his first pony.

He saw the cook and one of the waitresses in the kitchen, but no Wat Anderson. Beyond the curtain came the din of Newton's dinner rush. People had started eating again. Denise's restaurant had always been popular, but now it seemed busier. People got off the trains and wanted to see Perry Tuttle's dancing house. See where the "General Massacre" had taken place. That must have worked up their appetites.

A waitress took a slice of pie and a cup of coffee through the curtain.

Gary glanced at Denise. Maybe the Major was at a table in the dining room.

She nodded to the rear door.

"He's waiting in the alley," Cindy said.

Denise went to the door, put a hand on the knob. She waited

as Gary, worn out from the climb down the stairs, slowly crutched his way toward her. The door opened, and Gary breathed in fresh air.

"I'll bring you some coffee," Denise said softly as Gary stepped into the alley.

The Major sat on a chair, his back to a frame building that faced First Street. Gary glanced to his left at Poplar Street, but saw no traffic, and focused on Wat Anderson.

He had aged decades. Of course, he had always looked old, especially after the War. Now he appeared seventy. What was he? Fifty? That sounded right. His hair had been white since the War, but now it had thinned. But it wasn't the hair. It was the Major's face. Tired, worn-out, worried, ancient.

When Wat started to stand, mumbling something about letting Gary take his chair, Gary shook his head. He tried to smile. "I've been laying on my backside for what feels like half my life, Major," he said, forcing a smile. "Standing feels good, sir."

The Major did not argue, but settled back in his seat.

"Thanks for your telegrams," he said.

A mother and a fast-chatting young daughter walked down Poplar, but did not notice Gary or Wat.

"Of course, the newspapers have been full of . . ." He sighed. "Every neighbor within thirty miles have come a-callin'. Bringin' fruit cake. Pies. Ham. Like it's a gol-durned funeral."

Gary leaned against the pine.

"How's Lou?"

The Major snorted. "Better than me. But she's always been the stronger one."

Denise came out with a cup of coffee and a pot. She handed the cup to Gary, and started for the Major's chair. Only then did Gary see the cup on the dirt by his chair. He looked up, smiled underneath that bushy mustache, and shook his head.

"I'm fine, missy. Thank you, though." He nodded at the cup. "This will hold me."

Denise nodded, turned, and went back inside.

When the door closed, the Major reached down, picked up the cup, and stared at the door. "Lou had red hair when I married her." He pulled on one end of his mustache and looked up at Gary. "Remember when my hair was blacker than that thorough-bred stallion I had?" He shook his head and took a sip.

"Can I see Hugh?"

Gary nodded. "I'll take you to him."

"Finish your coffee first," the Major said. "And fill me in on how you busted your leg."

They hadn't moved Hugh to that caboose that had turned into Newton's jail. Not yet, anyway. The deputy rose from the chair next to the cot in the back of Hoff's store when Doc Boyd opened the door and all three men stepped into the storeroom. Gaston Boyd quickly pulled the door shut, and two other deputies slipped a large piece of heavy wood back into two U-shaped iron pieces that had been attached to the door's frame. A similar contraption barricaded the door that led to the alley.

Those weren't there to keep Hugh Anderson in.

The deputy nodded at the chair he had vacated, shifted the Henry rifle in his arms, and stepped away. Gary watched as the Major shuffled across the dusty floor, settled into the chair, and reached over to brush wet bangs off Hugh's pale forehead.

"How . . . ?" The Major's voice cracked. He coughed, cleared his throat, and started to ask again, but the doctor spoke.

"Fairly well. His fever finally broke." Boyd wet his lips. "I removed the bullets. There were no broken bones. His prognosis is—"

Someone in the alley knocked on the door.

The deputy with the Henry brought the rifle to his shoulder. Two others put their hands on the butts of their holstered revolvers until a voice called quietly. "It's me, Carson."

So the two deputies removed the wooden rail barricade, unlocked the door, but both put their right hands again on their pistols as one pulled the door open. And the man with the rifle did not lower it until the city marshal stepped inside. Almost immediately, two deputies locked and barricaded the door, and the other lowered his .44 and leaned against the wall.

Doctor Boyd gathered his composure and turned back to the Major. "Good. His prognosis is good. But these cases can turn suddenly. He needs rest." He stopped, found a handkerchief, wiped his forehead, and nodded at the newcomer.

"Mr. Anderson, this is our city marshal, Tom Carson. Marshal, this is the father of Hugh Anderson."

Neither spoke. Both nodded curtly, and their eyes revealed suspicion. But that, Gary figured, was expected.

Looking up at Gary, the Major let out a heavy sigh and shook his head. "This I expected of Rich, my oldest. But not Hugh. Not Hugh." He sighed again. "I guess I should have. He was reckless. I should not have put him in charge of the second herd. You were right, Gary. Like always."

"I was wrong, Major," Gary said. "Hugh did a good job. Made his share of mistakes, but, by thunder, I've made aplenty. On every drive I've ever led. And I've been doing this, sir, a long, long time."

He smiled down at the sleeping Hugh Anderson.

"After that set-to south of the Red, Hugh became a real trail boss, Major. And he saved my bacon. I'd be some buzzard's or coyot's breakfast if not for him, sir. That's the God's honest truth." He swallowed, sighed, and shook his head.

"If anybody's to blame for Hugh's actions at that dance hall, it's me. I was the one who kept telling him that a trail boss protects his men. Always."

Gaston Boyd shook his head. "Newton's to blame. Bloody Newton's the guilty party. Guilty as hell."

This time, the knock came from Hoff's store.

"Judge Muse," came the muffled but still strong voice.

Again, the wooden bar of wood was removed, the door pulled
open, another man slipped through, and the door closed and the
barricade replaced.

It was getting crowded in the storeroom, the air thick and stag-
nant. Gary leaned against the wall, then placed both crutches to
his right. He removed his hat and wiped sweat from this brow
with his shirtsleeve. The hat came back on, and he tugged up his
too-big britches. At least, oversized as they were, some air circu-
lated down inside. But it started to become suffocating in there.

Still, no one was going to open a door. And there were no windows in the cramped room. It reminded him of the room above
Denise's restaurant, where he had been stuck for half of eternity.

After giving one nod that must have been for everyone, the
stern-looking gentleman turned to the Major.

"Sir," he said, "I am Muse, Judge R.W.P. Muse, and you might
say—and most people do—that this is my town."

The Major stiffened. "Well, Judge, I am Major Walter Pool
Anderson of Texas. And I do not think much of your town, sir."

This, Gary feared, could go quite badly.

But the judge nodded. "For the moment, sir, we are in agreement." He found a snuff can, offered it to the Major, who shook
his head. "But it will be a fine town." The judge took a pinch,
and looked at the marshal.

Tom Carson cleared his throat. "Coroner Bowman held an inquest on the Sunday morning after the deadly encounter at Tuttle's establishment. The jury determined that Jim Martin met his
death at the hands of some person unknown and that Mike Mc-
Cluskie, alias Art Delaney, was killed by shots from a pistol fired
by Hugh Anderson." He nodded at the sleeping lad and looked
again at the Major. "This was one of the bloodiest affrays in
Kansas, sir, and the worst, some say, since Lawrence."

The Major stared at Hugh. "This was no Lawrence, sir, although I was involved in that senseless butchery. I was fighting
with honor, sir, fighting with honorable men and fighting against

brave and honorable soldiers. And the men I hire to drive my cattle are, likewise, honorable men . . . and boys."

He looked, his gaze moving from the marshal to the judge to the doctor and to the guards.

"But I have yet to see honor in this town. I see railroad men holding clubs. I see cowboys from Texas walking the streets, bold as brass, most of them carrying guns on their persons, many of them carrying more than one six-shot revolver."

His head shook.

"By God, Marshal, no one carries a gun in Abilene. Not when Tom Smith was the marshal there. And not now, from what I have heard, with that new lawman . . . that . . . that . . ."

"Hickok," Carson said.

"Yes, that is the name." The Major turned to the judge. "Cowboys get rowdy. They get drunk. They might even fire a shot or two, in the air. They dance. They gamble. They raise Cain. Such is their right, having spent months in a saddle, risking their lives." His face swung to Gary. "Tell them, Captain. Tell them about that poor hand you lost on this drive."

Gary hadn't expected this. He straightened, breathed in and out, and said, "Young kid. Named Casey Steer. One of my sons was his pard. Casey was night-herding. After spending twelve hours in a saddle all that day. Wasn't wearing a gun. But he had spurs on. Bolt of lightning came out of the sky. Killed him dead. Started a stampede that could have killed more of my men."

The Major nodded vigorously. "They are good boys, gentlemen. They work hard. But sometimes, after months in the saddle and with money in their pockets, they get a little wild."

Tom Carson sighed. "And what do we have here in Newton? Air tainted with the hot steam of human blood? Murder, unnatural, foul, staining pages of her brief history?" He shook his head. "The brand of Cain stamps its crimson characters on men's foreheads with horrible frequency."

Two of the deputies stared at the boss. Gary figured they

thought the same thing running through his mind. Tom Carson read too many blood-and-thunders, or he was already campaigning for reelection or reappointment or however they picked town lawmen in Kansas.

"Five men are dead," the deputy with the rifle said softly. "Five. And aplenty wounded. Done in or gravely injured by that boy of yours, Major, and whoever that other man-killing jackal was." He shifted the rifle, not threatening, just to find a more comfortable position, and said, "And now this town is full of Texans—your hard-working cowboys, with guns on their persons, and threatening to lynch our citizens from telegraph poles if we even put that boy of yours in jail."

"Yep," Gary heard himself say. "And tell me what your law . . ." He stared hard at Carson. "And your coroner." His eyes found Judge Muse, since Bowman didn't have the guts to show up for this parley. "Tell me what you, you, you officers of the court did about McCluskie."

"He left town," the man with the Henry said.

Gary nodded. "He left town. And came right back. Rode in a week later. And no one made any attempt to arrest him. No one made any attempt to take his guns from him. And this came right after he walked up to a Texan, yeah, but a Texan who you folks had made a special deputy. A policeman. For that bond election. McCluskie walked right up to him and didn't give him a chance. He shot him down like I'd shoot a hydrophoby wolf."

He found his crutches, put them under his armpits, and moved forward. "You call that law?" He nodded at the Major. "Come on, sir. It's too hot in this place for me. The air's foul. Like the gutless wonders in here. Except for your son."

Gary hadn't thought all this through. Two armed deputies stood by that barred door, and Gary wasn't sure he could get that heavy wood down. He was at the mercy of Kansans. And the Major didn't appear to want to leave his son's bedside.

"Captain Hardee."

That wasn't the Major's voice. Gary stopped, turned, and found Judge Muse staring at him.

"All we want," the judge said, "is for peace to come to Newton. There is no eye-for-eye here. We want justice. Justice and peace. And I think we can have that. I think we can make arrangements that will be to the mutual benefit of us all."

Chapter 37

Thus ends the third or fourth chapter in Newton's
bloody history—a town only a little over three months
old. Let its police force be strengthened by good and
honest men, and all violators of the law be made to
suffer the extreme penalties of its wise provisions.
Then bloodshed will cease. But if the worse than
beastly prostitution of the sexes is continued, and the
town is controlled by characters who have no regard
for virtue, decency or honor, it will not soon become
fit for the abode of respectable people.
—*The Abilene Chronicle,*
August 24, 1871

It rained hard that night. Gary Hardee sat back in that bed, listening to the drops pounding hard against the roof of Denise's
restaurant.

He wanted to go with them, but he knew that with these
crutches, and especially in this weather, he would just get in their
way. He lay in bed in his long-handle underwear and that cast,
sweating, even though the thunderstorm had cooled down everything in Wichita.

Maybe even the boiling blood of Kansans and Texans.

The door opened, and Cindy Bagwell stepped in, shaking herself dry. Her brown hair looked as though she had been dunked in a horse trough. Her blouse was wet, but not that wet. She had to have been wearing a poncho, blanket, or something. The shoes were muddy. Denise would give her grief if she tracked that mess in through the dining room.

She was out of breath.

Gary tried to push himself up, but she brought up her hands, shaking her head, telling him, "No, no, no, no, no." She held pencils and a pen in one hand, and a notebook in another. She moved toward him and sat in the chair.

"Denise is bringing coffee," she said, still trying to catch her breath.

"The devil with coffee," Gary said. His heart had to be pounding as hard as hers. "Tell me—"

"They made it." She giggled with excitement. "I don't know how. But they did."

"You don't know how? Weren't you with them?"

Denise came in, kicked the door shut, frowned at the mud and leaves and whatever Cindy had brought in with her, but said nothing. She handed Cindy one cup, splashed coffee into Gary's, filled Cindy's, and sat at the bottom of the bed. She still held the pot.

"Yes," Cindy said. She must have downed half the cup in two swallows. Some dribbled down her chin and fell onto her skirt. Not that anyone would notice.

"They made it."

She giggled. "It was so . . . exciting . . . and dangerous, too."

"Oh, brother," Denise said. But she got up, refilled Cindy's cup, and sat back on the bed.

"Marshal Carson came in first," she said, flipping back pages in the notebook, her face showing increased frustration as she looked at what she had written. Tears welled in her eyes. "I'll never be able to read all this. It's all wet. The ink, the lead, it's all . . . ruined."

Denise swore, put the pot on the floor, and crossed the room to the dresser. She found some paper there, grabbed a pen and a picture frame, and again sat at the end of the bed. Using the picture frame as a writing board, she said, "Just tell what happened. I'll take notes. Won't rely on my memory this time. Tell it. Now. While it's all fresh in your head."

With a nod, Cindy began.

Tom Carson told the three deputies to go home to their wives. "Not to a saloon, not to an eating house. Go home. And don't tell your wives anything, either. You've lost your memory. Or you've lost your salary."

When they left, Carson let Cindy into the storeroom. Mr. Hoff had gone home already. Judge Muse and Doctor Boyd were with Cindy.

"A few minutes later, someone knocked on the door. The marshal let them in. Didn't even ask who they were before he pulled the door open. I guess they had been waiting for the deputies to leave."

She guzzled more coffee, wiped her mouth, caught her breath, and continued.

"One said he was George Yocum. Lives in Howard City. The other was—"

"We don't care about their names," Denise cried out.

"Well, I do," Cindy snapped. "This isn't just for you, remember. This is for *The Wichita Herald*. Write it down. Yocum." She spelled it. "The other was Baker. He wouldn't tell me his first name. Or where he's from. I asked him if it began with 'A'—I was going to go all the way through the alphabet, but he said, 'A's as good as anything.'" She finished that cup of coffee. "I don't blame him. For not wanting his name to get out."

After that, Marshal Carson left. He said nothing to the men, did not even nod a goodbye. The door closed, and Judge Muse and Doctor Boyd reached under the cot and pulled out a litter they had made.

It was two o'clock when they left Hoff's store.

"Black as pitch. Rain falling hard. Thunder." Cindy sniffed, wiped her nose, looked at Denise to make sure she was writing everything down. "Doc Boyd covered Hugh with an India rubber poncho. We started walking. North. That was the judge's idea. So nobody saw us. Not that anyone would be out on a night like this."

They brought no lanterns, no torches. Judge Muse said any light might give them away. So it took a long time. The streets had turned into a mud bog. When they moved through grass, it was waterlogged, high and soaking wet.

"When we made it to the depot, the conductor was waiting. Major Anderson had paid him, I guess. He wouldn't talk to me. He opened one of the railroad cars; Yocum and that Baker fellow climbed up while Major Anderson and the conductor took hold of those ends of the litter. They slid Hugh inside. One of them pulled off the poncho and covered him with a blanket. I couldn't see which one. Then the conductor got into the car. He unlocked this closet, and that's where they put Hugh in."

Cindy caught her breath.

Baker and Yocum left. The doctor shook hands with the conductor, Judge Muse, and Major Anderson, and he left. The conductor closed the door. He nodded at the judge, and he and Major Anderson walked away.

"Judge Muse," Cindy said, "looked at me. That's when the rain stopped. The judge nodded, and said, 'The history of Newton is now to begin afresh.'"

Her head turned quickly to Denise. "Get that down just right. 'The history of Newton is now to begin afresh.'"

Turning to Gary, Cindy smiled. "I waited. The train got off all right. Hugh and the Major are gone. They'll be in Kansas City soon."

"That's good." Gary felt completely exhausted. "Hugh's safe."

He looked at Cindy, then Denise, and sighed. Dampness filled his eyes.

"And I don't even know if my sons are alive or dead."

Denise brought him a copy of the *Kansas State Record*, a Topeka newspaper, opened and folded it, let him take it before she pointed to a paragraph.

> *Hugh Anderson, the Texan "high priest," who sang that remarkable "death song" at Newton, is lying at the Gillis House in Kansas City, and may recover.*

He was moving around better now, his leg, itching like crazy, still in cast. The stairs weren't as hard to navigate, but it still took him forever to get down, and he made himself walk around the block every day.

That September day brough the first hint of autumn, and he sat in the dining room, sipping coffee and working on a bowl of Denise's potato soup, when the door opened, and Cindy Bagwell walked in.

That was an everyday occurrence, but the look on her face made Gary put down the spoon. She made a beeline for him, sat across the table, and reached inside her purse. He saw the envelope, which she slid toward his bowl.

"This came in today's post," she whispered. As long as Gary had known Cindy, she did not often whisper.

He studied the envelope, addressed to Miss C. Bagwell, Wichita Herald, Wichita, Kansas.

It had been torn open from the far side. Well, the letter was addressed to her. He wiped his fingers on the napkin, squeezed the paper with his left hand, and tapped the piece of paper out.

But he had already recognized the handwriting on the envelope.

* * *

Dear Miss Cindy:

Please tell our father that we are both red with shame.

But are fine and can see how far we have come.

And mistakes we have made.

Hope you are well.

Tell Pa we have a hard hill to climb.

But buffalo to eat.

Hope to see Pa soon.

Taylor had written it. He looked inside the envelope, found nothing there, no strange words or markings. He stuffed the letter back in the envelope and met Cindy's eyes.

"That's all there was," she whispered.

"Yeah." He tore the letter and envelope in half, then halved that, then again, wadded the remnants in his fist, and dropped it in the bowl, still half full with soup. He pushed the ball of paper down with his spoon, and began stirring absently.

Cindy wet her lips. She looked over her shoulder, but found only two railroad men at a table by the window, talking and laughing and eating roast beef.

Gary kept stirring the bowl.

"Do you . . . ?" she started, but Gary's head shook.

He pushed himself up, and Cindy got out of her chair. He found a dime and put it by the bowl, grabbed the hat he had set crown-down on the table, put it on his head, and reached for the crutches.

"Need you to do me a favor," he said. "If you can."

"I—"

"Don't say you can till you hear what it is. Get Denise. Meet me . . ." He jerked his thumb toward that pain-in-the-buttocks staircase.

The dentist frowned when Gary asked him to cut off the cast.

"Everhart," Gary said, "seven weeks is long enough. And I'm itching like my flea-bit barn cat."

"Long enough for many fractures," Everhart said, "but Doctor Boyd knows what he's doing, and if he says nine weeks."

"That's why I fetched you, Doc. You're cutting it off. Not Gaston Boyd."

"No, sir, I shan't do this. Yours was a serious, multiple—"

"Doc." Gary found his holster and tugged the handle of his Colt. "You really want to keep arguing?"

Gary paid for a wagon and mule, but the owner of the Dark Moon gambling hall bought them. That was Denise's suggestion. Since Gary, Cindy, and Denise couldn't risk buying the rig and alerting the law, her cook, Grover, got money and instructions to the gambler.

Once the wagon arrived at First and Poplar, the driver tethered the mule to a cast-iron weight and walked away. Gary started down the alley, hearing only snores from inside alley tents.

Finding an empty street, he sighed in relief. Even the gambler had disappeared. Gary could never repay that stranger. Or Denise . . . Cindy . . . Grover.

The rig was light and the mule looked sturdy. Cindy had grabbed Gary's valise and gun belt, Denise carried canteens and a basket, and Grover lugged the saddle, bags, blanket, and bedroll. The gear went in the back, the gun rig on the driver's bench.

Gary offered the cook a gold coin.

"No, sir," Grover whispered. "No, sir."

"Thank the fellow who bought all of this," Gary said.

"Yes, sir," the cook said, and Gary shook his hand before Grover walked away.

Turning, Gary smiled at Denise. "I . . ." But he couldn't find any words.

"Bring me a free steer next time you come up the trail," she said.

"I don't think you can drive this rig all the way home, Gary,"

Cindy Bagwell continued. "It's too far for you to go. Alone. How will you unhitch this team? You're still using crutches."

"But my leg can breathe without that cast that weighed more than that buffalo bull that caused me so much trouble." He slid the crutches into the back of the wagon near his saddle.

"There are two canteens," Denise told him. "And I packed you a basket of food."

"You're an angel," he said.

"I am not." She leaned against him and hugged him hard. "Be careful," she whispered.

"Thank you." He bent and kissed the top of her head.

He saw the tears in her eyes, but just for a moment, because she turned and walked after her cook.

When he leaned against the light wagon, Cindy came to him.

"How are you going to get . . . wherever you're going?"

He didn't answer. Gripping the side of the wagon for balance, he moved to the back of the rig, leaned his butt against it, and boosted himself into the back. He slid himself, dragged that bad leg till he hit the front bench, ignoring the pain, turned, grabbed the seat, and managed to pull himself up. He got his good leg over easily. The right leg proved harder, but he did it, though he was sweating and panting before he twisted around, and somehow managed to prop the leg atop the front board.

A pillow would help. But he could find one in Wichita. Pay a kid to fetch one out of a mercantile. Not here. No. Wichita. He had to get out of Newton before someone saw him and started to get suspicious. He wasn't completely certain Page Everhart wouldn't rush off and tell Doc Boyd, and Boyd might tell Marshal Carson.

"Well," he said, once he caught his breath. "This sure beats eighteen hours in a saddle all day." He pulled off his hat, ran his shirtsleeve over his face and forehead, and set the hat on his head again.

He looked down at Cindy.

"Undo the tether, please?"

Cindy did and came back to the side of the rig.

Their eyes met.

"I'll write you," he said. "When I get home."

Tears already streamed down her cheeks. He pretended not to notice.

"I never could have done this without you and her." He hooked his thumb toward the alley that Denise had taken.

"Tell Evan and Jim Riley goodbye," she said between sniffles.

"I don't know any Jim Riley," he said. He leaned down for her, felt her arms around his neck.

He did not kiss her on the top of her head, but he kissed her long and hard.

When she pulled away, he whispered, "See you down the trail," turned, flipped the lines hard, and cursed the mule into a trot.

The mule would have gotten a nod of approval from Moises Dunn. The rig? Well, it was light, and he could keep it going at a good clip. He rode hard, usually fast, in the mornings and after the sun began to sink. He let the mules, and his back and that itching leg, rest a bit during the heat of the day for a couple of hours—if luck found him in a trail crew's camp, rare this late in the year . . . or in a town if he wasn't quite so lucky . . . or, more often, under a shade tree or shadow if he could find one—and kept riding.

He fretted, constantly found himself looking over his shoulder, but never saw dust except from the last cattle herds on the way to market. In Caldwell, which barely even existed and which he scarcely recalled when they had come through after his tangle with a buffalo, he posted a letter to Jane. Then he crossed the Kansas state line into Indian Territory.

In eight days, he had traveled more than two hundred miles. He forded the Canadian River the next morning, and turned the light wagon off the trail when he saw the rise of Red Hill.

His palms sweated, making the leather lines slick. Remembering the buffalo, remembering Hugh Anderson, he stopped to catch his breath. His heart beat faster than he ever thought it could. Breaths became ragged. He wondered if his pump was about to give out. Then he saw the reflection of sunlight up Red Hill.

He drew the Colt, laying it beside him. A precaution. A figure rose on the hillside, but it was way too far away for him to make out anything. For all Gary knew, that was a mirage. A dream. A . . . ?

"Pa."

He spun around.

Taylor Hardee held only the reins to the horse he pulled behind him. Gary's oldest son looked nervous.

At the top of Red Hill, the wind blew hard. A cold wind with hints of autumn.

"Figured that was you."

Looking Taylor over, Gary nodded, lowered the lines, and felt his breathing return to normal, though his heart kept pumping hard.

"We weren't sure you'd figure out where we were," Taylor said.

Gary waved his hand in dismissal. "With the note you wrote, I'd have to be illiterate not to figure it out." He nodded at the water seeping out of the red earth. "How's the water?"

Taylor tried to grin. "Tastes like buffalo."

A horse whinnied, the mule brayed, and hooves sounded as Evan rode up, reining in on the wagon's right.

"Pa."

Gary nodded. He held out his right hand. His youngest son

kicked the gelding closer, leaned out of the saddle, and grasped Gary's hand. It was firm. Solid. A short, good shake. That boy was a fine man.

"Good to see you."

"Same," Gary said.

Evan straightened in the saddle, and Gary looked at Taylor again.

"I don't see a short gun on you," Gary said.

Taylor shook his head. "Figured I don't have any need for a short gun anymore."

Gary's head bobbed. "Never have had much use for this one." He lifted his Colt, glanced at it briefly, and shoved it into the holster. "Only good I've gotten out of it is scaring off a coyot' or two."

No one commented.

A raven flew over their heads.

Gary looked south. You could see a mighty long way from the top of Red Hill.

Taylor cleared his throat. "How's . . . what happened to . . . ?" He tried again. "Is Hugh all right?"

Evan added: "We read in a paper we found that he was shot up pretty bad, but expected to live."

"He was all right when I left Newton," Gary said, still admiring the view. "Hugh wasn't in Newton. The Major came up. We got Hugh to Kansas City. He might be back in Fort Bend County by now. I don't know."

A long silence passed.

Gary found a canteen, took a long pull, held the container toward Evan, who shook his head, then to Taylor, who said, "No, thank you, sir."

The wind blew harder. Gary could find not a cloud, not even a wisp of one. The blueness reminded him of Jane's eyes. He hardened himself and faced Taylor again.

"What happened to Jim Riley?"

Taylor held his father's gaze. "I don't know any Jim Riley." He grabbed the horn, and pulled himself into the saddle, holding the reins in his right hand, while pulling down his hat tighter with his left.

"How's Ma?" Evan asked.

Gary shrugged. Then smiled.

"Why don't we go home and ask her ourselves?" he said.

Epilogue

The sale of the Hyde Park property last week furnished a splendid opportunity for the truly virtuous to visit that place upon which they have so often gazed but would not venture near. The property was sold quite cheap, and nothing but a piece of hardware is left to mark the spot where one year ago was a den of brothels. Let persons who tell of Newton's early days make a note of this.
—*The Newton Kansan*,
May 29, 1873

Looking in the mirror after shaving, Gary Hardee ran his fingers over his mustache, still heavy, mostly dark, but the past couple of years had added a lot of gray. His hair remained thick, but not as dark as it had been. He splashed water over his face, toweled himself dry, and limped back to the hotel bed to find that nuisance of a paper collar that would choke him half to death.

It had been a lot easier to get dressed when he was bossing cowboys around, but now he was just an ordinary rancher. He found the tie—felt like a hangman's noose—got it on and straightened, grabbed the brown-striped coat hanging on the wall, planted the hat on his head, and opened the door. He sighed, remembering the walking cane. The temptation to leave it leaning against the wall struck him like it always did, but Jane would give him grief if she found out. That wasn't likely, Jane being eight hundred miles south, but, well, wives had ways of learning things.

He limped back, grabbed the cane. It did make him look like a man of wealth, especially in his Sunday-go-to-meetings, and he left the room, eased down the hall, stairs, and across the hotel lobby to hand his key to the bald gent behind the desk.

"Supper begins at five, sir," the man told him. "Ends at eight-thirty."

Gary chuckled. "Remember back when you could eat, drink, or do anything you wanted in this town noon to midnight?"

"No, sir." The clerk put the key in one of those boxes behind the counter. "I've always gone to bed promptly at eight, sir."

"How long you been in Newton?"

"Seven months, sir." He turned around and adjusted his spectacles. "Will there be anything else, sir?"

Gary gave up on this old fogey.

"Could you tell me where I'd find the *Newton Kansan* office?"

Once he peered through the plate-glass window, he thought about turning around. He hadn't told her he was coming, not even written a letter saying he was even considering coming. For all he knew, she had moved off to some other city. Newspaper writers and editors were like cowboys in one way: they never felt tied to one place.

But, well, he had spent money on a hotel and a train ride from Wichita, and even if she told him she wouldn't have a part in his proposal, it would be good to see her again.

He moved to the door, opened it, heard the bell singing, and stepped inside.

The smile that stretched across his face surprised him. There she was—or the spitting image of her—back to him, in a summer dress, waving a finger at a man who wore an apron and blue-ticking sleeve stockings.

"Be with you in a moment," Cindy Bagwell called out, and Gary knew it was her. He'd recognize that Southern voice anywhere. She jabbed her finger at a crumpled sheet on the table in front of the thin, bespectacled man. "Does that look like a capital T, Henry?" She jammed her finger near the bridge of his nose. "An 'M,' Henry. Uppercase. Eighteen points. Not a 'B.' What language is *Biscellaneous*, anyway?"

Gary didn't hear the man's answer. He said, "I want to speak to the person in charge."

"Mr. Ashbaugh's not here," she answered without turning, and took a step back. "You set type better, Henry, when—"

She stopped and turned sharply. Her eyes widened. Gary smiled, closed the door behind him, took a step forward, and removed his hat.

"Oh," Cindy said softly, spacing her words, "my . . . lord." She moved to a gate, pushed it open, stopped again, and blinked repeatedly, as if she were staring at an apparition.

"Been a long time," Gary said.

"Yes." She smiled, came to him, reached her arms around him, pulled him close, and kissed his cheek. Then she gave him a bear hug before pushing back and shaking her head.

"I can't believe it." Then she turned around and yelled, "Ashbaugh pays you to set type, Henry T. Price. Not gawk." She spun back and smiled. "What brings you to Newton? There's no cattle being shipped out from here anymore."

"I know." He hooked his left thumb toward the door. "Sold eight hundred head in Wichita."

Her eyes saw the cane. "Are you still driving cattle?"

"Actually, I took the train. Evan brought the herd up. I met him in Wichita." He wanted to hug her, but holding his derby in one hand and the cane in the other, he just grinned like a happy dog.

"Evan?" Cindy's head shook. "How's . . . Taylor."

Gary just nodded. Cindy waited. "Married. Got a little spread in Pleasanton. Good cattle country."

"My, my." Cindy shook her head.

They studied each other, then Cindy said, "Would you like to see Newton? It's changed a lot in two years."

"I'd like that a lot."

"Where are you staying?"

"Newton House."

"Good. There's a livery right back of it. I can rent a carriage. Give you the tour."

Gary shook his head. "You don't need to rent a carriage for me. I can walk. And—"

"And nothing," Cindy said. "Schuster's an advertiser. It won't cost you or me a dime. We'll take it off his bill next month. Come on. We have catching up to do. And you might give me a story— and a byline."

Gary stared, wondering if she had read his mind.

"I'll drive," Cindy said, and when Gary gave her that look of a Texan, she countered with an Alabama stare. "You couldn't find your way around Newton today. And Schuster advertises with me, not you. Get in."

The man who had hitched the horse helped Gary into the seat, and he slid over, still holding the cane, as Cindy was helped up. She found the lines, tipped the stable hand, and said, "We'll be back before dark." She whipped the lines, and the buggy pulled out onto Sixth Street.

They turned down Main, trotted past Fifth, crossed the iron tracks, and she slowed down, letting Gary look west and east. Gone were the scattershot buildings. Brick and stone had often replaced clapboard, picket wood, and tents. A few false-front wood structures remained, but instead of signs reading Dance Hall, Faro, or Saloon, he saw signs for Furniture; Garden & Nursery; Agricultural Implements; Groceries & Provisions; Stone,

Lime, Coal; Dry Goods; Hardware & Tinware . . . No women wearing next to nothing, and sometimes nothing at all, calling out to *Handsome* or *Sweetheart* or *Got a Dollar?*

Glancing at Gary's face made her smile. "They started spelling it H-*Y*-D-E recently. Hyde Park. Makes it sound uppity, or at least respectable."

Cindy pulled hard on the reins, stopping the buggy at the intersection of Poplar and Second. She pointed at the house on the southeast corner.

"There it is."

Gary's knuckles tightened on the cane he held. "Someone lives here?" He shook his head. She tried to think about how he must have felt. Perry Tuttle's dance hall was gone, replaced by a frame house, two stories, with a swing on the front porch, and a wrought-iron hitch post sculpted like a horse's head.

Yes, Newton had changed a lot since '71.

"Yes." She sighed. "But I doubt if the owners—I don't even know who they are—have any notion what stood here before they had this house built. Perry pulled down his lumber, moved it—I don't even remember where. Nobody remembers, or wants to remember, much about those days."

Gary spoke in a whisper. "I understand that."

Cindy wished she could forget a lot of it herself. Most of it, in fact.

He stared at his boots. He might have watched those boots till the end of days, so Cindy made a fist and moved it under his chin. Painting on a smile, she pushed his head up. He found her eyes.

"Would you like to eat some of Denise's cooking?"

Gary's eyes widened. "She's still here?"

Her grin widened.

"Found a better location north of the tracks," she told him. "Let's go. She'd love to see you. And I'm hungry."

"You're always hungry."

She laughed, clucked her tongue, and worked the lines. "You remember."

Once she had the buggy turned around and heading back toward Main Street, he said, "There's something I need to ask you. You don't have to say yes. It's . . . it's . . . well . . . criminy, I never should have—"

Well, now, I never thought you came all this way just to see little ol' me.

"Why don't you just tell me?"

Denise Beeber told the two cooks and the servers to help themselves to food while they had time, went to the stove, found a spoon, and sampled the soup.

"More garlic," she told Grover.

That bell chimed as the front door opened, and she stepped through the curtain that separated the dining room from the kitchen, trying to find a smile—which came instantly when the man and woman looked up.

"Eat," Denise called back to Grover. "And one clove. That should do it. One clove. Then eat."

A server started toward Gary Hardee and Cindy Bagwell, but Denise shot out her arm and said, "Don't worry, Kristine. These are my guests. Go eat. You'll get their tip. I promise."

If they tip.

Laughing, she moved across the hardwood floor, trying not to run, then hurrying, and wrapped her arms around Gary, hard enough that he almost dropped his cane, and stepped back, put her hands on her hips, and laughed.

"You look rich."

He chuckled. "I ain't. Never met a rich rancher."

"Hungry?" Denise asked.

"I could eat," Gary told her.

"Find a table. You picked the right time. And I know Cindy's hungry. She always is. I'll serve you."

They were drinking coffee when Cindy and Gary released a sigh, and said, "I came here, well, because I need some help."

A few years back, Denise's guard would have closed her off like palisade walls. But not now.

"It's Hugh Anderson," he said.

And now she knew why he came back.

"Two years have passed," he said. "People still talk about what happened at Perry Tuttle's place. As far down as Pleasanton. Even all the way to Fort Bend County."

Denise's head bobbed. "They talk about it in Kansas, too. Everywhere but here."

"Newton," Cindy said, "is good at forgetting what it doesn't want to remember."

"Railroad detectives have stopped by my place, asking me questions," Gary said. "Even a man who said he worked for Pinkerton came by November last."

"Where is Hugh?" Denise asked.

"New Mexico Territory," Gary said after a moment. "The Major won't even tell me what name he's going by."

"And Jim Riley?" Denise asked.

Gary waited, studying Denise with those penetrating eyes he had. "They don't look for Jim Riley in Texas. They've figured him for a railroad man, who wouldn't have the guts to travel to Texas."

"Riley killed more men than Hugh," Denise said.

Gary nodded. "That's why they figure him for a Yankee. Never came to realize that all Taylor—Jim Riley, I mean—was doing was trying to save his kid brother."

"Which," Cindy said, "he did."

"Yeah."

The legs of the chair scratched the floor as Denise pushed back. She looked hard at Gary, trying to find something that wasn't there. That had never been there. Dishonesty.

"Why would you want to save Hugh Anderson's hide?" she finally asked. "You wouldn't have that limp if not for Hugh. Bailey might still be alive. Lord, a lot of people might still be alive."

"He saved my hide," Gary said. "He could have left me there to die. Could have let buzzards pick my bones clean."

He made himself sip coffee and looked at Denise. "I didn't think Hugh would ever be a man, but he grew into one right quick. Like I said, he saved my bacon. He did what he thought was right that night here in Newton. And, well, I owe his pa, too. The Major dragged me away from death's door in North Carolina during the late war. Hugh Anderson pulled me out of a tight spot just south of here. And he was a pard to both my sons. And, I feel responsible. I gave him that scar across his cheek. And I kept telling him that a trail boss always protects his men."

Denise found Cindy's eyes. Held them for a minute, then heard Gary whisper, "And I'm tired of having squat assassins pestering me like . . . like . . . like your hard-biting buffalo gnats."

Denise shook her head. "You got who you need," she said, and nodded at Cindy. "She's the writer."

Gary agreed. "But you can help us. You're not just a . . ." His smile was the same as always. ". . . just a pretty redhead."

Denise stood. "Come on." She headed toward the kitchen. "This place will fill up in the next hour. My room's upstairs. I even have a window in this place. And I've got just what we need for some serious lying. We're going to have to kill Hugh Anderson."

She could hear the chatter and noise of a busy restaurant below. Denise didn't recollect how much Old Overholt she had downed, but at least tomorrow was Sunday. The restaurant, and every place in Newton except the marshal's office and the churches, closed on Sundays.

"Who kills Hugh?" Cindy asked, looking up with eyes that had trouble focusing.

"McCluskie's brother." Hardee slurred his words.

"I know that," Cindy whined. "But what's his brother's name?"

"Benedict." A belch followed Gary's suggestion.

"No," Denise said. "Arthur. Arthur McCluskie."

"Why Arthur?" Cindy asked; then the memory came to her. "Oh. Oh."

"Arthur dies a hero." Denise smiled.

"Like the king!" Gary beamed.

Denise and Cindy exchanged a quick glance, and both nodded in agreement.

"Arthur dies a hero," Cindy said, and wrote on the back of one of Denise's recipes.

Denise also came up with the place for the fatal battle: Medicine Lodge, Kansas.

But Cindy made it Indian Territory. "A hundred miles south of the Kansas frontier," she said, and started writing.

"I don't recall a settlement named Medicine Lodge in the Nations," Gary said.

"There is now," Cindy said.

She started writing furiously, stopped only to finish her glass of rye, which Gary somehow refilled, and took a hard pull from the bottle.

Grinning, Denise drank more whiskey. Arthur. Arthur would get his name once more in a newspaper, or many newspapers, if Cindy was right. It wouldn't be Arthur Beeber, but Arthur McCluskie, but he'd be a hero, die a hero, one more time.

Cindy laughed, picked up the paper, and read: "'At the faro table, I recognized Anderson, the Texas desperado, the horse-thief, the celebrated pistol-shot.'"

"Add," Denise tapped on the table till she got the phrase right, "red-handed murderer."

"Red-handed murderer." Cindy nodded. "I like that."

Gary pointed at the paper. "Write it down then. If it's good."

"It's great." Cindy scribbled.

"Will your newspaper run this story?" Gary asked. "I mean, I don't want to get you in trouble."

She giggled. "No, the *Kansan* can't print this. But do you remember . . . ?" Now she had to think of that name. "McNelly? Liam Mc—" Her head shook. She drank more whiskey. "No. You never met him. Well, I worked with him in . . . Wichita. That's right. Wichita. But he's at the *World* now in New York. He'll get it in the *World*. And everybody reads the *World*. And out here, in Kansas, they'll reprint it. They'll reprint this story in every paper. Well, a lot of papers."

She laughed again. "I'll have an article in the *World*. Me." Her head shook. "No. No. I'll have to use a pseu—, a pseu—a . . . a . . . a alias. *My* alias. Allegro returns."

She couldn't believe she, a newspaperwoman, was actually writing this. She had a job at the *Newton Kansan*, a good job. Cindy Bagwell had become respected all across the new Harvey County. Focusing on what she had just written, she thought she had never read worse prose in a half-dime novel. But, she kept telling herself, it might work.

"Of course, it'll work," Cindy said. "Cowboys and railroad men are idiots." She tried to find Gary Hardee, but wasn't sure he was still here. But she asked anyway. "You aren't offended by what I just said, are you?"

"Not at all," came a voice that might have been Hardee's or might have been her father's. She smiled. Her father was a good newspaperman. "It's a good story."

Maybe her father said that, too.

That was the last thing she remembered until she woke up late Sunday afternoon.

He saw the article, at least a mention of it, in *The Junction City Union*, and an even older version in *The Kansas City Times*, which he found in a stack of papers at the Kansas City depot. In Panola, he read about the Medicine Lodge duel in *The Western Spirit* when he got off the Katy to stretch his legs.

When he reached Dallas, he found the first article, published in *The Dallas Weekly Herald*, that doubted the veracity of the blood-and-thunder account. Having read Cindy Bagwell's piece, which the *World* did publish under the pseudonym Allegro, Gary wondered if anyone believed it.

Two men dueling, riddling each other with bullets, then stabbing each other to death.

And yet, to his surprise, when he finally got home in Richmond, he never heard anyone mention Hugh Anderson, Jim Riley, or Mike McCluskie, especially not McCluskie's brother Arthur, who never existed.

More people talked about Wild Bill Hickok's duel with Phil Coe, which happened in Abilene a month or two after "Newton's General Massacre." Or, currently, a gunfight in Ellsworth that left a sheriff dead after Gary's last trip to Kansas.

Gary Hardee took to ranching, staying home with Jane, watching her cook on her stove, make clothes on her sewing machine, and get those clothes cleaned perfectly in her Doty's Washing Machine and Universal Clothes Wringer, the last present he ever bought her from his earnings as a trail boss.

He left the bossing to Taylor, and later Evan.

In 1885, he served as a pallbearer at Major Wat Anderson's funeral. He wondered how Hugh took the news. Living all the way west in Lincoln County, New Mexico Territory, Hugh couldn't get to the funeral. It was warm and pleasant here in South Texas, but, this being January, New Mexico might be covered with four feet of snow.

By grab, it had been hard enough for Gary to get there himself, since the Major and Lou had moved way out into the Hill Country, settling in a town called Voca, where the Andersons had a nice place on the San Saba River.

Besides, there still was that chance that some private detective or A.T. & S.F. man would be spying at the funeral, hoping to catch or kill the man who shot Mike McCluskie dead in 1871.

Gary no longer needed the cane to get around. And he could still sit a saddle better than most of those boys punching cattle. His and Evan's cattle, longhorns, but more Herefords, these days. Taylor ran a small herd with his wife and young'uns up in Pleasanton. Evan had his eye on a girl in Galveston, and Jane kept asking him for a grandbaby she could spoil.

She could be persistent, Gary knew. Eventually, he figured, Jane would wear down Evan. Shucks, Gary wouldn't mind having a baby to bounce on his knee.

When he got back home after the Major's funeral, Jane fed him a fine meal, kissed his forehead, and he went outside and stood on the porch, watching the sunset.

He stood there, thinking back to 1871. Cindy Bagwell. He wondered where she was now. Denise Beeber. What would Moises Dunn have done had he ever tasted her biscuits or her coffee?

He remembered poor Bill Bailey, and he saw himself atop Red Hill, wondering what it would be like to die, and suddenly hearing Hugh Anderson's voice, feeling strong hands latching onto both of Gary's arms.

The door opened, closed, and Jane came to his side, and he smelled her hair. He had the urge to take her into his arms, kiss her, and dive into those pure blue eyes, so he turned to her.

She held two tumblers. Smiling, she brought one of them up toward him.

Rye whiskey. He laughed, took the glass, clinked it against hers, and stared at her.

"What's this for?" he asked.

She took the first sip.

"You always have a whiskey," she said, "when you finish a drive. Welcome home."

Author's Note

One of the bloodiest chapters in the annals of the old
West began on Friday, Aug. 11, 1871, in Newton,
Kan., the toughest town on the cattle trails that
season.
—Robert W. Richmond,
The Wichita Eagle,
April 7, 1957

That much is known, but the story of what came to be called the "General Massacre" is so steeped in mythology and lore—and official records sorely lacking—it's doubtful that a true account of the 1871 gunfight that secured the "Bloody Newton" nickname for the Kansas town will ever truly be written.

This, of course, is a work of fiction. Neither the *Times* nor the *Herald* existed in Wichita, but the *Vidette* and *Tribune* were being published in 1871. I have loosely followed the timeline of Newton's birth, and some quotes spoken by characters real and fictitious were pulled from newspaper clippings—thanks to Newspapers.com, NewspaperArchives.com, and the Harvey County Historical Society. Some characters existed in real life; most are from my imagination. The Hardee boys—Gary and sons Taylor and Evan—are real people, however, as are Cindy Bagwell and Denise Beeber, but in name only. Gary, Cindy, and

Denise were newspaper colleagues at the *Dallas Times Herald* (and Gary and I also worked together at the *Fort Worth-Star Telegram*) who graciously let me use their names; as did Gary's sons, Taylor and Evan. Names only. The descriptions and characterizations are my own inventions.

Likewise, the many historical figures featured here, including Major "Wat" Anderson and his son Hugh, are used fictitiously. Joseph G. McCoy, Jesse Driskill, Shanghai Pierce, Perry Tuttle, Judge R.W.P. Muse, Doctor Gaston Boyd, Tom Carson, Mike McCluskie (which might have been an alias), Bill Bailey, and a few others went through Newton, and so did Jim Riley, whoever he really was. With the exception of Evan Hardee's futile intervention and adding a twist to the Jim Riley legend, I have tried to capture the essence of the bloody gun battle at Tuttle's dance hall in the early hours of Sunday, August 20, as accurately as possible.

But, again, much of the history is more speculation than facts.

That said, the epigrams at the beginning of each chapter, epilogue, and this author's note, are pulled from actual newspapers. I even left the typographical errors.

Many Kansas cowtowns, including Abilene, Caldwell, Dodge City, Ellsworth, and Wichita, have embraced their rowdy cowtown history. But Newton? Not so much. Oh, historical markers still exist, but there's not as much pomp and pageantry as you'll find in other cattle towns. On the other hand, it's hard to find a whole lot to glorify in what happened that night at Perry Tuttle's dance hall.

That said, the Kauffman Museum offers a fine historical look at the area, and the staff at the Harvey County Historical Society was extremely helpful in my research for this novel. A big thanks to curator Kristine Schmucker and volunteer staffers Ronald Dietzel and Jane Jones for making me feel at home and answering tons of questions in person and via email.

Thanks also to the staffs of Chisholm Trail museums in Duncan and Kingfisher, Oklahoma; Cuero, Texas; and Wellington, Kansas; the Longhorn Museum in Pleasanton, Texas; Bullock Texas State History Museum in Austin; and Old Cowtown Museum in Wichita, Kansas. Nor could I have written this without assistance from Marvin "Woody" Woodworth of the Minco (Oklahoma) Historical Society and Museum.

Now, on to my source books:

Lewis Atherton's *The Cattle Kings* (University of Nebraska Press, 1972); Dena Bisnette's and Joe Gilliam's *Newton: Images of America* (Arcadia, 2013); Otto J. Boutin's *A Catfish in the Bodoni and Other Tales from the Golden Age of Tramp Printers* (North Star Press, 1970); Barbara Cloud's *The Business of Newspapers on the Western Frontier* (University of Nevada Press, 1992); David Dary's *Cowboy Culture: A Saga of Five Centuries* (Avon, 1991), Dary's *Red Blood & Black Ink: Journalism in the Old West* (University Press of Kansas, 1998), and his *True Tales of the Old-Time Plains* (Crown Publishers, 1979); Harry Sinclair Drago's *Wild, Woolly & Wicked: The History of the Kansas Cow Towns and the Texas Cattle Trade* (Clarkson N. Potter, Inc., 1960); J. Frank Dobie's *The Longhorns* (Bramhall House, 1941); Robert R. Dykstra's *The Cattle Towns* (Bison Books, 1983); Chris Emmett's *Shanghai Pierce: A Fair Likeness* (University of Oklahoma Press, 1954); David Fridtjof Halaas's *Boom Town Newspapers: Journalism on the Rocky Mountain Mining Frontier, 1859–1881* (University of New Mexico Press, 1981); Wayne Gard's *The Chisholm Trail* (University of Oklahoma Press, 1954); Walter Hill's *The Cowboy Iliad* (Marmont Lane, 2019); John Howells and Marion Dearman's *Tramp Printers: Adventures and Forgotten Paths Once Traced by Wandering Artisans of Newspapering and Typography* (Discovery Press, 2013); editor/compiler J. Marvin Hunter's *The Trail Drivers of Texas* (University of Texas Press, 1985); Joseph G. McCoy's *Historic Sketches of the Cattle Trade of the West and Southwest*, edited by Ralph P. Bieber (Bison Books, 1985); Darren J. McMannis's *Deadly Encounters: Murder & Mayhem in Harvey County, Kansas* (self-published,

2019); Nyle H. Miller and Joseph W. Snell's *Why the West Was Wild: A Contemporary Look at the Antics of Some Highly Publicized Kansas Cowtown Personalities* (University of Oklahoma Press, 2003); H. Craig Miner's *Wichita: The Early Years, 1865–80* (University of Nebraska Press, 1982); Judge R.W.P. Muse's *History of Harvey County, Kansas, 1871–1881* (Harvey County Historical Museum & Archives, 2011); Sam P. Ridings's *The Chisholm Trail* (Grant County, Oklahoma, Historical Society, 1985); James E. Sherow's *The Chisholm Trail: Joseph McCoy's Great Gamble* (University of Oklahoma Press, 2018); Dudley Dodgion Toevs's *Newton Remembering Yesterday Today: Romancing History, Newton, Kansas— 1960's Toward 2000* (self-published, 1994); Don Worcester's *The Chisholm Trail: High Road of the Cattle Kingdom* (Indian Head Books, 1994); and *Historic Newton Downtown Walking Tour* (Newton/ North Newton Historic Preservation Commission in partnership with the Harvey County Historical Society, 2019).

And a final thanks to Gary Goldstein, my editor at Kensington Publishing Corporation since 2007, and to Mojo's Coffee Bar in Newton, Kansas. I couldn't have written this without y'all.

—*Johnny D. Boggs*
Santa Fe, New Mexico
December 15, 2022